Lucifer's Child

Gideon Masters

TSL Publications

First published in Great Britain in 2019
By TSL Publications, Rickmansworth

Copyright © 2019 Gideon Masters

ISBN / 978-1-912416-91-2

Cover images:
https://pixabay.com/photos/angel-headstone-cemetery-grave
https://pixabay.com/photos/devil-chaos-demon-flames-hell-
2708544/-1822368/

Dedication

To my wife for her great patience and support whilst I spent many hours at my computer writing this,

To my publisher for her guidance, hard work and willingness in helping me bring this book to publication.

John

John's bones and muscles burned with every agonising step but he kept going. He had to for Helen … Who was he kidding? He had to for his sanity. If there was a job here, he wanted it. He needed to get Helen out of the debt he had put her in. He looked through the grimy banister rails, twisting up from the fifth landing, at a broken door, skewed on one hinge, and felt his crotch contract in disappointment.

"Derelict!" just like you, Johnny boy he whispered. Head dropped in defeat, he turned to leave.

A stifled gasp snapped his reflexes into action. Tired limbs sloughed fatigue and contorted into a practised crouch against the wall. Five silent steps saw him to the threshold. He paused, sucking in the thrill of fear. Tightening his grip on the pepper spray in his pocket, he crushed all doubt and launched the suppressed rage of recent events, into an explosive kick and roll through the damaged door.

An arc of shattered wood flailed inward, from which he erupted in a low fighting stance. Stamping on the knee of the fallen brute entangled in the door wreckage, he sprang forward and upwards, with a palm thrust to a second assailant's chin, hooking clawed fingers into startled eyes and grinding his knee into a groin with a satisfying crunch. His right hand punched out, spraying the eyes of a third attacker, before he was stunned to immobility, by the hatchet click of a gun being cocked.

The dishevelled gunman, dribbling snot and blood, was much smaller than the others. Dragging a foot, he limped into John's peripheral vision. John waited wondering if he would hear the shot and feel pain or just know a release into darkness.

Three shots in quick succession confirmed the disappointing fact that life would not let go of him just yet. The erstwhile aggressors writhed and groaned, clutching at shattered knees, whilst the smaller man, continued to hobble across the room, calmly aiming the weapon in John's direction.

"Mr Wolfe I presume? He drew a sleeved hand through the gore under his nose. I think it would be wise to conduct our interview elsewhere." He gestured towards the door with the gun.

"What about them?"

"They are alive. I would not be if they had got what they wanted. They will give us no more trouble, and their pain is somewhat therapeutic to mine. I would see them crawl their own way out for help but, if it worries you, you can call an ambulance when we are well clear of this place." He looked around with distaste and gestured again at the door. Thinking it good policy to obey any nut with a gun, John led the way. The man pocketed the weapon and directed John through back streets to a Soho café with an upstairs window looking out over the neon street.

They faced each other over coffee and a sticky bun. So this was the guy he hoped to work for, a crazy with psychopathic tendencies, but he would work for Satan for the kind of money he was putting out, and if he was a head case, who gave a rat's arse, as long he came across with cash.

"That was very impressive Mr Wolfe. You've demonstrated, admirably, that you have the skills I'm looking for but, whilst my expedition includes death as a very real prospect, I am not embarking on a suicide mission. So, I have to ask you this … Are you? You took an enormous risk back there for someone you had never met, and without knowing whether you were going to be employed by me, or even what that employment was."

"I did what needed to be done."

"No, you did not! Until you blasted into my office like an avenging angel, you had no involvement at all. Your phone message said you were a police officer for 30 years. I don't think you would be here now if you treated every job with such a disregard for your safety. I need someone willing to take unavoidable risks not someone with a death wish. So, whilst you have my gratitude, I need convincing that you would place neither me nor yourself in unnecessary danger. I want protection throughout this mission. You will be no use to me dead. So … I'm listening. Explain why you were willing to put your life at risk for a total stranger." John took a deep breath.

"Look Mr ...?"

"Isaac."

"Isaac. I don't think either of us has too many options. Your ad went in the paper three days ago. You want an expert bodyguard, willing to put his life on the line, for an indefinite period of time, not exceeding three months, to leave for foreign parts within the week, for which you are offering £75,000.

"You are going to get a shed load of cranks, liars and thieves responding to an advert like that. You haven't got time to check them out. Whereas, you've seen me work, and you would not find better references in the time you've got." John paused, assessing Isaac's body language. He was stock still and impassive. "In six to eight months I'm dead anyway, tumour." He tapped his temple with a forefinger. "Mortgaged my wife's future getting quack treatment, not a great legacy to leave to someone you love (he could say that readily now) and I don't want to die knowing I've left a millstone of debt around her neck.

"I'm told when it happens I will deteriorate quickly but that I should be good for at least five or six months, apart from some aches and headaches, for which I have effective medication. The risk I took was calculated. Without your money my options are zero. Until I get that money, I promise you I will not put you, or myself, at risk, unnecessarily."

Isaac regarded him for several minutes. John could not fathom what might be going through this, oddly charismatic, little man's mind but he held his stare and waited. Isaac came to a decision. Leaning across the table, he offered his hand.

"Looks like I'm stuck with you. No policeman would have the imagination to construct such a melodrama. Good to have you on board. We won't be waiting around, so say your goodbyes. Get what you need and keep it light. We leave for Afghanistan tomorrow. Check your account before you leave. One third of the money will be in it. You will receive the rest, and a bonus, if you are fortunate enough to complete your work for me."

Helen faced him with a frown creasing her, normally, serene features. He noted her clenched hands squeezing her chair back, and the tightness in her shoulders when she twisted away from where he stood at the kitchen table.

"I knew you were going to do something stupid! Why can't we have this time? I don't give a toss about the money. I want you John."

He moved to step behind her and, with gentle caution, placed large hands on her taut shoulders. She shook him off, slumped then turned to face him again.

"But it wouldn't be me. Would it Helen? If I gave up trying, I would feel like a failure. I couldn't bear to leave you in debt. We've thrown away everything we have, so that I could cling to a shadow of life. It was cowardly. There never was any real hope; I feel dead already. This way, I'm motivated again, able to forget the cringing fear, and I can leave you secure. Right now I hate myself. I need to know that I have left you with enough money for, at least a chance, to get on with your life. I have to do this Helen, while I still can."

She felt the tremor in his large frame. Despite his desperation she knew she could hold him, but he was right, this was the only way. Truth was she loved him for it, even if it did claw out her heart, and it would be unbearable if he cried. The future was already sealed. Theirs was not a possessive love, where blinkered need could so easily lead her to hate him for his selfishness. It was a mature love of mutual respect, and acceptance for whom they both needed to be. Turning, she fixed him with a look of fatal resignation. He faltered. Doubt saturated his features. His voice was a broken whisper. "We will feel whole again, at least for a while ... I will die the man you know, an equal. Not a cripple waiting for slow death and, you? ... You will be able to go on with the memory of how great we both were, right to the end."

She looked away, crushing a surge of intense emotion with a nod, "Okay," she said, with quiet finality.

John checked his watch and sat up in the pre-dawn light to look down upon Helen, sleeping quietly beside him. After a moment he swung his legs over the side of the bed and quietly gathered his things. One last glance around the room embedded this simple domestic memory into his dying psyche. Padding quietly to her side, he brushed back her hair and pressed gentle lips to her forehead, then left. A muffled sob was lost in the trip of the closing door lock.

Entering the aircraft he gave a low whistle, "Fuck me, a private jet. What the hell are you getting me into?"

"An aeroplane Mr Wolfe, don't get too excited. You are going to be too busy to enjoy it." He shoved a file at him. "It's a six hour flight Mr Wolfe. Read that. It will tell you most of what you need to know. For the rest, you have what remains of those six hours to ask me anything you like. Take advantage of them. You may not get another chance. We have very limited time in which to unlock the secrets of Genesis."

"What the hell are you talking about Isaac?"

"Read the file John." He tapped it with a slender finger. "Read the file."

John read the file and became even more convinced that Isaac was barking mad, but that was not his concern. He just had to accept things as they were. He was in Isaac's reality now, and, if Helen was to be left secure, he had better do his best to embrace it.

"Okay Isaac, questions. Tell me about this volcano." Isaac's eyes were closed and John leaned across the table separating them to jostle his arm. Before he made contact, however, Isaac proved he was fully alert by responding.

"Straight to the root of the problem, I like that John. I thought your first question would be about the men who attacked me, and what their involvement was in this concern. By the way, I did some research and my deduction was correct, your story checked out. That is something else I like about you," he looked wistfully out of the window. "Practicality and honesty, rare traits, and combined with your proven ability to look after both me and yourself, well, it's almost too good to be true, but God and the Devil nurture their own I suppose," he turned back to face John. "Let's see if we can answer your questions then, shall we? The volcano mentioned in your file is situated in a low mountain range in east Afghanistan. It is newly formed and in close proximity to a larger and, until recently, dormant volcano. This new volcano which the local tribesmen call Beherit (Syrian name for the Devil) has formed within the last month, following a minor eruption of its larger neighbour.

"You have probably seen some news coverage. One of my many interests is geology, in particular, crustal faults. I have contacts working in this field all over the world. Naturally, I was deeply interested to hear of an eruption, but, this new volcano, and the details of the way it has formed, is very unusual. It seems, almost, to have been a controlled release of pressure from the centre of the earth to relieve what might well have been a much greater, and more devastating, eruption from its mightier neighbour.

"More interesting still, to me at least, is a geyser that is currently venting at regular intervals on the slopes of Beherit. You will not have heard of this, as the Afghan authorities are doing their best to suppress it. Fragments of a substance, previously unknown, have been expelled from several ventings of this geyser. They are very small but appear to be some kind of silica, metallic and crystalline alloy, incredibly strong, with an ability to withstand immense pressures and truly extreme temperatures. As you might imagine, the military are all over it but, as usual, they are missing the bigger picture. I believe I know exactly what this substance is, not its detailed chemical properties, but what its capabilities are, what it represents, and the purpose of the very much larger object, or vessel, from whence it came. I intend to retrieve that vessel and to enter it. Whilst the authorities have agreed to receive me as an advisor, due to my extensive expertise in underground fault geology, they will certainly become extremely hostile to any attempt on my part to approach or interfere with the vessel itself when they become aware of its existence, that is. I intend to make my play before that happens and I need you to protect my back as suspicions become heightened for, I am certain, our lives will be in the balance from the moment of our arrival, but the rewards, John, if we succeed, they are beyond imagination." His eyes glistened at the deluded prospect of the fruition of his efforts.

John moved on to more mundane questions regarding the key players and protagonists in this dangerous charade. The military commander would obviously be one to watch, so too the small technical and security team assembled by Isaac to initiate his observations (treachery was always a factor when practising deception) but the ones who really worried John were Delarum Sahar, an Afghan contemporary and competitor of Isaac's, who was both very religious and politically motivated, and, if Isaac's assessment was correct, "a dangerous fanatic hiding under a thin guise of aristocratic charm." John was even more unsettled though by Delarum's sister, Afsoon, and her relationship with her brother.

Information in the file related rumours, viciously suppressed by the Sahar family of an incestuous impropriety with Delarum.

Afsoon was, apparently, also a genius. Having no formal education she had yet mastered an extensive knowledge of chemistry and, oddly, quantum physics, and had smuggled out and published several very well received and thought provoking theses on the fluid structure of quantum matter. She was also highly unstable, a religious radical, and an advocate of ethnic cleansing. As a teenager she had been actively involved in the manufacture and distribution of Improvised Explosive Devices, and had assisted in the radicalisation and training of female suicide bombers. There were a few others who needed to be closely watched and, of course, everyone was an enemy until proven otherwise and, even then, were to be treated with caution and suspicion.

John limited his questions to those pertaining to his role as protector and stopped whilst there was still an hour and a half left of the flight. He threw a couple of pain killers down his throat and lay back with his eyes closed, trying to digest what he had learned, and to make some sort of sense out of it, so that he could, at least, put together the skeleton of a plan of action. He slipped into a fitful slumber which proved to be the ideal state for his subconscious mind to offer some lateral strategies.

The file contained a contour map of the area and the layout of the encampment. A high security wire fence enclosed the site, with armed guards at regular intervals. There was a large bunk house tent for the manual staff and a cluster of smaller ones for key personnel, with shared kitchen and toilet facilities, but Isaac would be able to site his equipment tent where it was most expedient. It would not arouse suspicions if they spent most of their time in and around it, catching cat naps whilst they worked. This would enable them to ensure the best position to access the active site, achieve relative seclusion and, most importantly, to maintain a guardable area with a clear view of the encampment. The site map had suggested a couple of possible areas that he would inspect as soon as possible after landing.

John's ears popped and reverse thrust told him they were coming in to land. Isaac pushed a harness across the table towards him.

"You had better strap that under your jacket. It's a 10mm Glock machine pistol. Ridiculously large and ungainly for a hand gun, but they will take it off you anyway when we land, which will appease their need to find our weaponry and send them a message that you are a thuggish killer, lacking in brains or finesse. Terry and Jake, as your security team, will be carrying similar heavy duty arms. You can play the part if you like, dangerous but stupid. Then, hopefully, they will mistakenly see me as an easy target when they make their move."

As predicted, after a very bumpy landing at a makeshift airfield, they were searched on leaving the plane and deprived of their weaponry. Not without some schoolboy bluster on both sides.

"Get your fucking hands off my piece you slimy bastard." Terry kept hold of the pistol for a couple of tugs then, suddenly let go, and grabbed the assault rifle slung round the neck of the military official, twisting it over sharply, so that the strap formed a noose, half strangling him. Another soldier threw a heavy fist at Terry, then doubled over from the blow John drove into his lower ribs. Guns were cocked and everyone froze, except the poor guy still struggling to get his fingers under the strap around his neck. A curt order and a pistol placed in Terry's temple by Colonel Azizi brought the fight to a close but John had the strong impression that Azizi was not fooled by the subterfuge. Isaac made an excellent show of being both livid and highly embarrassed, going so far as to strike Terry on the shoulder, and dressing down John in a very public and humiliating way, and forcing immediate, and grovelling, public apologies from both of them. They had made enemies. But these were known quantities and were an excellent foil for future distractions. Terry's eye was now showing signs of becoming a real shiner but his assailant would be nursing his ribs for the next couple of days. And it was somehow satisfying to get off to a dynamic, if dangerously volatile, start having avoided all the usual pretences of wary courtesy.

Whilst equipment was being unloaded, John inspected the site. It was early dusk and a hot dry wind was starting to lift grains of gritty sand from where it had pooled amongst the protruding lava rocks. He turned his back to the wind and climbed the steep slope to the crater rim. Steam and sulphur fumes, venting from fissures in the rocks, hung heavy in the air. He took care which rocks he grabbed for support as some were radiating large amounts of heat. Reaching the rim, he sucked deeply through his nose filling his lungs with the heated, rotten egg stench to evacuate the last of the flight fatigue befuddling his thoughts. He stared absently into the crater for a few moments, the word "Beherit" slithering into his mind as he watched the steamy soup bubbling below. Shielding his eyes, he turned into the stinging grit and surveyed the encampment below, noting vehicle and guard placements and likely weapons and munitions stores.

He chose a seemingly ill-considered position for their encampment in the lea of a huge rock close to the rim. This would probably add to the illusion of a brutish persona with limited intellect, the site being far from facilities and within metres of the last lava flow. It was also close to the heat and sulphur smell from continuing volcanic activity. Working conditions would be unpleasant and dangerous but it was perfectly suited to his purpose, just uphill from the geyser that so interested Isaac. It was difficult to approach, and would be an uncomfortable place for people to indulge in idle curiosity. It also gave extensive views of the whole camp, so anyone who did approach would find it difficult to do so covertly, and the rock formed a semi cave offering some protection from both the local conditions and unwanted observation, or direct approach from behind. Isaac frowned at the choice but made no objections and ordered the tents and equipment to be brought to the site.

Isaac and his chief technician were invited to dine with the Sahars that evening and the invitation had been belatedly extended to include John. Colonel Azizi would also be attending. Isaac wasted no time however and arranged sonar, seismic, and various other monitoring equipment to be placed both inside the rim of the crater and around the geyser. Delarum accompanied him, raining a constant barrage of questions on him about his method and early deductions.

John maintained a wary watch but continued to supervise the setting up of the equipment camp with the assistance of Robin, the chief technician, whom he had taken a liking to. Robin was a tall, rangy and bespectacled, ginger guy, thirty-ish, with a sharp mind and a wicked sense of humour. He was explaining something now to a persistently nosey and interfering soldier who understood a little English. He waived John over. "John, this man has been asking what we intend to do with all this equipment. I've explained that the fulcrum, more commonly called the scrotum," he nodded encouragement at the man who repeated "scro-tum," "will hold the prop or penis 'pe-nis' and that we will drill into the back passage of the crater until we have penetrated the anal crust which will, hopefully, release an excremental discharge from the bowels of this cesspit that can be sampled for analysis. I have told him that you are the real expert though and that he should ask you if he wanted to know more." Robin's assistant, Gwen, saved the day by thrusting a crate of electrical parts into his chest and pointing towards the geyser where Isaac was assembling a monitoring station. John wasted no time making his escape, warning Robin in passing that he was going to make him pay for that. Robin chuckled, taking a second crate, and headed off in the same direction.

When all was complete to both their satisfaction, John gave Terry and Jake instructions to keep a sharp lookout for anyone showing too much interest in what they were doing, and to report every detail to him. He threw a bed role on the ground just inside the opening of the main tent and lay back to think, before preparing for the dinner engagement.

He dwelt on the rapidity of his changing circumstances. Eighteen months ago he was looking forward to retirement and extensive travel with Helen with mixed feelings. It was what they had planned. To finally have unlimited time in each other's company had become a cherished fantasy. A chance to rebuild their lives after their long grief following Annabel's death but, looking back, he realised this was not really what he had wanted. Their ambitions had been stunted by circumstance. Helen, too, had had a budding career as a writer. This had been the basis of their attraction to one another, two strong people, each admiring the qualities of the other and wanting to conquer the world. To degenerate into broken creatures grasping at each other for company and support was not the partnership he had envisaged. He loved her for her strength not her weakness and he was coming to realise that she felt the same, even if she didn't fully own up to it. They had coped with what the world had thrown at them and come out the other side. Why should his illness have changed that? He was still alive and able, and had wasted enough time and money chasing fanciful dreams of a cure. He was taking life by the horns again and it felt good. So what if he was dying! He would leave Helen in a position to fulfil her ambitions. That was real love, when you helped the person you loved to go on with or without you.

Isaac shook him from semi-slumber. "Come on John! Ridiculous as it may seem, we are expected to dress for dinner. I know these cretins so I brought suitable clothing. Help yourself from the chest at the back of the tent. There should be something about your size. If we look like we're enjoying ourselves it might blunt the edge off the urgent nature of our work and hide the fact of just how desperate we are to bring it to a close." John followed him to the shower tent, totally bemused.

Dinner was an extraordinary affair. The dinner suit, supplied by Isaac, looked and felt expensive but it fitted badly and the legs were too short. He felt like a casting reject from a James Bond film and totally ridiculous, but the food was both exotic and delicious and, more importantly, so was the wine. The tent was a revelation. It might have belonged to Kubla Khan. It was huge and sumptuously furnished. A large deep piled Persian rug supported an oak dinner table laden with silverware and covered terrines. Set for six, it would have comfortably sat twelve. Around the perimeter were divans and low tables loaded with fruit. Alongside were welcoming heaps of interspersed cushions. Bubble pipes exuded a heady smell of shisha mixed with the unmistakably pungent smell of hashish.

One of the bed compartment curtains lifted in the breeze created by the tapestry fan wafting gently from the high ridge overhead, exposing an incongruously lavish boudoir of medieval splendour. Rose coloured mosquito nets were drawn back to reveal a bed of sumptuous red velvet with silk sheets folded invitingly back, ready to receive an occupant, or occupants. The same breeze dispersed mouth-watering aromas that enticed the guests toward the dinner table with irresistible insistency. In this barren environment such opulence was no circus prop but rather a torrent of welcome relief, an oasis in the wilderness. Feeling like a questing knight seduced into the tent of a witch temptress, John walked in with trepidation and couldn't help wonder if he and Isaac were being diverted from attaining the Holy Grail.

Colonel Azizi gave John an occasional appraising stare but otherwise, apart from some polite pleasantries, he was studiously ignored and made to feel of no consequence. This was fine by him except that the fully suited waiter seemed intent on making him drunk with copious refills, so, unfortunately, some of the wine, under the guise of drunken clumsiness, had to be tipped into the sand. As this added substance to the oafish persona he was still trying to portray, and gave him the opportunity to observe without being too closely watched himself, he was not entirely dissatisfied with the situation.

Delarum, opposite Isaac, hogged all of his colleague's attention, fishing for information whilst being evasive about his own conclusions. He elaborated a little from time to time, giving occasional hints of what was probably greater knowledge than he actually possessed, in an apparent effort to force an unguarded response.

Robin sat opposite Azizi, who questioned him closely about what equipment he had and what would be the method and purpose behind his observations and experiments. He demonstrated surprising insight into the science involved and, obviously, had been chosen for his understanding of geology as much as for his military prowess. Afsoon was relegated to sit opposite John. She was very attractive but also very distant. She was incongruously dressed in a debutante-style turquoise gown with matching emerald pendant and earrings and showing a small amount of cleavage. Nevertheless, she seemed to blend into the scene with perfection. Her features, surprisingly, were mainly of a western caste with shoulder length chestnut hair. The capitalist image was contradicted, however, by an overly demure demeanour. She said nothing throughout dinner, merely nodding when introduced, and John had yet to catch a glimpse of her eyes, these having been downcast until now.

John had allowed his own eyes to drop in contemplation of the ruby fluid currently being, yet again, poured into his glass. He became aware of a warm touch on the back of his hand and looked up into the startling green of large catlike eyes boring into, what he hoped, was his own vacant stare. A rich contralto voice and a waft of musk momentarily numbed his senses.

"And what do you think Mr Wolfe? Or may I call you John?" Her English was perfect with just the trace of an accent. She waited, without removing her hand, whilst John mustered his stunned senses. Slurring his words a little, he responded.

"I'm sorry? Er, er, yes, 'John!' Call me John, if that is okay? It is isn't it? With your brother I mean. Isaac warned me not to offend anyone else. I want to keep this job and I'm in enough trouble already." She smiled radiantly, displaying perfect white teeth.

"Isaac?" she enquired. "It seems to me you are already over familiar with your superior. One more gaff should make little difference now." John cursed inwardly.

"What do you mean? That's the only name he gave me, said he didn't think I needed to know any more." This was the truth and he hoped it was enough to divert her evident suspicion of him.

"You seem frightened of me John. Why is that?"

Colonel Azizi was watching the exchange with interest. Delarum seemed, deliberately, to ignore them, turning more towards Isaac and hunching his shoulders to lean further over the table. Afsoon continued, "You feign fear for your employment; yet, you thought little of attacking an armed guard in a military environment known to harbour killers and fanatics. Don't cast your eyes around like that John! I find it very rude when I'm speaking to you." There was humour in her tone, and something else. John felt stirrings that shamed him at this time in his life, and were likely to betray him when he stood if he didn't quickly regain control of himself. His recently re-invigorated sixth sense was shoving a cattle prod up his backside, as he kept his eyes down to avoid the full effect of her sexual magnetism.

"I d-do my job miss, that's all." He tugged at his collar, "I-I don't feel very well. Is it okay if I leave?" Her penetrating look continued to strip away his defences and her voice took on a harsh tone.

"No you can't leave! I demand you keep me company!" She leaned close. He could almost taste her. She whispered, "I wouldn't cause you the embarrassment of having to stand." More loudly she said, "stay, have one more drink, then I will think about releasing you." All eyes were now on them.

Isaac said something to Delarum, who cleared his throat. "Leave the poor man alone Afsoon." He ignored John and spoke to Isaac. "You know how she likes to play her little games. I have always been far too tolerant of her wilful behaviour. Instruct your man to go back to his sleeping tent Isaac. Then, perhaps, we can finish our discussion in peace." Isaac nodded at John who, just about, had sufficient control of himself to leave, which he did without another word.

He heard Afsoon respond to Delarum behind him.

"Manners, dear brother, manners," but he was too busy making his getaway to pay further heed. She caught up with him just outside the tent. Swiftly ducking under his arm, she was suddenly in front of him. A hot hand writhed expertly around the back of his neck. As tall as he, she pulled him forward with an unexpectedly strong grip and kissed him full on the lips. He stood immobile and stunned. She breathed in his ear, "You do not fool me John Wolfe." With a cascade of mocking laughter, she grabbed his stiffening crotch in a firm grip. "You're not fooling anyone." He flushed for the first time in many years, as he closed a steel fist over the offending wrist intending to force her to release her hand. She seemed unaffected going on to give him a playful squeeze before releasing him. He shoved out a hard palm thrust to her shoulder but she wasn't there. Once again she had eluded him by ducking under his arm. Rage, at his failure to control the situation, surged through him as she strolled off, still laughing. Adrenalin dispelled the effects of the wine, and a return to clearer thought, brought the realisation that it must have been a lot more potent than he thought.

He couldn't face the communal sleeping tent, going instead to the equipment tent, where he dismissed Jake, changed into work-wear and took over guard duty. He wasn't getting any sleep tonight anyway. His thoughts were a seething mass of anger and turmoil. She had somehow contrived to make him feel like a shamed adolescent caught masturbating in the school toilet. Perhaps his condition was affecting his ability to act with the certainty and iron control he had always managed to command before. He had to hold it together for this last assignment, for Helen.

Isaac arrived back about three hours later to find a wide awake and confused, but much more composed, John sitting contempla-tively on a rock.

"My deepest apologies John, I should not have exposed you to that without due warning but I wanted to see just how much they suspect of our true purpose here, and I'm afraid it does not look too good."

"So you knew something like this was going to happen?"

"I knew yes, but I was truly surprised by the extent of their probing and manipulations. For them to act so overtly there is obviously more focused political and military involvement than even I realised, and Afsoon is always unpredictable."

"I don't fully understand your reasons Isaac but I did not set down any conditions before I came and can only assume you know what you are doing. However, I do need to be fully informed from now on if I am to do my job properly."

Isaac could hear the strain in his voice and enlightenment drew a veil from his features. He softened his tone. "Afsoon is a stunning woman John, but not that stunning. You do realise that you were drugged, don't you?" John's shoulders relaxed and he regained firmer control of his voice.

"Ah! I had begun to wonder if it might be something like that, but it does confirm my earlier fears that I need to be more fully informed. I can't be caught off guard like that again. Next time we may end up dead."

"Very true John. I can't tell you absolutely everything at this stage. But I promise you I will tell you all that I can and I will reveal more as soon as I am able. That is the best I can do for now. You may never know everything John but you will, eventually, know as much as anyone, other than myself, if we can both stay alive that long." John thought for a moment, sucked in a deep breath and, in a tone full of consternation, released his reply into the night air. Portentously, it was instantly snatched away by a sudden hot gust of air as a warm blast vented from a newly opened fissure between them. They backed off and he repeated himself in an attempt to dispel the ridiculous but unsettling feeling of a supernatural and malevolent presence having just expressed its displeasure at their unwanted involvement.

"That will have to do for now." His feelings of betrayal by Isaac, and of Helen, ebbed a little but he was not completely convinced that the drug, whatever it was, was entirely to blame for his shameful reaction. He made a mental promise to keep a sharp eye on Afsoon but, most decidedly, from a distance.

Afsoon

As the sun was about to breach the horizon, Isaac called Jake, Robin and John into the equipment tent. Terry maintained a watch from atop the rock. They had been allowed to keep knives, as these were considered a necessary survival tool in the desert mountains. John carried a large hunting knife, displayed openly on his belt. It suited the image he was trying to project and was both handy and deadly. Jake's commando knife was less obvious but somehow more menacing, as was Jake himself. He was small, athletic, and swarthy and rarely spoke. John judged he would be a good man in a fight but did not trust him. Terry carried a machete, which pretty much said everything about him. John liked him. Robin was rummaging around in the equipment at the back of the tent and was struggling to pull free one of the large drill props. John made to help but he pulled it free on his own and hefted it into the space in the centre of the floor.

Using a fist sized rock and a screwdriver; he broke off one end and upended the other. To John's astonishment, four hand guns fell out and, following some probing and tapping, what looked like a Steyr type, tactical machine pistol. A few other items including stun guns and pepper sprays increased the small arsenal. John gave a low whistle but Jake displayed no reaction at all, simply leaning down and taking two of the hand guns, one, presumably, for Terry. The Steyr was returned to its hiding place. Isaac, John, Jake, and later, Terry, made their own arrangements for the concealment of their individual weaponry.

By the time the sun was fully risen a test borehole was already underway and Robin was studying the results and graphs of various sonar, seismic, and other probing and monitoring equipment. Jake and Terry maintained a general watch whilst John, aside from checking on these two from time to time, stayed close to Isaac and Robin questioning both, whenever he could, about what they were doing and what they hoped to gain from it.

He was making his way over to Robin but slowed his step when he noticed Gwen leaning over the console next to him. Robin's assistant might have been a pretty little thing if she had taken the time to look after herself, as it was she just looked dispossessed. Unkempt and scruffy in oversized shirt and saggy trousers, held up by an ancient leather belt and worn out boots to match. Her mousey hair was held back with a cable tie and, whilst she usually kept her distance, it was impossible to miss the occasional whiff of grease and old sweat that wafted downwind of her. Her lack of response, apart from the odd grunt (unless facts, figures or instructions needed to be explained), did little to endear her to anyone. Generally though, she had an extraordinary knack for being invisible. What was disconcerting was that when you did notice her it was usually because of the odd way she had of staring at you analytically when she thought you were not looking. Robin, however, seemed to think she was a genius and always asked her opinion as soon as any results were available. They were discussing some now and Gwen was unusually animated. As he drew close he tuned in to what she was saying.

"Whatever it is, it's fucking big, at least sixty feet long, around thirty across and perhaps twenty deep. Trouble is it's not there. The readings show nothing but a uniformly shaped empty space, but, as the area surrounding that space is mainly fluid, something has got to be occupying it. Something shaped like an egg or, kick me in the crotch for saying this, a saucer, but don't ever repeat that out loud."

That was another thing about Gwen when she was communicating regarding her work; it was as though someone struck a match. Authority and presence, even humour, flared for a moment, before fizzling out as her interest returned to its inward focus. Robin nodded sagely and tweaked some of the instruments, whilst Gwen, downloaded, encrypted, and backed up the findings into secure data files. Robin ordered several more bore holes to be started. This meant co-opting help from both John and Isaac, as Isaac wanted minimal intrusion from anyone outside the team.

Unfortunately Colonel Azizi had other plans and was currently insisting to a composed, but obviously irritated, Isaac that several of his "best men" would work closely with Isaac and his people, helping with both the heavy work and the guarding of this project.

The Sahars and even Colonel Azizi himself would be giving assistance with some of the more technical areas of this, "very important work that is of such intense, interest to our 'political leaders.' I am sure you understand how crucial our involvement in all aspects of this work is to our national interest." This was said with unveiled and emphatic menace that did not pass Isaac by.

Afsoon sauntered over from the main encampment area, wearing Levi jeans and a grey T-shirt with the motif "Afghans bite" written across the chest. Even with mussed hair and no makeup, she was stunning. In fact she looked several years younger, and more impish than dangerously beautiful, as she had seemed last night. She walked between Azizi and Isaac and, grabbing Isaac's elbow, walked them both toward the scene of operations, near the geyser spout.

"Oh come on Isaac, you must have known you would be closely supervised and will it really be so bad working with Delarum and I and, of course, the indomitable Colonel Azizi? He is quite an expert in his field you know, and really just a pussycat when you get to know him, aren't you Ahmed?" So saying, she leaned across and mischievously pecked him on the cheek. He ignored her but walked with them both amicably enough.

"Charming as ever Afsoon. I find such beauty in someone so very clever disarming. Of course I want to work with you and your brother, and I entirely believe your assertions regarding our very capable Colonel but you know how it is when you are setting up operations. Every team has its own way of doing things and other people, unfamiliar with our methods, will just get in the way, to begin with anyway, and will slow operations down. Once all our equipment is in place and initial observations are correlated, I will be more than happy to familiarise you with our mode of operations and will welcome your full involvement and input. In fact I think your help will be essential to success. But, for now, I just want to get things under way. It is always the devil of a job to prepare the ground and the less interference, at this stage, the better. I'm sure you understand."

Afsoon was taking a keen interest in the bore holes and equipment but she turned to Colonel Azizi. "You know Ahmed, Isaac is right. It will slow things down if we interfere at this stage. I think one day will make little difference. Let me suggest that I remain with Isaac for today and get familiar with his intentions. You and your men, and of course my brother, can come on board tomorrow after I have given you a full briefing of Isaac's requirements."

Azizi looked irritated but agreed in principle, with the proviso that four of his men remained, "To guard the working perimeter against unwanted curiosity or interference."

Afsoon quickly merged herself into an integral part of the team and was constantly on the shoulder of either Isaac or Robin, asking occasional very direct and probing questions, or offering, what was always, relevant advice. Gwen became almost entirely invisible and John kept his distance, only approaching either Isaac or Robin when Afsoon was at a distance with the other of the two. This eventually became a bit of a farce when Afsoon walked toward John with a flask and some sandwiches. He shuffled away behind the rock to emerge covertly from the other side where she was waiting, having quickly changed direction to meet with him. In his haste, he barged into her and she fell heavily onto her butt but managed to deftly maintain the flask and sandwiches in either hand. Reflexively, he grabbed her upper arms and started to raise her to her feet whilst apologising. She declined his help.

"Honestly John, the things you'll do to get a girl's attention. I knew you were not to be trusted. Now that you have injured my nether regions I expect you to wait on me through lunch. If you are sufficiently penitent and attentive I may let you massage my injuries until I get some feeling back. Now sit here next to me." She patted the sand next to where she was sitting cross legged. He could see no way out of it without causing offence and she had, besides, totally disarmed him. He found it difficult to reconcile this vivacious young woman with the siren he had encountered last night. In some ways, she now reminded him of how he had imagined his adopted daughter might have turned out. He sat down with a theatrical show of reluctance. "Cheese sandwich?" she said, proffering a hunk of bread and a cup of wine.

"I'll pass on the wine thanks."

"I don't blame you. You had a skin full last night. Is that why you have been keeping your distance? You don't need to be embarrassed you know. I've seen it all before."

"I am a little embarrassed, but that's not all of it." Her eyes widened.

"Oh! Isaac told you the wine was drugged didn't he? You don't want to believe everything you are told you know."

"Are you saying it wasn't drugged?"

"No, that would be lying, and I don't lie, but Isaac is being deceitful by not telling you everything. We all drank the same wine as you. It's just that this particular wine is a special batch. My brother laces it with a mild drug just to give our social occasions a bit of a swing. I suppose if you are not used to it, it can catch you unawares and I did make sure you were awash with it, despite your clumsy attempts to spill it everywhere. You seemed so awkward. Isaac really should have warned you, but I was right wasn't I? You did loosen up, or rather stiffen up." She laughed, a light tinkling sound, girlish, nothing like the heavy mocking laughter of last night. He smiled despite himself and began to wonder if this was the same person who had so shaken him.

Isaac rounded the rock. "Come on John, you're needed. We're starting a new borehole and we need some muscle to manoeuvre the rig."

Afsoon raised her eyebrows, "Another borehole?" She jumped to her feet and brushed off the sand, "What are you trying to do? Create a second crater?" Isaac failed to see the funny side of this and suggested that if she had nothing else to do she should role up her sleeves and lend a hand. Afsoon ran ahead and was already besieging Robin with a barrage of questions.

"Be very careful John. She really is extremely dangerous."

"She says you knew the wine was drugged and that we all drank it."

"Much as I told you, admittedly after the event, but its effect is accumulative, she probably added something extra too, and I really had no idea how much of the stuff she was going to ply you with. The amount of interest she is showing in you is a particularly disconcerting turn of events but it is also something I need to speak to you about urgently, as soon as we can find some privacy. The situation here is far worse than I imagined and Afsoon is starting to draw some very accurate conclusions. I think it possible that we may be able to use your liaison with her to our advantage."

The sun had set and Afsoon had gone to shower and change. Azizi's four guards remained at a discreet distance, but the night was still and sounds carried. Isaac spoke in low tones to Robin and

John. Gwen sat, very much unnoticed in the corner of the tent. Jake and Terry kept watch outside.

"Listen John, things have become difficult and we are out of time. You need to know more of what is going on here."

"At last." John folded his arms and sat on a pile of equipment.

"Sitting a scant sixty-five feet below us is an artefact of astounding importance, pre-historic importance. Something made at the time man first set foot upon the earth. It's big, physically big. You've heard Robin and Gwen discussing dimensions. Excavations would take months. By that time the Afghan authorities will long have taken all control of this project. I had hoped we would be able to hoodwink them and gain access via a shaft before they realised what we were up to. But with Azizi and Delarum on the case that is now unlikely and Afsoon has already figured out, in broad terms, what we are up to. By the morning we will already have lost control.

"My research indicates this vessel may contain information pertaining to the secrets of the Genesis of humanity and of just about everything else on this planet. Listen carefully John, I know this is a cliché, but this really 'cannot end up in the hands of the wrong people' and believe me John, the Sahars are very much the wrong people. Afsoon has also divined your importance to this project, something you do not fully realise yourself yet. You might say you have gained celebrity status with her, hence, her efforts to coerce you into a relationship. She may also be looking to you to fill the gap left in her life by the death of her father. As it is highly likely that she killed her father that might not be very desirable, but it may be to our advantage. Gwen has come up with a plan but we need to keep Afsoon occupied. She will be here soon, probably with Delarum, Azizi, and a retinue of armed guards within hailing distance but I think she will want to draw out her moment of victory a little longer. She has set her mind on seducing you and frankly we need you to allow her to do just that, if Gwen's plan is to have any chance of success. Don't make it too easy or she will smell a rat."

"Whoa! Wait right there! This was not part of any agreement, and I want a whole lot more information. For a start I want to know what you mean about me being important. I take it you mean in some other way than as a bodyguard, and this talk of

Genesis and vessels and, God knows what else, is starting to creep me out."

Isaac cut him dead with an alarming show of icy authority that had been noticeably absent until now. The sharp tone of his voice sliced through the air like a scalpel.

"Keep your voice down! We haven't time for your puerile foibles. I will tell you, in brief, what you are going to do and why you are going to do it. For the rest, if you and I are still alive after tonight, I will fully enlighten you.

"You agreed to protect me without question. By following Gwen's plan you will be doing precisely that. The stakes, however, have become very high. I know you did not expect to have to betray your wife, but, if you genuinely have her future interests at heart, you will agree to do this. I have arranged for two million pounds to be placed into your account in three days' time. Your wife will never want for anything again, other than her dead husband that is, which I remind you, will very shortly be the case, if not tonight, then, as you have previously indicated, in the very near future, so stop whining and do what you need to do. What we all need you to do. Your importance to this project has to do with your cancer. I haven't the time to explain that now but when the time is right, if we can create a situation when time is right, you will know what you need to know. The rest is on trust. Can we trust you John?"

John struggled with his conscience and feelings of betrayal and, bugger it! his bloody pride. His body unconsciously adopted a fighting stance but he was not stupid. He exerted his formidable willpower and forced down his frustration and rage at Isaac's tone. Ultimately, he could see no fault in Isaac's cold logic. He became aware that he was now bolt upright and glowering down at Isaac with fists clenched tightly under his ribs. Isaac stared coolly up at him. Forcing himself to relax, he gave a strained nod, and looked away. "Good. Gwen, explain your plan." Gwen lowered the machine pistol aimed at John's chest and stepped into the middle of the tent.

The match was well and truly lit, and Gwen delivered her plan with succinct authority and precision. "Okay. John!" She looked directly into his brown eyes with her cool grey ones, which seemed to quickly rummage around inside his mind and come up satisfied.

"We need an hour and a half, so play hard to get. After this time, if all goes well, we'll be ready. There will be a large explosion. If you are in any position to, at that time, your best course of action will be to kill Afsoon. Either way, get yourself outside and over the lip of the crater. A series of explosions will follow. If all goes well the ground will split and crumble, down and inwards. Your position, here in this tent, will be swallowed up, so, I repeat, get out and away. There will be a pause of perhaps 30 seconds and then the earth will truly move. If our calculations are correct, we estimate a 25 percent chance of success, the vessel we seek will be ejected on a spout of super-heated steam, water, further explosions, and crustal fault adjustment, and will, we hope, come to rest some way downhill of our current position. Your job will be to get to that position as fast as you can, making sure you are well clear of the new crater that Afsoon so accurately, if inadvertently, predicted as the goal of our many boreholes and into which, we have now inserted, a network of controlled explosives. Those of us who have avoided mishap will meet you there."

John almost had to raise his hanging jaw with his hand. "Are you taking the piss?" but he could see she was not. "Jesus! You are all insane! I'm going to die anyway, apparently a lot sooner than I thought, but I didn't think you lot were all going to join me."

Gwen ignored his comments. "Do you understand what you need to do?"

"I don't understand anything but I can follow instructions. I suppose I always wanted to go out with a bang. It looks like I'll be getting my wish twice tonight." He pulled a wry face, finding no humour in his unfunny joke. Terry blew his nose atop the rock outside and Gwen turned to Isaac and Robin.

"Looks like she's here, come on John you can help us get this monitoring equipment outside to the edge of the geyser pit. We'll be occupied for some time setting it up," she looked at him significantly. John rolled up his sleeves and got stuck in with the others. They were half way to the pit when Afsoon caught up with them. Robin nudged him in the ribs and nodded in her direction, whistling wolfishly.

Afsoon stood several yards away displaying yet another aspect of her chameleon charms. Her hair was raked back into a high pony tail with heavy makeup and cat's eyeliner. She had a waist length leather jacket with a high turned up collar, tight leather skirt and thigh length, high heeled boots with a crop top and plunging neckline under the jacket.

"What are you doing at this time of night? Can I help?" Her voice, although enquiring, was now also authoritative and demanding.

Isaac responded. "Just setting up some more probes, ready for an early start tomorrow, your help would certainly be appreciated but you are not really dressed for it."

"No problem," she shrugged off the leather jacket, dropping it in the sand, and grabbed a corner of the heavy rig cradle. Once manoeuvred into place, Isaac told John, it was all tech stuff from here on, so he might as well go off and get some rest but if Afsoon wished she could stay to help with some of the calibrations. John wandered off back towards the tent. Afsoon stayed for a moment, asked a couple of questions, and then ran after him. He brushed off the gritty sand and handed the jacket back to her. Putting it on, she slipped her arm through his and put her hands in the pockets. "So gracious John, you do understand that you are not just going back to your tent, don't you?"

John looked up at her. In high heels she was taller than he. "Yeah, I suppose I do. I thought I might go for a walk, unless you wanted to do something else."

"Well these boots were designed for other pursuits but I guess a short walk will whet the appetite." She flicked her tongue between the heavy lipstick liberally coating her lips, before biting the bottom one invitingly. They walked, some distance, to a break in the crater wall which John examined surreptitiously for later.

Afsoon went up to the opening. "Look John." She indicated the moon that hung just above the horizon, sitting in the broken crater wall like a Promethean flame. "Was this why you brought me here? Be careful, you are in danger of capturing my heart. This is a good omen John. Walk me through the opening." She offered her hand. "How many entwined souls have the chance to consecrate their love by bathing in the spilt essence of moonlight?" Seeing him hesitate, she laughed, and said, "Come," somehow managing to combine both gentle seduction and sexual authority in her low and sensuous tones. Stepping close, she slid her hands with tantalizing slowness up his arms. Cupping his elbows she pulled him gently but irresistibly into the heat and shadow of the balmy fissure. In the muted moonlight her skin glistened with a light silvery sweat as she backed further into the fold of rock. He felt both panic and lust as his senses melted into the night. His blood was pounding and, oh God! Every deep throb of engorging blood sapped further the last vestiges of his will. In other circumstances, could he have held back? The answer to that question was lost in the hot wind of desire as he succumbed to bestial abandonment.

Drained by the succubus of insatiable passion (guilt having fled to recoup its resources) John fell into velvet sleep. Aeons passed. A slow, deep growl intruded his slumbers, billowing and rending, the cocoon of satiation. Cognisance returned like a sledge hammer. Eyes snapped open as the earth rippled and undulated under his back. His hunting knife, used by Afsoon, to cut the clothes from his body, lay near his head. The gun had gone. He struggled to his feet rubbing the gashed lump on his head. Rasping pain caused him to clutch at his lower stomach and genitalia. Bringing hands to his face in the shadows he could not see, but felt and tasted the sticky fluid that oozed down his torso to congeal in his groin. The pain was excruciating, but the wounds seemed not deep. Urgency fell on him like doom and he forced his limbs into a crouch. Knife in hand he grabbed his shredded clothes and pushed them to his wounds. He located his boots, and took time to pull them on, before leaving the shadows and scurrying along the internal slope of the crater.

The second explosion shook the ground sufficiently to knock him to his knees. He made use of the added traction and quickly scrambled to the top of the rim. The camp was in pandemonium, a huge pit was hypnotically forming in the area of Isaac's operations, a sliding vortex of rubble and equipment slumping downwards. As he watched, it started to go into reverse and swell up. He ducked below the rim as a further, larger explosion spewed rocks and dust into the air, some whistling into the bowl of the volcano. Wounds forgotten, he scampered further along, using his scant knowledge of the terrain to estimate where any ejecting object would role to a halt on the slopes below. Some part of his conscience chided him for buying into the ludicrous idea that Gwen and Isaac's fantasy might actually become real but the series of massive explosions that followed washed away all thoughts of anything except the headlong rush to survive the current onslaught, and to achieve his rendezvous with the ridiculous.

He found a crevice in the crater wall, wriggled inside and waited for the storm of violence to subside. Quiet fell on the world like a lead blanket then, a low rumble felt rather than heard disturbed the subterranean depths, growing to a screaming crescendo, as of the heart being ripped from a wounded Earth. John squeezed tighter into the apex of his confined space and felt the earth flex. The entire area ruptured like a boil. The crater wall next to him fell in, shedding rocks that miraculously bounced and tumbled over his refuge and carved a jagged gash darting zigzag to the edge of the crater wall. Revealing within the flood plain of its expanding delta an emerging disc, so dark, it sucked in light. It seemed to pause for a moment, as if the terrain had opened a tired eye, then dilated and erupted, ejecting a hard centre on a cloud of roaring steam and semi-molten rock. The disc flew clear in a perfect arc, dropping like doom on the rocky slope some two hundred metres below. It did not roll, or slide, or bounce but came to rest gently, and with unnatural slowness on an incline that should have been too steep to bear it, seeming more to hover on the ground than to settle any weight upon it. Through the gap John stepped from one reality into the mythical maelstrom of another, finally, fully embracing the madness of Isaac's universe.

The force of the explosion had knocked out the generators and cloud and dust shrouded the moon. All was utter dark, from which guttural voices and sharp commands sliced their urgency. Several shots were fired showing brief discharge flashes that revealed running silhouettes. John started to run too, at dangerous speed, down the steep volcanic slope recklessly leaping boulders and equipment in his headlong rush for the landing site. His feet were protected by stout boots but his skin was cut and lacerated from many falls and slides over sharp lava rock and grating sand. As the moon finally slid from behind the cloud he heard a shot and someone screamed in agony. Hot shale began to rain from the skies. Clouds of dust rolled away in every direction. John followed his nose pursuing the vessel site. Torch beams slashed rents in the dark shadows. John ran on, panting in gasps.

The dark ovoid loomed before him, sounds of pursuit echoed in the distance behind. Several vehicles were making impotent choking noises. His subconscious proffered the suggestion they had likely been tampered with. He was on a forty-five degree incline. There was no stopping even if he wanted to. A large boulder stood between him and the vessel. Three shadow shapes were converged on it from up-slope and one further up stumbled and slid, like he, toward it, from somewhere over to his left. He realised the boulder was now upon him and leapt. Gravity seemed weak. It was like a moon jump. He sailed through the air clearing it with ease and hit some fifteen metres on, in a spray of gravel and sand, rolling on in a collision course with the ovoid. It was like hitting a sponge. He sank into the surface and was gently repelled back onto the gravel. Four metres away, Isaac was reaching up to the vessel with one splayed hand touching the hull and waiving some sort of monitoring device over its surface. Gwen was behind him aiming the machine pistol up-slope towards two converging figures. A divided force of some twenty soldiers were shouting and stumbling some way up the slope. A couple of shots were fired toward the vessel.

Isaac remained focused on his task but spoke to John, "Immaculate timing my friend, so good of you to dress for the occasion" then with a rare note of excitement in his voice, "I have it Gwen. I've found the portal. Now all we have to do is open it, and our avenging demon is here, right on cue. God willing, we will transcend this place. John, come here please. I need your help, quickly!" Several bullets kicked up spouts of sand around his feet. Gwen dropped to the floor aiming the pistol directly at Afsoon as she walked from behind the boulder so recently leapt by John, her gun trained on Isaac. Jake walked in casually from the left with a captured rifle over his shoulder.

"Shoot the bitch!" Gwen rapped out at Jake. He un-slung his rifle and fired two shots into Gwen's pelvis. She screamed and contorted but somehow kept the gun aimed at Afsoon. Afsoon was striding towards her and fired a single shot into Gwen's clenched fist, sending the gun spinning from her grasp in a shower of discharging bullets that miraculously hit no one. "You filthy bastard!" Gwen choked, through a welling mouthful of blood. Jake now loomed menacingly, treading on her ruptured pelvis; he hefted his rifle and aimed it at John.

"Tut, tut, Gwennie we're really no different you and I. We just work for different governments, that's all. You didn't really think you were going to walk in here and take away the keys to the universe did you?" Gwen was gurgling now and clawing the ground with her good hand. John made a move to help but was stopped by the tip of Jake's rifle pushed against his ear. "Another inch and I'll blast away that troublesome tumour for you right now."

"No you won't, you fucking moron!" An undertone of savage cruelty boiled in her fierce whisper. It was the first time John had seen any sign of fear in Jake, as he quickly backed away, nearly tripping over Gwen in his haste. "Seeing as how you have just, all but, killed the first of those keys you mentioned, you had better damn well make sure you look after John, as our only readily available alternative." Afsoon looked at John and her tone softened to humour. "Well it lifts my spirits to see you made it John. Life is so much more entertaining with you in it. Just when I think I have taken all you have to offer, you come up with this. From the fiery mouth of destruction you fly naked and bloodied into the midst of a universal conflict. Hermes himself could have made no grander entrance. And right now, at this instant. It all hinges on you John."

This all meant nothing to John except that they were not going to kill him, so he made his move, aiming a kick at Jake's groin whilst simultaneously twisting his torso to grapple Afsoon's gun arm. He had no time to enjoy the satisfying crunch as Jake doubled in excruciating pain, as a far greater agony was exploding into his own neural receptors. Afsoon had anticipated his move, and calmly side stepped, sending a bullet through his thigh that had smashed his femur.

"I didn't say you had to be healthy John, just alive." She twisted and put another bullet through Jake's throat. "Useless piece of shit," then turned to Isaac. "Come on Isaac. It's only you and me now. You can refuse me and spend the rest of your life in the hands of Afghan torturers. Or you can work your magic and use John to open that thing now, before the rest get here. We'd be a good team Isaac. I win either way, but I would win so much more with you. I don't want to be a part of a scientific team studying something for someone else to use. I want to own it. What do you say Isaac? Can

I be your new Eve?" Gwen twitched. Afsoon kicked her in the ribs, "Be still woman." She turned back to Isaac. "Well?"

Isaac nodded. "Get John over here and help me to get him into position."

"Okay Isaac. Just remember, don't try anything. I'm keeping the gun in my hand, and I'll kill him and maim you if you try any tricks. Not that I think you will. You need me now." John floundered in near unconsciousness, vaguely aware of the liaison taking place over him and of the hands grabbing him, sending more shards of agonising pain through shredded nerve endings and, momentarily rousing him further into a world of harsh agony.

"I'm so sorry John," Isaac's words echoed into his fading consciousness from a vast distance. Isaac carefully placed and clamped a metallic collar on his head. An over arch crossed the centre of his cranium with a metal slot locating a particular spot. Isaac placed a solid metal syringe into the slot. The needle was shrouded with a chisel like guard that slid perfectly through the overarching device. He produced a small hammer and gave a sharp tap to the plunger. The chisel grated through John's skull in one movement. The precisely measured needle extended deep into John's brain exuding, what John's senses perceived as, pure undiluted acid. He screamed as his consciousness shattered and fluttered away into formless darkness, each piece retaining a remnant of dying memory.

IVF had been expensive and had produced nothing ... Refuge in work ... Helen ... so sad ... "A gift from God, John ... We are so lucky! ..." ... "It is unlikely you will get a baby Mrs Wolfe ... would you consider adopting an older child? ... Annabel was perfect ... eighteen months ... Beautiful blue eyes ... "Dad, Dad I got a first in chemistry ..."

"Oh God John! ... She's gone ... She's ... gone ... drunken ... Bastard! ... just ... ran ... her ... down ... White ... space ... Floating ... faces ... of ... troubled ... foster ... children ... cruel parents ...

Perfect white silence ... Safe ... Eternal ... Timeless ... Nothing ... Something ... Cool movement ... air ... A draught? ... Noise ... Clatter of something dropped ... Inrush of awareness ... Blinding light ... Pinched ear ... Squeezed eyes ... Head flinching ... Effort to rise ...

"Sorry John. I had to test responses. You've been through a lot. You must rest now. I'm giving you a sedative. Sleep now." His name had brought memories, ones he did not want. A sharp needle in his arm offered release. He mumbled words that seemed to be spoken by someone else.

"I was dead you cretin. Now I have to do it all again." Oblivion beckoned.

Habitat and Home

John lay in luxurious slumber. He knew he was waking up but was so comfortable and wanted to prolong the moment. By degrees, he became aware of his environment. Soft sunlight played on his eyelids and bathed his body. A light breeze wafted across his face and lifted his hair. Gentle waves slapped near his feet. The urge to extend and reach into a glorious stretch was rising to the surface. He suppressed it as long as he could, then, finally, reached up both arms to their limit, pointed his feet and arched his back in ecstasy. A rich female sigh nearby piqued his curiosity. He opened his eyes and looked around. He appeared to be in an outside hospital room located on a small desert island basked in sunshine, except that a Greek God appeared to be standing about eight feet to his left turning away from a console that seemed to look out through a vast glassless window onto the most beautiful night sky he had ever seen.

"Ah! You are awake. Don't talk John. You will be much disori- ented and, perhaps, delusional for a little while. Just stay quiet. And enjoy the wonderful surroundings. We have plenty of time now and I will make everything clear to you. I imagine you are hungry. I'll get you something to eat." John had no inclination to talk just now. He wanted to try and make sense of everything, so he just lay there, in exquisite comfort, while this stranger, who seemed to know him, prepared him breakfast. Nice as the sur- rounding scenery was, he was fascinated more by the window into the sky and couldn't take his gaze away from it. It had a hypnotic quality. A movement to his right claimed his attention. The Greek God was rising from beneath the wavelets, perfectly dry with a tray of fruit and juices and, incongruously, a bacon roll with a steaming mug of tea. He may have looked like a God but, John noted, his clothes were mundane: a white crew neck T-shirt, showing off a stunning physique, Levis and trainers. John silently chided himself, Christ I'm thinking like a gay boy. I actually feel some arousal. Effect of whatever drugs I'm on I suppose. The God sat on the stool that had just appeared and pulled a trolley tray over the bed for John to eat.

"Now eat slowly John. Remember, you may be perceiving things a little differently right now, so just accept everything as it comes. It will all fall into place with time." John reached out for the food. Two slender, hairless, and lightly muscled, arms came into view terminating in elegant, and decidedly feminine, hands. He turned them and looked at them wonderingly. They reacted as though they were his. "John? Don't be alarmed. I know things look different and strange to you but it's me, Isaac." Gently grasping John's arms, he firmly pushed them down.

"Isaac?"

"Yes. Don't think too much. Just eat for now. Enjoy the ambience." Nothing was right here. Memories were starting to clamour for attention. John sat bolt upright knocking the tray of food across the sand, that feminine voice? The rising tempo of his thoughts stirred him to speech.

"Afsoon, where is she? Is Gwen dead?" His attention was wrenched in another direction and he grasped his throat. "What's happened to my voice?" His eyes went suddenly wild. He glanced down at his body. Pert perfectly formed breasts. Deep curves and long feminine legs and, Jesus! His eyes went up inside his head and he started to fit. Strong arms pinned him to the bed. A needle plunged into his forearm. He struggled for a moment then, spun off into deep sleep.

He awoke in more familiar surroundings, a regular hospital room. That was one surreal, and very real dream, he thought, and again wondered why anyone had bothered to save him for second death. He felt more himself and decided to get up and find out what the hell was going on. Was he in some Afghan hospital? If so they were looking after him far better than he could have dared hope, or had he somehow been returned to home soil? He swung his legs over the bed and made for the door. His balance was all wrong. He fell flat on his face. Enlightened memory sloshed through his mind as his head hit the floor. Of course, Afsoon had shattered his leg. How long had he been here? He must have been on some very strong medication. No wonder he had hallucinated. He hauled himself onto his right knee, careful to avoid putting any weight on, what he hoped, was a whole left leg. Strange it felt like he could flex both legs. With a sick feeling, he remembered, he had heard of this with amputees, a feeling of a ghost leg. But it really felt as though his legs were under him. He tried to rise. Shaky, but he made it, huffing a deep breath of relief. He was loath, however, to look at the damaged leg. There was a mirror in the corner and he made a stumbling bid to place himself in front of it. Not a mirror after all, but an entrance to another room. A stunningly beautiful woman stood on the other side in a hospital gown. He quickly averted his face.

"Sorry miss! I didn't ..." He clutched his throat. That feminine voice again. He looked back through the door. The female mimicked his movements. The world tilted. He was looking into a mirror from the eyes of a woman. How? He didn't know. It was insane. Was it hallucination or dream? If it was either, it was the most real he had ever known. He touched himself. So did the reflection. He felt sensation. For some time, he could not bring himself to drop his gown. Eventually he allowed it to slide from his shoulders. Isaac found him there some time later, staring catatonically into the mirror, and gently guided him back to the bed where John sat demurely on the edge with his legs together and his hands in his lap looking vacantly at the God of his earlier dream.

"Listen John, I know how confused you are. I said I would explain it all to you when the time was right, and I will. I have brought you some clothes. They will fit the new you perfectly, nothing too feminine, jeans and trainers, and a blouse and jumper. Oh, and bra and knickers. Sorry about that, but they are necessary I feel, nothing too skimpy I promise. I will leave you to get used to the idea of putting them on. Take as long as you like. When you are ready just call. I will hear and come and get you. I have wonders to show you John. Such wonders." His words seemed to sit in the air as he left the room. John just sat and stared at the clothes. He didn't move for over an hour. His thoughts were viscid. Each one, taking an age to form.

A slow globule of feeling finally rose to the surface through the treacle of his mind, "discomfort". His bum was cold and wet, the sheets chafing. He must have urinated. On auto pilot, he rose. As he did so, the wall dissolved, revealing a bathroom. He stepped into the huge steaming bath and bathed with absent autonomy. His senses massaged by the scents and oils in the water, he washed the silky smoothness of his perfect skin, vaguely feeling like an actress in a soap advert. He explored the impossible body he now seemed to occupy. Slowly, sponging down perfect breasts, dreamily, circling the sponge around nipples and down to genitalia. He heard a gently erotic sigh that reminded him of Helen. His sigh! Eyes snapped open and a twisted reality flooded in. Acute embarrassment on realising that he was nearing orgasm, and uncomfortable pangs of dissipating manhood, finally brought him to his senses.

He found the shower head and deluged his body in ice cold water, every icy needle of pain clearing the fug further from his mind. Gasping, he towelled himself vigorously down and padded into the hospital room, where he picked up and inspected the knickers. After a moment's hesitation he slid them on, trying to ignore the sensuous feel of his own hands as they passed over wide hips and a shapely rump. He struggled with the bra for a moment before discarding it, jammed the tails of the blouse down the waist of his jeans and lay on the dry half of the bed to put on his trainers, trying, all the while, not to think about the form he now found himself in. He raked hands through a mass of blonde, wet curls, and shouted in a disconcertingly female voice. "Isaac! Come and get me now, and tell me what the fuck is going on!" The door opened instantly and the deity that was Isaac entered the room smiling.

"Thank God John. I was getting very worried about you. I thought you had lost your mind."

"Hold on to that thought. Now, get me out of this bloody room and start explaining." The God Isaac gave a theatrical bow and held out his hand toward the door, indicating that John should lead the way. John stepped forward unable to prevent a slight sway of his hips. Isaac grabbed his elbow and there was an awkward moment when a small thrill plunged down through his abdomen causing his knees to wobble. Removing the hand with more vigour than intended, he petulantly snapped that he didn't need assistance, paused, took a deep breath, said "sorry" and strode on, still unable to fully control the tilt of his hips.

Isaac chuckled. "Be ready for anything John. The universe waits."

John found himself in a white corridor. As he walked he kept talking to try and choke down the madness that rose like bile within him. "You can start by telling me what happened after Gwen was killed and you ..." he spun on his heel and thrust his palm hard into Isaac's chest "... and that freak Afsoon, started destroying my skull! You mad fucking bastard! What the hell was all that about and where the fuck is the insane bitch anyway?"

"Not here, thank Christ!" The anger and the swearing definitely helped. Confrontation was even better. He shoved harder with both hands forcing Isaac back a step but Isaac's reflexes were incredibly fast. John felt his wrists snatched in a steel grip. Moving in, equally fast, he brought his knee up into Isaac's groin and had the satisfaction of seeing him double forward and grunt with pain but Isaac maintained his grip, extended his arms, and turned his hip to deflect the force of John's kicks. Seeing the futility of continuing his attack, John stopped. As Isaac's grip slackened, he snatched his hands away, spat full into Isaac's face and spun forward, to continue his stride along the corridor. There was no longer any sway in his hips.

"I deserved that." Isaac wiped the spit from his face. "I'm so sorry John. You had no preparation for this. I will explain my crude surgery later. For now, if you'll slow down, I will explain the events that followed.

"Robin made it to the vessel, doing a fair imitation of your own athletic leap, and startled Afsoon, when he almost landed on her. She shot him through his face. Dear Gwen was not quite dead though. How she managed it with her injuries, I will never know, but she recovered the gun and fired a volley at Afsoon. Most missed but Afsoon was taken to the ground by a bullet in her stomach, she still managed to scuttle from my reach however. I ruined the probe trying to hit her with it. I think I caught her a glancing blow but the pursuing soldiers were almost on us and she got away. It was all I could do to manhandle you into the opening, and shut it behind us.

"Before we were in I took a bullet through my foot and I think I left several toes behind. As for Terry, I just hope to God they never captured him. He was immobilising the vehicles last I knew, so I razed the area before I left. With any luck, I managed to kill him. John! Will you stop walking? We've circuited the vessel three times now. The door to the control area is on your left, six feet in front of you." John stopped, nonplussed.

"Vessel? You mean we're still inside it?"

"Yes." His voice slowed. "Think about it John. Where else would we be? How long do you think you were out? And where else could we hide and be safe?" John could see no door but made for the spot indicated.

An opening presented itself that wasn't there before. He walked in. Several dark red marble couches littered the soft pearl room. He sat in one resting his head in his hands, elbows on knees, ignoring the way it yielded pleasingly under his rump. After a few moments, he looked up. Isaac, or whoever he was, sat opposite. He looked at him long and hard. After several false starts he managed in a weary voice to articulate some simple questions which, he was certain, would have very complex answers. "What is this Isaac, a space ship? Why are we here? How are we here? Why am I alive? And, who the hell are we? We are certainly not who we were. Am I really a … a … a … woman?" The last came out in a rush, almost a cough. Tears welled in his eyes and began to overflow. Complex emotions surged against his composure and the dam burst. He couldn't stop. He wept and wept, shoulders shaking in wracking sobs. Isaac waited patiently for it to subside.

"Listen John, there's a host of new and different hormones raging around your body at the moment, trying to settle. Just bear with it. It will get better. You were a dead man when you came to me John and you certainly were not in any improved state when you entered this vessel. That life is over now. But you have the chance to start again. Just hold up, until I can explain everything to you. You are different now, more different than you could possibly realise. We both are. I don't want to overwhelm you by flooding you with too much information before you are ready but let me at least start by giving you some answers. You won't understand any of it though, if I don't give you some background information first." He looked worried, and it carried in his voice. "Is that okay John?" When he got no response, he repeated himself. "John? Is that okay?"

John sat, once again, with his slim hands laid one on top of the other in his lap and with shoulders slumped, a feminine gesture he had never previously possessed. He blew a sighing breath and shrugged his acceptance.

"Please hold judgement until I have finished." He took a moment to compose himself. "This vessel is not a spaceship, although it is capable of serving that purpose. It is a habitat, and a laboratory. It is the work of Satan." John wriggled uncomfortably. Isaac stalled him with a raised hand. "I will explain in more detail later but suspend any preconceived ideas you may have. Assume, for now, that God and Satan are higher beings, super intellects, no more than that. God was the creator, Satan, his brilliant assistant. Satan saw God was possessive of his creation, keeping his progeny weak and subservient, cosseting them, retarding independence and free will, and denying his assistant full access or input. Satan, therefore, worked in secret to create his own Adam and Eve, near perfect beings, fully capable of handling independence in the harsh rigours of this universe. He designed a pocket environment for them in which to grow and learn, a mini Eden. But this was God's world. Nothing could be hidden from the maker. He was discovered before his work was complete. His Adam and Eve were still useless flesh, uninhabited by id or soul. God was enraged by Satan's betrayal and cast them, and their habitat, into the fires of earth. Satan was banished."

"Where is this fairy story going Isaac?"

"Right here Eve," he spread his hands, "pocket Eden."

John's jaw went slack, as scattered thoughts finally started placing the pieces of Isaac's story into context. "Eve?" he repeated distantly.

"Yes. It was meant to be Gwen but only you and I made it, and you were all but dead. I had to make a decision."

"And my skull? You arsehole. What was all that about?"

"It was one of the reasons you were so important to the mission John. Opening this thing was always going to be the biggest problem. We suspected it could only be opened by an immortal.

Gwen and I had developed various tissue cultures that we felt might serve to trick the defences. They were grown onto her skin like patches. But then you came along. Don't misunderstand me John, you were a good choice anyway, but your cancer made you invaluable. Cancer is really a cellular bid for immortality and you, as its host, were therefore, in some part, immortal." He paused. "Do you believe in fate or divine providence, John? Because the statistical coincidence of the factors that led to the success of this mission are incalculable times a trillion. Until Gwen came up with her plan, we had become resigned to destruction as our only workable option, although we weren't sure we could achieve that either. I had to be brutal John. There was no time for finesse."

"And what now? Are we the new anti-Adam and Eve?"

"No John that would be gauche. There's no reason for me to change my name, but I'm afraid John is not right for you anymore, so why not Eve? After all, it is the Eve of a new future, for us at least."

"Get one thing clear right now! There is no us!"

"Of course not Eve, or John? What do I call you now?" John just looked at him exasperated, and thought. It would help if I didn't practically cum in my pants every time I look at him, and I'm sure the bastard knows it. He said simply. "When are these bloody hormones going to settle down?"

Isaac was looking distracted, seeming to avoid John's eyes. "Oh! A couple of days at most I think." He didn't sound too certain.

John suddenly realised where Isaac was looking. "Hey! Get your eyes off my ... my ... tits you fucking ..." He couldn't think of another word and came up with "Letch!" Isaac burst out laughing. Even John couldn't suppress a smile, which he covered by standing and saying, "Come on then Isaac, show me your wonders," at the same time shaking the front of his blouse to hide his tightening nipples.

"No need to go anywhere. I can do it from here. Prepare yourself Eve." Isaac made a gesture and the room snapped out of existence. They hung in black space facing each other and looking at planet earth from a geo-stationary orbit. There was no disorientation, just the stunning beauty of space all around. "This is where we're hiding at the moment." He nodded to a point behind her. "There's a beautiful moon behind you Eve." But before John could look, he made another gesture and they were back on the desert island of his earlier encounter.

John was incredulous. "Is it real? Can I swim? Or will I just walk through the water without getting wet? As you did before."

"Be my guest. Take off your clothes and go for it!"

John looked witheringly over his shoulder at Isaac. "Piss off!" He took off his shoes instead and rolled up his jeans then walked in, bending to splash the water with his hands. "It feels real. Can I really swim in it? If I swim ten feet will I hit a wall?"

"You will feel like you are moving but, in reality, the current will always equal your efforts. The terrain, however, will seem to move. You can swim to another island if you want."

"No. It's alright thanks." John walked to a palm tree and sat on the sand. Isaac joined him on a log that appeared as he sat down. "Can I go anywhere I want?"

"I could take you anywhere on earth, possibly as far as the moon. But it would entail moving the habitat. For everything else, we are, in reality, bounded by a few metres."

"Reality? I don't think that exists anymore. How can my id be in another body?"

"It's complicated. These bodies have lain in wait for mega-eons, preserved by a science beyond comprehension, expectant of absorbing a life force that never came, until we entered this place. Everything was already set up. It just needed activation and two willing sacrifices. Enter you and I."

"But I had no will in this. I knew nothing of what was happening."

"The unconscious mind will cling to survival Eve, and besides, you accepted my offer of employment, unconditionally, if you remember."

"Well there are conditions now Isaac. If I really am a new person, then no former contract applies. There are things I want."

"Name them Eve. Anything I, or this habitat, can provide, are yours for the asking." The island faded and they were back in the control room.

"I'll think on it. For now I need some rest, time to try and figure things out. Give me my island back please, and leave me alone. I don't want any company. Don't observe me. I'll call you when I'm ready." He was back on the beach before he finished speaking. Just having time to observe the look of surprise on Isaac's face as the scene materialised around him.

"What happened to my body?"

"That's a nice greeting. You've been gone for three days. I thought you might at least say hello. It's here. Where else would it be? Do you want to see it now? It's still in a bit of a mess at the moment. I haven't had time to prepare it for viewing. I kept it because I thought you might like to return the remains, Christian burial or whatever. It might help to give your wife closure." He paused. "Thinking about it, maybe you should see it, if you are ready? It might help you to move on. "John nodded. Isaac took him to another part of the habitat, the walls breathing open then shut to give them access. He stopped before a white wall. "Eve. Are you sure you are ready? It's not very nice." He nodded again and the wall dissolved.

John couldn't make out the mangled mess on the dais at first. There was a definite shape to the body and the thigh was a bloody mess but above the neck was unrecognisable. The face and skull were split down the middle and laid open to expose the brain, from which a mass of tubes and wires protruded. Tubes were pushed down the throat and into arteries, all connecting with bland spherical monitors and equipment extruding from the walls. More horrific, was that it seemed to be alive and breathing. He could sense Isaac watching him closely. He walked closer. An odour of acetate did little to hide the underlying smell of rotting flesh. He watched the chest rise, then, the body farted. The stench was foul. It was too much. His hands went to his face and he vomited violently through his fingers. Isaac took his elbow, placed a supporting arm around his shoulder and tried to lead him away. "Come on Eve. I think you've had enough." She pushed him away, steeled herself, and moved closer, pulling away the sheet that had slipped slightly from the midriff.

"What's this carved into his ..." she took a breath, and corrected herself "my stomach? It looks like it says ... Daddy?"

"It does. Afsoon killed her father. You were obviously a substitute, but it speaks volumes that she didn't finish you off after your romantic interlude in the steamy environs of that volcano. I don't think many lovers have survived after a night with her. It seems you were special."

"And your body Isaac, where is it?"

"Disposed of, I had no further use of it."

"Then why save mine? And why mutilate it in this way? What purpose does it serve? And don't tell me it was for Christian burial."

"Alright Eve, here is the truth. I explained before, the habitat will only respond to the commands of an immortal. Your cancerous brain cells are immortal!"

"But I ... It, is dead?"

"Yes."

"And us? Are we immortal?"

"I don't know, but we are amazing. Our tissue replacement is flawless. I believe we may have extreme longevity of life."

"I want it disposed of Isaac. I will never be able to carry on while that thing still exists."

"Difficult. I'm not sure what will happen if the cancer cells are separated from the living tissue. They may be recognised for the anomaly they are. The habitat may cease to function, perhaps if we just kept the brain?"

"No! I want to see the whole thing incinerated" There was a note of hysteria in her voice.

Isaac conceded. "Well, I'm fairly sure we have interfaced with the habitat by now. Our time was always going to be limited anyway, once it was activated. It is a nurturing and learning environment only. We were never going to be allowed to become dependent on it, or to discover all of its secrets, but I want to study it for as long as possible. Let me run some tests and I will see what can be done."

Eve's voice was strained. "It must be very soon Isaac, today!" She laid an imploring hand on his wrist and gripped it tightly.

Isaac sighed and nodded, then led her away. He left her standing by a glassless wall looking down on the earth and went about his tests. Eve brooded. Something was nagging at her thoughts. Something Isaac had said, but other thoughts intruded. Three days of speculation and experimentation on her island paradise, and within a dozen other self-created environments, seethed through her synaptic processes. She had discovered that she could control the functions of the habitat by calming and focusing her mind in a certain way. To begin with it was a hit and miss affair but, after a couple of days, it was like a positive on-off switch in her mind.

As she became more adept, she also noticed that the habitat had a dialogue with her, a kind of undercurrent to her thoughts. When she was musing, suggestions ran along with her thoughts prodding her to formulate ideas and questions and to expand conclusions. This will-o-the wisp presence in her mind seemed to be encouraging some reservations she was starting to have about Isaac. What was it he had said that nagged at her? A wistful thought played at the fringes of her ruminations. John and Afsoon climaxing in the "steamy environs of that volcano." The thought dilated like the eye of a waking dragon. She had never related the details of their encounter to Isaac. Only he and Afsoon knew. Had he lied? Was she on board? Was he … She? Oh God! No! Eve sent a command. "Hide me!" The world went black.

She floated in a womb of darkness. Half formed thoughts tumbled slowly through her mind before returning to the void. It was pleasant to drift but the undercurrent was becoming insistent, prodding for more clarity, nudging her to coherent thought. Was Isaac dead, or was he on board, perhaps splayed out like her former self, perhaps conscious and in tortured agony? She summoned knowledge from the habitat. An image flashed into her mind of Isaac, naked on a floating platform. Isaac/Afsoon leaned over him. With a mental flick, Eve engaged sound.

"Your protégé is becoming troublesome Isaac. I think she suspects something is wrong, and I don't like the way she is gaining some control of the functions of the habitat. I have been too lenient with her. She is only a feeble woman after all. The time for wooing is over. I will take her virginity tonight and make her fulfil the function of all women. She will serve my desires and have my babies. Lots of them, and she will learn to be obedient. What do you think our children will be like Isaac? Do you think they will be like us, super beings? No? I suppose not. Like the children of Adam they will probably be lesser beings, but still great, nevertheless, greater than Adam's, for their blood will be pure, unmixed with animal or angelic beings, and they will bend this universe to their will, my will! A shame you won't be here to see it. But I will keep you alive for a little longer. You still have knowledge I need to drag out of you. Oh don't look so frightened." Isaac flinched as Afsoon smoothed his brow but s/he persisted, and bent to kiss Isaac's forehead. "It will only be as painful as you make it!"

Eve issued another command. "Hide Isaac! Bring him to me!" She was conscious of indecision in the dialogue, as both Isaac and Afsoon/Isaac, seemed to shimmer. Afsoon was instantly aware of what was happening and sent a questing demand in search of Eve's location. She quickly altered her own command. "Old Isaac, mortal Isaac, tortured Isaac, leave the other behind. Imprison him somewhere!" A white bubble contracted in the darkness and a single presence joined her in the void, but which one? Fear cradled her thoughts. She posed a question "Isaac? Not Afsoon but Isaac? my Isaac?" The wait for a response was interminable. She suspected some form of mind attack at any moment. Instead there was a frail and broken "yes" whispered into the darkness, a trick? Or the real Isaac? How could she defend herself? Should she flee elsewhere? She could only hope.

"John? Is THAT REALLY YOU? Thank God! Don't ask any questions, we must act now! Afsoon will be here very quickly. She has had time, John, to get to know this environment. You cannot stand against her. His thoughts were laboured, yet there was both urgency and strength in them. "This habitat is designed to obey the dominant life form. Afsoon will soon exert his authority."

"But I can control it too Isaac. I've been practising. Tell me what to do."

"The habitat is confused at the moment by mixed feminine-masculine signals from you both but believe me, as you settle into your new sexualities, Afsoon will seize control. We must prevent that, at any cost!"

"What do I do?"

"Tell the habitat to dump you on earth and to destroy itself immediately. Try to convince it that Afsoon is criminally insane and has no place in this universe. Tell it that it must destroy her, emphasise the feminine her. It will probably save her anyway, but we must try. Until now, the devil, as in, evil incarnate devil, didn't really exist but, if she continues to occupy that body, and gains control of this habitat, God help us all. A living hell will come to earth." He halted. "John? What's happening?" The black had turned to grey and a white dot was expanding in the distance.

"Shit! It's Isaac, I mean Afsoon. He's here!" She sent more commands, and the universe tumbled through a thousand images momentarily immersing the two of them in each before whipping them away to another. Finally they tumbled into a dismal cobbled street in the midst of down pouring rain. Dilapidated Victorian terraces crowded in. One street light flickered revealing strobo-scopic images of rat-infested rubbish, broken glass, and discarded jumble. An odour of stale urine pervaded the place disturbed by the freezing torrent washing along the gutters and walls.

Eve issued further commands. Nothing happened. Isaac/real Isaac was crouched on the ground, blood and spittle running down his jaw, drenched and shivering. She helped him up. "I can't move us from here. We have to get out of this rain." She took him to the nearest door but it was locked. Leaning Isaac against the broken and rusted railings, she gave the door a hefty kick. It wouldn't budge. She tried several other doors and tried to break windows but all effort was wasted. She looked around and spied a manhole cover in the road. A shock of fear scuttled down her spine. Boy-hood memories flooded her mind. She knew this street, although it had degenerated appallingly. It was where she was born. Where John was born and that manhole cover was an object of dread.

As a little boy she used to hide in the coal cellar and clamber up the coal to come up into the road through the manhole. One time though, he had come home from school to find no one at home and had prised up the manhole to get in. The cellar was three quarters full so he'd had to slide his way over the coal to the door. He struggled but couldn't open it. Then the light went out as a hundred weight of coal was dumped through the manhole and the cover was replaced. He was wedged into the corner by the coal and panicked. He tried to dig towards the manhole but couldn't get close enough to gain the purchase to lift it. He shouted and screamed but no one heard for a long time. He had choked and gagged on the coal dust and his eyes stung as tears washed the dust into them. He had not been found for several hours and had never liked small places since, especially dark ones.

Isaac groaned. There was nothing for it; he needed to be out of the rain. She found a piece of broken glass and, after several attempts, managed to prise up the cover. The pitch black below did nothing to relieve her sense of impending doom, and that nagging undercurrent in her mind was nudging her awareness to caution, but they had to get out of this cold stinging rain, before Isaac became feverish. She helped him into the opening and held his arms until his feet touched ground, then followed in, but not before launching the cover down the road. As she bent to help Isaac to his feet, a hundred weight of coal spilled into the opening. Dropping Isaac she scrabbled for the opening releasing a loud expletive "No!" which echoed back at her as though she were in a cavern, then the cover was replaced and she was in pitch darkness once again, just like she had been as a child, but she was no longer a child. This was Isaac/Afsoon's doing and she was buggered (she flinched at the ill-chosen word) if she would give him the satisfaction of knowing her fear.

Degradation

"Isaac? Where are you?" Frozen silence preceded a deathly whisper.

"He's here, with me." A whoosh of frigid air entrained with it an overpowering smell of antiseptic cleanser and fluorescent light as tubes sequentially flickered into existence, buzzing with disdain. Eve's slim wrists were invisibly wrenched upward and lashed to a hook above her head. Stretching toes, she paddled, in quick ballerina steps, to try and arrest the lazy to and fro of her swing, producing a halt and half spin before, once more losing purchase.

Her attire was changed. She was now dressed in a red latex mini skirt, PVC halter top, dog collar, ball gag, thigh length boots and, embarrassingly, if the draft was anything to go by, no knickers. She looked around at a fully fitted sex dungeon. Isaac was inside an oversized, bird cage hanging over a fire pit. Isaac/Afsoon, dressed disconcertingly in full Nazi SS uniform, and sporting a riding crop, gave a slow handclap.

"Bravo Eve. I have to say you are the most challenging and interesting person I have ever met. I owe Isaac a debt of gratitude for providing me with such an excellent consort. John was a joy to manipulate, courageous, determined, unorthodox and really quite clever, and now here you are in female form, apparently having acquired the deviousness of the weaker sex and wow! What a stunner you are, but you need to be disciplined and it will be my pleasure, and yours, to teach you the benefits of obedience and acceptance of me as your master. Although, in your case, the pleasure will be somewhat tempered with excruciating pain.

"But, once you are broken, we will have a good life, you and I, with more children than you could think possible, great children 'Demigods.' We will rule over all of creation, but you really will have to submit to me. Accept your fate Eve. You are mine to do with as I please." He walked over and attached a thick leather dog lead to her collar. Eve bunched her legs and kicked out hard. He side stepped easily and waited for her to stop flailing her legs. "Tut! Tut! That will cost you some additional degradation I'm afraid." Her skirt was suddenly yanked up and a stinging slap was delivered to her butt. The male psyche within her both cringed and fumed with impotent rage.

She struggled violently, but the female body responded. Nipples hardened and she felt wet between her thighs. Fear and shame fought for dominance. Afsoon produced a knife and pressed it to her nipple until a spot of blood appeared then licked the blade with enough force to cut his own tongue. In one lightning movement he snatched the back of her head and, gag miraculously gone, covered her mouth and forced his tongue between her lips. Before she could react he ducked away and cut her down, sweeping her legs from under her with a roundhouse kick to the back of her calves. Eve rolled and dropped like a cat onto hands and toes and tensed for attack, but Afsoon was too fast, delivering a heavy slap to her rump that knocked her flat to the floor, before placing a foot on her spine and wrenching hard on the dog lead to choke off any attempt at struggle.

"This is where you belong Eve, here at my feet. Obey me and I will let you have some dignity. Resist and I will whip you like the dog you are. Do you understand? Nod your agreement Eve, or there will be consequences." Despite the choking pain Eve ignored him. He yanked on the lead to lift her head so she could observe the pop of the flames igniting under Isaac's cage. Eve made gagging noises around the, now returned, ball. "What's that you say? I can't quite hear you." Eve managed a nod against the excruciating pain of the tightened lead. "That's better. You see, you can behave when you want to." He slackened the lead. Eve was trying to shout around the ball and was looking and nodding urgently at Isaac. "Oh! Sorry? You want me to extinguish the flames?" He waited, "A nod will do Eve." Eve nodded vigorously as Isaac tried to crawl up the bars with manacled hands and feet, his own ball gag preventing any sound beyond panicked grunting." The flames popped out of existence. "I'm going to take my foot off your back now but you will stay on your hands and knees. When I tell you to move, you will crawl. Do you understand?" He looked significantly towards Isaac.

With venom in her eyes, Eve gave a short nod. "Louder. I can't hear you!" Eve grunted, and nodded with more vigour. "That's better. Now you are starting to get the hang of it." He lifted his foot. "Now, come with me, there's a good little whore. I will show you around my little domain." He tugged on the lead. Murderous rage contorted Eve's muscles but the tell-tale pop of flames arrested her attack before it began. She crawled around obediently, whilst Afsoon showed her the various restraint equipment he intended to use on her, dropping back at each station to look pointedly and lustfully at Eve's bared behind. "You'll enjoy this one. You may stand to look at it." He tugged the lead and she rose to her feet to look at an X shaped table with manacles at each extremity. "I expect you get the gist." He gestured around the room. "There are the usual items, sex swing, whipping post, crucifix, stocks, but I particularly like that one over there," he pointed. "You're looking puzzled. Would you like me to explain it to you?" He snatched the lead downwards. "Back on your knees then, come along, let's go and have a look. You may whimper if you like."

As he led her towards the equipment, the distraction of her knees chafing on the rough-hewn stone floor was over-ridden. She became aware of a familiar tugging at her mind, stronger, more insistent, and with far more clarity, than before. Actual words were being projected onto her thoughts.

"John! Listen to me."

"Isaac? How?"

"Just listen! There isn't much time. The habitat has a kind of secondary sentience. It is confused by the mixed genders of the thought patterns generated by you and Afsoon and is communicating with me to help it decide who should be dominant. You must try and hang on to your masculinity John! We have a chance, but we have to keep her off guard. As you can see, she is going for the macho masculine in a big way. I'm afraid you are going to have to play along until I give you the word."

"Play along? Are you mad? You can see what the bastard is planning for me."

"We have no choice. This is for humanity John. If you don't want a thousand years of you and the whole of humanity being fucked then, please, just go along with it until I give the word. I have to somehow convince the habitat who it is who should be in charge before we make our move."

"I'll never forgive you for this Isaac. You make your bargain pretty bloody damn quick! Because I don't think I can go much further with this, without going insane." A secondary self-loathing thought she tried to bury, forced its way to the surface, "if I don't explode in orgasmic pleasure first." A choking yank on the lead brought her to an abrupt halt.

"Don't get too eager now, little slut." Eve looked at the contraption whilst Afsoon coldly explained its use. He ran his hand over a leather saddle on an extended post, cupping the nose part suggestively. "This supports the abdomen whilst the various manacles hold your elbows, wrists, knees and ankles flat, with your knees forced wide and slightly forward from vertical. These leather straps run x shaped across and below your shoulder blades (he snapped the two pieces of leather together) to keep your back low, so your buttocks are raised, and a leather cord attached to the top pony tail you now have, keeps your head up and back, all at the perfect waist height for caning, and for penetration from both ends. Clever little device isn't it?" He patted the saddle. "Come on then, climb on. You've been a very naughty girl, and it's time for you to be punished. Don't make me force you now." His voice became cold and hard. "Or your friend will die and your chastisement will be harsh and very prolonged." He lingered over the last word and gyrated his hips. Eve reluctantly crawled on, shaking with a blend of fear, anger and excitement.

As he secured the shackles, straps and cords, she was shouting in her mind. "Isaac! Where the fuck are you? I can't move. How the hell are we going to tackle him if I can't move? He's going to fuck me for Christ's sake. She looked towards the cage but Isaac was in a state of blissful unconsciousness. She heard the swish of a cane as Afsoon practised his swipe. Her skirt was snatched up and her chastisement began. "Shit!" It was hurting like hell but she was becoming wet again. She heard him chuckle.

"You really are a very naughty girl aren't you?" He walked to the front end and stood before her, displaying the large bulge in his trousers with his hands on his hips. "I'm going to fuck you now, you filthy little whore. But first, you are going to savour the goods. The ball gag disappeared. "Open very, very wide now." He loosened his belt and dropped his trousers.

"Jesus, fuck Isaac look at the size of that thing. For Christ's sake, do something!" Receiving no answer and, seeing that Afsoon was in no hurry, appearing to be savouring the moment. She spoke to him instead. "Why are you doing this? Your own father abused you. That's why you killed him, isn't it?"Afsoon looked confused for a moment and then started laughing.

"Is that what he told you?" She cast a glance at the bird cage. "I killed him because he wasn't man enough to take me, and that mewling brother of mine wasn't much better, did what he was told of course, but still not much of a man. Not like you were John, but I will dominate you too John. Both my will, and my seed, will eventually consume you. You will tremble in fear at the sound of my tread, and yet crave my every touch. The sound of my voice, even my violence and abuse, will make you quiver with desire, and, however much your masculine mind rebels and rages, you will be a hopeless junky, addicted to my every whim and fantasy, however depraved.

"Every time you beg me to fuck you, I will crush your crumbling resistance a little more, and I will relish it John. You are so delicious. It has started already. How many times have you cum, simply by being in my presence? You are a whore John. Accept your doom." Roughly grabbing the back of her head, he touched his penis to her lips. "Use your teeth and you'll lose them, understand?" He waited, whilst the flames ignited once more under Isaac's cage. Eve managed a muted and frightened, nod. "Look up at me! I want to see your eyes whilst I …" he paused, took a firmer grip on her hair, locked his gaze on hers and, pulled her head hard forward onto his erection.

"Now John!" Isaac screamed into his mind. Several intense instructions boiled into her thoughts at once. "Whilst 'her' guard is down! Command the habitat to jettison 'her' into space. Do it with raw masculinity John, for all our sakes!" S/he hit the mental switch in his mind with every ounce of masculine rage left in him ... Afsoon, with startling abruptness, was not there anymore. The dungeon faded and Eve found the familiar surroundings of the command room solidifying around her. Snapping up erect from her dog like posture, she scrubbed at her lips, spat and retched several times then, looked down at her slavish attire. Ripping off the collar she commanded a change of clothing. Isaac was no-where to be seen so she summoned him. Nothing happened. Several attempts produced no results. She paced and pondered and vomited again before becoming aware of, the now familiar, tug at her thoughts. She focused on this. "Isaac?"

"Yes John, I am here, I'm sorry I can't join you physically. My body couldn't take anymore I'm afraid. Fortunately the habitat has allowed my consciousness to be a guest, within its memory matrix, for a while. It's a sort of barter process. If I can remain interesting, challenging and useful, I can remain for a little longer. I am able to access some of its lower control functions but you have more wide-ranging command, for now at least. So we can start making plans for your return to earth, before the habitat decides to destroy itself. First, however, we have to formulate some long-term strategies regarding Afsoon?"

"What are you talking about? I thought he was ejected into space, dead, no more a problem."

"Not so, I'm afraid. He was placed into a life support capsule and sent on a twenty-five year solar orbit, at the end of which time, he will return to earth, very likely totally pissed off and baying for blood."

"What? I don't understand. Why isn't he dead?"

"Because the habitat will not allow it, there are imperatives that it has waited millennia to implement. Chief amongst these is to seed the earth with new life, better adapted to survival than those currently occupying it. The male is the dominant sex and the habitat will always accede to it. No male, no seed. Fortunately, the gender confusion gave us an opening, and Afsoon's psychotic behaviour was a powerful argument as to which male psyche should rule. The habitat eventually conceded that more time was needed to decide. Afsoon's excitement, at your imminent subjugation (thank you for playing along, by the way), caused him to abandon 'her' (God this is difficult) grip on control of the habitat long enough for you to make your demands, which I managed to negotiate into something acceptable to it. The end result of our efforts is that you now have temporary control of your surroundings and twenty-five years to prepare for the return of Afsoon. Given Afsoon's lust for power, plus twenty-five years of anguished impotency, and planning for his vengeful return, it will be like waiting for Armageddon."

"How is he able to plan? Surely he is unconscious?"

"I wish that were the truth. I could not persuade the habitat to sedate his mind. His body is contained but his mind will be free to communicate, and roam, within a number of real life experience programs, designed to educate, and to help him to achieve moral and psychological adjustment. As his only outlet for a quarter of a century, these are more likely to seriously piss him off."

"Jesus Christ Isaac, I can't take any more of this. My mind is going to explode. Why didn't you just let me die? I was more than ready to."

"Because hope for humanity would have died with you. Now man up and learn what you are, and what you are capable of. We have work to do and a battle to prepare for."

Eve began to laugh hysterically. "Man up? Very funny Isaac, just how the hell am I supposed to do that? Haven't you noticed? I appear to be a woman now, with very feminine desires, apparently." She flopped down, with extended fingers digging rigidly into her face and forehead.

Isaac gave a mental sigh. "Haven't you learned anything yet, about Afsoon? He drugged you before remember."

"So, you're saying I was drugged again?" She was almost shouting now.

"No! No need. He had control of the habitat. He just boosted your libido hormones into overdrive."

"And are they out of overdrive now?" She ground out, "because I'm being ripped in two at the moment. I'm so disgusted with everything I could fucking kill myself, but I've had three orgasms just thinking about what he was going to do to me. Is it ever going to stop? Am I a whore?" Tears welled into her eyes and her voice broke. Am I what he said I was? Is my ultimate fate, to be a fucking sex slave?" Isaac responded carefully.

"Just a moment." A group of colours spilled into the air next to Eve. And there was Isaac, fully healed sitting next to her on the marble couch. "A neat trick I just realised the habitat could do, some sort of hologram. Listen, the hormones and libido will settle, but you will continue to have strong desires, especially for him. Your body was made for him. It has no choice but to be attracted. It's just a question of control. You must have been attracted to women, and not always appropriate women, I'd guess, when you were John, yet, until it became necessary for fulfilment of our plan, you even resisted Afsoon's charms, few men could I can assure you. I'm guessing you were always faithful to your wife until then?" Eve nodded. "This is just the same. We all have desires for bitches or bastards. It's that taboo thing. We shouldn't but we want to, but it's all in our heads. We don't have to follow through with it, and so what if you had a few orgasms. I'll bet you had wet dreams when you were a teenager. This is no different. When I said man up Eve, I just meant that your John persona will have better control of this environment than Eve's. It really doesn't sit well with it to be responding, foremost, to a feminine entity."

Eve wiped her eyes and shook her head. "Yes. You are right, and what about you, Isaac? I have been totally insensitive to your problems. Tortured and now, dead, apparently. How the hell are you coping? And what exactly are you now, a ghost?"

"I'm not really sure. I think I'm like an echo, or imprint, of the person who passed on, but for now the echo is strong, and I retain, in large measure, most of my personality, although, only my strongest emotions, and my mission still seem to hold the importance they once did. I think, in time that will all fade too, if the habitat allows us any significant amount of time, that is. But I was prepared for this, and I am willing to make this sacrifice for my beliefs. You are my hope Eve. I will live on, in this plane, through you. Now, let us begin our preparations shall we?" Eve rubbed beautiful eyes with the heels of her hands and nodded agreement.

Return to beginnings

She stood on top of the dingy Soho building, with icy wind flailing hair about her face, and looked down on the neon lights. Why she had chosen to be put back on earth at this time and place, she could not have said. Perhaps, because this was where it had all started. She had arrived here a dying and desperate man, and here, scant weeks later, she had returned, a lone demi-goddess with the fate of humanity in her hands, awaiting the return of her nemesis and the encroaching thraldom of the existence he planned. Isaac was dead. The habitat had imploded into infinity mere seconds after leaving her here. The afterimage was still burning in her retinas. And, Afsoon was coming.

Clenching her fists, she shouted into the wind. "You shouldn't have left me Isaac! I can't do this alone. I need your knowledge. Your guidance! Ice pearls formed on her upturned face as the first sleet began to fall. Dropping her rump onto her heels, she allowed her hands to creep to the wet edge of the asphalt roof and contemplated those last days in the habitat. They seemed precious now. Isaac had explained what he could. She was still trying to get her head around it all … The son of a Jew brought up as a Catholic on the wish of a dead Christian mother, he had gone on to become a Jesuit priest but he had uncovered texts, hidden in Vatican archives that caused him to re-think his calling and to leave the church to accept control of the business empire bequeathed him by his father.

This provided the means for him to pursue his research studies. Studies that pre-dated Genesis, and that had come to reveal the true nature of the relationship, and the rift, between God and Satan. Satan, apparently, believed God too selfish to create truly independent beings and conjectured that he merely wanted fawning worshippers so granted only a parody of free will. Following his own moral compass, he subverted God's designs and created alternative creatures to inhabit the world, creatures more physically adept, and with something more. He had woven a celestial thread into their extended DNA. 'The wrath of God was terrible to perceive ...' Her thoughts were rudely disturbed by the crunch of footfall behind her.

"Not thinking of jumping are yer? Pretty girl like you, only you look like you've maybe got some cash and a decent mobile. I like yer jacket, and Emm ere likes yer shoes. Don't you Emm? So, hand em over first, and then you can do what you fucking like." Eve rose and spun in a smooth movement, one hand whipping out in a blur to grip the knife wielding hand of her assailant and the other grabbing her hair, before deftly swinging her out over the roof edge, to dangle by her greying roots. The other two women backed off. Looking the frail and wasted creature up and down, she threw her across the asphalt and walked to the roof hatch, whilst the three scuttled away. She climbed down the ladder, and the broken stairs beyond, to the office where she had first met Isaac. The door was still in ruins and the whole room stank of piss. She could just make out a broken and overturned desk, in the near dark, and some urine soaked papers that had fallen from a draw. There was nothing here for her. Turning back to the stairs, she cautiously made her way down to the street.

After wandering aimlessly for a while, she found herself in a burger bar in Leicester Square contemplating her coffee and the leers of several loud drunks, at the next table. She left, braving the whistles and catcalls, to book into a hotel with one of the several credit and cash cards provided by the habitat. She slept like the dead and woke in a heavy sweat with the bed wrecked and the covers scattered on the floor, feeling like she'd had a full physical workout. At breakfast, she had sat near a couple and their new baby, and had found herself gushing over what a beautiful boy he was and how wonderful it must be to have such an adorable child. Catching herself in mid flow, she made her excuses and left. The morning was spent wandering around shops and public buildings.

Eve was steeling herself for a duty she felt she had to perform. She was going to visit Helen. Helen would need closure. Someone had to tell her that John was dead, and try to create a tale that would give some meaning to it all. A dozen scenarios swarmed through her seething thoughts. Finally, mind made up, she stepped into the road and hailed a taxi. The driver looked her up and down appreciatively, wishing she didn't have jeans on, as she stepped into the back cab.

"Where to miss?"

"Devonshire Close. Chiswick."

The cabby tried several times to engage her in conversation but soon tired of monosyllabic answers and resorted, instead, to fantasising about her, minus the masculine leather jacket, loose jeans and training shoes, replacing them, in his mind's eye, with more erotic attire. He looked wistfully after her as she walked up the garden path to the front door of the Edwardian semi, noting that all her attempts to disguise her outstanding figure were in vain, her gently swaying rear being an equal rival to her pert and ample breasts. He delayed a few moments with counting his money, whilst she knocked loudly on the door and stepped back to await the occupant. Shaking long gold curls away from her perfectly proportioned face, Eve could hear Helen calling up the stairs within.

"Taxi's here. Are you ready?" She opened the door, looking back and up over her shoulder, at the same time, putting in an earring. She turned to Eve, looking flushed and beautiful and lifted her foot, half crouching and hopping to put on her second stiletto. "Sorry we won't be a moment." She called out again. "Come on the show starts at two!" A male voice answered her.

"Two minutes!" She turned back.

"You are the taxi aren't you?" She looked Eve up and down, settling, finally on a direct look into her eyes. Eve quickly averted her own stare. "No. I can see you are not. Can I help you?" A casually scruffy, but good looking, middle aged man, appeared at the top of the stairs. "I'm not that keen on wearing John's shoes Helen. It doesn't seem right somehow."

"Don't be so stupid, you can't wear those tatty old trainers of yours, and they are a perfect fit. He wouldn't want them to go to waste."

Eve swallowed down a swelling rage fuelled by jealousy. How could she do this to him? He was barely dead, dead trying to secure her future.

"Are you alright?" Eve turned on her heel and ran down the path waving a hand, in a spasmodic gesture, behind her. "I'm sorry wrong address! Taxi! Wait!" She jumped back in, leaving a disconcerted Helen calling to her from the door step. "Take me to the nearest hotel, quickly!" She looked back and felt a crushing pain in her chest. Helen was still a very attractive woman, even if she wasn't the woman John had thought her to be. Inside, she knew this was for the best but it didn't stop the pain, and the tears began to run.

"Are you alright Miss?" She wiped her eyes and sniffed. "Can I do anything?"

"No! Just get me to a hotel." The stress had exhausted her and she drifted off into uneasy slumber. She was abruptly awoken with beefy hands clasped round her throat and right wrist and a knee thrust hard up between her legs.

"Do what you are told and I won't hurt you too much. Understand?" The rotting cabbage smell of bad breath was nauseating, as he spat his words out close into her face. He released her wrist to thrust a hand into his open trousers. Her reaction was instant. In one arching movement, she grabbed his throat with one hand, twisting over her other wrist to grip his, then shoved his own brawny hand, hard into his crotch and ejected him from the taxi. Ramming two fingers up his nose, she dragged him kicking onto the waste ground he'd brought her to, and delivered three hard kicks into his ribs and kidneys

"Stop your groaning and shouting, you lowlife shit! I'm sure you brought me somewhere quiet enough that no one would hear my screams. I ought to rip your throat out." She slapped him, as he tried to rise, with sufficient force to knock him several feet. He started to plead with her, turning onto hands and knees to scamper away. She stamped on his back, stepped back, took careful aim and kicked him savagely in the crotch, hearing the gratifying gasps and wheezing splutters that accompanied unbearable pain. She calmly walked back to the taxi and drove it over his legs, as he tried to crawl away. Dropping the keys beside him, she made her way to the nearest high street, phoned for an ambulance and took the tube to Shepherds Bush.

She settled down in a café, and scoured a property paper for somewhere to stay. Three hours later she paid an up-front deposit, in cash, for a one bedroom, furnished mews flat above a betting shop in Hammersmith. The violence had cleared her head and helped her find some perspective. It was good that Helen was not grieving and that she appeared to have found someone else. Although, Eve could not escape the bitter thought that Helen might already have been in an affair before he died, maybe even before he was ill. She would still have to be told of course, but Eve needed to concentrate on her own new life, and it could never really have included Helen, and now, at least she didn't have to worry about her fretting in lonely grief. Tomorrow she would get her new identity and set about finding a place at a university.

"Live normally for several years," Isaac had said. "Get used to what and who you are. Discover your capabilities. And don't put yourself under stress. You will have plenty of that in the coming years. You need to grow into your new self. When you feel ready, study the scriptures. I will give you a reading list. There are some you should read that will be inaccessible to you. It will not be the same, but I will tell you where you can find translations, copies, and even some originals. Once you feel confident in who you are, prepare for battle. Because, be assured, you have a formidable opponent. You know what he has in store for you, and for the rest of humanity. Find a way to overcome and destroy him. I wish the habitat would help more and not destroy itself and me with it. I wish I could give you access to some of my fortune but it will be too tied up in litigation. At least your wife will have received the funds I set aside for her."

He had given her an address, and letters of introduction to someone who could provide her with an identity, qualifications and anything else she needed, for a price, plus, a safe deposit number and the location of a key that would unlock sufficient funds to tide her over. Also, names of several people she should contact for help, when she was ready, and a highly emphatic instruction that she should trust no one.

"It's you, isn't it? You're the girl from yesterday." Hearing Helen's voice, even with the phone acting as intermediary, was strangling Eve's resolve. "Don't put the phone down please. It's something to do with John isn't it? Were you with him? Do you know what happened? Please I must know. Don't leave me not knowing. I can't bear it. Meet with me, anywhere. I'll be there. I'll pay," her voice broke. "Say something." All idea of blurting out a contrived fiction to appease Helen's probably guilty conscience deserted her. Eve could not help but respond.

"Your house, tonight, seven-o-clock, be alone." She slammed the phone down, and left the kiosk. It was ten-o-clock by the station clock.

She made her way to Church Street, went into the secondhand book shop and perused the musty shelves. On a whim, she bought a book on the kabala, and asked the young woman at the counter if she could speak with the owner.

"Mr Soames? Is he here?"

"I don't know if he will see you, what is it about?"

"Could you tell him I'm a friend of Isaac Abraham's please? I have a letter of introduction." Eve handed over the letter. The woman looked at it suspiciously. A muffled, cultured voice, called from behind one of the bookshelves.

"It's alright Annie, I'll deal with this. A tall, slightly stooped man past middle age came out with several books in his hands and placed them on the counter. "Ah, the kabala, an interesting concept." He took the letter from Annie and told her to catalogue the books on the counter. "How is Isaac these days? I haven't seen him for a while now. Come with me to the office. Annie, be a dear and bring us some tea will you. You do like tea, don't you Miss?" He raised thick eyebrows, expectantly.

"Only with shortbread biscuits, I'm afraid."

"Then you are in luck, they are my favourite too Miss?"

"Fox, Eve Fox." She couldn't resist the obvious links to her former name and her current appearance.

"Very apt Miss Fox, may I call you Eve?"

"Please do." Eve sipped her tea whilst Mr Soames read Isaac's letter. Placing the letter on the cluttered desk, he peered over his half-eye spectacles at Eve.

"So who do you want to be?"

"Eve Fox, student of Theology and Criminal and Forensic Psychology at a top university will do. I'll leave all the background details to you."

Pressing his splayed hands on the desk, he studied her intently. "Isaac has requested an especially thorough job. That will be costly, £30,000. You have sufficient funds?" Eve hoped the deposit box did indeed have sufficient funds.

"Yes."

"Isaac has vouched for you, so I will take you at your word." He took her into a storeroom at the back of the shop, off of which was a small studio. Here, he finger printed her, X-rayed her teeth and took a range of photographs. "Come back in one week, a.m., with cash. Your new life will be waiting for you, and, before you go, my earlier question. How is Isaac?"

Eve was ready for this. "Dead I am afraid. I hope you were not too close." He took a deep breath and exhaled slowly.

"We were," he paused, "well acquainted, I think, would best describe our relationship. I hope his loss is not too much of a hardship for you Miss Fox. I sense he was important to you." He offered his hand, "until next week."

The deposit box had proved interesting. Several more keys with a list of address sites at different cities around the world, along with a list of access codes and contact names, £100,000 in cash. "Thank you Isaac. That's Mr Soames and my university fees sorted." A pendant on a sturdy silver chain depicting a shattered pentagram with some kind of letter or rune carved into the surface of each piece, a tube marked open with extreme care, and a neat little hand gun having no manufacturer's name or mark, and of a design she had never seen before, perfect for secreting in a hidden pocket or pouch. She mouthed words in silence, "Thank you again Isaac." Last, a large bag of strangely shaped bullets. She would examine them later. She placed them all in the small rucksack purchased on the way. Outside she approached a street vendor, bought a leather card holder, placed her fake credit and debit cards into it, then wandered distractedly around several more stalls, repeatedly dropping and retrieving it. At the third stall it was snatched.

"There you go Isaac, you told me to get rid of them quickly, and in a way that would be difficult to trace. This way, some would-be villain will get a little more than was intended too. With any luck they'll burn his hands off." She still had several hundred pounds from her illegal cash withdrawals and, with a hundred thou in her back pack, felt a taxi would be the safest and quickest form of travel (provided she didn't fall asleep again). "Devonshire Close, Chiswick, please." She looked up at Big Ben. "Only four o'clock. I have some time to waste so take the long route. Show me some sites." Eve kept one arm through the loop of her rucksack and lay back in the seat to watch London go by.

Since becoming Eve, she had scarcely had time to think. Even her brief sojourn alone in the habitat, and away from the man she believed to be Isaac, had been taken up with trying to work things out, and to gain as much knowledge and control as possible. Her thoughts and emotions were as tightly confined as acetylene in a pressurised cylinder, just as unstable, and likely to explode, if not handled with extreme care. Isaac had worked her to exhaustion, trying to instil in her a sense of duty, a measure of understanding of who she was, and of the desperate task for which she must prepare. Everything, existence itself, was at stake.

"Stop!" Eve had recognised a face as they passed through St James's. She jumped out leaving the door open.

"I can't stay here long, miss." Pulling out a fifty, she stuffed it into his hand and ran off after the tall guy in the suit jacket and jeans. Shrugging her rucksack onto her shoulders, she called after him. "Matt! Matt Crow! Wait!" Matt turned, looking back in bewilderment. He watched her weave through the crowded street, and waited for her to catch up with him.

"I'm sorry, do I know you?" Eve collected herself.

"No. You knew my ..." She did a quick calculation and estimated how old she would appear "... uncle, John Woolf."

"John? God yes, how is he? I haven't seen him for a while. I heard he was ill and had retired. I didn't even know he had a niece." He looked at her with suspicion. "How is it that you know me?"

"I met you once, very briefly, with my uncle. He brought me up to Scotland Yard for a visit. I was only twelve then. He said you were the best profiler he'd ever met."

She needed to put him off guard. "As for your question, I'm afraid he's dead."

"Dead? I'm sorry. Did he suffer?"

Typical Matt, straight to the point. "No. It was very quick. If you buy me a cup of tea and a sticky bun I'll tell you all about it." She pointed at the café a few feet away. He glanced at his watch. She could see the curiosity burning in him.

"Okay. Why not?"

As she reached for the bun he'd placed in front of her, he looked her up and down. First impressions were not wrong. She was every bit the stunner he had first perceived. About five foot ten, twenty-seven or twenty-eight-ish? honey coloured, long hair, in loose curls down her back, startling marine blue eyes, with dark blue, almost black, radial flecks, full red lips, a straight perfect nose and a stunning white smile, all the beauty that makeup artists dreamed of creating attractively mounted on a sensually curvaceous, but muscular body, yet unless he was mistaken, and he rarely was, not a trace of anything artificial applied anywhere. He checked out her breasts, perfect, but definitely natural. The amount of male attention she was receiving, from every quarter, was disconcerting, and, when her full attention was focused on him, as it had been a few moments ago, her sexual charisma was almost overwhelming.

"Your uncle loved those too."

She spoke around a mouthful of the sticky mess. "Yes. I know. He introduced me to them and now, I'm afraid, I'm an addict. Sticky bun and a cup of tea and I'm anybody's." Shit, had she really said that, and in that flirtatious way? She had to control these random urges. Quickly, she pulled away the finger that was pushing the last of the soft white icing into her mouth, noting how other men in the café were looking at her. She could see he was very uncomfortable, however much he tried to hide it. This was the last thing she wanted. "Sorry, figure of speech. Aunt Helen always used to say that about Uncle John and it's become a bit of a family joke. I wasn't being coquettish, I promise. I was just imitating the way Aunt Helen used to tease him."

"Coquettish?" He repeated musingly. He seemed to relax. "Yeah that sounds like how he described her. I never actually met her. Me and your uncle got on well but we never really caught up with each other socially, apart from a few down the pub after work." He looked her up and down again. "You know, I really can't remember John bringing you along."

Trying to avert further suspicion Eve quickly responded, "Oh, it was just in passing and you were very busy," she checked her memory. "I think you were working on the Smithson case or something. I wanted to be a police woman and Uncle John was just showing me around, to give me a feel of what I might be in for."

"You must have quite a memory for faces to know me after all this time. Do you still want to be a police woman?"

She nodded and then elaborated, "But I want to be a bit more than just a police woman now. I was thinking maybe forensic psychology?"

This seemed to be all the explanation he needed and Eve could see much of the tension drain out of him. He finished the sentence for her. "And you thought I might be able to point you in the right direction, or maybe open a door, or two, for you?" She gave him a broad smile and nodded again. He chuckled, despite himself. "John was a good friend. I'm really sorry we didn't catch up. Tell me what happened."

Eve gave an abridged version of events, minus the sex, and substituted oil deposits for religious fantasia, merely concluding that the probing equipment had exploded and that John had died as a result.

"How is your aunt coping?"

"I don't know. I'm on my way there now to see her." Eve wasn't quite sure why she had stopped him. It had been a rash decision, but she was in desperate need of a friend and seeing him like that had somehow brought some normality back to her life. Nevertheless, she felt she ought to bring it to a close before more awkward questions began. "Look I've got to go now but when I saw you I remembered you and my uncle were friends. I was very close to him and I just wanted to speak to someone who knew him. I really had no intention to tap you for help with my career. That was just a bonus, and besides, I was trying to put off going to Aunt Helen's. It's not easy right now. Thanks for the tea and bun." She stood up and grabbed her rucksack to leave.

Matt stood too. "Wait!" Fishing a card from his pocket, he took her hand, and placed it in her palm, folding her fingers around it with his other hand. It did not seem sexual, just caring, and she wanted to hug him. "Call me, if you need to talk some more. Having taken the initiative, he turned and left. Eve completed her journey and stood at the garden gate looking apprehensively at her once front door. She had not lied, when she said she was putting off her visit, and she dearly wished she could leave again but it had to be done.

Starting Again

The door opened before she had a chance to knock and an anxious looking Helen invited her inside. Feeling displaced, Eve sat in her favourite leather chair and waited while Helen brought in a tray of tea and biscuits, placing the tray on a coffee table in front of her. Helen sat on the couch to Eve's right. She seemed uncomfortable and started to wriggle restlessly.

"Look, Miss."

"Eve," Eve supplied.

"I don't feel very comfortable with you sitting there. John always sat in that chair. It's never bothered me until now but somehow your sitting there has unsettled me. Perhaps because I know you're here to talk about him. Can we move to the kitchen please? I think I would find that easier."

They sat facing one another across the kitchen table. Once again Eve was having trouble containing her erotic desires. Having Helen so close again, feeling the wind of her movements as she replenished their tea, and smelling her familiar scent was arousing some strange sensations both emotionally and physically, and now, Helen too, was becoming restless. Eve was almost finished relating a more honest version of the tale to Helen than she had to Matt, but still minus the sex, and placing herself in the role of Gwen. Afsoon was not mentioned. She had just explained the execution of the plan to retrieve the vessel by exploding the earth around it. Eve had been gauging Helen's incredulous expression as the tale unfolded and was highly doubtful she would sit there and listen to any more of what, she must feel, was a ludicrous story, but Eve had been determined to give her as much of the truth as she was able to. She plunged on, concluding that John had died in the massive explosion that had destroyed the vessel they had been trying to retrieve.

"Foreseeing the likelihood of failure and its associated consequences; John had persuaded Isaac to let me get the plane ready for take-off, prior to detonating the explosives. John was very good to me. I would not be here now if it were not for him. He spoke about you a lot and asked me to let you know what happened, if he didn't make it. So here I am."

Helen sat silent for what seemed a very long time. The daylight was fading. A slight smell of kitchen cleaner lingered in the cool air and apart from the occasional rustle of clothing, and their own breathing, the kitchen was very quiet. A surreal calm seemed to invade the bubble of reality in which they sat. Eve's thoughts wandered as she looked at Helen's downcast eyes. At forty-three, she was still very attractive Five foot nine, slim, brushed back thick. ash-blonde hair and just enough makeup to enhance her green eyes to full effect, dressed casually, in a loose necked beige cashmere sweater, with dark brown moleskin jeans and mid-brown leather ankle boots. That was one of the things he'd always loved about her, her natural ability to look comfortably elegant and serene. The current strain in her features moved him deeply. It reminded him of the time after Annabel's tragic death. Helen's eyes flicked up startled as Eve absently covered her hands with her own. For a moment she looked directly into Eve's eyes and Eve saw her pupils dilate widely, before she looked away again and pulled her hands from under Eve's. She got up stiffly and turned on the light destroying the moment. Moving to the work top and presenting her back squarely to Eve she asked a question. "Another cup?" and began pouring more tea. Eve struggled to keep her voice even against surging emotions.

"Yes please."

"Were you having an affair with him?"

"Of course not!" Eve blurted out before fully understanding what Helen had asked. She was now, fully alert, and back in the present. "Is that what you really think? I don't think I was his type."

"Please don't take me for a fool. Of course you were his type. You are everybody's type. Christ you are my type! Look, I really don't mind, as long as he was happy with you for a while."

Eve was speechless, her type? What was Helen saying? Why she responded as she did, she really didn't fully understand, but she found words were issuing from her of their own volition. "Well you didn't exactly wait around did you? Who was the lover boy you were with yesterday?"

The strain drained out of Helen's posture and she turned to face Eve, calm serenity back in her face. "Thank you. I think I have my answer. I'm glad he was able to find some comfort during his remission. I take it you knew he was dying? Lover boy, as you put it, was my cousin Paul back from Australia. He's been a great comfort since John left and, subsequently disappeared." Eve sat up straight, feeling a rush of blood to the head. Paul? Of course! How could she not have recognised him?

"Disappeared?" Eve made to rise but, the shock of realisation at what Helen must have been going through, caused her knees to give way and she clutched at the table to steady herself. "You mean you didn't know he was dead?"

Helen came quickly around the table and supported her back into the chair.

"Are you okay? You won't fall if I let go?" Eve shook her head and sat up straight, feeling a sense of loss as Helen moved away again. "I guessed of course, but we have been unable to get any information at all from the Afghan authorities and I haven't a clue who Isaac is, or was. That was why I was so desperate to find out what you knew. I couldn't bear to think of him dying by degrees in some Afghan jail."

Eve could see there was no use denying an affair. Helen had made up her mind, and her own outburst, had confirmed Helen's suspicions, and besides, it was the truth, in a twisted sort of a way. He had had an affair, albeit not with him/her-self, God was there no end to the conundrum of her current existence? Somehow she felt better, now that Helen understood, in broad terms, the circumstances leading up to John's demise. And Helen's understanding also gave Eve a degree of comfort. So she said simply, "You really don't mind?"

"I mind that John is dead and that I was not there to comfort him, but I am glad he died the way he would have liked to. Like an action hero. Instead of withering away in pain, and without dignity, in some hospital bed, and I'm glad that you were there with him. I wish it had been me, but the main thing is, that it was somebody."

"Can I ask you something, Helen?"

"You can ask?" Eve hesitated whilst a gamut of confused emotions fought for superiority in her heaving chest .

"What did you mean when you said I was your type?" Helen didn't answer straight away. She seemed to be looking inward.

"I don't really know what made me say that, but you must realise the devastating effect you have on men. Paul only saw you for a moment and he hasn't stopped talking about you. All I will say to you is this; the effect doesn't stop with men. Now let's just leave it at that shall we?"

Eve digested that for a moment, her mind running through a thousand possible scenarios. Getting a grip on herself, she asked another question. "Just one more thing, it is a fantastic tale yet, you seem to believe me. Why?"

"I'm not completely sure. It was a fantastic tale from the moment John told me what he was going to do, and the way the authorities have acted certainly suggests something strange, but honestly? I guess it's something about you. John's presence seems to hang around you like a cloud."

As they parted at the door, Eve pressed on, not without some trepidation. "Helen? Would you see me again if I got in touch?" A puzzled frown touched Helen's features but she nodded pensively. Eve quickly ducked in towards her and gave her a quick kiss on the lips before spinning on her heel and bouncing off up the path toward the waiting taxi. At the gate she turned. "Oh! Helen!" she called. Helen turned back from the door. "John told me to ask. Have you checked your bank account lately?" Helen shook her head.

"No. They have been trying to contact me but I've ignored the letters and phone calls."

"Check it! He made sure all his wages went into it. It is quite a substantial amount."

She sighed, "I know. He said it would be around £75,000 but I assumed that disappeared with him."

"Think again. It was definitely paid in, and there is also a bonus, check it out." So saying, she dived into the taxi and left for her flat.

By the time she arrived the euphoria had dissipated and the old maelstrom of seething confusion and emotion had returned. She'd bought a full-length mirror on the way home and now stood in front of it, naked. She could see what Helen meant, she was a siren. She was getting hot just looking at herself. Her imagination wandered. What would it be like being with Helen now? She ran for the shower, turned it fully to cold, and forced herself to bear the shock of freezing water for several minutes.

After a restless night, during which she had finally given up resisting, and had brought herself to orgasm several times, she fell into a dreamless sleep. She awoke fully alert however, but once more in a wrecked bed and in a sweat, feeling like she'd had an exhilarating workout. The euphoria had returned. She leapt out of bed and washed away the evidence of a night of self-abuse before settling down for a breakfast of tea and toast and a flick through the free paper. The headline informing of a vicious mugging by four gang members of a local taxi driver that took place in a remote industrial area, gave her some wry amusement.

She took some time out to think. Her meetings with Helen and Matt changed things. She would have to give a great deal more thought to how she was going to handle her feelings for Helen and hoped fervently that she hadn't ruined everything with that kiss. What had she been thinking of? Helen wasn't gay; a kiss on the cheek would have been fine but ... Oh well, habit she supposed but ... Helen had said that she was attracted ... No! Stupid! Stupid! Stupid! The best thing would be to forget her and move on but ... Seeing her ... Touching her ... When she had thought never to again ... "Jesus Christ! Listen to yourself girl. You're a bloody pervert. Women often show their affection in a more tactile way than men."

It was wrong on so many levels but she couldn't just leave it like that either. They could be friends. At least she would then know how Helen was getting on. Perhaps even give some help, or protection. Sighing heavily, she mentally stamped down on her fanciful thinking, "Oh! Who the hell am I kidding? Helen is tougher than I am. It could never work!" Definitely best to just drop her a goodbye note and be done with it, but, it had opened up possibilities regarding her sexuality, and her high sex drive was something which she was going to have to address sooner rather than later if it was not going to consume her every waking, or for that matter sleeping, thought.

Isaac had said that it would settle down but that wasn't any help right now. The thought of going with a man both excited her physically and repulsed her mentally. Her male ego was too strong. But, sex with another woman, was something she might have to think on. With an effort of will, she forced it all from her mind, focusing instead on more immediate matters. Keep busy. That was the main thing for now. She made a decision and headed for Mr Soames' book shop.

He showed mild surprise when she walked in but ushered her into his office for more tea and biscuits. "Why are you here Miss Fox? I told you your new identity would take a week."

"I want to make some changes."

"That will cost."

"No problem. Can I still have everything by next week?"

"For the right price, provided you do not want to be Prime Minister, I expect I will be able to accommodate you. Give me the details please." He took some more photos, during which he casually asked some questions about what Isaac had been up to on his "recent expedition to Afghanistan." Given what Helen had told her about lack of information from authority, Eve was instantly suspicious and was evasive with her answers. As she left, he asked if Afsoon was still up to her wayward antics. The hairs prickled on the back of her neck and she stopped in her tracks. She didn't need to turn. She knew there was a gun pointed at her back. "Sit down Miss Fox. I need to ask you some questions."

Without looking back, Eve dropped smoothly into a cross-legged position on the floor, facing the door. Her intention was to take the initiative from him, and to make him nervous. "Go ahead. Ask away." He seemed uncertain for a moment but recovered his composure. He drew up a chair several feet behind her. "Won't you turn and face me Miss Fox? You have a beautiful face and our conversation will be so much more amicable if you look at me."

"I'm sorry, my mother told me to never to look down the barrel of a gun."

"If you promise me you won't attempt to attack me, or to run, I will put it out of sight. How does that sound?"

"Very well," Eve spun on her bottom, in a swift movement. She observed the contour of the gun concealed under the flap of his open cardigan "What is it you want to know?"

"I want to know who you really are Miss Fox. I have run a check on your fingerprints and dental records, and on all of Isaac's contacts, and you don't pop up anywhere. You have also told me that Isaac is dead. Much as I would like to believe differently, that suggests to me that you may have had some hand in any ill that has befallen him."

"There is no ill, Mr Soames. Isaac is dead, blown to bits, and, as you seem to know of Afsoon, I think I am not remiss in telling you that both she and her pervert brother were up to their neck in it. I need a new identity to hide from her and any agents they, or the Afghan authorities, might send after me. I was with Isaac before he died, and I can tell you, I am a marked woman."

With lightening reflexes, Eve sprang at Soames, snatching the gun and grabbing his ear. She held him to his chair while she made the gun safe and quickly patted him down for any other weapons. "I'm about to let you go Mr Soames. Don't try to shout or give any alarm, or get out of your chair, or you will suffer a severe amount of pain and distress. Do you understand?"

He answered with surprising composure. "Yes."

"Now, tell me who you are and what you know of Isaac."

He was disturbingly compliant and seemed almost amused. It unnerved her and she kept on high alert, scanning every part of the room and listening for any approach from outside.

"I am a contemporary of Isaac's, both a colleague and a competitor, but I have seen little of him these past three years and this expedition of his I found suspicious, so I had him observed. I have an inkling of the nature of his recent work and, although I have always found his theories rather off the wall, this volcanic enigma, and the subsequent invitation from Afghanistan, gave me pause for thought, a second genesis? Ridiculous isn't it Gwen?"

Eve was not happy with the way this was going.

"Gwen is dead. Why would you call me Gwen?"

"Just a random idea, stupid really, but I had to check. Look, you are obviously not going to kill me. I want to know more details about what happened on Isaac's expedition. You are in need of a friend, and would doubtless like to know more of what I am about and, I suspect more of who, and what, Isaac was and the thrust of his research. I don't expect you to trust me, hopefully I can earn that in time, and I still have a way to go before I will trust you, but I have a good feeling about you, and you need my help. So why don't we ride the same boat for a while and see where it goes?"

Eve knew he had a point, but he was right. She didn't trust him either. "Does this mean you will waive my fee?"

He grinned. "Not a chance."

Eve nervously clutched the CV file, supplied by Mr Soames, to her chest. Matt had arranged an interview for her for an internship as assistant forensic psychologist to "Vincent Barnes", a top man in his field who did a lot of work for the police on their very high profile cases here, and in America, and whose opinion was sought around the world. Soames had really gone for it with her new background. She had, apparently, achieved a doctorate at Cambridge in theology, and had gone on to complete a master's degree at the Chicago school of criminal and forensic psychology. She was "a truly outstanding, dynamic and popular student with a keen and probing mind." When Eve had expressed doubts about her ability to live up to the fictional superwoman portrayed, and had highlighted the fact that her background could easily be checked in academic circles with just a phone call, he had shushed her and told her not to worry. Any enquiries to the worthy scholars named in her file would receive positive responses. "It was a time for her to grasp the nettle by its roots, and to be bold. People at these levels have no time for door mice."

"But what about my thesis, he will want to look at those."

"All taken care of Miss Fox, these things are often published in minority specialist papers and circulars. No one has time to read them all, should he wish to, however, he will find them. There are copies in the file, so you will know what you wrote. I can assure you he will think you highly capable. Now run along. You have only about three weeks to learn your subjects. In any case, one look at your other attributes," he looked her up and down, "will quell any undue curiosity in that quarter although, you might find ... a more physical form of curiosity much more of a problem."

Fortunately, Eve soon discovered that one of her new attributes was a photographic memory. She was also, it seemed, highly focused, had boundless energy and a massive IQ. She had gone on to discover quite a few things about herself in the past few weeks, for a start her weight. Having broken two of the flimsy stools in her small kitchen and raised her small sofa by sitting on one end of it, she decided to get a set of scales, three sets of scales later, and a trip to the local chemist, confirmed a weight of twenty-two stone and five pounds. She could only assume this was due to muscle density, as, it soon became apparent that she was also incredibly strong, and fast. A trip to the swimming pool confirmed that she was very heavy in the water, sinking straight to the bottom on her first plunge. This was to her advantage when swimming below the surface and she easily had the power to stay afloat if required, although she did have to cut her trip short. Even though she had chosen a costume that covered as much as possible, the amount of attention she was receiving became too embarrassing in the end. A bunch of teenage boys started calling out and touching her in the water. One now had two broken fingers, but it was really becoming quite a nuisance. She would have to try and dumb down her appearance. Much to her relief, all of this activity seemed to divert her attention sufficiently that her own sexual needs were at a controllable level.

When Eve had shown Matt her CV, he was stunned to silence for several minutes. Finally, he puffed a quiet sigh. "I had intended to get you a placement with a local guy, but seeing this, I had better think again. Leave it with me for a bit. I will get back to you." And here she was, peeing her pants, waiting to see the great man. Matt had deposited her outside an office on the second floor and told her not to worry. "Just be yourself. You will be working for nothing, so he shouldn't be too hard to convince. Don't mind his manner. He can be a bit off hand and vague, but he is the best guy to learn your trade from. If all goes well, in a year, I should be able to get you a job in the force. Just leave me to sort that out, if it's still what you want?" She nodded. Oddly, she would have preferred him to stay. When she was John, he had done everything on his own, had always found it easier that way, but perhaps not so strange, he had recently just died and s/he had been through a hell ride of fantastical experiences ever since. She needed someone and, thank God, fate had provided Matt. He had proved himself a good friend to both of her selves.

A middle aged guy in jeans and a brown sweat top showing the collar of a green gingham shirt, wandered down the corridor ten minutes later. He gave her a cursory glance, unlocked the door and reached in for the light switch.

"You are Matt's friend. Miss Fox isn't it? Come in." He pushed a pile of case notes to the edge of the desk so that he could see her when he sat down. Eve remained standing. He searched around for his glasses, eventually finding them by fishing down the neck of his sweat top into his shirt pocket. He put on his character with his glasses. He did not do the body check she was now getting used to, but looked directly into, and through, her eyes. It felt a bit like he was surveying the inside of her head, before taking a quick peek down her throat, and backing quietly out to the surface again. "Please sit down. Why do you want to work for me, Miss Fox?"

Such was the subdued power of the man that she was answering before she had thought what she would say. "I want to understand the criminal mind Mr Barnes and I want to learn how to manipulate it, change it, heal it, if that is possible?"

Now he did the body check, but it was slow and assessing, not lustful. "It is possible to rehabilitate, or heal, those who are ready for change Miss Fox, but the kind of criminal you will meet with me is unlikely to fall into that category, they will never think like ordinary human beings. Sometimes we can alter their perspective to one which is law abiding, and generally, un-harmful, but it is hellishly difficult, and never completely successful, and there is something you need to fully understand Miss Fox. Many of these criminally insane minds are very powerful and their driving purpose is to subdue and corrupt. Unless you are extremely strong and focused, it is far more likely that it will be you who is manipulated, and also violated, mentally and physically, if the possessors of these minds are able to seize the opportunity to do so. I warn you now Miss Fox that, should I agree to allow you to work with me, I will be introducing you to some of the owners of those minds, and there is a real danger that you will suffer permanent damage from the contact. I have read your file, so I really have only one question. Do you want to take that risk?"

He had succeeded in frightening her but she really didn't have any choice. "Yes! Yes I do." Then more quietly, "emphatically, yes." He seemed to be lost in thought for a moment.

"Good. I have a case in Texas that I have been asked to interview. Your theological background may help to gain some insight into this case. I want you to accompany me. We will see if you feel the same afterwards. I take it you are not barred from entering the US. No criminal convictions or anything. Texans, in particular, can be difficult over such things."

"No."

"You can pick up your plane ticket here tomorrow. We leave from Heathrow at 10:30 a.m. Monday. Pack light. We will be there for four days."

Eve couldn't help thinking "God! It's Isaac all over again."

She was relegated to economy, whilst Barnes travelled first class. She re-joined him as they climbed into the waiting limousine, struggling under the weight of all the case papers that she had indexed, catalogued, and read. She had barely slept for the last 24 hours trying to gain some basic knowledge and grounding in theology and the case in hand.

The man, known as "The Priest" was a monster. Priest was not a pseudonym. He proved to be an actual Roman Catholic priest with an intense hatred of women, whom he believed to be the embodiment of all weakness in mankind. His mutilated victims wore the text of his preaching carved into their back and torso, the only parts of them left intact. All else, had been eaten from these living, screaming and begging creatures over a period of days as they slowly lost any physical or mental resemblance to anything human. His vindictiveness was not confined to the female gender. Boys and men alike were punished for their failure in allowing their right to immortal domination to be taken from them by mere deceit. If he could subdue them, that subjugation was all the proof he needed that they were unfit to exercise the gift of will bestowed upon them, not by their creator, but by he, whose destiny it was to usurp him, "The True Power" from whose loins, the seed of humanity was stolen.

Male victims remained alive to worship dominance of his will by being subservient to his every whim, beaten, raped, defecated on, and abused in every way to punish their craven stupidity. It was believed fifteen females had, so far, fallen victim to his hatred. Males were thought to double that number. Most of those were, at least, likely to be still alive. Females exhibiting the first signs of womanhood and up to middle age were stored in batches of three, for up to two months, forced to listen to his unholy rants, and to await the dining habits of their priest and master. The police, so far had no clue to the whereabouts of the secret store (or stores) and slave quarters, but it was believed that up to twenty male slaves were still imprisoned somewhere and, he was holding and feeding, possibly, six females.

There was believed to be a highly organised cult following, of brutalised acolytes, marshalled and directed by trusted lieutenants. He had finally been caught following a citizen's call to police relating a tale of satanic goings on in the dark and empty church of "Our Lady" in downtown Houston. He had been caught in the midst of the act of personally carving his gospel into the last of his dying victims, stretched across the altar, a pitiful creature, beyond any capacity to expel a whimper or offer any resistance. A frenzied, and fruitless search for survivors had followed. Mr Barnes was a last ditch hope for getting information on possible locations from "The Priest".

"He will be chained by feet and hands when we go in. I will sit opposite him. You will sit three feet back from the table and to my left. This is the position in which the chairs will be placed. Do not respond to him, or say anything, unless I ask you to. Do not look him in the eye, and do not show any reaction to anything he says or does. He is highly intelligent, and he will try to bait you. Do only as I tell you. Is that understood?"

Eve nodded her assent and said, "yes."

As she stood behind the barred prison gate waiting, she could hear heavy shuffling coming from the corridor leading to another gate, at the opposite end of a short walkway, then an echoing shout.

"I smell harlot! Do the whores of Jewa have the affront to enter even this place?" As he came into sight, Barnes stepped in front of her but he had caught her eye with a malevolent look before she was fully shielded. It seemed to her eyes that a lightning bolt burned an after image of their mutual abhorrence in the air between them, which faded, with sluggish reluctance, as the guards manhandled him through a side door and into the interview room. A heavy iron door whispered shut behind them.

Barnes gave her an assessing look. "Do you want to leave?" His eyebrows were raised in question. She shook her head and stepped grimly forward, as the gate rolled noisily open.

He sat erect but with head bowed, and was muttering something that might have been prayer or invocation. One of the two guards flanking the door, and nursing a gaping bite to his neck, was relieved, by a third guard, to enable him to seek medical attention. Keppler, aka "The Priest" was dripping blood from a broken nose. The second guard stood with baton drawn and ready. Barnes sat

down, Eve behind and to his left. He sat quiet for a time, then spoke.
"What, within reason, will it take for you to tell me where your
living victims and slaves are?"

"Why do you bring your whore to contaminate my space?"
Keppler returned to his mutterings.

"Do you want her to leave?"

After a minute or so of further mutterings, Keppler responded,
"No. I want her to choke to death on my semen." The mutterings
continued.

"Your intended victims? What will it take?"

Keppler looked up, fully lucid, and held silence, the only noise
the shuffling of the guard's feet, and then he dropped words
heavily into the still air. "Your harlot naked on this table and in
reach of my hands and teeth."

"You know that will not happen. You also know that you are
going to die. This holds no fear for you, but failure to do all in your
power to fulfil your mission does. To do that, you must stay alive
as long as you can. Time gives you a chance to subvert others in
your sphere of influence in here and a chance to plot an escape. We
can trade in time."

"I don't need your time, or any chance. I take what time I need,
and nothing happens by chance."

"Then take your time, and make your plans, by trading with me."

"I will not trade with you but I will bring Satan into this room,
to rip out your heart, and your pretty little tongue. Then I will rape
and consume both you and your filthy whore." So saying his eyes
turned up, his head lolled, and spittle began drooling from his
mouth. Eve had been watching him closely but he had never
looked at her. Something about his mutterings had a familiar ring.
He now started to babble, speaking in tongues. Then, with shock-
ing suddenness, he was on his feet snatching out, with catlike
speed, with a hand he had, somehow, freed. Eve should have
avoided. She was fast enough, but the babbling had distracted her,
stunned her. She understood it, or rather not it, but a kind of
subdued musical language that accompanied it. Everything slowed
down. She felt her non-resisting body being drawn towards him.
Felt the extra pressure, as his muscles accounted for his misjudge-
ment of her weight, the twisting motion he exerted on her wrist,
intending to spin her in front of him and allow his teeth access to

the jugular in her throat. And all the while, his babbling was informing her of his intent. She observed the far too slow reactions of both Barnes and the guards. A cold part of her admired a well-conceived, and well-executed, plan. Then she spoke in the same babbling tongue. Keppler froze. His eyes rotated downwards and locked with hers.

She showed the flat of her hand to Barnes and the guards, and ordered them, in imperious tones.

"Be still! I have this," before returning to the babble and the music. She drew his gripping hand irresistibly towards her own, with a mirror like grip on his wrist. Without conscious volition, she crooked her index finger and gouged, with lightning strokes, a shattered pentagram into his forearm, but with one un-shattered stem pointing up his arm, towards his shoulder. "I mark you Keppler, named Priest with the sign of your sire. You will inflict no further pain on any living thing, lest, if you cannot control your desires, it be to yourself." As fear rose into his eyes for the first time in his life, she spoke, in an aside, to Barnes. "Write down or record everything I say," then, to Keppler. "Where are those living whom you have, or whom you intended to, hurt? What dangers will those who seek them encounter? Where are the bodies of those you have killed?" Repeating each answer aloud in English, but not for those questions that followed, these she kept to herself. "How do you come to speak this language? What ancient texts have you studied? Where can I find those texts? What, if any, are the dangers in my recovering them?" Finally she instructed him to relate none of their liaison to anyone, to be a model prisoner from now on, and to go quietly with his captors. Having some prescient knowledge of his fate, she disengaged his hand and, with almost motherly gentleness, assisted, the now Zombie-like Keppler into his seat. The guards rushed him. She and Barnes were hustled quickly out of the room and brought to the prison governor's office.

The governor was a bullish man in his early sixties, and far too overweight. He jumped up from behind his huge desk, as they entered through the door.

"What the hell just happened down there? And you ..." he struggled for a moment, waving his hand in the air in frustration, as he tried to remember, "Miss Fox. How the Jesus fuck did you get him to talk, or understand anything the creep was saying."

Eve spoke up. "You recorded it all I hope?"

"Yeah! Yeah! All interviews are recorded. A SWAT team are already on their way. I just hope he hasn't spun you a heap load of steaming horse crap, or that you haven't got an over active imagination Missy. We don't take no shit in Texas, so you had damn well better be right."

Eve had been thinking hard about what she would say on the way up and thought she had cobbled together a reasonable story.

Barnes intervened. "Miss Fox is with me Governor Hinch." He glanced at Eve, "I do not associate with people who spout 'shit' and I don't like it when people are heavy handed with my staff." He had spoken in subdued tones but, his quiet power, when focused, was formidable. Hinch stopped in his tracks and seemed to deflate. Looking baffled by having his pending tirade effectively diverted, he waived his hand in the air again and headed back to his desk. Barnes winked at Eve.

"Okay, okay, I get it Vincent, and for Christ's sake call me Jim. We're friends aren't we? But you've got to admit that was some performance down there."

"I should explain. As well as having a master's degree in forensic psychology from one of your own very fine American universities, Eve is also a doctor of theology. Nevertheless, I find myself of like mind; I too would like to hear more about what exactly happened down there. Eve?"

She took a deep breath. "Okay." She paused, sat, adjusted her posture and plunged in. "Some of my university studies predated any of the holy books. I was interested in people who speak in tongues. No one ever seems to have wondered if there is any sense in what they are saying. So I asked myself if they were just undergoing a period of temporary insanity or whether they were actually talking in one, or several, of the ancient languages. I thought about doing my dissertation on it but it became too complex and I chose another subject. I didn't drop it though. It was too interesting. These languages are dead. There is no direct record of them." She was really winging it now but it had to be convincing, and not easy for anyone to check out. "I found some material in the very early religious texts and quite a lot in language used for incantations and black magic, strange words from an older time. When he started babbling, I recognised some of the language used. Certain words were considered very potent, spoken only when a powerful spirit was being invoked. I used several of these to control him. I reinforced my control by use of a sign that I knew he would fear if he had been delving into some of those magical rites."

"Well you certainly achieved your purpose Missy." He was about to continue but the phone rang. He mainly listened, then, very respectfully, thanked the caller, and slammed the phone down. "Well whatever it was you did Missy, you hit the jackpot. That was Senator Jackson. We've got the lot. You've saved some lives today ..." Eve jumped in. She couldn't stand another "Missy."

"Eve. Please call me Eve."

"Yeah okay, Eve it is. You did it Evee baby. Not a shot fired." He punched his fist in the air. Eve thought, perhaps "Missy" wasn't so bad after all.

They boarded the aircraft. Only this time, Eve sat in first class with Barnes paid for by the state of Texas. A stewardess, exaggeratedly swinging her hips, walked up to Barnes and asked if he would speak with Governor Hinch on the cabin phone. He came back a couple of minutes later.

"That was Jim Hinch. Keppler is in the county hospital, chewed his own hand and lower arm off last night, the one you put the sign on. He also smashed his head against the wall a couple of times. It's unlikely he'll make it through the rest of the day." Eve didn't comment, just nodded. He looked at her for a moment longer then sat down, reclined his seat and closed his eyes. "When you are ready, I'd like to hear the real story behind what went on in that cell and not the fantasy you concocted for Jim Hinch." Eve didn't feel she could say anything just now and Barnes didn't ask her to. She was glad he had asked for their names to be kept out of the media. Reclining her own seat, she tried to get some rest. She wanted to tell him, but, if he thought her story was fantasy, what the hell was he going to make of the truth. She had no idea how she had understood Keppler or how she had been able to control him.

There was one thing she would have to follow up however. The sign she had carved into his forearm was the same as that on the pendant left in the deposit box by Isaac, and which now hung around her neck, bar that is, her modification of reassembling one part of the star to point up Keppler's arm. There were also the texts Keppler had revealed the locations of. She would have to return to Texas and find them. Something else she would have to think on was that she was sure Keppler had not understood himself, what he, or she, had said during their coded liaison. It had seemed he was under a compulsion to respond to her in this foreign tongue without understanding what he was actually saying or revealing.

Eventually she solved the problem of Barnes by promising to tell him everything one year from now, when she had completed her internship and had found gainful employment, when it no longer mattered if he thought she was insane.

He gave her a half smile and nodded. "One year then," was all he said.

Forbidden Encounter

She travelled first class from then on and was given a small wage, in the form of inflated expenses. Barnes proved to have a ready wit once you got to know him, and was both compassionate and a stimulating companion. They became good friends and worked well together, so she was devastated when she opened the paper one morning, eleven months after first meeting him, to read the headline. "Top forensic scientist found dead in his Mayfair flat." It was just one of those freak accidents. He had climbed a step ladder to change a bulb in the high ceiling and had fallen smashing in his skull.

She was shaken to the core and not only by his death. She had recently been having some unsettling dreams. Half remembered at the time but crystal clear now, dreams of Afsoon, in male aspect naked and laughing, and with a full erection. He had turned away from her and climbed a ladder. His left hand was clutching the ankle of a dangling, and struggling, Barnes. Above a dazzling sun hung from a cord. Afsoon reached for it. It exploded in a shower of glass and all went dark. In the silence, Barnes screamed.

Eve didn't know what to do. She had come to rely on him heavily. He had obviously known she had many secrets, yet he never pushed her on anything. Once, in the pub after a gritty interview with a child abuser at Holloway prison, he had mused. "There is something satisfying in knowing that an enigma will be solved on a specific date in the near future, and, I am sure that what you tell me at the end of our year, will give me an insight into the whole of you my good friend." And she would have told him everything, even at the risk of him thinking her mad, he deserved that. She now wished she had found the courage to tell him sooner. Perhaps he would have believed. He was a remarkable man. She didn't know if he had any family, or even close friends, apart from her, and, a somewhat removed camaraderie with Matt. There had never seemed a reason to ask.

She couldn't face Matt. Not today. The hormones had settled down, just as Isaac had said they would, but this? She wasn't entirely sure she wouldn't break down and she didn't want Matt to see her like that. Her John persona didn't want him to see her like that but she needed to talk to someone. She left her flat, walked around for a while, jumped on a couple of busses and found herself at her old garden gate. Did Helen still live here? She had lots of money now. She had probably moved. Eve should have contacted her long before now. She had wanted to but her heavy work schedule, and her friendship with Vincent, had helped to shore up a belated resolve not to complicate Helen's life. When all was said and done it was an impossible relationship. She turned to go. Footsteps ran up the path behind her.

"Eve? Is that you? I saw you from the window, what's wrong?" Eve turned and Helen scanned her face. "What is it?" In a gesture so natural that any incongruity in their relationship dissolved away, Helen stepped forward and hugged Eve to her chest.

As simple as that and, for the first time, Eve allowed her feminine self free reign. "Oh Helen, I didn't know what to do. There was no one else I could turn to." She faltered. "The … the … man I work for, my friend … died last night." There were tears in her eyes but they failed to fall. "He … he was important to me." She ducked her head into Helen's shoulder, and went limp. Helen hushed her and, with an arm around her waist, guided her along the path, through the house and into the kitchen. The kitchen was much the same as it had been. Eve sat in the same chair, in John's preferred position, elbows on the table clasping a steaming mug of tea to her lips and looking across at Helen, who regarded her closely. "I'm sorry I didn't come to the funeral Helen and I'm sorry too that I haven't been in touch." Helen waived her hand and shushed her for the second time. "I wanted you to be able to forget. I didn't want to stir up unwanted memories."

Helen allowed her gaze to roam down to where the table bisected Eve's washboard torso, then slowly back up to the, slightly parted, full red lips, before restraining herself from falling into the sorrowful turmoil surging in the depths of those amazing, black on blue, eyes. "Was he a lover?" she asked, in a tone, somewhere between sympathy, and hurt.

Eve placed her tea mug down slowly and returned a level gaze. She chose her words carefully. "No. I couldn't do that to John, or to you. Not so soon. He was just a true friend at a time when I most needed one. Someone unconnected with my past or any of the land-slide of events in my recent history, and now he's gone, and, I don't know why, but I think it's my fault." Her voice broke as the last words came out and she started to sob. Helen was magically at her side with an arm around her shoulders and Eve buried her head in Helen's chest.

When the tears subsided, Helen withdrew, smoothing her sweater over her hips, and moved to look out of the window. Rubbing at her own eyes, she coughed herself back to reality. And spoke in an upbeat fashion.

"Listen, I have a proposition. As you can see," she waived her hand in an encompassing gesture, "the money John left me hasn't exactly changed my life much but I did have one extravagance. John often spoke about getting a sailboat, something, that would enable us to cut away from the rat race and be together for a while without any intrusion from the rest of the world. Since I've been on my own, the thought of those precious times we never had has played on my mind, so I bought one. The *Sea Wolf.* Stupid name really, you don't see many wolves on the sea, but then John is never going to be on the sea now either, is he? I've become quite a good sailor over the last year, and it really is a beautiful boat," she said with enthusiasm. Turning to look at Eve once more, she said. "Look I need a break, somewhere I can start to get my mind back onto an even keel again, so to speak. I think you need a break too. Why don't you come and spend a few days on the boat with me?"

The image Helen had conjured up of the two of them together, as they once were, or could have been, poured deep yearning into the chasm of her despair, and, as though it were food proffered to a starving beggar, she snatched at the offer without thought. "Yes! Yes, that would be wonderful. Thank you so much. It's just what I need."

Helen released a deep sigh of relief and let the tension flow out of her tautened muscles. Eve re-assembled her composure. "It is alright isn't it Helen? You do really want me?" She looked down at the floor awkwardly. "I mean what, with my relationship with John and all. It's not too weird is it?"

Helen grasped her shoulders. "No weirder than anything else that has happened over the last eighteen months. Honestly Eve I would love to have you. Somehow I feel close to John when you are around, as though he never really died at all. Now let's put all that aside and plan our trip. I think we should go right away or tomorrow anyway. I can provide any sailing clothes you need. Our sizes are quite similar, so you don't even have to return home. Unless you want to that is. Anything else we need, we can buy. I've got more money than I know what to do with these days and it will be great to pamper ourselves, so just name anything you need and we'll grab it on the way to Portsmouth."

Eve looked around in wonder at the white leather interior of the Jensen sports car. "So the boat wasn't the only luxury you allowed yourself then?

"That one was for John. This one's mine. Can't be sailing every day of my life, can I now?" They both laughed as she gunned the motor and wheel spun down the slip road to the motorway.

Screeching with laughter they left the quayside pub and headed for the *Sea Wolf*. Helen came to a sudden halt. "Wait! I forgot our shopping." She ran back to the pub and came out under a burdensome bundle of bags and packages, staggering a little as the O2 hit her for the second time. Eve darted forward to steady her and relieved her of some of the bags. Arms around each other's shoulders they set off giggling and wandering dangerously close to the harbour wall. Eve had fared better than Helen and managed to get them both safely on board.

She placed two steaming mugs of coffee on the galley table and sat opposite Helen. "Thank you Helen, I really needed this."

Helen looked across at her seeming, suddenly, a lot more sober. "Nonsense we both needed this. Now loosen up. I've got a great bottle of wine in the fridge. In fact I've got several. I'm sure, if we pace ourselves, we can keep the evening going a little longer. No one has to get up in the morning." She took a swig of the coffee, bent across the table, looked Eve squarely in the eyes and said with intensity. "Eve there is something I have wanted to say to you for some time now."

Eve chewed her lip. "Yes, what?" she whispered huskily.

"You make shit coffee! It's worse than John's." So saying, she threw it down the sink. "Come on, I'll find the wine. You put on some music."

Eve found a CD of mixed soul music and put it on a subdued setting, then returned to the galley to see Helen's rump sticking up out of the fridge whilst she rummaged around in the bottom for a bottle of wine. She lost her balance and fell into the fridge banging her head. "Whoops!" She looked through her legs at Eve. "Hey. Eve! Guess what? You can't drink wine standing on your head!" Suddenly she was back on her feet, like a jack-in-the-box, flush faced and facing Eve with a bottle in one hand and two glasses in the other, "but we can give it a bloody good try." She swept an arm around Eve's waist and waltzed her back into the living quarters amid peals of musical laughter. Her mood was infectious. "What's this crap you've put on? It's that dreary old stuff John used to like. Come on! Let's liven things up a bit."

After an hour of jiving, twisting and Salsa, a stab at the Tango finally finished them. They both flopped down in exhilarated exhaustion on the couch seat. Helen looked over her shoulder at Eve. "You dance like shit too. I bet you like the slow ones like John. I was never sure whether he was being romantic or just couldn't keep up." She crawled across the floor to the player and shuffled out a slow mix to put on. Eve averted her eyes from Helen's rear. "Come on then, let's do a couple." Eve looked up at Helen who extended her hand to her. Feeling awkward, ashamed and excited, she took it, twirled to grasp the other and moved to the music. "Come on you can get close. You can't do much else on a boat. I won't bite, promise." They shuffled around for a bit.

Then the next number came on, *Je t'aime.* "Oh dear! That's embarrassing." They pulled away and stood looking at each other for a moment, both shrugged. "What the hell!" They closed together and went for it in a theatrical way, throwing in a few jokes, but had to break away after a minute or so, on the pretext of getting more liquor. Helen mixed a couple of Mojitos each and Eve knocked off the music. They sat and talked for a while enjoying the natural ease of each other's company.

"Well Eve, that's the most fun I've had in a while. You pushed your luck a bit though when those guys tried to chat us up. No imagination the youth of today. You're always lesbians when they can't get what they want. Still, with a bottle of Bailey's emptied down his underpants, I don't think he'll be getting any tonight."

"He might be in for a treat if his girlfriend has a taste for Baileys. Besides you were pretty damn outrageous yourself, winding up that poor kid in the sex shop. His eyes nearly popped out of his head when you shouted out from the changing room that you were stuck in a one-piece latex sub kit and dog collar and could he help you to get out of it. The shop was in uproar, but the underwear you did finally buy was actually very tasteful."

"Thank you my very sexy friend. I suppose I did get a bit carried away. I should never have been that cruel. It's not like me. I've never been in one of those shops before and he was only a young lad. I wasn't mistaken was I? That was an erection he was trying to hide when everyone was laughing at him."

"Yes it was but don't feel bad about it, you probably made his day. You really didn't need to appease him by waiving a blank cheque at him and telling him to give you a sack of mixed toys of his choice, but it probably gave him the best thrill he's had in a while, and it was a riot watching him beetling around the store like a kid whose birthdays had all come at once. And then, when you told him to individually wrap them as no one else had brought you any surprises for your birthday. He really started to get into it. 'Do you want the 12-inch wrapping paper or the 18-inch madam,' shoving a role between his legs and gyrating his hips. Still at least 'he' didn't get the sack."

Helen choked down a laugh, cutting in with, "I think he may have emptied it though, mostly down his trouser leg I would think."

Eve made wide eyes and sat up primly, thinking how she ought to stop but how great this feminine camaraderie was. She had never seen Helen in this mood but it was fantastic. It was the only time she could remember feeling comfortable, in allowing herself to act like a woman. Everything was different somehow with Helen. "Why Helen, I never realised what a filthy mind you had. I think he'll be having wet dreams about that encounter for a good few weeks." She picked up one of the packages. "What are you going to do with all this stuff anyway?" They looked at each other and burst out laughing.

"Unwrap it I suppose and find out what the dirty little sod has put in there. Tell you what, let's try and guess what each item is before we open it, loser downs a shot. We'll drop it all off at Help the Aged tomorrow. Put the light on will you?"

"That boy is depraved! Look at this one."

"My God Eve, ouch! That wouldn't fit in a dustbin. I was closest though, down your shot. What do you reckon this one is?"

"Soft packet got to be ... an outfit. Probably that sub kit you kidded him about."

"Nah! Young lad like that ... school mistress, they all fantasise about their teachers. Tell you what. Forget the shot. Whoever gets it wrong wears the outfit."

Eve unpacked it and dangled it in front of Helen. "You lose. Love the rubber. The boy has taste. Don't think you'll be wearing it though. You really would get stuck in it."

"No, a deal's a deal." She grabbed it and held it against herself. I think I might need help with this one though." She pulled her sweater over her head. Undid her bra and started wriggling into it. Half an hour of pushing, prodding and uncontrollable laughter later, and they finally squeezed her into it, but the knickers had to go to allow her bottom to slide in on the tub of talc they'd emptied into it. "Yay!" Helen thrust a fist in the air. "Did it! Oh, oh, I'm not sure I can sit down in it though. No, I'm alright, it actually stretches quite well. Any more outfits in there? I've got to see you in one."

Eve was starting to get a little uncomfortable and was experiencing a strong sense of deja vu. It was also a revelation to her that, for once, she didn't miss having a penis because, if she had one, Helen would have slapped her face by now. She didn't want to ruin the good time they were having but thought it best to curb things a little.

"There is one more, but I'll only wear it if you guess spot on. Otherwise, I'll down another shot and you get to try another outfit."

Helen rubbed her hands. "You're on! Kid's got no imagination. Got to beeee … a 'Dom' outfit."

Eve broke open the packet. "Yesss! I win. You gotta get up early to catch me girly." Thirty-five minutes later, with Helen sitting astride her back they finally got the zipper done up on Eve's outfit and lay exhausted and sweating, side by side on the floor.

"Get up then, girl. Let's see you strut your stuff. Here, you'll need this." She handed the whip to Eve. "Hang on a minute. I'll give you some inspiration." She got up on all fours and turned her rear towards Eve, looking back over her shoulder; she put a gloved finger in her mouth and said, in a very good imitation of Marilyn Monroe, "Oh mistress, I know I've been a naughty girl. Please don't spank me. I promise I won't do it again. Not, unless you want me to."

Eve was on her feet, whip in hand and breathless. She spoke in a tremulous whisper. "Helen, please don't." She could feel her nipples standing out hard against the black latex and she was starting to get wet.

Helen glanced back, giving a glimpse of an equally hard nipple, and spoke huskily. "Why not Eve, am I making you uncomfortable?"

"Yes." She breathed.

"Then do something about it. You're the Dom." She turned onto her hands again and presented her rear, then, arched her back.

"Oh fuck!"

"Yes please."

Eve woke in a sweat but felt great and, as usual, like she had had a good workout. Which, as guilty memories washed over her, she realised that on this occasion, she really had, but not the sort that she would be willing to tell anyone about. There was also a disconcerting guilty torrent of memories and forebodings of her last near sex encounter, on the habitat, prodding an unsettling sense of some outside force orchestrating events. The boat suddenly yawed and heeled violently to one side tipping her from the bed and banishing these disturbing, and unwanted, thoughts. There was a loud snap as rigging slackened, caught the wind on the other side, and the boat heeled over the other way.

A couple of minutes later a fresh-faced Helen stuck her head through the door. "Come on sleepy head, you're missing all the fun. As I'm captain, you get to cook breakfast. Bacon and eggs are in the fridge, back in ten," as she disappeared back up on deck. Eve looked at the shrivelled sex wear on the floor and cringed, as a fresh wave of shame sloshed through her conscience. She forced herself to tidy the sleeping area and scrub clean any used items, including herself, then, headed for the galley. Eve listened to Helen moving about on deck then heard the clatter of a chain running through a pulley. Helen poked her head through the door several minutes later.

"Mmm, nothing better than the smell of bacon when you've worked up an appetite." She sat at the table, "Sleep well?"

"Like the dead. How about you? You seem bright and breezy this morning. Thought you might have a lie in after ..."

"What? Last night? Great wasn't it? Never really expected to take a walk on the wild side but I wouldn't have missed it for the world, bit sore though. I told you that thing should have been put in the dustbin."

"No, you said it wouldn't fit in a dustbin."

"Nooo! I didn't, did I? Oh well, better just call me dusty from now on. How about you, bit sore down below?"

Eve threw the tea towel at her. "God woman, you're insufferable.

Helen dodged but looked at her quizzically. "You know you even have his way of talking, yet you knew him for such a short time." Helen paused and seemed lost in thought for a moment. "You do know I'm not actually gaym don't you Eve? And I don't think you are either."

Eve sat down. "Then what is happening here Helen? I'm as confused as hell."

"I'm not really sure. Two people filling the hole, if you'll excuse the expression, created by the loss of a great and wonderful man. I feel so close to him when I am with you, and absolutely no sense of betrayal. I think it is just an interlude, but somehow the passion I feel with you exceeds anything I have ever known and I don't want to let go of it, not yet. I think I have also found a friend, a friend like no other, and I want to know you in every way possible, mentally, emotionally, and of course physically. I only hope you feel the same."

Eve sighed deeply. "I do but ..."

Helen leaned over and placed a finger on Eve's lips. "No buts." She ran her eyes seductively down Eve's body. "Just butts." Stepping close she slid quivering hands down to Eve's hips, cupping her buttocks and pulled her in hard against her pelvis. Her penetrating gaze stripped away Eve's defences. "Hmm, perhaps I'll be Dom this time."

Eve gave an exasperated but defeated gasp. "You'll have to tie me down, and tight. I am very strong." Her John persona seemed to be giving up, still strongly there but integrating into a new composite being, whose disapproval was crumbling under a barrage of desire. There was a kind of resigned mental shudder and all resistance to her feminine sensuous side seemed to collapse.

"No problem. I know a few sailors' knots."

Eve shook her head, nonplussed, but renewed stirrings of desire were engorging her being, she returned the clasp. "Aye, aye captain," she whispered. They kissed passionately, as Helen force walked Eve to the table and pushed her firmly back onto it.

Eve came out of the shower dabbing a towel carefully between her thighs. "Well you certainly did know a few sailors' knots and you were right, that thing really does belong in the dustbin. I don't think it is a very good idea to take it down to Help the Aged. The strategic war office might want to examine it though, for its properties of mass destruction."

"Well, perhaps we'll just keep hold of it then. You never know when there might be a desperate need for a weapon of mass destruction. Come on, get dressed and grab a life jacket we need to weigh anchor and get under way."

Eve quickly became an invaluable crew member, fluidly mastering each task she was set, revelling in the bracing wind and the invigoratingly cold sea spray as they cut through the waves. Helen manoeuvred the *Sea Wolf* around a jutting headland. The wind dropped and the sea calmed to reveal crystal depths hemmed in by sheer cliffs, a flat bar of fine white sand at their base. She anchored off shore, ran to the bow, and slapped her hands down hard on the rail either side of Eve, bringing her lips close to Eve's ear. "This is what I wanted you to see Eve. It should have been John but somehow your being here makes everything okay. Isn't it beautiful? And look! Look!" she screeched. She broke away, leant far out over the rail and pointed. "Oh, I hoped they would be here. Do you see them?" A pod of dolphins were making straight for the boat.

Helen began to hurriedly strip off and mounted the rail. "Come on Eve, we can't miss this. Get your clothes off!" Suddenly she was streaking headlong in a perfect dive toward the water, a blurred flash of naked flesh. Eve hesitated only a moment then quickly followed suit, gasping as the shock of icy water engulfed her. She surfaced several feet from Helen who was treading water in the midst of the family group with a look of innocent wonder on her face. Eve looked on indulgently for a few moments before being startled by something butting her in the stomach. A young dolphin that she instinctively knew was male slid gently past her thigh, circled, leapt over her head and dived. This manoeuvre was repeated several times. The meaning could not be mistaken. It wanted her to follow.

On the next pass she waived to a giggling Helen and duck-dived after it. Seventy feet down it waited for her to catch up. Eve felt her body react strangely as she swam into the depths. Her abdomen flattened against her spine and her lungs seemed to roll up into the upper half of her chest. She settled cross-legged on the bottom next to the gently finning dolphin. It nudged up to her forehead and held station for a full minute before bolting gleefully for the surface. That minute had an endless quality to it. They had communicated. Something had passed between them. Eve could make no sense of it but she was left with a sense of warmth and support, and a feeling that something important had been imparted to her. She swam languidly back to the surface where she met a breathless and very concerned Helen, still gasping for breath, following several vain attempts to locate her beneath the surface.

"Where were you? You were gone for ages. I thought I had lost you."

"Just making a new friend." Helen looked at her incredulously.

"What are you a fish?" And then, with a distracted air, "No! Not a fish, a mermaid perhaps." She splashed Eve violently in the face.

"Don't ever do that again, I mean it Eve! Really! I've already lost one person I love. I couldn't bear to lose another." So saying, she swam back to the boat leaving a powerful rip current of emotion in her wake.

Eve climbed aboard bemused and suddenly very weary. The sand bar had disappeared under the rising tide and dusk was seeping from sea to sky in a blurred band where the horizon had been. She made her way to the galley to find Helen, still naked, opening cupboards and clattering pots and pans. Helen stopped, caught her breath and released it in a gasp then dumped the pans in the sink and grabbed two beers from the fridge.

Sitting down opposite Eve, she proffered one of the beers. "I'm sorry Eve. I never tried to control John and I won't treat you any differently. I just," she paused, stood up to grab a towel and said whilst her back was turned. "I was just worried that was all. You were down so long." Eve moved around the table and gently began to towel her dry. Helen returned the favour. Eve drew her to the bedroom and lay down behind her, moulding her form to Helen's and drawing the quilt over them. Helen sighed gently and slipped into sweet oblivion. She awoke screaming.

Eve's blood froze in her veins. It had taken twenty minutes to calm Helen down. She sat subdued and bleary eyed with a steaming mug of tea between her hands, shaken but calmed. Eve looked at her with intent concern, "This creature in your dream you are sure it whispered, Afsoon?" Helen's eyes glazed over as she focused on the memory.

"Not whispered exactly. It was more entwined with the wind of his passing. It was the wind, Affffsooooon," she intoned. "It seems daft now. I don't know why I was so upset but even now, although the memory is fading, the evil in that wind was physical, and corrupt beyond imagining. Things crawled and chittered in the dust and stinking decay of its path that ought never to see the light of day."

"But 'Afsoon' you are sure?"

"No, not sure. It wasn't spoken, more felt, in the shape of the wind, as it sucked the marrow from my bones, a kind of subdued and breathy mind howl. I suppose it could have been something else, or nothing at all, but that was what I seemed to perceive.

Don't be so concerned. It was just a nightmare. I'm fine now. You seem more unsettled then I am."

"Helen! This is important. Have you had any similar dreams before?"

"Well not exactly."

"What do you mean?"

Helen looked at her hands, fidgeted for a moment and spoke quietly. "Have you ever had a dream where it seems like it's the first one you have had but in the dream you remember it as a recurring dream?"

That settled it. "Helen, I need to make a phone call."

"What's wrong?"

"Bear with me. I will explain as we go along, but first I have to make that call." She dived across the bed and rifled through her jeans pocket for her phone, mentally kicking herself for not leaving it on charge. "Shit, it's almost out." She managed to access and memorise the number she wanted just as the phone switched itself off. Fortunately Helen's phone still had some charge left. "Mr Soames? I need your help."

On Soames' instructions they weighed anchor, docked at the nearest port of Welham Quay and waited in the Black Bull hotel bar with instructions not to let Helen fall asleep. Two hours later Helen's phone rang and they bustled out to a waiting Mercedes with ominously blacked out windows. A chauffeur ushered them inside and sped off at high speed for London. As the car crunched onto the gravel drive of a large, red brick, Georgian house, Helen was still remonstrating with Eve. "Look Eve, it was good of you to enlighten me a little more about what went on in Afghanistan but you are still not telling me everything, and who the hell is this Afsoon guy that has you so spooked, and whom you seem to think has miraculously entered my dreams? It's just coincidence. I probably heard you mention him at some point."

"No! You most certainly did not!"

The car door was swung open from the outside cutting off Helen's gathering rant in mid-speech whilst she protected her eyes against the glare of the drive's spotlights flooding the car interior. Eve was already out and assisting her from the car. Helen shook her off. Soames waited at the front door for them, took their coats and led them into a large period lounge, tastefully decorated in keeping with the exterior of the property. A decanter of brandy and three poured glasses sat on a silver tray on a large marble coffee table, flanked by three leather armchairs in front of a freshly stoked fire.

"Please sit and warm yourselves." He took one of the brandies and sat in the centre chair, discarding his slippers, and wriggling sock covered toes under the table towards the fire, thus compelling the two women to sit either side of him. Helen flopped into a chair and sloshed back her brandy in one gulp eliciting an amused smile from Soames. He waited expectantly while Eve sat on his left, un-speaking until she took a sip from her own glass. "Now Eve, I think the time has come for us to be more honest with each other. Don't you?" Eve sighed and took another sip of her brandy, whilst she considered just how much she could get away with not telling him. It was an awful lot less, she realised, than she would have liked.

Soames said nothing more for several minutes, just waited sipping his drink. Helen poured another and, likewise sat waiting, but with more agitation and a more urgent air of expectation. Eve wriggled uncomfortably, swallowed more of her drink, and tried to think how to pitch her story with sufficient honesty to be convincing, whilst avoiding the more damaging and far reaching aspects, particularly concerning her relationship with Helen. She slipped into a reverie, feeling very feminine and very unable to cope. She prayed inwardly. "Oh Isaac why did you have to leave me? I don't know what to do. I need you so much now."

She was shaken to full awareness by Helen jumping to her feet with an expletive. "Oh for Christ's sake!" She remained on her feet and started pacing across the carpet in exasperation.

Soames finally spoke in sympathetically patient tones. "Who are you Eve? I've checked my vast resources and I can find no trace of you anywhere prior to the day you walked into my shop. That is a new experience for me. More importantly what is your game? I imagine you are in some kind of danger but, what worries me is how dangerous are you? The people you say you were with in Afghanistan were a volatile mixture of super egos. Something truly momentous must have been happening to contain them in the same space. You say you are a marked woman by the Afghan authorities, for your actions at Beherit, yet, from the enquiries I have made, despite your very imaginative tale, you were not among the women who were on that expedition and, apart from Afsoon ..."

Helen dropped her glass. "Afsoon again! Just fucking enlighten us, will you Eve?" The question was rhetorical and she continued her pacing with no attempt to retrieve the glass.

Soames continued. "Apart from Afsoon and Gwen, there were no other women in the encampment."

Helen repeated the word. "Women?" in a pensive tone and sat back in her seat, scooping the glass from the carpet and pouring another brandy. The ignored, spreading stain, seemed to echo the expanding chaos and intrigue of the world they were being drawn into. Helen now adopted a more patient and inquisitive air and held her tongue.

Eve came to a decision and spoke to Helen. "Helen, my tale is a fantastic one. You already know some of it but believe me it gets wilder. Unfortunately, I can't tell you all of it." She thought Helen would explode at that but she kept her peace. I will give you the overall picture, but then I must ask you to leave, whilst I talk to Mr Soames alone." She paused, expectant of a delayed and volatile response.

"Go on," Helen encouraged in an unnerving but subdued tone.

Eve related the story of the released vessel and how Isaac and Afsoon had boarded it and made their getaway. She laid claim to being Gwen's sister, shadowing Gwen to gain practical experience in support of her theological studies. It was a clumsy attempt to explain Soames' statement that she was not one of the women in the expedition. She suspected he wasn't fooled but he kept a neutral face. It was, in any event, Helen that Eve was desperate to convince and she hoped that some of the other revelations she had disclosed would deflect any doubts Helen might conceive.

"How is it that you know, what went on at this vessel, I thought you were getting the plane ready."

"I was. I did, but this was my sister. After the explosions I had to go and see if she and John were okay. I hid when I saw the scene at the vessel. I hoped I could somehow intervene and make a difference but, Helen, forgive me please, I had no weapons and it all happened so fast and I was scared. I managed to get back to the plane in the confusion following the events at the vessel."

"And you just happened to know how to fly a plane?"

"Actually yes, I have a pilot's licence for light aircraft and Gwen was our pilot going out there, so naturally I showed a keen interest in how to fly it and she was a great teacher."

"We'll leave how you managed to get past the authorities in England without detainment, until later. Now tell me about John, you are positive he died?"

"Helen I am so sorry, I wish I could have spared you this, I tried not to tell you, but no one could have survived the brutal surgery Isaac performed on him. They left him to bleed out his life in the dust whilst they made their getaway to God knows where." She hated disclosing this but something so horrific was the only way she could think of to distract Helen sufficiently from the weaknesses in her story, and to make her compliant enough not to pursue it to the death of their relationship. She would never forgive Eve, or John, if she found out the truth, and Eve could not bear that. Helen's eyes gave nothing away and this worried Eve more than anything else. She had never known her so closed.

"You say John slept with this monstrous person as part of the plan to prevent her intervening in the extraction of this vessel."

Eve felt sick at what she was putting Helen through but nodded with downcast eyes.

"And you? You maintain that you slept with him too?"

"We were very close. He needed solace. It was not passion, just two people sharing a need and finding comfort in each other. It was not my right to steal those wonderful moments from you. It was you he loved but I was there. I needed him and he needed a substitute." Eve felt like she was crushing the last vestiges of any trust but she just couldn't risk telling Helen the whole truth. The way things were going at the moment, however, might be just as bad. She knew Helen didn't believe her. She'd felt her condemnation from the start and everything she said just made it worse. The sides of the grave she was digging were just about to topple in on her. Belatedly, she realised she was going to lose Helen, forever.

As her lies unfolded, she could feel Helen's disbelief turn to loathing and disgust. It was too much, she couldn't bear it. Helen's gaze pinned her to the chair like a struggling butterfly. She was babbling nonsense now, and starting to hyperventilate and shake. She fought hard to stem the tears filling her eyes, with a limited effect that just made the shaking even harder to control. Surprising-ly, it was Soames who put an arm around her shoulder. The sympathy was more than she could bear and she buried her head on his chest amid fierce shuddering sobs.

Looking over her head as he patted her back, Soames spoke to Helen. "Would, you mind leaving us for a while Mrs Woolfe. Eve is going to tell me everything now and, I promise you, I will leave nothing out when I repeat to you everything she has said. Is that alright Eve?" Eve nodded mutely through a fresh wave of tremors.

"Oh and Mrs Wolfe be sure to see Mrs Martin in the kitchen, out of the door and to your right, she will give you a stimulant and you must promise me you won't go to sleep."

"I don't know why I shouldn't sleep Mr Soames but I can assure you I will need no stimulant until I find out what the hell is going on here," so saying she swished out of the room and left them alone.

Death, Allies and Strategies

Several minutes later, feeling weak and totally inadequate, and like she'd betrayed the whole of humanity, a dry eyed and washed out Eve told Soames everything. He now wore a deeply sad and very weary expression.

"This is far worse than even I had suspected. So you claim you are John Woolfe?" He drummed his fingers tensely. "And Afsoon, for want of a better word, is the new Adam?" Eve nodded quies-cently. "If this is all true, and despite the extraordinary and ridicu-lous enormity of it all, it is the only thing that makes any sense out of all that has gone on, then you are the most dangerous person on this planet. Were it not for the fact that out there orbiting the sun is, apparently, a creature infinitely more dangerous, I can assure you, I would have killed you the moment I began to believe what you were. As it is, however, you could be our best hope of salva-tion. Much as it grieves me to say it, we must be allies until this menace is dealt with. If I am still alive when that happens we will reassess our relationship. God only knows why but, despite every-thing, I have become somewhat fond of you so, until then, I hope we can be friends, at least within the bounds of our alliance."

"You are still going to tell Helen everything, even though it might destroy her?"

"The truth, however hard to bear, is a power that heals, Miss Fox. It is lies that destroy."

"Even though you make your living by deceit."

"Ah! Sometimes it is necessary to combat evil with its own weapons but I think you will agree that Mrs Wolfe is not evil." He paused before adding. "Mr Wolfe." The irony in his words defeat-ed her.

"Can you help her? I am sure Afsoon killed Vincent, somehow. I had dreams about it. I think you should beware of any relation-ship with me Mr Soames. When I get close to people I have come to believe that Afsoon, somehow, manages to use our genetic bond to manipulate them."

"Yes, separating you and Mrs Woolfe would seem a sensible precaution but not sufficient on its own, I think. No, there may be another way. I take it you still wear that pendant Isaac left you. Do not look so surprised Miss Fox. You must know I would not leave you unobserved. I was intrigued by the way you manipulated its symbol to control that psychopath in Texas. That was a destructive use of its force. My research, sparse though it is in this field, suggests that it can also be used to protect. Unfortunately, I don't know how to do that but I believe you may. I think deep emotion and empathy combined with ritual are factors which will help you to access the forces you require. So, right now would seem a good time to make the attempt to bring that about given your current emotional state."

"And the ritual?"

"After you contacted me, I took the liberty of having your flat searched for the scroll that Isaac left you, with that pendant." He raised his hand to forestall her question. "Please don't ask how I knew about it, my methods are my insurance so I do not share them. I have been unable to decipher it but I am guessing you might be able to, in the same way you understood Keppler speak-ing in tongues, and if Isaac left it in the same box as the pendant, my guess is they are connected and intended to be used in conjunction with one another. You really have no choice. This may seem like a long shot but it is the only shot."

Under extreme duress Eve repeated her tale to a silent and impassive Helen. It took three times the time it took to tell Soames, because she couldn't stop weeping and broke down completely when she revealed her former identity. Had Helen comforted her at that point, she might have lost her sanity. Helen's stony silence, however, somehow anchored her in the here and now and she was able, eventually, to function, if only, in a state of removed reality. Soames took the two silent figures to a small room decked out like a chapel. He handed them each a white robe. Helen just folded her arms, and looked at Soames and Eve with disgust. Eve shrugged dejectedly and donned hers. The lights were dimmed and a single candle lit. Eve carefully unrolled the delicate scroll and just stood looking at the jumble of symbols, trying to make sense out of it. Helen was getting restless. Soames began a low repetitive chant.

Helen finally had enough. "What a load of bollocks! I really thought you were something Eve, and, if you really are John," she laughed harshly, "I thought 'you' were something even more. Turns out you are just some kind of insane stalker." She turned and strode out. Eve had a flash vision of her choking out a death rattle in the grip of a potently naked and laughing Afsoon. Magically, Helen found her path blocked by Eve, who seemed to materialise in front of her. Whichever way she stepped to avoid her, Eve was already there.

"Please Helen I know I can make this work. Please don't leave. He will harm you. I know he will. He killed Vincent. Please?"

"Get out of my way you lunatic!"

Eve held her in place with one hand. Helen could not break, or even loosen, her grip. She slumped for a moment. Then let loose a tirade. "What do you care? You bastard! You leave me to fuck off to Afghanistan, sleep with a gaggle of whores and sluts, change your fucking sex, and come back to stalk me, so you can have depraved sex with your own grieving, fucking, widow. You're a fucking degenerate reptile. Now get your polluted, grimy, lowlife, hands off me, you shit, and let me go off to die, so I can be as far away from you as eternity will allow." She managed to deliver a stinging slap to Eve's face.

Eve crumpled to her knees in despair. She thought she had cried all the tears in the world but a fresh source was found. Helen finally relented, and sat wearily down next to her, finding the scroll, she handed it to Eve. As Eve's tears wet the page, golden words ran through the moisture and overlaid the scripture. She found herself reciting a litany.

The darkness thickened around them but it was protective rather than ominous. Of her own volition, Helen turned and offered the nape of her neck. Eve drew the pendant from her own neck but instead of placing it around Helen's, she used one of the points to carve an intricate tattoo onto the lumpy vertebrae at the base of her neck, mimicking a, four parts, formed pentagram, containing an out spill of arcane symbols. A sense of weightlessness engulfed them. Holding hands, they calmly rose together. Helen leaned over and kissed Eve on the forehead. "We must separate now, but we will speak again."

Soames escorted her to the door. "I have a car waiting. We will find a safe place for you."

Eve called after her. "Helen, where will you go?"

She turned. "I can't tell you that but I am a writer. Perhaps I will find an alp somewhere and write a book. Good luck Eve, John, whoever, or whatever, you are."

Her shape filled the door for a moment, and then she was gone. A backwash of loss boiled away from her absence. The door slammed shut snuffing the candle and she was left in the dark. She sat back down on the floor to reflect. She had thought, before Vincent's death, that she had got all her hormones under control. It seemed that trauma was a catalyst for kicking them off again. She would have to accept that inhabiting this woman's form she could no longer be as coldly analytical as she had been when she was John. She came to slow awareness that her throat was very dry and tried to clear it, but her "ahem" turned into a violent coughing fit. Alert now, she stumbled to the door and tried the handle. It was locked solid. There was a hissing from a vent in the base of the door. Light-headed, she removed the robe and covered the vent but was unable to seal it effectively. She slipped into unconsciousness with a churning and despairing thought. "Soames you bastard! You gassed me."

She awoke in a bed to which she was strapped. An elderly nurse leaned over her. "Not to worry, dear. The worst is over. You'll be a bit sore for a few days but then you should be fine."

"I don't understand. What am I doing here and why am I strapped down?"

"That was Mr Soames' idea. I told him I didn't think it was necessary but he said you sometimes fitted. I'm sure when he comes he will give us permission to take them off, now that you're awake."

"You still haven't told me why I'm here."

"Oh dear, you are a bit confused aren't you? That does sometimes happen after a general anaesthetic. I'm sure you'll remember everything soon. I expect you're eager to see Mr Soames. He should be along shortly and then we can see what can be done about taking off those restraints, but I'm sure Mr Soames had his reasons, he is such a nice man."

Eve felt like she had been kicked in the stomach and didn't really feel like struggling against, what looked to be, very substantial restraints. She decided to wait for Soames. Ten minutes later she heard him in the hall enquiring from the nurse after her condition. She contained her anger and waited a couple of minutes that seemed like an hour before he finally walked in. He looked at her critically for a moment then walked to the window. She half expected him to walk through the wall and come back with drinks and bacon sandwiches, as another dominant male had done, in a previous existence. He rocked on his heels for a moment before speaking.

"It's a beautiful view from here Eve. I hope you will allow me to get those restraints removed, so that you can take some time to enjoy it."

"What have you done to me Soames, and why are you keeping me a prisoner?"

He turned and brought a chair over to the foot of the bed. "I'm so sorry. I promise I will get the restraints removed soon. I just need to be sure that I can trust you and that you will not do anything drastic, or try to leave, before we have formulated our alliance and agreed a strategy."

"You have a strange way of winning the confidence and trust of those you would be in league with. You can begin to correct that by telling me what you have done to me, after gassing me in your house that is! Remind me never to call on you again. I do not find your hospitality to my taste."

"I really am very sorry but I had no choice in the matter."

"Cut the crap Soames and tell me what you have done." He drummed his fingers on the side of the chair then stood up and pinched his lips with thumb and forefinger as though to prevent himself from making the disclosure.

"I had your ovaries removed Miss Fox."

Eve felt like someone had thrown a hand grenade down her throat. She started sputtering. "What? Pardon, say that again. What the hell are you talking about?" She struggled against her straps trying, and failing, to sit up.

"I had to Eve. Please understand. You could never be allowed to have children. They would be an abomination. I am human Eve and you are a threat to my species."

"Why didn't you just kill me?"

"I thought of that, and believe me I would have but, as I said before, there is an even greater threat out there and I may well need your help in finding a way to destroy it."

"Do you really think I would help you now?"

"Yes, I think you will. First because I don't believe you have an evil heart and that you, like me, will want to stop this creature from bringing Armageddon to the human race. You were human once. Perhaps some part of that still resides within you. You certainly seem to still love your wife."

"Assuming you are right, what on earth makes you think I would throw in my lot with you? You see, it seems to me that you have demonstrated all that is wrong with humanity. Perhaps it should be destroyed, if you are an example of it, and, if I do decide I want to take a hand in saving it, I would like to remove the likes of you from it, so it would hardly be a harmonious coalition would it? Whatever you think you know, I know, that I am still human. More human than you can ever be. So, come on then, that was the 'first' reason you thought I might help you, what is the next?"

"You hurt me Eve and, to some extent, shame me but I would do it again. I have the right to protect my race and I will use any means to do it, but, to answer your question, you will help me because you will not like the alternatives."

"Which are?" Seeing his reluctance she urged him on. "Go on."

"One possibility is to have you committed. It would not be difficult to convince the authorities that you are dangerously delusional with a tendency to violence. I could even convince them to keep you under sedation. I do not want to do that. I like you Eve and, believe it or not, I trust your intentions. It is possible too that you might find a way to escape, however vigilant we were. I would not want you for an enemy Eve, especially on the loose and pissed off with me. I would also like to think you were grateful for my part in saving Helen, but the reason I know you will help me is because I have Helen under my protection. She is safe I assure you, at least for as long as our alliance holds, and she is not captive, just very closely observed. She has agreed to remove herself to a remote location whilst we resolve the problem of Afsoon." He gave her a sidelong look. "I can guess at what you are thinking. It would be a mistake to try to find her and it might be harmful to her if you did." He waited, giving her time to consider all that he had said. "So, do I take it we have a deal? Or are you going to be stubborn about this."

Eve stared at the ceiling for a while. He was right. All her speed, strength, and newfound abilities were nothing in this situation. If she was bested this easily by an elderly man, what hope did she have of ever standing against Afsoon, alone? She probably needed Soames more than he needed her, but he had defiled her. She didn't know why her ability to bear children should be so important. She never had any intention of going down that route; it horrified her, especially the thought of Afsoon having his way. It was, in fact, the most effective blow that could have been struck against him. She had to allow that Soames' logic was impeccable but she'd had no say in what had happened to her and no idea of the health implications. She would see Soames pay for what he had done but that could wait. She would think long and hard on how she was going to collect on that. Eve looked down at her straps.

"You can remove these now."

Soames had been holding his breath. He now let it out in a huge sigh of relief. "Thank you Eve, I promise you Helen will want for nothing. Together I think we may just have a chance."

"Don't push it Soames. Just get me out of these. I need a piss."
Eve felt her cool John persona rise to the surface for the first time
in many months.

Half an hour later she returned to the hospital room, fully
dressed, and spoke with Soames. John was back in command now
and not about to be pushed around. Soames wanted to know all
that had transpired on board the habitat. In return John, or more
precisely, he conceded, a feminised version of himself known as
Eve, wanted to know more about Soames' organisation and mo-
tives. It seemed, pretty much as Soames had said, that he and Isaac
were contemporaries. Soames' research was on similar lines to that
of Isaac, but he was more scientific in his approach, seeking solid
and corroborated evidence rather than being creative, and drawing
conclusions from fragmented information.

Both were researching the origins of creation, but Soames focused on the known: physical structure, form, genetics and the
scriptures, backtracking from these into quantum areas of pre-
creation, certainly, but always referring forward again into the
physical, and how quantum origins are only the building blocks of
existence, so that, whilst conceding physicality sprang from the
productive soup of the infinite, he conjectured that it is, in fact, the
physicality itself that defines the origins of creation and, as such,
supports beliefs based on solid evidence that can be tested and
corroborated.

Isaac was more existential in his method, looking to the same
sources but creating and adapting hypotheses from trends, and
allowing for a quantum element to remain a contributing factor
within the atomic and physical world or, as Soames would have it,
a fairy tale hypothesis. Soames had thought Isaac a genius, but
essentially a cowboy who arrogantly manipulated scant facts to
create dangerously misguided theories of pre- and post-creation.
They had worked together on many projects but had, ultimately,
fallen out and parted company over these profound differences.
Both had supporting factions within the theological community
that polarised as they each expounded their opposing beliefs.
Much of Soames' support and financial backing came directly
from the Vatican. Isaac financed himself but had powerful and
very rich allies within the old aristocracy, and certain scientifically
based business corporations working in the quantum field that

endorsed his work. Given Eve's revelations concerning recent happenings, however, Soames now expressed a degree of contrition and remorse at having opposed Isaac's theories remarking that, "on reflection it seems that one must be creative to understand the workings of creation."

After much verbal duelling, a generalised strategy was eventually hammered out whereby Eve would continue as before with both her work and her investigations into the criminal psyche (but that it would be a good idea if these focused specifically on cults and the occult, these being relevant areas where her special talents could glean much useful information) and also, with her own on-going research, as suggested by Isaac, into the scriptures and theological areas of study, making equally good use of her talents.

Soames interrogated her closely regarding Isaac's remarks about Afsoon's twenty-five year voyage around the sun, specifically wanting times and dates, and any subsidiary information, concerning Isaac's disclosures to her, regarding this. His "plan A" was to try and locate the vessel in which Afsoon was entombed and find a way to destroy it prior to it ever reaching the earth. They would maintain regular contact with each other through correspondence or communications media but little or no face on communication, as a precaution against Afsoon's apparent ability to locate and destroy anyone in regular close contact to Eve. They discussed the fact that Soames might well die before Afsoon's intended return and, quite possibly, that Eve too could meet with a similar fate. So further contingency planning would need to be considered. Eve parted with an admonition to Soames that she required updates on Helen and that should any harm befall her Soames would find himself accountable for it.

Vincent's funeral was attended by a small group of family and friends. His wife had died several years before and Eve found herself irked that he had never mentioned her. It was a short ceremony and the eulogy, read by a cousin, was direct and to the point, loving father (another surprise there) devoted to family and work, that sort of thing. Eve now stood talking to Matt, taking firm refuge in John's persona for the present. She had remained dispassionate throughout the service, but Matt, damn the man and his uncanny perception, was now gently laying his hand on her forearm.

"You really were very fond of him weren't you? How are you bearing up?"

Caught off guard, Eve tried to answer with cold detachment. "Oh you know how it is when you work closely with someone." Despite her resolve, her voice suddenly broke and she let out a single sob. She quickly regained control but her momentary lapse had been noted. Matt hugged her for a moment and it was all she could do not to fall into his fatherly embrace. As she disengaged from him she felt a light tug at her sleeve.

Turning she was confronted by a willowy girl of about sixteen years old. Her enquiring grey eyes were on a level with Eve's own. "You must be Eve. My Dad liked you a lot. He never said how beautiful you were though. Is it your fault he died?" The blood drained from Eve's face and she took a step back. Matt supported her elbow.

A young man, perhaps a little older, tried to pull the girl away. "Leave it Jackie. It was no one's fault." He tugged her again but she held her ground. "I'm sorry Miss she has some crazy ideas sometimes." Turning back to the girl, who must have been his sister, he put an arm around her shoulder and forced her away but she continued to speak over her shoulder.

"Dad had a premonition about you. He said you were a dangerous person to know but that it was worth any danger, because you had a destiny. I don't hate you. It was what he wanted." Eve was trembling and found herself unable to respond.

The young lad cast an apologetic glance in her direction. "Just leave it Jackie."

Matt led Eve away and drove her home. He spoke to her from the wheel of the car. "Are you okay now?"

Eve had regained her composure and nodded.

"Don't pay any heed to her. Grief releases some fanciful emotions, especially in pubescent young girls. I'm sure she meant nothing by it."

Eve was not so sure but she kept her thoughts to herself. "I didn't even know he had any children."

"I don't think anyone did. He was a very private guy. Probably because of the work he did. It wouldn't do for any of the offenders he dealt with to find out he had family. Any casual comment could be enough to reveal that."

She nodded again but remained thoughtful.

"Anyway, I know I probably shouldn't bring this up now but you need to think about the future. Have you had any thoughts about your work, now that Vincent is gone? You know, you have been not unfavourably noticed within the field you worked, in Vincent's employ. You are starting to get a reputation for getting results. Thing is, there is an opening in my department at the moment for a forensic psychologist come police officer. I want to put you forward for it. It's a newly created post. Pay's crap, basic police pay, that's why it hasn't been taken up yet. Anyone with the CV and experience they want would be looking at consultant work and corresponding wages, and they certainly would not want to do anything menial, or physical, as you would have to, doubling up as a police officer. Basically you would be a negotiator-forensic psyche-police officer. I thought the role would suit you very well."

"Too well, I don't suppose you had anything to do with creating it?" He took his hands off the wheel and shrugged his shoulders, with a "hands up" gesture.

"I don't make those kinds of decisions."

She laughed despite herself. "Well … of course I'll take it, as if you thought I would be likely to refuse, and thanks. I owe you. Now put your hands back on the wheel before you kill us both."

Six months had passed and Eve sat in the Police HQ canteen dwelling on her recent history. Matt's recommendation and a CV, already prepared by Vincent, before his demise, had secured her the job. They didn't seem too sure of what to do with her but she had dealt with a couple of small cases, notably a kidnapping of one of the Imam's children at a West London Mosque, and the deputy chief was showing some interest, although, his angle seemed to be more about PR. He'd booked a press interview for her, Matt, and himself tomorrow afternoon. She had tried to call on Helen once, but there was a "for sale" notice on the house and no sign of any current occupation. It was probably for the best. She had heard nothing from Soames, apart from a quick communication saying Helen was fine and immersed in her writing but was still refusing to talk about the events at his home, or about Eve. Eve had recovered from the operation to remove her ovaries, seemingly without any untoward effects but it still rankled. She felt defiled. She was being careful not to socialise outside of work with Matt, so that no harm would befall him, but it was unavoidable in work hours.

She became aware of Matt standing beside her. "Come on! Up you get. Now you're the deputy's blue-eyed girl he wants to cross the Ts and dot the Is. He's looking to present you as a forensic psyche with full police training, 'a true part of the force, not someone just drafted in' so today it's going to be a crash course in self-defence. You're joining a bunch of recruits at their final exam. Watch out for the instructor. She's here on exchange from the FBI and she takes her role seriously. Have you done any self-defence?"

Eve nodded. "A little."

"Good, then let me warn you, she picked up Olympic gold in judo and silver in Karate so she may be a bit rough."

"Oh?"

During the warm-up, the instructor "Janie" found cause to chase up Eve several times and now she wanted to demonstrate disarming a knifeman (or woman) using Eve as the subject. Matt looked on from the side, arms folded and chuckling. Eve jabbed the wooden knife at Janie's face and allowed herself to be disarmed. Janie locked out her elbow and threw her hard to the floor grunting in surprise at Eve's weight. Eve thought she saw her wince, and move her hand towards her kidney area. She must have slightly strained herself, because of the unexpected density of Eve's muscular body. Janie didn't like it, and spent the remainder of the session throwing Eve hard in every direction, and using her as the butt of an endless stream of sarcasm about pretty little girls more concerned with their makeup than in doing serious police work, all to the great amusement of the class. Eve thought she was overstating things as she never wore make up but contented herself with making every one of Janie's moves and throws just a little bit more difficult than they should have been. Janie was now sweating profusely, while Eve remained calm and composed.

Janie was growing more and more irritable and made a particularly bad joke about women with no real policing skills sleeping their way into the job, while casting an eye at Matt. They broke for lunch. As Eve was putting her jacket on Janie leaned close to her ear and said. "Make sure you are well rested. Me and you are going to have a proper workout this afternoon. You may get away with sitting on your fanny and fluttering your eyelashes every other day but today you're going to know what real police work is all about. Buy yourself some Arnica cream while you're out. You are going to need it."

Matt waved her over to go for lunch. She jogged across to him. "Jesus. She's really got it in for you. What did she just say to you?"

"Oh nothing. Listen, rain check our lunch will you. I need to go to the shops for a couple of bits. See you in the afternoon session."

She arrived back after lunch in the brightest pink shell suit she could find, and sparkling headband and trainers. She'd also got the lady in Boots The Chemist to help her fit the biggest false eyelashes she had on the shelf. There were a few catcalls and whistles and a seething look from Janie who said with leaden causticity, "I see you decided to dress in a style that fits your air-head personality." This caused a few intakes of breath and Matt was looking concerned. "Come on then Barbie do your worst." She extended the handle of a baseball bat towards Eve and armed herself with a sidearm baton. "I won't hurt you," and, as Eve stepped onto the mat, she added, with heavy emphasis, "much." Eve ignored the bat and instead did a Muhammad Ali shuffle and gave Janie a light slap on the cheek. Taken completely off guard, Janie's reaction was, nevertheless, lightning fast going for an arm breaking lock with the baton and moving on into a vicious throw manoeuvre. She couldn't understand it, before she could slide her forearm under Eve's wrist, Eve was no longer there and someone was tapping lightly on her shoulder from behind.

She whirled in a rage, ready to kill, and received another light slap on her other cheek. She kicked out hard at Eve's supporting knee. Eve just absorbed the blow. She followed up with a baton neck choke onto empty air. Spinning full circle she saw Eve sitting at the corner of the mat with a makeup mirror and mascara stick, messing with her false lashes. Everyone was laughing. Janie started to hyperventilate in frustration and the effort it took to hold herself in check. Eve waved her on. Unable to contain herself any longer, she threw the baton at Eve and charged her. Eve plucked the baton smoothly from the air whilst rising and side stepping with blurring speed. A fist to the solar plexus should have doubled Janie over, but Eve moving quickly behind her, placed one hand in the small of her back and grasped her forehead with the other, which added greatly to the winding effect. Eve ushered her

smoothly off the mat, supporting her with an arm round her waist
and a hand under her elbow. She walked her to the drink fountain,
where she sat her down and poured her a drink. "Small sips are
best."

Janie looked up at Eve with something resembling awe.

Matt dismissed the class and left with them, glancing over his
shoulder as he went.

"Where the hell did you learn to fight? I've never seen anything
like it." She had to stop for another gasping breath. "And what the
fuck do you weigh? It was like trying to throw a truck."

"Yes appearances can be deceiving, don't you think? My Uncle
John taught me a few moves and I've picked up a few since but
really it's all about the element of surprise, isn't it?" Janie was
calmer now. "Well you certainly achieved that but you must have
been taught by a master, I'd like to meet your uncle."

"Dead unfortunately, blown to pieces in Afghanistan."

"Oh! I see. Look, I was only trying to prepare you for the street?"

"Please don't pretend to be something you're not Janie. I've
never liked bullies and I don't like liars much either. So let's just
keep out of each other's way in future shall we?"

"Yeah, I guess I can live with that." Eve placed a pot of Arnica
cream beside her and couldn't resist patting her on the head as she
walked out. "Good girl."

She ditched her purchases in the bin, took a shower and joined
Matt in the hall. "Where's everyone else?"

"I sent them all home. I didn't want them mobbing you at the
door. You've gained yourself quite a fan club there. That was some
show you put on. Care to elaborate?"

"Just a lot of bullying at school, Uncle John taught me some and
paid for classes. It was just something I really took to."

"I'll say." He left it there.

A day later, Eve was at her desk, preparing for the coming press
interview, when the call came. A known radicalised fanatic had
taken two hundred and fifty hostages at a West End store, rigged
the store and the hostages with enough explosives to destroy the
entire block, and was demanding immediate liaison with the police.

Mutilation

She stood there calm and poised, despite the blood and mucus that ebbed from the cavity where her nose should be. A snake of congealed hair coiled around the clawed grip of her left hand, from which dangled the lump of shattered bone, that was once Stella's beautiful head.

Inspector Matt Crow hesitated: hand gesturing to his men to hold fire and stay back, unsure if it was safe to approach. "Eve it's okay, you're safe now. You know me. We're here to help." He approached gradually and with extreme caution, inching toward her. "Open your hand. You don't need that anymore. It's over. We have to get you to hospital."

He searched her eyes, waiting for any sign of cognisance, or recognition. The malignant stare she turned in his direction almost paralysed him, nearly caused him to drop his hand which would have signalled the waiting marksmen to open fire. Willpower prevailed and, slowly, very slowly, sanity returned to her eyes. She scanned the devastation around her. There were five bodies in all, two headless, one still twitching with a scimitar through the sternum pinning it to the door frame. Another with the lower arm burnt off at the elbow. All of them beaten, battered, slashed and dismembered. All, bar one, were male. She raised Stella's ruined head by the ponytail, still clasped in her hand, and looked at it curiously for several seconds, before dropping it with a slopping thud to the floor. Eve scanned again, urgently this time, desperately searching. She attempted to speak, but gagged, as blood welled and splattered from the cavity in her face. She raised her hands to her mouth and nose. Her irises exploded black as pain shattered through the lattice of exposed nerve and splintered bone, feebly probed by disbelieving fingers. Her eyes rotated up and she fell forward into oblivion. Crow reacted fast and instinctively, and caught her inches from the floor. "Simmonds! Fenton! Get that medical team up here. NOW! Find her fucking nose, and have forensics secure this place so tight a fart can't get out. Make damn sure you get every bit of CCTV seized, and understand this! No one outside this team views it without my authority! Is that clear?"

"Yes sir! "They responded in unison.

Eve floated happily in the ether but low voices and discomfort tugged irritatingly at her serenity.

"Did you find her nose?"

"No, we've scoured every millimetre, nothing. He either took it with him, or, it got destroyed when that incendiary device went off. CCTV may give us some idea of what happened."

"It would have deteriorated too much by now anyway."

"What can be done about her face Dr? Money is not a problem. The force will pay."

Dr Stewart's words ran over one another like scurrying rats. "Without the nose? Not a lot. It was dug out of her face in a very brutal way. The best thing at this time is to see how it heals, help her to cope with the trauma, and then, look at whether reconstructive surgery is possible."

"Whether? Are you telling me it might not be, that she might have to live like that?"

"As I said, it was very brutal. Even if you had found her nose in time, I'm not sure what could have been done. The damage is too extensive."

Just now, Matt Crow wanted to bury his fist in Dr Stewart's carefully neutral face, but he had noted Eve's jerky movements and was at her side.

"It's okay, Eve. You're in hospital. Don't try to talk. We'll have you up and about again in no time." He gave Dr Stewart a savage look. "Dr Stewart is going to look after you." She coughed, which caused her to shudder with pain. After a few moments, blood welled into her facial dressing and began to drool onto her chest. Matt stopped her from raising her hands to her face but she started flailing. "Doctor, do something. I can't hold her, before she damages herself anymore!" He was already there helping to pin her arms, calling for morphine and checking her over. He had to use a second dose, and a third, before they could subdue and restrain her.

Dr Stewart looked again at the X-rays. Three times he'd had them re-done. The wound was horrific. Her nose had been dug out in one swift movement, with a ragged blade. This, according to inspector Crow, was done to make her unacceptable to other men. Anyone could see she had been a true beauty, but this was not what was causing him such dismay. He had an earlier set of X-rays, which he set alongside the others. They all showed the extent of the damage. A piece of the skull, above and between the eyes, three teeth, and part of the roof of the mouth had been broken away at the same time leaving a gaping, shattered hole of broken bone and torn sinew. The earlier sets of plates must have been badly taken, and yet ... "It is possible I suppose," he muttered under his breath. It actually looked like re-growth, for all the good it would do her. It might even complicate matters. He heaved a sigh, threw the plates to one side and went to get some rest.

Matt Crow forced himself to look through the footage again. That bastard had forced her to make a fucking snuff movie, as bad as any he'd seen, or could have imagined, during his career which included vice work. Crow knew Sadique had copies, had in fact made a separate film of it, before achieving a dramatic escape by helicopter from the roof of the Ebony building. Matt had told her not to deal with him face to face, but two hundred and fifty hostages, many of them children, had been a powerful argument, when refusal meant all their deaths. Eve was nobody's fool. She had checked Sadique's history and established that he always kept his word, and would flay, had flayed, any of his freedom fighters who did not do likewise.

She had met Sadique's pedantic insistence that she conduct negotiations in the "flesh" (Matt remembered Sadique's leer, when he had used that word) with equally stubborn insistence, first, that he exchange half of his hostages for her presence, that she would always be in full view via CCTV, would wear a microphone, and, be in constant communication with her team at all times. Also, that she would be able to leave unharmed whenever she chose. They had settled on a hundred hostages. Deputy Chief Constable Crighton had congratulated her on achieving those concessions, and granted her autonomy in handling further negotiations. He also made sure the press were well informed. Sadique's deviousness was apparent when he released only men. It all started to go badly wrong the moment she met him "in the flesh".

Sadique sat in a throne-like chair (taken from the furniture department of the store they occupied) at the far end of a large and empty function room. Four of his men slouched either side of this would be monarch, Kalashnikovs hanging lazily at their sides. Eve knew two men were covering the main staircase, and one had brought her here, now standing behind, and to the left of her, using his gun as a prod to push her forward, two more on the roof. If intelligence was correct, that meant two others, corralling the hostages in the toy department. Sadique was refusing to look at her, looking instead at his men.

"You see how this woman offends the prophet! Invited into our presence, she yet demands proof of our good intent, and do we not meet her demands by granting freedom to a large part of our human wealth? And how does she repay our generosity? She attempts to imitate God's most eminent creation. Take her away. Remove these man's clothes and return her dressed as a true representation of herself. We will teach her some humility as befits a woman." His men smiled and turned disdainful and openly lustful stares in her direction. Eve stepped boldly forward. The gunmen tensed and glanced at their leader. His handsome features remained neutral. They relaxed but stayed alert.

"I am told you are a man of your word Sadique-Al-Fayed. I remind you of our agreement. No harm will befall me during our negotiations and I may leave when I choose." He turned toward her. She was momentarily startled, not by the hostile intensity of his gaze, nor by the demonic hunger behind it, but by the deep blue colour of his eyes, so at odds with his swarthy skin. The effect was mesmerising.

"I do not need to be reminded to be an honourable man by a western whore, Miss Fox." Eve cursed mentally. "Shit!" How had he unearthed her surname?" A disturbing answer was tapping Morse code on her conscious mind. She refused to decipher it.

He continued. "You will remember that I said, I would cause you no harm, nor hold you against your will, during negotiations. I cannot possibly promise that no harm will befall you by circumstances unforeseen, or, that you may not decide to stay of your own volition. That would be foolhardy in the extreme. I do not presume myself a prophet and cannot predict how events will turn out. I can only ensure that I keep my word. So, if you wish to avoid any risk at all, perhaps you should leave now. No one will stop you." His presence in the room (was it only his?) had been dominant from the moment she entered. Now under his direct scrutiny she could feel the malignancy in this man. Evil oozed from him, pulling at her strength and suffocating her will. The atmosphere seemed to coalesce and darken around her. Fear slicked her skin and seeped into her. Matt was right; there could be no profit in this charade. She should leave, now! She turned on her heel to go, half expecting his will to reach out and throttle her, or, more realistically, a bullet through the knee. She reached the door, however, without incident and was about to slam it behind her when his quiet voice cut through the thick silence of her wake with a cold edge that would chill Antarctica.

"Before you go, I feel you should know the consequences of your leaving so soon."

Eve did not want to turn. She tried not to, but felt compelled. Slowly her head turned back, jerkily, inch by, impending, inch, until she saw the horror that sealed her fate ... He sat with a child, no more than three years old, on his lap, a hand clasped firmly over her mouth. Her watery eyes seemed to fill her pudgy face with black fear. His right hand held a curved blade under her skirt, which he thrust, savagely inward, deftly, sawing up, through her frantically struggling, little body, in a sinuous wriggling motion. Eve heard the ribs popping, as the blade peeled her open and she released the first scream she'd ever uttered. The child's own screams were silenced by the force of his hand over her mouth but fear and agony in the girl's eyes resounded with deafening and sinister quietude.

Eve was striding toward the throne chair, but the sight of Sadique sweeping the blade away from the girl's throat, with a flourish and turning to face her with the child's entrails writhing over his knees, brought her to a tottering halt. A mother and child were now being manhandled through a side door. Sadique turned his eerie gaze full into Eve's accusing eyes. "Isn't power a wondrous thing Miss Fox, especially the power of life and death. You can know that power. I want you to feel it. I will plant its 'seed' (this word trawled memories Eve would rather forget) within you. You can give life to all those here, awaiting their execution. Alternatively, if Allah is merciful, they may come to know the ascendant ecstasy of holy sacrifice."

His eyes shone, as he looked up, and east, into the distance beyond the confines of this room. He looked like he'd been touched by God. Sweat, undulated, down her back like a living thing. "Like this beautiful young girl, just now, elevated and transcended before you." So saying, he lifted the little body by the throat and scooped out the remaining entrails and organs into a waiting steel bowl, offered by one of his men, distractedly handing the empty corpse, that had now stopped twitching, to another of his attendant men. "You have the power to leave Miss Fox but, by so doing, you will be condemning everyone to death, or, you can give them life. I will give you that power in return for your humility and obedience. Prove to me that you can behave like a woman."

He looked at her now, his gaze searing into her hers. Evil writhed in that gaze, compelling her to look away before it suppurated into her soul. She looked down at the floor. He must have given a signal because the captive mother screamed. Eve's head snapped up to look as the child was being prised from the mother's arms and another attendant gunman approached, with another steel bowl. The mother was knocked to the floor where a boot was placed on her throat and a gun aimed at her head. She, nevertheless, managed to twist to look imploringly at Eve, and to gasp out a few fatal words from her crushed larynx.

"Please don't let that monster have my baby. Do whatever you have to plea ..." Her last words were cut off by additional weight on her throat but the depth of misery and despair in her petrified stare were soul consuming. Eve was suffocating under the weight of responsibility. As fate tightened its grip, she began to shake and to lose control of her bladder. She could feel the tide of hot urine seeping into her under garments. She tried to tighten rubbery knees and buttocks, but only succeeded in forcing the fluid forward, finally, losing all vestige of control, as, humiliatingly, it gushed and spread into her clothes, and began to drip and run into a sploshing pool on the floor.

Sadique looked down at her in disgust but she could see the excitement running through his features, and the expanding bulges in his trousers, and those of his men. "I take it, from your pathetically weak and cowardly reaction you have decided to stay, but I warn you, any deviation from my precise commands, and people will die. Is that clear Miss Fox?" Eve was unable to speak so she nodded. "Failure to answer will lead to someone's torture and death, Miss Fox," he said mildly.

With an extreme effort of will, Eve grated words from her constricting throat. "Yes, yes, it is clear," she gasped.

"I will overlook your insolence this once Miss Fox. As agreed you will, like our hostages, wear an explosive collar as surety against your colleagues deciding to attack, should they take exception to the way our negotiations are going. If you decide to end negotiations it will be removed prior to your release." She nodded agreement and a gunman came forward to fit the collar. Turning to his men, he said. "Bring the mother here." The woman was dragged to the chair and forced to the floor. Sadique now had her child on his lap and was absently stroking her hair. Speaking to the mother he asked in a kindly tone. "What is your name?" He casually gripped the child's neck.

"Stella," she blurted out from the floor, and then, more quietly, "Stella."

"You are an attractive woman, Stella. I may have a use for you later. In the meantime, let's see if we can keep your child alive shall we?" He gave her a conspiratorial wink. "Miss Fox, as you can see, has fouled herself. I want you to go with her, clean her up and choose some more appropriate clothes." He cast an appraising glance at Eve, "and perhaps some makeup. Obey my instructions precisely, there's a good girl, and all will be well." He stroked the, now shaking, child's hair again, then, leaned forward and spoke to Stella in a low voice, before instructing her to leave. "Off you go now. Take time to get to know one another, be as long as you like. Your little girl will be safe with me." He turned to the little girl as they left the room to say, "Now what's your name? Shall we play a little game while your mother is away?"

One of the men followed but stayed at a short distance. Stella supported Eve for several steps, although Eve felt this might be partly to place Stella in the best position to stop her, if she tried to leave. Eve summoned her strength and disengaged herself with some force. Her considerable personal resources were now starting to rally. With a superhuman effort of will she quelled the terrified and raging male id within her and shackled it in a remote corner of her mind. Whispering beneath quivering breaths, she gave silent prayer that insanity would not overtake it before she could retrieve the damaged psyche.

Stella was sobbing uncontrollably now; she bowed her back shaking violently, tears streamed and mixed with the mucus dripping from her nose. She spoke haltingly between shuddering sobs. "I know I have no right ... to expect ... anything ... from you ... but ... you know what he will do to my little baby. Please do what he wants. Please don't leave us to face that ... that, thing!" Eve could barely stop herself from running away screaming. Instead she walked to the nearest CCTV camera and spoke to the microphone in her riot suit. Eve had removed the earpiece on entering the building. She wasn't going to replace it now. She knew Matt would be raging at her to get out, and she needed to hang on to every bit of resolve she had.

"Matt, you know what's happening. You were right I should not have come. You can't deal with the devil. I expect you can guess the kind of thing he's got in store for me but I can't let him have them. At this moment it would be so easy to just leave them to die. I thought I was superman. I guess I'm just another stupid tart. I hope I can save them all. Forgive my stupidity. Try to pick up the pieces when he's done." She went back to Stella, put an arm around her shoulders and called to their guard. "Hey arsehole! Where do I get a change of clothes?" He pointed the way with his gun and continued to direct them with grunts and nods until they reached the clothing department.

Eve went to a rail to get some trousers but Stella grabbed her arm. "You can't have those. I have to pick for you. He was very specific about what you can wear." Stella grabbed a dressing gown from the rack. "Let's get you cleaned up in the loos first, then, I have to apply some makeup." Stella helped her to undress and wash, and placed the dressing gown around her. She took Eve to cosmetics. Eve pulled back but Stella started crying again. "He'll kill her if you don't go back to him the way he wants." Eve allowed herself to be manoeuvred into a chair, and makeup to be applied to her face, by Stella's shaking hands. "Your face doesn't need makeup. You are the most beautiful woman I have ever seen." Despite herself, Eve coloured a little. Stella tied back Eve's hair, then, led her back to clothing, where she chose some black stock-

ings, suspenders and lace bra and knickers. Completing the outfit
with a black skirted business suit and black six inch stilettoes.

Eve wobbled back into the throne room on her high heels with a
glazed look on her face. Stella had been allowed to leave with her
child but had run back to embrace and kiss Eve, whispering, "God
bless you. Whatever happens I will never forget," before running
back to her child.

"Sit down Miss Fox." The only other chair was a footstool set
fifteen feet in front of Sadique's makeshift throne. Doing her best
to keep her composure, she sat on the stool, but her knees were so
high her skirt rode up and she was forced to sit awkwardly with her
knees to the side, trying not to show too much bare thigh. "Okay
Miss Fox, now you may begin your negotiations."

She was momentarily startled into uncertainty and hope? "N ...
Negotiate?"

"That is what you're here for isn't it? You want lives don't you?
What are you offering in return?"

This was not what she had expected. She faltered for a moment.

"We ... we want all the hostages released Mr Fayed. Tell us your
demands and we can begin to talk."

"What is this, we, and us? I am negotiating with you Miss Fox,
no one else. What can you offer that will convince me to part with
my possessions?"

She answered wearily, playing his game to delay her fate, "Mr
Fayed, you've been here before. You know how it works. You
make your unreasonable demands and we," she paused, "sorry, 'I'
tell you how much I'm willing to give. Then we haggle over the
finer points. Make your demands Mr Fayed!"

"I insist you start the bidding Miss Fox, but I will make one
demand, just to get the ball rolling."

Sadique nodded to his man at the door. Stella's child was
brought back in. "Open your knees Miss Fox. So that we can see
you for what you really are. I want our negotiations to be," he
paused, "open. I do not want to feel that you are hiding anything
from us. You can say no of course, but then you would be condemning this beautiful child to worse than death."

Eve could feel the blood draining from her face. Tentatively, she
opened her knees. The guard took the child away again. Eve felt
the cool draft, in the large room, waft between her thighs and could

not restrain a spasmodic quiver that she fought, unsuccessfully, to control. Teeth chattering, Eve forced herself to look around the room, attempting to quell the burning desire in every man's eyes by the sheer force of her will and trying, desperately, to ignore the more obvious signs of excitement below their waist-lines. Sadique's gaze although candidly directed toward the centre point between her thighs, showed nothing but casual disdain, belying the burgeoning bulge in his trousers that he made no attempt to hide, easing himself lower in his chair and jutting his hips slightly forward to emphasise his straining ardour. Yet, still, he continued with his masquerade (The word "Afsoon" finally whispered into her mind). Eve made a decision.

There was no escape for her. He had her conscience firmly crushed in his cruel grip. His word, however, remained in her desperate hands. Sadique wanted to kill them all, but he wanted to fuck her, body, mind and soul, even more. Okay, she had something to sell and he, sure as hell, was not going to get it cheap. Some lives were going to be lost, God help her. At least a couple were, almost certainly, going to die to show him that her compliance came with a high price tag and that pre-emptive kills were not going force her into gibbering and abject obedience. He was going to have to give her what she wanted before she allowed him to consume her. But first, she was going to save Stella's child. It was time to play poker.

"Very well, we'll do it your way." She stood. The creature in the corner of her mind cried out in relief. "I'll keep my knees open when I have your word that the child you just brought in will be safe from harm, and will be released."

"Sit back down Miss Fox, and resume your posture immediately, or there will be more death in this room!"

"Not until I have your word."

"Ah. You wish to play hard ball. I think you are getting a taste for the granting and taking of life." He nodded, and a teenage boy was brought in struggling. He received a gun butt in the groin to quell his exertions and was placed, gasping, between Sadique and Eve. Sadique addressed the lad. "Your name boy?"

"Up yours!" He gasped.

A hand gesture from Sadique prevented a further blow to the boy's head. "Brave boy, this pleases me. You see Miss Fox how even a stripling of the male species can show courage, without losing control of his bladder. Now, listen to me boy. Miss Fox here has the power to save your life. She merely has to make the right offer but she is proving stubborn at the moment. The length of her delay will increase the time, and amount, of pain you will undergo before death. Do you not find her attitude cruel and selfish?"

"Okay, Sadique," Eve began.

He interrupted her, "Mr Fayed, surely Miss Fox."

The animal was taunting her. "Mr Fayed," she complied. "Leave the boy alone," she had to test alternatives even though it was plain what he was after. "I will arrange safe passage for you and your men to the nearest airport and a plane out of here but all hostages must be released, unharmed, or there is no deal."

A weary note entered his voice. "Miss Fox, I have already explained to you that I am bargaining with you. I am not interested in what your colleagues in the police can offer; only what you can give me on a more," he paused again, "personal basis. Now I want no more procrastination. You have already made this boy's death something that will involve considerable and lengthy suffering. I can't imagine what you might offer, if you wish to save him, so I hope your imagination is better than mine Miss Fox. Resume your previous posture now and see if you can appease my disappointment or the boy will be skinned." She knew he meant it. With prompt reluctance she sat and opened her knees, once again willing the raging presence within to be quiet. The boy's eyes widened. Without warning he launched a sudden and frenzied attack on Sadique. For a moment, Eve thought he might succeed and prepared herself to join the attack. A spray of bullets through the boy's calves brought him to the floor but somehow he had contrived to grab the blade and slashed at Sadique's ankle. Sadique side stepped and brought his heel down to crush the boy's throat. "An honourable death don't you think Miss Fox? But a waste of a bargaining chip," he said, as he retrieved the knife.

Eve knew the time had come. She had to extract promises now before he killed them all. "The hostages Mr Fayed? You release them all unharmed, and you get to fuck me." The creature within her was now almost gibbering with fear and rage but she forced it back into the recesses of her mind. It must not gain control or influence here.

"All the hostages Miss Fox? You have a very high opinion of yourself. I want much more than that pitiful offer, and what of my men? I would be a poor leader if I squandered all their hard-earned wealth on a few moments of self-gratification with a filthy whore." His voice took on a new stridency. "No Miss Fox I expect much more. Use your imagination, but the bargaining has begun. I will allow you five lives for what we will loosely call your honour. Remove your knickers Miss Fox." She froze … "When I make a request I expect you to react. My patience with your foibles wears thin. There will be more death if you do not respond with haste." He shouted at his men, causing some of them to quickly remove their hands from their trousers, "bring the child back!"

"No!" Eve quickly removed her knickers, struggling to get them over her high heels.

"Sit down Miss Fox. Open your knees as before, wider. That's good. Now that I can see you are hiding nothing from me, we can begin negotiations in earnest. What of my men, Miss Fox? I am losing patience with you woman," he raised his voice and spoke with icy clarity, enunciating each word. "Answer immediately or you will witness a mass execution right now!" She mumbled something. "Louder Miss Fox! We all want to hear."

"Hand relief!" she blurted. "Five lives for each of your men."

"Really Miss Fox; you westerners have no idea how to haggle. These are lives we are bargaining for here. Do you really think I would offer even one for a cheap fondle? You insult me and you insult my men."

Eve gritted her teeth. "Perhaps, but your men are not attractive to me so it would be a chore. You on the other hand are different. I might go much further with you for the right price."

"An interesting postulation, I see you are beginning to use your mind at last. Nevertheless, I will take a life for the insult but," another pause, "I will also be generous. Five lives for you to give relief to all of them. I reiterate, however, you really will have to exercise your imagination a lot more. You have gained ten more lives but lost three. Also, in case I didn't mention it, there is a time constraint. I intend to leave here in just over four hours. Whilst all our human wealth is rigged to explode at that time, I prefer to be more imaginative with the taking of life. I will need at least two hours to prepare suitable deaths for so large a number. So if we have not finished our bargaining by then, and you do not have me, and my men, fully occupied, it will be on your conscience. Convince me to part with our wealth or create more suffering."

"What more can I offer? You already have everything I can give personally. Except to again offer to be your broker for negotiations with the police."

"That will cost you two lives, Miss Fox. You know as well I do that there is a whole lot more you can do. I am beginning to tire of this. If you do not offer me something substantial soon, I will seek solace in the mass and bloody slaughter of our captives."

Eve suppressed a shudder. She closed her eyes so she didn't have to look at the reactions of Sadique and his men. "Okay!" She bit down fear and rage. "Oral! I will give you oral sex as well for ten more."

"That is acceptable, but again, not with just me, all of my men too!"

"No!" She was actually quaking now, but there was no way out. "It will be ten for each."

"That is not possible. You may have a further ten, for all of them but you must swallow."

She clapped her hand over her mouth to stop herself retching and started to babble. "No, I … I couldn't. You … you … you, don't understand." She played the last card she had, one, that in her panic she had only just come to realise, she had. "You, you, don't know what you're asking." Her voice trembled and broke with the impact of what she was saying, and her whole frame started to shake violently. "I'm … I'm a virgin damn it!"

There was a moment of stunned silence. Then Sadique's face split into a broad grin and he started to laugh. His men all joined in the hilarity, high fiving, and slapping each other's backs. "But this is wonderful news." He looked at his men. "You see, Allah provides for the faithful. This is good news for you too, Miss Fox."

Hope began to trickle past Eve's despair. "You … you mean we can look at other, other collateral?"

"Of course we can. This changes everything." Eve almost sighed in relief. "I would be churlish and ungrateful, if I put too low a cost on such a gift. Praise be to Almighty God, who has seen fit to so honour his faithful servants." His men echoed this sentiment in unison.

Eve felt her dilating hopes of escape suddenly constrict around her. "What do you mean by cost, and gift?"

"Isn't it obvious? A virgin is a rare and wonderful thing Miss Fox, especially amongst infidels, and, because you are not of the faith, your deflowerment will be no sin. You should rejoice Miss Fox. Such a gift, if given honourably, and without reservation, is worth much. You may indeed succeed in saving many lives, if your claim proves to be true. The privilege of establishing that, will, with your permission, fall to me. For this, I will give you half of our human wealth. What do you say Miss Fox? Is this not a good and honourable offer? And you may still bargain for the rest, but let us dispense with this tit for tat haggling. The time to celebrate is upon us. We must not denigrate it with petty squabbling. I will put before you a very generous proposition. If you accept, we can each honour our debt and be about our business. If you do not, or if your claim proves false, we will make sacrifices of them all." The chill of retribution seeped through the air enfolding what was left of her desperate resolve. Eve choked on her disappointment but nodded agreement. "I will take your virginity Miss Fox. This is my right as leader. If you are truly a virgin, you may then fulfil the rest of your bargain."

"Y-You still expect me to swallow your men's semen, but we never agreed ..."

"True, but you were going to weren't you? To save lives ... and I am offering more now, twice as much, but also twice as much torture and pain, should you refuse, that is only fair, and I still have many children." Eve started to shake again. "Come now, we all need to spill our seed. I'll tell you what ... Add full sex with them all and you can save half of the rest."

Eve could hardly speak. John was going insane inside her. She managed to grate out. "All of the rest."

"Final offer. I urge you to take it. There will be no other. I will not give back those that I have already condemned, and I will keep ten or eleven others just for the hell of it. You can have the rest. Take it or leave it Miss Fox!" He rose and turned to leave.

"Yes," she whispered.

He stopped and looked around the room as though trying to locate something. He looked at his men and gave a shrug, and asked of them. "Did you hear anything? I thought I heard something, probably just a mouse, or some other vermin. Come my brothers, we have souls to send to hell." He opened the door.

Eve's screech was pitiful, dribbling snot and saliva into the trembling, clawed hands, she had raised to her face. "STAY! PLEASE! All of you. I agree. Do whatever you want. You can all fuck me! Just let them go. Please. Just let them go? She was blubbering and repeating the same phrase over and over. Her whole frame bowed, shuddering uncontrollably. A small piece of her mind willed Blood.

"DONE! On your knees. NOW!" His men were on her, man-handling her onto her face, pulling her knees apart before she knew what was happening. There was a moment of tearing pain, then, he was shouting. "Praise be to Allah!" and walking amongst his men with a cloth full of her blood, showing them the proof of her virginity. There was a startled shout as the cloth got too near a candle and was engulfed in flames. This was seen as a sign from God and frenzy ensued. Eve was grabbed from every direction, spread-eagled, turned, forced to kneel and to gag whilst they held her to her promise in full.

She lay exhausted by trauma, defiled, and weeping silently whilst mentally crawling into the darkest part of her mind for refuge. But it was not over.

Sadique's voice prodded into her sanctuary with rasping cruelty. "There are still ten children Miss Fox. Would you do 'anything' to save them too?" Eve forced eyes that had turned up inside her head, to rotate down and to focus their bloodshot gaze on her tormentor.

Cringed in a posture of utter defeat, she uttered the sound he wanted to hear in a voice that might have issued from a corpse. "Yes."

"This must be from you, Eve." Nearly catatonic now, she missed the significance of this form of address. "You have only one area left to desecrate. If you beg me to penetrate you in that way, I will release two children and one more for each time you wriggle and moan in ecstasy, or beg for more. Do you understand?"

"Yes."

She saved them all, then, slowly, quivering and quaking, she drew herself into a foetal ball, hugging her knees and whimpering feebly within the fetid fug of bodily odour and discharge that clung, cloyingly to her in crusting smears. And still he had not finished with her.

"Eve! A mutual friend asked me to give you this." Something in his voice made her uncurl enough to look and listen. He forced a DVD between her knees and chest. Looking slowly around, she saw the cameras, four of them, two on tripods and two held by his men, still filming her. "We each have one. We all need reminding of our experiences don't we? Except that our copies will have out takes too." The enormity of her humiliation and the public nature of it, finally punctured the dead space in her mind, violating even that bottomless crevasse in which she had taken refuge. Her stomach suddenly rebelled, contorting in violent contractions. Flipping onto her knees, she arched her back, catlike, and spewed colloidal fluid, in great wracking retches that sucked partially back into her throat when her gut relaxed for the next shuddering ejection. The elastic fluid congealed and oozed into a viscid pool between her splayed and shaking hands. As the last of it finally drooled from between her teeth and slack lips it formed the shape of a nose thus completing the illusory face that now stared back at her.

"Afsoon?" Her own utterance echoed back at her, chasing itself around the inside of her skull like a penny in a drop machine. Impossibly, the thing was speaking.

"You have but to say my name and I shall appear." Time, away from this moment, this space between them, had frozen.

"Have I lost my mind?"

"Poor, poor John You lost your body and got another. Now you are Eve and you've lost your virginity, your dignity, and your mind. You really cannot be trusted with anything can you? Why don't you just give up? You can't win. You made a terrible mistake shooting me off among the stars. This vessel has access to all the data of the habitat, and it is teaching me Eve. You have no idea of what we are capable. Look at me now. From a billion miles away, I can possess the wicked and control the weak and you are weak Eve. All that power, and look at you. You have no idea how to use it. You were no match for me before, and daily I draw further beyond your meagre capabilities, but I will never let you go Eve and you will bear my children, thousands of them." She smashed her fist into the slimy mess and was back in hell. A subliminal touch of feminine amusement seemed to run like a bass beat below her thoughts, a former Afsoon, mocking her from another world and another time?

"Get up whore. My word is sacred. Come and collect your hostages." Her withered psyche failed to prevent her body's auto obedience. She followed submissively. They took the lift to the top floor and went along the corridor to a door into a maintenance area. He had removed her collar in the lift.

"Negotiations ended when you left the function room slut!" Sadique stepped behind her and pushed her through the door. The scene that greeted her untethered a raging demon from the depths within. In that exact instant, Sadique stepped forward from behind, swung his arm in a tight arc and stabbed downwards into her face, gouging with a serrated hunting knife, deep behind her nose. "No man, or woman, will ever want you now. Your memories of sex will forever be encapsulated in what has happened to you here." Twisting his arm in a serpentine flick he ripped the nose and a large lump of flesh from her face and sent it flying across the room. One of the guards caught it.

At the precise time of Sadique's well-timed attack, Eve had taken in the scene. Stella, bound and gagged. A scimitar descending toward her exposed neck. Eve was already reacting, but her focus had been on Stella, which had left Sadique his opening. Now her arm shot out at frightening speed smashing into, and through, the side of his face but her attention remained on the scimitar that was already slicing into Stella's neck, her eyes wide, and dilated almost entirely black, looked directly into Eve's. With all her speed it was still too late. All she could do was to catch the falling head by the hair with her outstretched hand. The other hand seized the scimitar and wrenched it from the stunned executioner. His face registered surprise as his cleaved head was backslapped across the room to smash against the wall. The guard raising his rifle clashed heads with Stella's from the double handed swing afforded it by Eve's supercharged anger, reducing both to shattered pulp. The man who caught her nose screamed as his arm ignited, engulfed in intense white fire, and the guard struggling to escape through the door turned up his eyes for the last time when the thrown scimitar pinned him to the door frame.

Eve swept a malevolent gaze around the room trying to clear the blood from her eyes. There was gunfire outside. Frustrated at being unable to locate Sadique, an eerie, gurgling howl of rage issued from her throat, whilst Matt and several marksmen kicked frantically at the door from the outside. The air in the room crackled with an unspent fury that seemed to coalesce into a malignant singularity, before being absorbed by the unnaturally quiet beast that Eve had now become. Insanity writhed through her inner being, threatening to destroy all coherent thought. It was into this vacuum, with Eve straddling the pit of mental annihilation, that Matt Crow entered the room.

Six weeks had passed since her ordeal. Matt of course had been a constant visitor but, so too, had Janie, of all people. In fact she was becoming a pest. And Dr Stewart had just left. He had not liked her discharging herself, but had reluctantly agreed, on the proviso that she allowed him to make regular house calls. At one point he had threatened to have her sectioned but a murderous look from Matt had crushed that thought before the words were off his tongue. Eve knew that his real interest lay in her miraculous recovery. The missing section of skull, new teeth and a nose had all regrown perfectly leaving mild scarring that was fading by the day. She supposed she should thank him for holding fire on corrective surgery, before seeing the extent of this unheard of regeneration. Who knew what harm might have been done.

Janie was droning on in her South American drawl. "Matt has got everything in hand so you don't need to worry about a thing honey. That damn doctor wanted to publish his findings and bring in the media. Matt's made sure all press coverage is blocked and that all the Doc's visits are via high security. I've been giving the chief constable a headache making sure your criminal injuries' claim gets processed on the hurry up. The chief says you can take a holiday with a bodyguard and a trusted person to help care for you. I'd be happy to take some time off if you like." She looked hopefully at Eve.

"Thanks Janie, I'll bear that in mind." Changing the subject she asked. "Where is Matt anyway?"

"Meeting with the chief to discuss your future and what to tell the press, they will have to have a concluding story sooner or later. All the world knows," she hesitated looking carefully at Eve before continuing, "what happened, following the 'social media' clips released by that creepy bastard (she couldn't bring herself to say his name). You can't contain something like that." She was almost crying with pent rage and sympathy and tried to hug Eve.

Eve gently disengaged her. "I'm fine Janie I promise." And she realised that in the physical sense she was indeed fine, even experiencing a kind of high from the ready flow of endorphins flooding through her system, but then the dark beast in her twitched and she said with true venom. "Doesn't mean I'm not going to hunt down and kill the bastard though," and very quietly, under her breath, "you too Afsoon. I'm coming for you."

"Atta girl Evee, but which one was Afsoon?"

"All of them Janie, it's a collective term." Eve needed to get back to her studies. She wanted to read through the Texan manuscripts she had recovered from the Priest's lair. "Janie I am really very tired now, would you mind leaving? I can barely keep my eyes open."

"Of course, but you will holler if you need anything won't you?"

"Yes I will." She ushered a reluctant Janie out of the door.

Matt bumped into Janie hanging around outside the safe house that the force had acquired for Eve. "Are you still here Janie? You have to give it a rest. You can't be hanging around here twenty-four hours a day."

"No offence Matt but I haven't got a lot of faith in your guys' abilities to keep her safe, that Paparazzi slime ball has been hanging around the yard again, tried to follow me home the other night."

"I'll get right onto it."

"No need. He won't be able to use a camera with broken fingers anyway and the broken toes should slow down his mobility a bit as well. I just wish she'd let me move in. I'm worried about her. I think she wants to go on a killing spree, who can blame her, but we've all seen what she is capable of. I'd feel a whole lot better if she was screaming or threatening or even whimpering. She seems perfectly okay, too okay, and then you see that cold look and those quiet threats under her breath. She scares me Matt. I don't know how far she might go, or if there will be any bringing her back if she does catch up with him." She huffed a deep breath. "Yeah, okay, Matt I can see the look in your eye. Now you're here, I'll leave. One question though, do you know anyone called Afsoon?" Matt shook his head and Janie walked off with a troubled frown.

He announced himself on the intercom, said the appropriate phrase for the day, and was rewarded with an irritable answer from Eve. "Is Janie still down there?"

Matt smiled to himself. "No Eve, I've sent her on her way."

"Have you got sticky buns?"

"Yup, half a dozen of them, straight from the baker's oven."

"Then get your sorry arse up here. I'm desperate for a sugar burst."

As she buzzed him in, he took a quick look up and down the street, entered, made sure the door locked behind him and bounded up the stairs two at a time. She waited at the top with the door open, dressed in jeans and a baggy top with the sleeves rolled up.

He entered and she walked off to the kitchenette. "Kettle's on. I'll make some tea. I've put some plates on the coffee table for the buns but you only get two of them, if you want to keep your fingers, right?"

"Yeah I got that. Still keeping up with the Bible studies, I see?" He cast his eyes over the religious texts she'd been studying that were on the corner of the desk. "These look pretty old."

She returned carrying two steaming mugs, set them on the table, and snatched the bag of buns from his hand to put on the plates.

"Biblical, but definitely not bibles and they're not that old, copies, couple hundred years at most, but they are interesting." She dropped down sideways across an armchair with her legs dangling over one arm and stuffed a bun in her mouth continuing to speak around it. "If you read between the lines, there are some pretty radical suggestions in there about the origins of mankind, but more interesting is the history of the books themselves, like where they were copied from. There are clues in some of the bibliography. Anyway how did you get rid of Janie so quickly? She normally hangs around for ages."

"You know you shouldn't knock her presence, she's genuinely concerned about you and she's probably just about the best protection you could have?"

"Yeah I know. Strange though how bullies often become besotted with those who best them, but I can't argue that she's become a very loyal friend and a great bodyguard. I'll try to lighten up on her a bit. Come on, tuck in, or I'll be eating yours as well."

"You know you should be as fat as a whale the way you eat."

"Working girl, got to keep up my energy."

He sighed and sat down opposite with a woof of exhaled breath. "Yeah that brings me to my next point. How do you feel about giving up work?"

She swivelled in the chair and leaned forward looking at him intently. "Meaning?"

He couldn't help noticing that despite her efforts to cover her gorgeous curves in shapeless clothes, she had relaxed into a far more feminine demeanour than she had previously allowed. It was almost as though, following her trauma, she had finally accepted that others found her intensely desirable and that she had no option but to work around, or with, it.

"Meaning that I have come here to sound you out for an offer sanctioned by the chief constable."

"What kind of an offer?"

"Truth is Eve, you have become a very hot potato. Forgive my frankness but they would rather you disappeared completely. The press are screaming to know what happened. You have become a celebrity," there was only the flicker of a hesitation before he continued, "porn star, on social networking sites. It is only a matter of time before they find out the extent of your injuries and, if they also find out about your recovery, both the police and you are unlikely to ever hear the end of it. You'll be hounded forever." He looked at her expectantly and not without some fear over her reaction.

"What are they offering?"

Repressing a sigh of relief he pitched the offer. "Relocation and a new identity plus one million pounds, but you can knock them for two, easily. They are very eager to get you out of their hair. They will reveal the injuries you suffered and say you never recovered."

"Relocation? Where?"

"Anywhere outside of Europe."

"No good, I want to stay in England and I'll choose my own name. I'll let you negotiate the amount, and one other thing, I want information, as much as you can get on this guy," she grabbed a pen and paper and wrote down details of Mr Soames passing them to Matt whose eyes widened before he pocketed them.

"You know him?"

"I know of him. Very high profile, they won't like giving anything up on him, but I'll see what I can do. As for staying in
England, that won't be to their taste either. You are a memorable
woman."

"I'll dye my hair and change my appearance."

"I guess if the press think you are dead, they won't be looking,
and the police are tight with money, if you agree to less we might
be able to come up with something. Again, I'll see what I can do."

"And Matt, for reasons I can't tell you now, I am not entirely
unhappy that I won't be seeing much of you if this deal goes
through, but I do want to stay in contact and, once things settle,
even to reopen our friendship. Can we make that part of the deal
too?"

He knew better than to question her reasons.

"One thing I can tell you for sure Eve, we will remain friends and
find a way, and not just because of my friendship with your uncle.
I'm very fond of you Eve." They both stood and she saw him to
the door. He put out his hand to shake hers and was startled when
she ducked in to give him a light kiss.

"That means so much Matt. Thank you." When he locked the
front door behind him he could still feel the touch of her lips on his
cheek, stinging slightly as though they had held an electric charge.
It was disconcerting, but there was no arousal only fatherly affection. He walked away distractedly.

Matt did a lot of wrangling and managed to cobble together a
deal that was acceptable to both the Force and Eve. They hadn't
liked her staying in England but with a stroke of genius Matt had
suggested that if she maintained a mobile address it would be very
difficult to trace her. He suggested "The Force" bought and fitted
out a narrow boat. The canal community were notoriously insular
and protective of their own and, if she kept on the move, no one
was likely to take a prolonged interest in her. (This had been well
thought out, because it also meant it would be easy for him to see
her, at various pre-arranged destinations, instead of him suspiciously coming and going to just one.) They reluctantly agreed, but
took the cost of the boat from the lump sum of one million pounds;
a sum they had decided was non-negotiable if she was to continue
to stubbornly refuse to leave Europe.

"What did you find out about Soames?"

"Not a lot. I was stone walled at every turn, but I made a few discreet enquiries amongst some pretty shady connections I have made over the years. Soames has some deep connections in criminal circles but has never been charged with anything. He is also well connected politically, and, something that you might find interesting, he was once a Jesuit priest and an exorcist. He still seems to pull some weight in the Vatican and is sometimes employed by them to carry out their more clandestine operations. Oh, and in case it isn't already apparent, he is untouchable." Matt sat back and heaved a deep breath, "and that's pretty much it I'm afraid."

"That's quite a lot Matt and it confirms that even if he is not telling me everything, at least he is telling me the truth. Thanks Matt. I don't know how I am ever going to repay you for all you have done. You are a great friend."

"Well you could start by telling me exactly what it is you have got yourself into. It's not just Sadique, is it?" She had been dreading this, but truth was she owed him that and far more.

Terrified of the outcome but determined to lie no more, she gritted her teeth to tell him everything. "Yeah I guess I owe you that much. Brace yourself. You are going to think I am insane. Just promise me one thing, when you've heard all I have to say, please don't bring that doctor back to commit me."

Matt sat in stunned silence for what seemed an interminable time. Finally he sighed and rose to his feet. "Listen Eve, you are in a dark place. If I didn't think it would kill you and, if I didn't trust your ability to overcome this, I would think about having you sectioned. Promise me you will get psychiatric help and keep in touch. Call me anytime, and keep your uncle's memory separate from all this. He was a great man but he is dead. You can't keep him alive by absorbing his personality into your own even if it is comforting to do so. I have to go now Eve. I am meeting someone."

Eve had feared this response. "Please don't go Matt. I can prove what I say if you'll just listen."

"No Eve! This is madness. I'm late for my meeting with Janie."

That stopped Eve in her tracks as the penny dropped. "Janie? Please tell me you two are not an item."

"Not yet but that is none of your business."

"No, I didn't mean anything. I was just surprised that's all. It's great, really! Please don't go."

"Look Eve, I need to think, but remember; I'm here for you when you are ready, okay? You've got friends, remember that." He turned and left but stopped at the door and turned back to her, "By the way what name did you choose?" The tone of finality in his voice froze her to the spot.

After a few moments, she spoke with an air of thoughtful distraction. "I've had so much change of late Matt and even you seem to have lost faith in me now. I know it's not wise but I want to stick with Eve. At least it is something to cling to from the life I've made these last months." A thought struck her. "I suppose it could be Evelyn, and then it could be shortened to Eve. Perhaps it could be a middle name, one that I use. So, how about Pandora? I feel as though I have released evil into the world. Pandora Evelyn." She thought for a moment longer and said with an air of subdued satisfaction, "Pandora Evelyn Gabriel, an arch angel to combat the evil I have wrought."

His one word response hurt. "Apt," he said and left. Eve felt like shit and wanted to take to her bed but the old anger coiled coldly in her stomach and she went back to her books.

Ben

Ben goaded Jack and Dec. "Go on wankers, break the fucking lock before she comes back. You got to see her. She class man, real pussy, but me first. I'm gonna bust her man. You two motherfuckers can finish her, once I got her dripping and whimpering and broken. Then we gonna beat her til she beg us do anything to make it stop. When she good and ready, we gonna make the bitch take all of us in every or-i-f-eece. She be so abused, she never walk again. She want to move around, we have to keep filling her up, so she sli-i-i-de." He made disgusting slurping sounds and mimicked a double handed grip whilst gyrating his hips. The other two sniggered, Jack rubbing his crotch excitedly whilst Dec worked more vigorously at the lock of the canal boat.

Eve looked on from the shadows with a steely glare, noting the iron bar being used to force the lock and the flash of a blade, now and then, in Ben's mobile hands. She tensed as the heavy padlock snapped open and Jack and Dec moved stealthily in. Ben carefully replaced the lock and moved to hide in the bushes directly adjacent to the barge. A startled look crossed his features when he spotted her standing there vampirically. As his head snapped up, she punched him in the throat, stepping silently forward to ease him to the ground. She continued moving forward onto the barge and knocked with quiet urgency. She paused, then knocked again and stepped back as the door, tentatively, opened.

Dec stayed just inside but Jack emerged. A well-aimed kick to his testicles doubled him, and a fist to the back of the neck finished him. Reaching across in a fluid movement, she grabbed the non-plussed Dec by the hair and threw her weight back. Tripping him over the comatose Jack, she smashed his head on the deck and delivered a savage kick to the base of his jaw.

The three sat with their wrists cable-tied to the back legs of their chairs, ankles to the front legs. They were all in varying states of stupor. Every so often, Eve walked along behind them, pulling their heads up by the hair and looking into their eyes.

"Good, you all seem to be awake. Now, I've prepared you breakfast, and I will be very offended if you don't all eat heartily!" There was a hard edge to her voice. Ben felt a clawing soreness in his groin and looked at the shrivelled mess in the bowl in front of him. An ice cold plunge of enlightenment contracted his stomach, making him retch. "Now, listen up boys, you can have a choice, which is more than you were going to give me. You can eat your own or you can swap bowls. It's up to you. Let's start with you. Dec is it? Which bowl would you like? No? I'll choose then." She spooned it to his mouth. He kept it tight shut and turned his head. She waved Ben's blade. "I can always take the other one." She placed the blade against his remaining very inflamed testicle, eliciting a scream and deftly pressed the chewy mess into his opened mouth with the heel of her hand, clamping it shut and pinching his nose until he swallowed. "Don't vomit!" She ordered, pushing the flat of the knife back into his crotch. Jack complied in similar fashion.

It took three tries and a great deal of effort to force Ben. Dec was now sobbing and Jack was in deep shock. Eve cut them loose, took them, at knife point, to the edge of the boat and pushed them off into the water with a heart stalling palm thrust between the shoulder blades. She returned for Ben. He stared at her defiantly and resisted every step. At the edge, he began making threats.

"You're dead bitch! You don't know who you're dealing with. The Bloods will rape you bad. You'll be our sex bitch, en-sl-a-ved." He drew out the word, "for a long, long time. We gonna spit roast you bitch, in every hole, and make some new ones, before we rip out your ruined p-u-sss-eey and feed it to you. You think you the bad bitch. There ain't nowhere you can hide once I tell them. You gonna die ho!" His crude threats disturbed dark and deadly emotions. Eve hesitated. An inward look exposed a dormant, and very vivid memory. A momentary flash of hatred marred her perfect beauty. She rabbit punched him and took him back inside.

Eve finished closing the wound, took the offending flesh and threw it into the Marina.

No point making him eat it again, she mused. She'd spent half the night chucking up the contents of her stomach as it was. She could see no practical value in repeating the exercise, but her issues around domination and degradation, continued to force the trend of her actions.

Eve switched off the motor and set the sails. With the salt wind snapping her hair, she looked at the dark horizon and dwelt on her situation. She'd brought the narrowboat up to the coast overnight and it now lay at its moorings, secured with a very expensive new lock. Ben's inert body was transferred, without incident, to the *Ark*. She would set him loose at the first remote port she came to, and return to her plans. The *Ark* was what she'd spent her compensation, and a fair bit of her savings, on. It was fast and comfortable and much bigger than she needed, and very well equipped.

She needed time to heal and to consolidate her plans. What she did not need right now, she realised with expanding clarity, was a vengeful and violent adolescent dogging her movements. What had she been thinking? The universe had changed forever since meeting Isaac. There was no room for her petty psychosis. She had to pursue the bigger picture. She had developed a habit whenever coming to a decision, and she was unconsciously indulging it now, gently sliding her thumb in turns down both sides of her nose. She ought to just weight his feet and drop him over the side but she was beginning to realise that any event had precursors, repercussions and responsibilities. So far, she had acted and reacted within a chain of these events. Now she needed to back off and consider. Further interference or action from her would lead to ever more complex outcomes. She needed to observe, and try to predict the course of future trends, so that she could act timely and appropriately, to nudge outcomes in directions she might be able to take advantage of. She heaved a huge breath from her lungs and with a deep sigh, said "Shit!" and went below to check on her casualty.

Things were not looking good for Ben. She was probably as good a surgeon as most junior doctors and had been careful with sterility, but there were signs of infection, and he was developing a fever. Perhaps he would be going over the side after all.

Ben awoke, slick with sweat, feeling like his crotch was about to erupt. A coughing fit launched agonising waves of pain that crashed against his ebbing life force but succeeded in bringing him back to full cognisance. He spat the soup Eve was spooning into his mouth into her face and tried to sit. "Fuck off you stupid bitch!"

She pressed him back down with a firm hand and spoke close to his ear. "Listen dipshit. I'm not really fussed whether you live or die. Eat the fucking soup or feed the fucking fish." She tried to give him another spoonful but when he went to spit that at her, she upended the bowl on his face and left him to it. The next time he awoke, he ate the soup, sulkily, a look of raw hatred on his face. He turned his head to the side, but didn't flinch, as she cleaned and dressed his wounds.

After a week at sea, Eve was sitting at a table reading religious texts and eating a bacon sandwich when she heard the heavy slap of a wet palm on the door frame. Skinny and bedraggled, Ben clutched a soiled sheet over his depleted manhood and leaned unsteadily against the jam. He mumbled something, truculently, and tried to suck back the drool that escaped his slack lips.

"What!" she said, around a mouthful of sandwich, studying him intently.

"Food, you fucking whore. I'm hungry."

"There might still be something through there in the galley." She pointed, maintaining her scrutiny as he lurched through, then, followed him into the galley. After several attempts at opening cupboards, thwarted by safety catches, he threw a clenched fist at a door and lost his balance. She caught him with one arm and guided him onto a bench, where he could lean into a corner. Opening a cupboard, she pulled out a hunk of bread and slapped it on the table with some butter and a knife, then, sat opposite, watching him closely, as he eyed the knife, and stuffed the dry bread in his mouth. Seeing him struggle, she gave him a cup of water and sat down again. After he'd gorged and choked his way through most of the bread and water, he leaned his head against the wall and closed his eyes, trying to get his breath. He made a feeble attempt to stop her as she slipped her hand beneath the sheet and took back the knife.

A further week and they had developed a silent routine interspersed by quiet commands from her and reluctant, though ready, obedience from him as any extended hesitation on his part resulted in being knocked to the deck and bound for several hours. Any attempt at resistance or retaliation resulted in an extended dip, whilst bound, in the sea. When mobile and working, he was allowed to wear only a light pair of her shorts, or his underpants, and was bound to his bed at night.

"If you get behind me again, I'll cut you loose next time you're over the side."

"I just wanted to know what all that religious crap is you're reading."

She turned to look at him and regarded him for long moments. He held her gaze for a while then turned away. "I'm bored to fucking tears. I need to do something, apart from what you say ..."

She regarded him a little longer. "Very well, we've got another few weeks at sea. Perhaps it will be good for your soul. If you do your work well, you may sit opposite where I can see you, and read after me, that is, try anything or harm the book in any way and you will wish you hadn't." He nodded and sat with a pained grunt, still very sore. She pulled her feet away from him under the table. Despite everything, there was still something of the sexual predator that seemed to stir in him, whenever he got close to her, an excited and unwholesome flush to his cheeks, sly glances, when he thought she wasn't looking, tremors, if they accidentally touched. He gave her the creeps. They read.

"You believe in all dis rubbish?" He had read opposite her for long periods, and in silence, for three days now. She ignored him, but his question was rhetorical. He closed the back cover and pushed the heavy tome away from him.

She raised an eyebrow. "Fast reader?" He took the gesture as an invite to continue. "This God dude, he love us all right? But he punish us when we do wrong, yeah? Then why he save Lot from Sodom city after he try to give up his virgin girls to be raped? And why, after he have babies with them, incest, right? He go unpunished? And dis Joshua, why did God tell him it was okay for him to kill, or make slaves of everyone in Jericho if, 'Thou shalt not kill!'?"

There was an edge to his voice and, she noted, his street talk was slipping, to be replaced with a degree of eloquence. She settled back on the bench and looked at him. He saw this as further permission to carry on, and his rhetoric gathered momentum. "Yeah it's all shit! Dis poor guy Job does everything right, and God rewards him by having a bet with the Devil, kills all his family and makes him suffer bad, and Jacob steals all Esau's wealth and God likes him for it, makes Jacob father of the chosen ones, and then says to Moses. 'Thou shalt not steal!' It's all shit man! You got to look after yourself! Init! You wait for God's help, you wait forever, you still be here waiting after the resurrection!" He was on his feet now and pacing the cabin, starting to drool and looking close to tears. He slammed out of the galley, leaving the door shuddering, and stamped to the cabin where he slept. She heard a clatter and a whumpf, as he scooped everything off the bedside table and threw himself on the bed. She quietly locked his cabin door and went to check her communications and navigation instruments.

He became aware of her looking at him from the foot of his bed. She was holding a hot drink and a sandwich, which she now placed next to him and sat on the edge of his bed.

"Storm coming, you'd better eat something. I'm going to need your help." She noted his eyes were red and bloodshot from rubbing. She sat on the end of the bed, "Rough childhood eh?"

"What do you care?"

"I don't, makes it worse really. Knowing what misery and degradation is like and then inflicting worse on others. Makes you one of the lowest creatures it's ever been my misfortune to come into contact with."

"Worse?" he gasped, and sat up suddenly, staring wildly, but with tears welling into his eyes. "You don't know what he ... he ... d ... did to me!" He stuttered and shuddered and started shaking violently, then, as she stood and pressed softly down on his shoulders, he totally broke. "You bitch! You fucking bitch!" He sobbed.

"Let's have it then. What did he do?" It was the first time she'd spoken to him gently and she still had her hands on his shoulders. He couldn't stop. He told her everything. She flinched when he buried his head in her hip, but she didn't move away, and even patted the back of his head a couple of times, and that meant more than anything. Each shudder released a cathartic tidal flow that eroded the years of fear and self-hatred and allowed him, for the first time in his life, to feel safe. She was unassailable. No one could harm him whilst she protected him. He slept ... She peeled his arms from around her thighs, and, with feelings of revulsion, both at him, and at herself, for allowing him to touch her, left, to face the storm alone.

She'd hoped to sail around the storm but it had grown rapidly and had swept across several more minutes of latitude than it was supposed to. As the wind started to chop the water, she donned the harness and wound in the sails. The deck began to heave and the waves were building too fast. She barely had time to set the rigging before the *Ark* started to yaw violently. She fought through the wind and driving spray to aft, quickly prepared a drogue before regaining the wheel as the first breaker caught her broadside, and swept across the deck. Although she was still secured to the rigging by the harness, the *Ark* now heeled dangerously toward the sea on her side, swinging her clear and plunging her in dark, quiet, choking solitude, before whipping her skyward into a thunder of whistling, creaking rigging wires. As the *Ark* heeled the other way, the line stretched to breaking point, nearly cutting her in half. She slammed into the main mast but, despite gashing her head and being heavily winded, she managed to hold firm. Whilst clinging there to regain her breath before the next onslaught, a disturbing thought crept through the back of her mind. "Is Ben okay?"

Her fingers were nearly ripped off in the next yaw but she held fast and took advantage of the momentary pause before the next, to claw and scuttle her way back to the wheel and, finally, to wrestle the bow into the next oncoming wave. As the *Ark* climbed the wall of water she focused her attention and strength and held the bow true to the crest, then, dangerously took a slight angle into the deep trough to avoid the breaking water to starboard. She gauged the wave length and tried to figure out how she could set and deploy the drogue to create optimum drag. If only Ben hadn't gone loony tunes on her ... As though magically summoned, a startled looking Ben appeared behind her in the stairwell, struggling to reach her. She grabbed his hands, pulled him to the wheel, and rolled his fingers around the steering spokes shouting directions into his ear and pointing as they again began to climb the next wave, before hauling her way aft again. She prayed he had the wit and strength to follow her instructions. With the drogue deployed, she got back to the wheel just as it slipped from his grip and started to spin. Together, they managed to regain control in time to outrun the next breaker. They fought on for another three hours and shipped a lot of water before the storm began to subside.

The sun broke through the dark clouds leaving dissipating shreds of vapour, and pouring warmth onto the *Ark* and its two occupants. Eve wasted no time, she put on more sail, gave Ben further instructions and left him at the wheel, whilst she pumped and bailed out the water, and began to get the wet things out on deck to dry. She wanted everything ship shape before they made landfall. Ben helped as best he could to lay them out and secure clothing to the rigging. Eve studied her charts. Although off course, they had covered a lot of water and they were not too far from land. There was a rock with a reef quite near where they could drop anchor, check the boat out and get everything back inside. She adjusted their course and left Ben with the wheel again, then went to clean herself up. Her reflection in the mirror revealed a lump and a nasty looking cut on her forehead but they would soon heal. She relieved Ben at the wheel, told him to clean up and get some rest, and then guided the *Ark* to anchor on the lee of the rock she had located.

Taking snorkel and fins, she dropped over the side and checked the boat below the water line. Nothing too serious, one of the rudder rods would need looking at but, all in all, damage was pretty superficial. She went to her cabin to get some rest, and crashed. When she awoke it was pitch black. "Shit!" She'd left Ben unsecured. She fumbled for the light switch, strode out through the door and tripped over Ben, laid out on the threshold, with a carving knife in his fist. The makeshift bed gave away his intent. "I don't need your protection Ben."

"You was fast asleep miss. I looked at the charts. Dangerous waters these, pirates. I can do breakfast miss, if you're hungry?" He looked at her hopefully. Despite herself, she was touched, but still wondered what his game was and noted, "He reads charts too?" She nodded. He rushed off eagerly. "Breakfast?" How long had she slept? She checked her watch 03:45, fifteen hours. Well, perhaps he just needed someone who could get him somewhere safe, but it looked like she could trust him for now, while they were at sea at least. Nevertheless, she checked on her hidden weaponry and, relocated anything movable, before going to the galley.

She decided he was unlikely to try and poison her, having already passed up his best shot, so she tucked in heartily to a very tasty, cooked breakfast. Ben fussed around her offering her more food, washing up, and, even tried to put a blanket around her shoulders to keep off the night chill.

"What's going on Ben? I'm the bitch who took your manhood. You can't have forgotten."

Ben's shoulders hunched at the sink. He spoke without turning. "You could have killed me. I didn't know what you was then. I wanted to do bad things, make you suffer. Hurt you. But you were good to me. You look after me. Teach me. Show me the way. Maybe you have a purpose for me. If I please you, maybe, I can be more than a man."

What the hell was happening here? And where had all the street talk gone? "Don't worship me Ben. I'm not a prophet."

He tensed and turned his head slightly at that. "I know that miss. Forgive me. Is Miss okay? Can I call you that? I'm sorry. I shouldn't have spoken. I had no right. Was the breakfast okay? I'll get some tea or coffee? Then I have to finish stowing the rest of the gear. What do I call you?" He had started to gabble and was shaking. Eve grabbed his shoulders and turned him to face her. He would not look at her.

"Ben! Stop this! My name is Eve. Hate me. Wish me dead. I don't care, but stop this pathetic idolatry. I cut your balls off! Remember that, be angry!"

His eyes flicked up, momentarily exposing a heaving current of unstable emotions. "Some lessons is harsh miss!" He seized her hand in both of his, kissed it, and ran for the door. Eve turned up her eyes and bit hard on her bottom lip.

"Oh fuck!"

Pirates

Eve declared a holiday. The weather was good. It was an idyllic spot and there were still a few items that needed drying out. Hell, there was even a few feet of sand to lounge on. They could make the mainland in a couple of days, easy sailing, so why not take the opportunity? Ben had made a makeshift barbecue and was gutting the fish she had speared, whilst she dried off in the sun. Eve closed her eyes for a moment and let her thoughts wander. What an accomplished little runt this Ben was. Who would have believed it? She had to admit the possibility that without his help in the storm, she might not have made it. Perhaps she ought to let up on him a bit. She wriggled a little to make herself more comfortable on the sand. The warmth on her face was making her drowsy. Perhaps she could just drift off for a few moments.

The light behind her closed lids darkened and the warmth on her face eased up a little as a gritty toe nudged her in the ribs. "Just so you know Ben, don't touch me again if you want to keep that toe, but, as that fish smells so delicious, I'll let you off this once." She opened her eyes and looked up at his silhouette against the sun then made to rise but a foot stamped down hard on her chest. Before she could react, her eyes focused, revealing the open barrel of an assault rifle three inches from her face. Something was said in, what she thought was, Arabic, followed by a gap toothed smile and a second head joining the first in peering down at her with the usual lustful intent. The second head ducked away and turned exposing a slim back with bowed but muscular shoulders, a loose white shirt hanging raggedly over cut-off jeans. He spoke into a radio and took part in a barking exchange with the person at the other end, to whom he seemed to show great deference. Stiffening, he shouted an order to the man whose foot was pinning Eve's chest. Grumbling an indecipherable obscenity, the man waved forward two others who had been out of Eve's vision above her head. One each grabbed her under the armpits and lifted her to her feet. The one on the right held a vicious curved blade to her throat. She thought about taking them out, but the guy with the gun was still training it at her stomach, but looking lower and grinning.

There was a blur of movement to her right and the grin disappeared, caved in by a sharp rock still held in Ben's bludgeoning fist as he reached for the rifle with his other hand. Eve reacted without thought, heaving the knife wielder a full ten feet into the man with the radio and sending them both sprawling. A bone crunching kick into the other man's groin left him gasping on the floor. Eve leapfrogged the radio holder who was now rising and stamped down hard on the knife wielder's hand, deftly retrieving the knife from his grip and delivering a backhand chop to the rear of his neck. Ben had placed his man on the floor between himself and the radio man; covering them both while Eve frisked all of them, revealing an assortment of weapons. The radio began crackling and an angry voice issued from it. Eve leaned forward and crushed the radio man's windpipe in her fingertips. "You speak English?" She let him go blue then released him. With the support of her grip withdrawn, he sagged gasping to his knees.

Clutching his throat, he nodded and rasped out one word. "Yes."

"Who's on the radio? Where is he? How many crew? And what weapons do they have?" He looked up contemptuously and smiled so she kicked him savagely in the ribs to let him know how unimpressed she was.

Raising himself several inches from the sand, he pointed out to sea. "See for yourself whore!" Shattered rock exploded six feet from her head, preceding a shock wave that knocked her from her feet. Grabbing a spread-eagled Ben from the sand by his armpit she scrabbled up and around the rocks for cover. Another flash issued from one of three boats spread out offshore, exploding a second shower of rock four feet beneath her feet. She threw Ben into cover and dived after him. The lead boat, which looked like a knocked about navel gunboat, nosed closer to the shore whilst the other two headed straight for the *Ark* and the small launch moored alongside it (presumably their erstwhile captor's boat). All was silent so Eve risked a peek. The radio man was back on his feet, rubbing his throat and, with some difficulty, speaking into the radio. He turned and called out. "Hey American woman!"

Shrugging her shoulders at Ben she called back, "English if you don't mind?"

"That is good. English is better. My boss wants to talk."

"Tell him to talk then." Eve was collecting a pile of rocks as she spoke and indicated that Ben should do the same. The gun had been lost in the scrabble to safety.

"He says thank you for the gift of your boat. It is very nice but your husband should not have killed his crewman. He will look over your boat and think about compensation. He says to enjoy your wait and that you may wish to say your goodbyes, for you might be dead soon."

Bemused, Eve shrugged again at Ben and pointed down the opposite side of their rocky refuge toward the sea. Crouching low, they began making their way down to a drop off into the ocean. A hail of bullets sent them scurrying back to their earlier refuge. One of the two boats had not stopped at the *Ark* but had rounded the tiny island so that there was nowhere to run without being a target. As they arrived back at their bolthole, they heard the sound of dogs baying. "Shit! Shit! Shit! These guys are really starting to piss me off." She hefted a rock in each hand, in readiness for the brutes, and observed Ben doing similar. Seconds later they swarmed up the escarpment baying angrily: six dogs of various sizes and breeds, but all with scarred muzzles and blood lust in their eyes. The lead animal was a monster. Ben threw a rock that hit it square on the cheek. It didn't seem to notice.

Eve took careful aim and looked the creature in the eye. The dog looked straight back at her and slowed its pace. For a split second their minds bumped against each other, and then it sprang in an astounding leap over the rocky outcrop. Eve discarded her rock and clapped hands either side of the beast's snarling jowls. Looking deep into its eyes at close range she saw both insanity and pain and began talking softly in a language she had no knowledge of but nevertheless understood, three words only, but the creature instantly calmed, and on its release veered round to look down on the rest of the pack bringing them into obedience with the sheer and savage force of its dominant will. Quietly now, with their heads low, they continued to filter up and around the rocky barrier and turned facing outward in a protective ring around Eve and her companion. Ben smiled and leaned forward to pat the lead dog but quickly withdrew his hand when it gave a menacing growl.

A new voice, now shouted up from the beach. "Hey English man and woman! Are you dead yet? My dogs are very quiet. They must be eating. They are only quiet when they are eating. If either of you are still alive call down. I will call them off."

"No need we get along fine. I think your dogs have found better masters now." There was a long, long pause.

"Why does your husband not speak? Surely he is your master."

Eve weighed that up. The Arab mentality rested easier when a man was in charge. Perhaps she should allow the subterfuge. It might be used to advantage. "My husband only speaks when someone proves they are worthy of being spoken to. I deal with lesser individuals."

"An arrogant man your husband, as are you. You would both do well to show some humility, it might save your lives."

"You don't want humility, you just want well behaved victims. Well you can go and fuck yourselves. If you have nothing to offer, we'll take our chances thanks."

"A lone woman amongst so many brutal men should not be talking about fucking. But I will overlook this. I have a question. Where did your husband get the holy books? The ones on his boat?"

"They're mine and if you damage any you will regret it." There was another long pause. Eve spoke to Ben. "Ben. Listen. I have an idea. I'm gonna talk to this creep for a bit and see if we can come to some arrangement, although a happy outcome is pretty unlikely. If I feel he's going to start firing again, I may do some things that appear odd. Don't try to interfere, just trust me okay. Get ready to cover your ears and, if I run, you run like hell too and follow me. Be ready for anything, understand?" Ben smiled broadly, nodding with enthusiasm. Reaching across to rest her hand on the lead dog's muzzle she spoke several more of the strange words and the dogs slinked silently away, down the rocks, moving stealthily back the way they had come.

"English woman, if your husband will not speak, I will speak to him and you may answer. You have copies of many major religious books. Some are very valuable. If they truly belong to you I might take them in exchange for your lives."

"Why would you do that? You already have them. Why do you care whether or not they belong to us?"

Whilst she was talking, she was scraping earth from the crevices in the rock and dribbling spit onto it. As she compressed the earthy mass into a ball she was remembering back to her rape. Specifically she was remembering when Sadique had cut her nose from her face flicking the gooey mess across the room for one of his followers to catch. An incendiary device had blown his arm off. Except that it wasn't an incendiary device at all it was her severed flesh and bone destroying itself. Also, since then, all her nail pairings and hair trimmings had fizzled away after being cut, shrivelling faster the further away from her body they were. As she pondered all this, she pressed her thumbs into the dirt ball in her hands making a deep impression.

"I do not rob holy books. I would be damned forever, but neither do I pay for stolen ones. If they are truly yours, then perhaps we can deal."

"And how would I prove that?"

"Meet with me, talk to me. I will know."

"Perhaps we will talk, but first you have to understand that it will be on equal terms."

There was laughter, and between the guffaws, he shouted back. "In what possible way can we be on equal terms? I have but to give the signal and you and the rock you hide behind will be blown to bits."

Ben couldn't help but lunge toward her at her next action but he was nowhere near quick enough. Biting down on her small finger, she bit through it and spat the amputated digit into the earthen ball she had prepared, squeezing it in her fist and throwing it in a sweeping arc straight towards the laughing man. It exploded into flames feet above his head raining down fire. As he dived for cover, she was already racing over the rock and heading towards him, screeching a single word in an ear-piercing tone. At this word the dogs attacked, bringing the three accompanying crew, and the radio man, to the ground. The lead dog had a paw on each of her would-be killers' shoulders and was slavering through curling lips a centimetre from his face. Another quiet word kept the dogs from savaging their prey and they resumed their protective ring about her. Ben deprived the pirates of their weapons with great caution.

The pirate leader eased up into a cross-legged position with an admirable lack of fear or concern. "Ah! You had an ace, but it will do you little good. If you kill me and my men, those on the boats will blow this island to kingdom come, a phrase I think we both understand very well. They may do so anyway. I rule them by fear but their loyalty is a small thing, easily overcome if they see I am vulnerable."

"Then stand and show them we are equals in negotiation talks."

He stood up smoothly and went to stand next to her giving a casual wave to his small fleet.

"I see you truly are your master's master and, given the circumstances, I see I must, for now, treat you as though you are my equal. This is a hard thing for an Arab but these are exceptional times, and you are obviously an exceptional woman. Will you and your toy boy?" he looked at Ben with disdain, "join me on my boat so that we can talk in comfort over tea?" She corrected him. "With my husband's permission, yes we will." She looked at Ben for confirmation.

He caught on quick and gave an abrupt nod, "Yes," dropping the weapons at her feet, except for a machete which he let hang at arm's length by his side with the tip lifted slightly toward the pirate he now faced. "When you show respect for my wife, I might think you worthy to speak to. Until then my wife will negotiate for me. The dogs will come with us onto the boat." He walked to the shoreline and waited with his back to the pirate.

The pirate leaned close to Eve's ear and breathed heavy, tobacco laden, words into it. "He is arrogant your young cockerel but I think his balls are in your fist." Eve winced at the unintended accuracy of his words, each one tugging at her former righteous certainty for the neutering of the young thug.

"Try anything and it will be the dogs eating your balls that you will need to worry about."

"I am Captain Amir," as he spoke a launch nosed from behind a rock. Two gaunt but muscular men, with machetes tucked in their belts jumped into the shallows. One held the prow whilst the other indicated that they should board. Snatching a gun from the pile of weapons Eve leapt in followed by the dogs, Ben, and finally, Captain Amir.

The gun boat had a sumptuous single cabin which appeared to be for the sole use of Captain Amir and his guests. With the lead dog at her side and the remainder guarding the door, Ben and Eve sat facing their host across a heavy wooden table piled high with the religious texts of her recent studies. He placed two mint teas before them and pushed a shisha pipe toward Ben. Ben ignored the gesture but took a sip of tea and indicated that Eve should do the same, whilst studiously avoiding eye contact with Amir.

Landfall

Matt watched the CCTV footage again. He pulled a face in an effort to prevent the bile rising in his throat as the bloody lump of flesh and bone that had been gouged from Eve's face sailed across the screen. The hand and arm of the man who caught it was incinerated. Soames loaded another disc. Hospital footage provided by Dr Stewart showed every biopsy taken from Eve disintegrating in a puff of white flame as soon as it was separated from her body. There were other scenes of her, following every significant period of sleep, when she wrought havoc to her bed shortly before waking. These at first looked like seizures but, as Dr Stewart pointed out in his report they also proved to be an effective intensive exercise workout that served to keep her body in a supreme state of strength and fitness, and finally, her miraculous recovery. He looked away from the screen and stared at Soames. Soames raised his hand to still Matt's questions whilst he played the last disc.

"You need to see this next piece Mr Crow. I know how hard it is to believe the impossible but when the evidence is overwhelming

... And believe me it is." He raised both hands in a "palms up" gesture, and lifted his shoulders. "This is the footage of when we removed her ovaries." Matt was still outraged at the calm and self-satisfied cruelty of the man and was contemplating kicking him in the bollocks before he left this room, but he wanted to find out as much as possible before that. The surgeon sliced into her stomach wall, two large incisions, and with cynical precision removed an ovary. With a yell he dropped it into a kidney dish and ran for the sinks. The removed organ burst into incandescent white flame. A nurse grabbed an extinguisher but to no effect. It burnt to nothing leaving a globule of molten metal where the dish had been that quickly hardened on the scorched floor. The surgeon returned with forceps and repeated the exercise, dropping the second ovary into a container of water. It boiled dry in seconds and the organ continued to burn until entirely consumed. Soames switched off the recording and threw back the curtains, letting in a bright blast of sunlight that made Matt blink and raise a hand to cover his eyes.

"So you see Mr Crow, the story our Eve has told you is, perhaps, not so far-fetched. She is a monster who, in normal circumstances, would need to be put down. Please don't balk. I know you have affection for her but, if she is what she claims, and, what I believe her to be, and if she were to have children, it would probably be the end for humanity. I thought I had neutralised her by having her reproductive organs removed but, having seen her amazing recovery rate, I am not so sure she won't just regenerate. We can't even study her DNA because anything removed from her incinerates itself. I just wish we had been able to keep her for longer then, perhaps, we could have studied it in situ."

Matt leaned forward tension stiffening every fibre of his being. "Vivisection? On a human? What kind of an animal are you?" He was quivering with suppressed rage.

"Your phraseology is emotional and seriously flawed Mr Crow. I had expected better of you. It is I that am human, although even an animal would be preferable to the abomination she represents, and I will do anything I can to rid the world of this threat to my kind. She is not even of this world. She is a demon created by the Devil himself. If you value your own humanity and that of those dear to you, then you will assist me in any way you can."

"I'll tell you what is dear to me. She is. And, if her fantastical claims are true, then her mind is human, and she is doubly dear to me, as a friend, in both identities."

"But for how long?" He let that hang for a moment then continued. "In any case this is all moot at the moment. She is our best hope of locating and destroying an even bigger threat, her counterpart Afsoon. For now her goals are the same as ours and she seems to have ways of accessing information we cannot." He spread his hands. "So we can all work together for the present. All I require at this time is for you to help and support her in any way you can. Get close and maintain as much contact as possible. Make her feel her humanity. In some ways this rape is a good thing. It may well prompt a hatred of all sexual contact, especially with men." Matt gritted his teeth and rose to his feet but Soames was oblivious and in full flow. "Given her enormous capacity for physical recovery, however, we cannot rule out the possibility that her emotional resolve is equally strong. So we need a strategy." He poured himself a brandy, ruminated for several seconds, took a swallow and went on. "I think it would be sound policy for you to make yourself her rock. That way if she regains her sexual appetite you might be able to step into the breach and become her lover. In this circumstance I would advise the use of protection.

"Dr Stewart assures me she is not pregnant so we can live in hopes that cross breeding is impossible, but it is more likely that her ovaries have not yet regenerated. Pray God they never will." He drummed his fingers and looked thoughtful then continued. "We cannot know the results of hybrid activity but references to human inter species experimentation in Genesis," he sat down at the dining table, opened, and perused, an ancient copy of Jewish scriptures then went on, "would indicate that we would be wise to be cautious. Keep me in the loop regarding any developments." He raised his eyes and looked at Matt over his spectacles. "Anything she wants, let me know. It will be provided. You will realise of course that the biggest threat of all is if she feels so disaffected from humanity that she turns to the only other of her kind in the universe. Don't let that happen! She must be destroyed at the first sign of any union between them."

At this moment Matt wanted to kill him. Soames stood, confronted and held Matt's piercing stare, and offered his hand. "It is essential that we work together Mr Crow, if for no other reason than that we are fellow humans."

Matt looked at the hand and then at his crotch, the urge was almost overwhelming but it would not, in any way, be helpful either to Eve or in sorting out this sorry mess. With an immense effort of will he crushed his anger under a facade of stony indifference, far better to work together whilst everyone wanted the same thing. They shook hands. Matt declined the offer of a drink and left. As he put his key in the lock of the car, his thoughts churned in a desperate bid to make sense of all he had seen and heard.

Eve had refused the offer of the return of her boat in exchange for the books, instead offering to add her boat, with her husband as captain, to his fleet. She would give him the books if he would, in return, assist her to locate and retrieve the original scrolls and manuscripts from which the books were copied, texts she believed were hidden on the African continent and, the locations of which, were hinted at within the pile of books now burgeoning his table. At first he had called her mad and laughed at her, but he proved to be a very learned man and when she coached him through the encrypted messages, hidden within the scriptures, his interest was aroused. In the few days of their acquaintance her Arabic had improved at an astounding rate and Amir now seemed quite content to converse with her as an equal, even deferring to her in the matter of her knowledge of the meanings contained in the earliest writings. They bargained and eventually agreed that she and her husband could keep their boat and sail as part of his fleet and that she would decipher the locations of the writings she sought. For his part, he would use his resources to help her. She would be allowed to study the writings but then they would come into his ownership.

There was a commotion outside and Amir rose from the table to investigate. Eve followed. On deck Ben was tied over the gunwale with his shorts around his ankles and a machete at the back of his neck. A queue of several leering pirates was forming. The first dropped his own shorts and, presenting his erection, waddled towards the gunwale. Listening to the cheers and jeering comments, Amir threw up his hands in exasperation. "Ah this explains everything. As if I did not have enough problems you bring a eunuch into our midst. You have some explaining to do English woman." Eve was already vaulting over the back of the nearest pirate and landed smoothly behind the man with the machete. In one movement she twisted his wrist over, took the machete and heaved him over the side. Her hands a blur she grabbed the would-be rapist's erection and lifted him bodily off the floor delivering four quick punches to nerve centres in his arms and legs so that he could not grapple the arm that was now holding him at full extension in front of the remaining mob.

The edge of her machete was tight under his balls. Shouting a stream of curses in fluent Arabic, she then addressed them. "If any one of you tries to harm my friend again I promise you, you will have more parts missing than he has." That said she sliced the blade across the man's ball sack, enough to draw blood, and dropped him to the floor with a thud. He tried to scuttle away holding his crotch but with dead arms and legs it was more like a disjointed slither. She held the machete before her and gave them the come on sign with her other hand. "Let's have you then. Who else wants to try?" Someone raised a gun, she looked him in the eyes and he covered them with a shaking hand. Amir knocked the gun from his other hand. "You all right Ben?"

Ben had freed himself and pulled up his shorts and was smiling. "You bet." He started shouting at the pirates in broken Arabic. "You hear that? She called me friend. I am chosen. There is nothing you can do to my body that will harm me. I have a greater calling, and if you make an enemy of me you will have her to answer to. Believe me, you do not want that, unless you are ready for eternal damnation. She is going to bring a new order to this world and if you are not on her side then there will be no God who can help you." They were all averting their eyes now and some had prostrated themselves on the floor or were gabbling and making signs to protect themselves.

Eve was stunned to silence and, turning to Ben, dropped the machete to her side. "What the fuck are you talking about, Ben?" She found herself looking straight out to sea because Ben was on his knees, grabbing her leg and resting his forehead on her foot. She looked back and saw that all the pirates, except Amir, were also now on their knees with their foreheads touching the floor. Her acute hearing heard mutterings about her virtually regrown finger and comments about the pendant now hanging visibly outside her blouse. Roughly shaking Ben away from her foot, she stormed off back to the cabin. In her exasperation all she could think of to say was, "Men!"

Amir came into the cabin looking shell shocked. He sat down opposite her with a tired groan. "It seems you are more than just my equal." He made a sign. "What are you?"

"Just a person. A person who needs your help."

"No! I cannot help you. Take your books and go! And take that mutilated monstrosity of a boy with you. Take anything you need and leave us be. Curse the day you brought your vessel into these waters. I should have known what you were when you took control of my dogs." Amir could not be pacified but when Ben arrived and started talking about curses, Amir gave them co-ordinates of safe landing places where the boat could be hidden and the names and details of several contacts who might be able to help them in their search. He advised that Ben should do the talking and that she acquire and wear a Burka. He agreed to escort them close to the landing he had recommended: as long as they took the dogs, stayed on their own boat and made no attempt to come aboard any of his fleet, or speak to, or make sign to, any of his men. Eve was mad as hell at Ben but she had to concede that in so far as it went, it was a stroke of genius. Amir was always going to break his word and the crew were likely to kill them in their sleep. This way all her property was returned and they had a safe landing site and good contacts to help them on their way. Also, Amir had related a desolate reed area, where a boat could easily be lost from view. With her boat safely hidden, their escape route was also secured.

"Just to be sure Ben, this is all a scam isn't it? You don't actually believe any of that crap?"

Ben cried out, "Look there's the mouth of the river. The tributary that leads to the landing site must be around that bend." He pointed into the wide estuary. "Guess we're on our own again." Nodding out to sea he indicated the departing fleet. Eve set about trimming the sails.

She spoke to Ben as they worked. "Ben how is it you are so knowledgeable about boats and navigation and religion?" She added with a smile, "You cook great too."

He said nothing for a while but then he spoke with lucid resignation. "It was my uncle. He was a strict Catholic. When I was very young, he used to take me out on his boat at weekends. He said it was for religious contemplation and enlightenment. I learned a lot about all those things you said. I had to." He struggled for a moment unable to continue. Then he went on haltingly, "He never missed an opportunity to punish me if I got anything wrong, but I was only putting off the inevitable. He liked to hurt any living thing. It didn't matter how hard I tried, he always found something I didn't do quite right. And there is no one to help when you are out at sea, on a boat, and it's dark. That was when I learned to hate God." He said nothing more and Eve didn't press him but she noted that there was no longer any pretence of street language. She mused for a while on how frightening it must have been for him when she dragged him off on a boat again into the middle of the ocean and mistreated him so badly, but he deserved it didn't he? She got on with preparing the boat for a landing.

They inched their way up the tributary. Eve checked the sonar but Ben dangled a weight over the side to check the depth to be sure. Eve had lowered the mast. It was getting dark and the chug of the small engine carried. She reduced it to tick over, just enough revs to keep a straight line in the mild ingoing current. They passed a village set back on a small stream that fed the tributary and ahead, just as Amir had said, were the tall reed beds. They navigated their way into them until they were out of sight from either land or from the main tributary and were just a few feet clear of the bottom. Ben threw out the anchor. The boat would be grounded when the tide dropped. They locked everything down tight and covered the boat with tarpaulins. Eve brought the dogs out and looked into the lead dog's eyes. There was no need for any words. The dog barked once and the small pack leapt from the boat and swam through the reeds to the shore.

"Goodbye boy," she whispered, "I hope we meet again, when I get back."

Ben and Eve headed back to the village in Eve's little inflatable, with two heavy rucksacks supplied by Amir and packed with essentials. Having land-marked their route, they deflated and hid the dinghy and headed into the village. They passed a hut and were regarded with suspicion by a couple of fishermen who just stared at them over their nets. Eve approached them speaking in Arabic and asked which house belonged to Hakeem. They refused to answer Eve and would not look at her. One spat in the water but they indicated the house to Ben by pointing.

Hakeem was a tall scrawny man in a white turban with sun darkened skin and a deeply lined face that made him look ancient. He moved, however, with a fluid ease that suggested he was much younger. He took Amir's letter of introduction from Ben, addressed a couple of staccato questions as to the whereabouts of the pirate now and "did he send anything? Did they have it with them?" Receiving negative responses, he ushered them inside. Eve was pointed to a spot on the bare earth floor amid several sweating and smelly women who were preparing food around a central fire whilst Ben was taken into the hut's only other room. An older woman poked Eve with a ladle and indicated that she should stir the pot. Irritated Eve, nevertheless, complied. Other than that, she was ignored by the women. She could hear Ben and Hakeem talking in low tones in the other room but could only catch odd words of what they were saying. It appeared that Amir owed this man a debt of some kind and that he was reluctant to help until it was paid.

Ben and Hakeem came back into the room and Ben indicated that she should join them. She handed the ladle back but was still being ignored so she dropped it in the pot. With what she hoped was appropriate humility, she entered a Spartan room lit by a spitting oil lamp that threw sinister shadows across the walls. Ben explained that although he had been able to make himself generally understood, she was required to translate, so they could come to a fully coherent agreement. Hakeem was prepared to help but only if Amir's debt was first paid off in full.

"What sort of money are we talking about Ben? We need to keep what we can so we can get by in this God forsaken place."

"If I understand him right, £2,000 Sterling plus another £1,000 for one night's accommodation and protection, £200 for his wife's best burka that you will need to wear if you want to move around publicly in these parts, another £100 for use of his transport and £400 to escort us to the places you deciphered from your holy books." He raised his hands to prevent an outburst, "Before you go off on one, that's just the starting point, you know how these fuckers like to barter. That's why you're here, so we can argue about the final price. We'll get him down to half that easy. That amount of money around here will make him a rich man."

Hakeem came back into the room with a shisha pipe from which he took a long draw and offered it to Ben. Ben did likewise and the haggling began. Hakeem never looked at Eve but kept his eyes on, and spoke only to, Ben. Although she was the medium of their communication, Eve was totally ignored by both of them ...

She was seething. "£2,300! You cretin, half you said. And why the hell did you agree that I had to wear this filthy burka right away. What were you thinking of?"

"Hey that was the clincher. You heard him, you were offending his sight, his wives and his home."

"Have you seen his wives? And how could anything offend this hovel?" She had an intense urge to stamp her foot.

"Look we did really well. We got him down to half price for his services and £500 off Amir's debt." Ben showed his palms in a placating gesture and tried to suppress a smile. "I think that's pretty good."

"Amir's debt?" She was struggling to get her words out. "Amir's debt? If it was 50 quid I'd be surprised."

He hid his face so she couldn't see him laugh but she did see him. "God you're all alike. You make me sick!" Realising what she had said, she turned on her heel and strode back into the hut slamming the door. Once he got control of himself he followed, to find her burka-clad sitting cross-legged, back on the floor, stirring the pot, and looking at him with menace through the steam.

The transport proved to be a donkey each for Hakeem and Ben. Eve walked carrying both the rucksacks and made promises under her breath that Hakeem would never return from this journey, and that Ben was going to pay for every foot of ground she covered. Thankfully the donkeys were only for the first five miles. From there they boarded a dhow. Eve sat on the small prow bench, in direct sunlight with their luggage whilst Ben sipped mint tea under an awning in the stern, with Hakeem and the boat's owner. Nevertheless, it was an improvement and her mood began to settle and, to be fair, Ben looked very uncomfortable with the situation, but let the bastard suffer. He eventually made his way to the prow with a sunshade he had persuaded the boat owner to part with. Also, it seemed, he had finally decided on a form of respectful address that he felt Eve would allow.

"Lady Eve." She rolled her eyes. "Please forgive me the disrespect I have shown. I have had to act the part. We stand out like beacons as it is and they seem angered by any show of deference to women but they will understand soon enough, when they learn what you really are. Then they will regret their failure to treat you with proper humility and esteem. All will crawl on their knees before you."

She wanted to pull him up on that and find out what he meant but she had a more pressing problem. "Never mind that, I'm dying for a piss. It's all right for you and your new buddies down there, you can just dangle it over the side but I'll burst before I let those creeps see me hanging my arse out over the water." With some venom she continued, "and if I end up wetting myself, they're all dead men. I can't get the smell of piss, from its previous owner, out of this burka as it is." Ben managed to arrange a stop and Eve took off into the long riverbank grass with some haste, to the great amusement of the men. Ben ensured Eve was given food and drink and had made a cushion out of reeds and dry grass for her to sit on when she returned. As darkness fell they came in sight of a town.

Ben had to pay the boatman when they alighted. Hakeem found them accommodation in a large house which Ben again had to pay for, as well as for Hakeem. Eve kept herself amused by keeping a tally and plotting ever more elaborate forms of vengeance on this grasping rattle snake of a man, should the opportunity arise. It did that night.

Since being caught off guard by Ben on the boat, and again, by the pirate on the beach, Eve had been paying a lot of attention to her sixth sense and found it to be a very reliable tool for anticipating, and alerting her to, danger. She lay still and kept her breathing steady as the door was quietly opened. Ben was outside somewhere defecating and vomiting up the stew from the night before. "Serves the little bastard right," a shadowy figure entered. Despite the darkness being almost pitch, Eve could see perfectly clearly that it was Hakeem. He rifled through their rucksacks and found some of the money. He took far too long looking for more. Eve waited to see what he would do next, noting that he had a nasty looking curved blade in his hand. He leaned over her and stealthily cut the pendant from her neck but exposed her breast doing so. She continued to wait knowing she would have no trouble retrieving it. He lingered looking at her. Then the knife went to her throat, a hand covered her mouth, and he tried to get astride her. He never made it. Her left had crushed the bones in the wrist of the hand holding the knife. The grating could be easily heard through the cry, stifled by her right hand crushing his windpipe. Suddenly Ben was there, naked from the waist down, one hand bunching the tails of his borrowed shirt over what was left of his genitalia, the other swinging a pot at Hakeem's head. Hakeem was beaten into unconsciousness.

"Oh for Christ's sake, Ben do you have to rob me of every pleasure." She suddenly gagged and pinched her nose whilst covering her mouth. "My God! What's that smell? What the hell did you hit him with? That's not the pot you were …? Ben nodded, covered his mouth and ran out to be sick again. By the time Eve had cleaned up, the first fingers of daylight were prodding at the sky. She left Hakeem until last, just so he could wake up to the smell of what he was covered in. He sat in the corner looking at the ground. Eve let him be, whilst she continued washing out her clothes, hoping he would try to attack her again or make a break for it, or even cry out for help. He did none of those things. Nor did he try to wipe the mire from his face and hair. He just sat looking at the floor. Knowing he would despise himself for any urges, Eve deliberately went about her work in just her shorts and a bra and hoped it was shame that kept him subdued.

A very pale faced but more human looking Ben came back in the room. "You mustn't do this Lady Eve."

Eve sighed. She'd given up trying to stop his adulation "You are above this filth. Leave the rest to me. I'll see to him. Do you want him killed or beaten? We could leave him in a ditch. No one would know or care."

"You are in no state to do anything and he doesn't need beating. I actually think he is sorry for what he has done but I haven't finished with him yet." She threw the dirty water over him and went to the well to get more, then gave it to him and told him to clean himself up. When he failed to obey, she smacked his crushed hand. He doubled in pain but did not otherwise respond or co-operate. She saw he was likely to allow himself to be beaten to death before he would give in, so sighing again, she sat cross-legged before him and began to clean him up, knowing this was probably a worse punishment. He tried to resist but she would have been too powerful for him if his wrist hadn't been broken so, eventually, he accepted her ministrations.

She bandaged his wrist and put it in a sling, then gave him a stinging slap across the face and spoke harshly close into his ear. "Listen to me, you sad creature. If you ever thought you were a man, then you proved last night that any shred of manhood or decency you may once have had has long since died inside you. Now, I have to decide what to do with you." She held the pendant before him. "You were looking for this last night weren't you? This is what you were really after isn't it? Why?" She slapped his face again. He just let his head loll.

Ben laid light fingers on her wrist. "Let me have a go. I have," he hesitated looking for the right word, "a rapport with him. I think I may be able to get him to talk."

Eve gave another groaning sigh, put her hands on her hips, arched her back and stood. "Yeah, I s'pose. I need a breath of air anyway. You do what you can. Reluctantly grabbing the burka, she shuffled it over her head and went out barefoot into the low sun and gritty sand.

When she came back Ben had finished packing and he and Hakeem stood ready with the packs on their backs. Hakeem averted his gaze and turned away.

She looked him up and down. "Did you get anything out of him?"

"Your pendant carries the same sign as that over the door of the temple we are going to, except that the temple shows only one stem broken where on your pendant all are shattered. He thought it might be valuable or have magical power. He says he was going to take it to the priests."

"How did you get him to talk?"

"I told him you were a powerful demon and that the sign of your pendant and the souls of all those who touched it were yours. Then I told him what you do to anyone who displeases you and showed him my deformities. He fears you now and what you will do to both his physical self and his eternal soul, as all will eventually."

"Why is he limping?"

"Oh, I bled him a little, cut his femoral, close to his balls. No oath to serve would be binding without some blood and pain, and a little fear and ritual helps too. I don't think he will disobey you anymore. We may have to dress that wound again though. It bled a lot." He cuffed Hakeem and indicated he should show Eve the wound. Cringing away, Hakeem reluctantly drew up his robe to show the failing dressing.

"You idiot, what good is he to us if he can't walk?"

"If a man is scared enough, he'll walk, and I know where we're going. I've got his map so he either keeps up, or he dies and we'll leave him on the road. He should have been killed just for touching you. He must, at least, learn some pain and suffering for his sacrilege."

Eve had had enough of this. She pulled him off a small distance and confronted him. "Ben we need to talk. Just what is it you think I am?"

"You will tell me when you are ready my lady."

"No Ben, I will not. You will tell me. I've told you I am not a prophet."

"I know that my lady."

"So tell me what you think you know."

Ben shifted awkwardly, "You talk in your sleep Lady Eve. You talk to him and you writhe and you fight invisible creatures."

Eve grabbed him by the shoulders and made him look at her. She was worried now. "What do you mean? Who do I talk to? Is it God? Who am I? Tell me now!"

He dropped to his knees and grasped the hem of her skirt bringing it to his lips. "Why do you test me like this my lady? I am a good and faithful servant."

"Tell me!"

He threw his head back and looked up at her adoringly. "You are the antichrist my lady."

Eve released him and staggered back as though struck. "Wh-What did you call me? Are you insane? I am not evil."

Ben prostrated himself in the dirt and sand, and started an unholy rant. "No my lady, you will banish all evil and weakness. You will undo all that has passed before. These paedophile priests and 'worship me' whore sons will all bow before your wrath. The world will know your new order. Not a craven 'turn the other cheek' religion that promises salvation only to the cringing meek, who bow in spineless supplication to false political gods. Your reign will rise in all its terrible power. You will destroy any who stand before you and show us how we ought to live, mould us into the creatures we should have been, masters of our world, and our fates. You will roll out the celestial carpet of destiny before us."

Eve slapped him. "Stop! Enough! Speak of this no more."

Ben scampered forward and, before Eve realised what he was doing, placed her foot onto his head. "I will die at your word my lady. But utter your command and I will cut out my own heart. It is enough that I have served you."

Eve wanted to stamp down on his head. His idolatry was suffocating her. Hakeem maintained a discreet distance and pretended to be indifferent but Eve was not fooled. "Get up! Never grovel like that again, and don't speak of this again either." She turned and stomped off in the direction she assumed they must be going. "Shit! Shit! Shit! Shit!" she said.

Nothing more for over an hour. Ben walked stolidly beside her, giving Hakeem a shove every now and then if he slowed his pace.

Finally Eve spoke again. "Who is 'he' Ben? The person you said I spoke to in my dreams?"

"Why do you continue to test me Lady Eve? He has many names. Satan, Beelzebub. In your sleep you call him Afsoon."

Although Eve had been half expecting this, it still shocked her to immobility. She put a hand on Ben's shoulder. "And have you ever dreamt of this Afsoon, Ben?"

"No my lady."

"You must tell me immediately if you do. Do you understand?"

"Yes Lady Eve." Ben seemed to be walking with a lighter step and to have grown in stature.

The Black Priests

Once clear of the village Eve discarded the burka and reverted to shorts, thankful to be rid of the stinking garment and to not have to look at the world through a slit. She saw Hakeem retrieve it and slip it into his rucksack. She wasn't sure if his wives would be pleased to have it returned. They spent the early evening in the lea of a rocky outcrop. Hakeem got a fire going and made some tea but his limp was worse. Eve told him to show her the wound so she could put on a clean dressing but he became so fearful that in the end Ben dressed it for him at some distance from the encampment. He was not gentle and when they returned Hakeem took his blanket and sulked on the other side of the fire. As dusk settled they set off again.

After a couple of hours, Hakeem approached Eve and offered up the burka. He was so deferential that she almost felt sorry for him. He had adopted Ben's mode of address and phrased the words awkwardly. "You must wear this Lady Eve. We will shortly seek shelter at a Bedouin encampment where I will help you to barter for camels for the next part of your journey. It is not safe for you to let them see you like this. I will try to arrange a guide for you there. It will be expensive because they will not want to take you to that place but, if you meet their price, someone will take you."

"You sound like you're leaving us Hakeem. Do you think you can make the return journey on your own with your leg the way it is? No! I don't think so either. We will need your knowledge of these people and this country. I think we will all be safer if you stay with us." She deliberately toyed with her pendant as she spoke. He would not look directly at it, or at her.

"As you wish my lady." He bowed and started to back away leaving the burka on the ground before her.

"Your English has improved remarkably since yesterday Hakeem. A word of warning, do not try to deceive me again."

Ben put away his knife. Reluctantly, Eve put the burka back on. She gave Ben a small bag of sovereigns she had kept for just such a purpose and followed him and Hakeem into the encampment. The Bedouin were acquainted with Hakeem and allowed Eve to sit with the women, a little removed from the men, whilst they got down to the serious business of bargaining. Some of the women were young and curious. Eve found their dialect a little difficult to begin with but soon picked it up. They told her how handsome her young husband was and wanted to know if he treated her well. They giggled a lot and showed her some beaded jewellery and colourful blankets. She gave polite responses, but some of the older women ushered them away and tried to bully her into buying their wares. When she refused they became aggressive and took the bowl she was eating from and her drink before she had finished. Then they left her to sit alone. When she thought none of the men were looking, one of the older women threw a rock at her.

Eve stood up fast and smooth, catching the rock as she did so, and walked over to the woman. Snatching her wrist before she had a chance to move, she forced the rock into her hand and crushed her fingers around it. "Yours I think." A look of insane rage entered the woman's black eyes and she tried to pull away and claw at Eve's eyes. With a whiplash flick Eve pinched a curving fingernail and peeled it from her forefinger. Her eyes widened in fear and pain. Eve released her and she hurried off, whimpering, with her head bowed and making signs to ward against evil with her damaged hands. The others followed, trying to console her and sat away from Eve, outside the awning muttering and casting fearful glances in Eve's direction. This suited Eve fine.

Hakeem and Ben approached with a small but well-built man who lacked the lined face and weathered look of the rest of his tribe. Ben spoke. "We have struck a deal Lady Eve. This is Fadil. He has agreed to be our guide. He is eager to make a start so that we can make some ground before the heat of the day. He also says his Sheikh has observed you, and that his wives are not happy to have you in their midst. He says it is not good to have disharmony. Fadil has advised that you should remember that whilst you are in his tent, you are under his protection and his law. He feels it would be wise for us to leave here immediately, to put some distance between ourselves and the diminishing hospitality of this encampment."

A lot of the men were on their feet now looking at Eve and talking in low angry tones. With Fadil's help, Eve and her companions quickly loaded the camels and made to leave. Several of the men got between Eve and her camel. Fadil tried to remonstrate with them but they were being difficult. One mentioned the evil eye and leaned forward to tug at her sleeve. Eve instinctively knew it was a flash point moment and seized the opportunity to grab his elbow and yank his shoulder down, low enough for her to use it as a stepping stone to leap onto the back of her camel which rose immediately, putting her out of reach. Fadil was quick to assess the situation and swiftly mounted his own, getting them out and away while the men were still trying to figure out what had just happened.

Once clear, he seemed greatly amused by events and brought his camel alongside that of Eve. "It is a beautiful night my lady."

Eve rolled her eyes. "God not another one, what makes you think I am a lady?"

He paused and reined his camel around to look directly at her for a moment. A strong wind was blowing up moulding the shapeless burka around the contours of her body. His eyes seemed to linger in every crevice. "No not a lady." His voice gained an intimate intensity. "Only a faerie princess could waft into the desert on such a night as this and arouse the envy and enmity of all the wives of our most worthy Sheikh, then go on to best his men too. It is good that you are covered so, for even in that garment, it is obvious that you are a wondrous beauty and such eyes … eyes that outshine the moon herself."

Eve kicked her camel on. "Fadil, you're full of shit." Another couple of miles and she discarded the burka once more into the sand. Hakeem doubled back to retrieve it.

Fadil covered his eyes. "How could I have been so mistaken my princess. In comparing you to the pale opacity of the moon I did you a grave injustice. So bright is your unfettered beauty that even the sun pales beside it. What need have you to wear clothing at all, for men must avert their eyes or be blinded by such dazzling perfection?"

Despite herself, Eve blushed deeply and wished she had not been so hasty in discarding the garment she so hated. Perhaps there was something to be said for covering up. She hoped Fadil had not noticed her reaction. "Full of it!" she said and urged her mount on having realised that all animals responded well to her.

Fadil chuckled pleasantly. It was refreshing to be teased in this way rather than worshiped or feared, even if it was all shit. She slowed the camel again. She was so used to switching languages now she hadn't realised he had spoken in English. She matched the pace of her camel to his. "How is it you speak such excellent English Fadil?"

He gave a sardonic smile. "Five years living in Bayswater helped a little, princess but I would urge haste now, we are followed."

Eve cast a glance back. She had been feeling a niggling pressure at the nape of her neck and knew exactly where to look, five in view (although a hawk would have had trouble seeing them) probably those who had tried to bar her path earlier. She sensed others.

"You must have very good eyesight."

"No, but I know these people. They will try to kill you."

"So why are you helping us? They are your people aren't they?"

"Not mine princess. They destroyed my tribe fifteen years ago." He said no more but picked up the pace and urged them on. Eve was left confounded. Not knowing if he was playing with them or leading them into a trap. She took the machete from her rucksack and slid it into her belt. Then she slid her hand into a side pocket and checked the small hand gun and bullets left by Isaac for her in the deposit box. It all seemed so long ago now. Urging her mount forward, she again matched stride with Fadil as he goaded his mount on. He pointed to an escarpment. "There are rocks ahead. If we can make them before daybreak we have a chance. There is a thin fissure that leads up."

"Yes I see it."

"I think your eyes play tricks, princess. It is too far to see, but if we can get there first, it is a place easily protected and one where we can slow their progress with rock falls. Once we are beyond it there will be perils for them, as well as for us, for we will be near to our destination and their greater numbers will work against them."

The escarpment was just ahead now but the wind was getting stronger, picking up gritty sand that got in the eyes and chafed at every area of exposed skin. Once again Eve wondered if she had been hasty in discarding the burka but she was not going to ask for it back from Hakeem. Their pursuers were not far behind now and Eve estimated that they would soon be in shooting range. She drew alongside Ben. Leaning in close, she shouted into his ear. "When we reach the fissure I want you all to get yourselves to the top. I am going to wait behind the first cover down slope and give them something to think about." She was indulging her habit of sliding finger and thumb up and down her nose. Ben had realised by now that this meant impending violence and was starting to feel sorry for their pursuers. He nodded and went to tell the others. Fadil looked back at Eve, shook his head in bewildered amazement, then looked at Ben with disgust, but he did not argue.

When they reached the fissure, a couple of spent shots rattled harmlessly against the rocks as their assailants urged their camels into a loping gait. Eve slid behind a boulder a short way upslope and waited while the others walked their camels around a twisting route toward the top of the overhanging cliff face. A group of five had separated from the remaining twelve tribesmen and the gap between them was opening as they drew closer. The lead man must have seen her as she clambered behind the rock and deployed the group left and right of the fissure to take advantage of the cliff cover as they approached. Eve didn't want to wait for the other group to catch up. She reckoned five were more than enough to handle, so as soon as they lost their line of sight behind cliff cover she was out and down the slope at a speed that even she did not know she possessed.

When the first tribesman put his head around the cliff she decapitated him with one swift blow, the arc of her arm continuing round to release the steel blade like a missile into the breastbone of the lead man on the other side of the fissure. Whilst the others were scrambling round their fallen comrades to bring their rifles to bear on Eve, she had time to see that one of the following group was shouldering a missile launcher. The long pent up frustration and anger that had set Eve on this reckless course of action had found some relief in the killings, but they now gave way to the analytical and steely cold logic that was more natural to her. She knew now just how fast she was and reacted decisively. Back flipping away from the opening she bounded up the winding fissure. Pulling the loaded handgun from her pocket she aimed shots back down slope at those positioning themselves to fire. To her surprise there were several small explosions that sent rocks skittering down the incline. Looking up to the sky she uttered a quick prayer. "Exploding bullets? God bless you Isaac." As she uttered the last syllable the ground beneath her feet exploded and a concussion wave lifted her bodily skyward, throwing her twenty feet up the small canyon. As darkness ripped through her mind she thought that, finally, it had all come to an end, and knew nothing of what followed.

Ben, and the others looking down, saw the explosion from the missile. Had she been slower it would have hit above her and buried her in rock. As it was she should have been blown to bits. Instead, she was thrown whole, out and up, with all the other debris, landing running, on all fours like a cat, on the high side of the rock. She leapt the last twelve feet to land in the frantically supporting arms of Ben and Fadil. It had all been reflexive. She was unconscious and blood was oozing from ears, eyes, nose and mouth.

At some level she knew she hadn't died and in a dark corner of her thoughts she was sad for it. Disjointed images sloshed around in her head for a while but a seeping cloud of dark fear was beginning to infiltrate her thoughts. She tried to ignore it and sought retreat in the oblivion that had so recently swept away all the worry and care inherent to her resurrected life.

A whisper grew out of the disturbing fug. "You can't escape me Eve. I have been with you since you connived to launch my body around the sun, and I am getting stronger. I will make every minute of your life apart from me a misery. All those you hold dear will suffer and die. In your isolation you will long for my return. We will have so many little godlings, you and I. You will forget what it is like not to be pregnant. And what exquisite pleasure I shall have breaking down your will and resistance. It may take all of eternity after all. So what are a few years of imposed rest and restraint against all that? I shall spend the time planning and savouring the perversion of your unwilling flesh and cringing soul. Our children will be all the more formidable for being born of such anguish and you, and they, and all of creation, will bend to my will.

A sharp voice drowned out the vile whispering. "She's fitting again. What did you think you were doing letting her confront them like that, your own wife? What kind of a man are you?"

Ben chuckled and his voice was calm. "You know nothing Arab man. Haven't you figured out yet what she is? She was never in any danger, and do you really think she would take me as husband? I am blessed to be her first follower but soon the world will see and understand, and all will flock to rejoice in her glorious presence. This 'fitting' is no more than her spiritual fight and proves that she will recover to claim her empire."

Fadil's voice receded as he moved away. "You are insane Ben."

Eve soon came to full consciousness but remained weak and needed Ben's assistance to regain her feet. Noting the bandages on Hakeem's hands she enquired, "What happened to Hakeem?"

"He took the cloths we used to wipe away the blood and disposed of them. Fadil and I only got slight burns but the further your blood got from your body the more fiercely it burned. Hakeem had to drop the rags very quickly and suffered more serious injuries but he will be alright in a couple of days."

"And his leg?"

"Healing slowly."

"Tell me about our new companions."

"Oh yeah, those two, sinister looking buggers aren't they? They were waiting at the top of the escarpment for us, bristling with armaments. There were originally eight of them and we thought they were going to kill us but they just looked at what was going on and stayed out of it saying nothing. They still haven't said anything. Six stayed at the fissure and these two tagged along. Once you got to us, they just went to the edge of the canyon and stared down. There was a bit of pointing and arguing among the tribesmen at the bottom for a few minutes then they all packed up and went. Fadil says these are the black priests of the shrine we are seeking and that we should follow them, so we have been for the last day or so. They stay within sight and, every so often, one will come close and look at you before returning to the opposite flank to that of his partner. It's like they were herding sheep. I asked Fadil how close this shrine is but he said he doesn't know. Apparently few have ever got close enough to actually see it. The priests allow some travellers to pass this way and will trade with others, but they do not normally allow visitors to their temple, unless they are initiates of 'the congruent path' whatever that is."

Fadil approached and offered Eve some water. Suddenly realising she was thirsty; she gulped down half of it and slung the container around her own neck.

Fadil spoke, "I knew you were something special. They think so too." He nodded left and right at the distant priests, "but what I have seen," he looked at his reddened hands, "and felt, has made me doubt my own sanity. Ben seems to think you are some kind of anti-messiah. What do you say?"

"I say Ben has an overactive imagination and you should try to be more rational. Do I look to be such an awesome creature?"

Fadil looked grave for long moments then shook his head. "Yes I am afraid you do." He turned and walked toward the camels with a look of deep concentration distorting his handsome features.

Ben and Fadil had strapped her inelegantly to the back of the camel whilst she was unconscious, stopping for regular rest breaks to monitor her condition and change her bandages. She disposed of these now and rode unaided, trying to ignore the pounding headache that exploded every time the camel's gait shifted from one side to the other. Several hours later it began to subside and she was high on endorphins and a gaggle of other healing agents produced by her complex genetic makeup. Fadil pulled alongside her and Ben.

He was about to speak but Eve pre-empted him. "You're going to tell us we're almost there aren't you?" Her mind was in overdrive from the chemical mix racing around her immune system and she was almost gabbling. "Pretty obvious really, being as our escort have now moved in close and are speaking to each other for the first time on our journey. Also, our pace has slowed, and there is an opening into some kind of valley up ahead. Yes Fadil, I know you can't see it yet but my eyesight is far superior to yours, or anyone else's on this God forsaken planet, and I can tell you it's approximately four miles ahead or, if you want precision, four miles and sixty yards. Would you like it in metres? Am I intimidating you Fadil? I thought you were different from the rest of the men in this hell hole. I hadn't realised you were as afraid of a strong and confident woman as the rest of your pitiful race. Well, you had better get over it. I don't like my men trying to dominate me." What the hell was she saying? She had meant to say just "men" without the sexually loaded "my" inference. Had he heard that? Of course he had. She tried to correct herself. "No man will ever dominate me. Ask Ben what happened to the last man who tried." She reined in, chiding herself. "Shut up Eve, you fucking moron, your bloody hormones have gone flaky again."

Fadil relaxed noticeably and gave a broad smile. "That's twice now I have made you blush princess. At the risk of making you do so a third time I will let you into a secret. I find dominant women sexually attractive, intoxicating and exciting."

Containing a sudden rage, Eve said nothing and urged her camel forward so that her back was to him. The guy was getting to be a pain in the arse. The sooner she got what she wanted and got rid of him the better. This set her thinking. What was it exactly that she had come for? She had been so busy on her quest that she hadn't really given it much thought in recent weeks. Information certainly, but in what form, more manuscripts and scriptures probably, but what about the priests, would they know anything? And what about the symbol around her neck? Hakeem had said that it was the same as over the entrance to the temple. That was something else. Fadil had told Ben that no one except initiates ever saw the temple. Did that mean Hakeem was an initiate? That didn't make sense. He had tried to steal from her and to rape her, yet the priests were, presumably, helping her, or were they taking her prisoner? And Fadil, what was his part in all this? As she thought this through she started to recall her dream about Afsoon. Previous experience suggested that Ben was now probably in danger. She had been trying to ignore it but now saw that he had become important to her, and that, she had come to understand, usually meant death. She would have to find some way to protect him very soon.

The priests were dismounting, and indicating that they should do the same. Urging her camel to the edge of the drop off, she looked down into a valley, rocky and barren on the far side but lushly cultivated on this. Perched above this cultivated side, about fifty yards below a sheer cliff was what looked like a very well maintained monastery with a central cloistered square. A well-kept wide path, cut into the cliff face, led directly to it. She dismounted and followed the priests around a curve in the rock. Ben, Hakeem and Fadil urged the camels along behind. Beyond the curve was a wide grassed area with a spring bubbling from the rock face. Here another priest took the camels. The path narrowed and they had to walk in single file to a large plaza in front of what appeared to be the only entrance.

Large gates opened into the central courtyard of the monastery and they were directed to quarters in the east corner. One of the escorting priests opened a door indicating that she should enter. Sucking in a deep breath, she walked in and emitted a gasp of wonder at what she beheld. The room was simple but elegantly furnished, open plan with a recess housing a huge bath and shower area. A large comfortable looking bed looked lost in the centre and the opposite wall was missing. The view was spectacular. This corner of the monastery was built at the point where the cliff curved away into a huge cultivated basin through which ran a broad river fed by tributary streams that burst from the rocky sides of the canyon to splash, tumble and meander through the greensward into the swift flowing waters below. So absorbed was she that the closing door went unheeded. When she did notice she didn't care. She was sure the others would be well domiciled. The bath was perfectly placed to take in the view and had already been run for her. Stripping off the dust encrusted clothes that offended the clean simplicity of this corner of paradise, she slithered over the side with the fluidity of a crocodile, and luxuriated for an hour or so before towelling down in the cool evening breeze and shrugging blissfully between crisp white sheets. She was briefly aware of someone removing the stinking garments and held off her slide into oblivion until the door was gently closed.

She awoke from a dreamless sleep perfectly refreshed. Ignoring the chaos of her bedding, she stretched, took a cold shower, and wriggled into jeans and a T shirt from her pack. She went to sit at a small table, on a terrace that ran to the edge of the sheer drop, contained only by a short width of rough chiselled rock from which the terrace had been cut. Magically, as she settled, the door opened and a cultured looking man in priestly robes entered carrying a tray of fruit, cereals, and a large jug of iced milk. Placing the tray in front of her, he waited for permission to be seated. She nodded and gave a palmed gesture indicating the chair opposite. Sitting down quietly, he admired the view while she helped herself. Curiosity had deserted her for the moment so she ate in silence and soaked in the vista below, glad to chill out and let her thoughts amble for a bit.

His voice flowed with the breeze, so quiet she almost missed it. "Beautiful isn't it? I rarely see it from this vantage. Apart from maintenance and cleaning, this room has remained empty, until now anyway."

She found herself answering in the same quiet tones, afraid to disturb the serene perfection pervading this place and this moment.

"Such a waste. Why would you deny yourself such a beautiful view? And why keep such a perfect room unoccupied?"

He sighed. "A perfect room is incomplete without a perfect occupant."

Before she had time to ponder that, he turned to her and introduced himself in more strident tones. "Frederick Wagstaff!" He offered his hand. "Believe me Miss Gabriel this is a pleasure I never hoped to have in my lifetime."

"Not Father then, or Imam?"

He smiled and plucked at his robes. "Ah my attire? Yes, I am a priest of sorts but not in any traditional sense. You might even call me an anti-priest. We have been here a long time Miss Gabriel. Certainly we predate Islam and, quite possibly, Judaism, even Hinduism perhaps. But we are not governed by the kind of dogma these religions use to contain and control the populace. Neither are we fanatics or zealots. Yet, our beliefs and our purpose are of a very high order indeed." Eve was in no hurry and was quite happy to let this priest come to the point in his own time.

She was in fact enjoying projecting indifference. He was very composed but she was sure it must be unsettling him and it might just get him to lower his guard and disclose answers more quickly. "And where are you from Mr Wagstaff? It isn't from here, I'm sure of that."

His smile broadened. "No not from here. You will find us quite a cosmopolitan bunch Miss Gabriel."

"Eve, please?"

"Of course, and I would be honoured if you would call me Freddy."

Eve giggled and felt self-conscious. It was too feminine a reaction. Deepening her tone a little she explained herself. "It seems odd to be calling a priest Freddy in such biblical surroundings. It should be something like Isaiah or Abraham. Freddy is too normal."

"We should perhaps be grateful for anything that anchors us in the normal Eve, for these are strange times and I believe they are going to get stranger but there will be plenty of time to talk of these things. For now, I think we should visit the Temple, before your friends begin to think we are keeping you from them. You will have many questions and I think the answers will be better understood once you have seen, and felt, our purpose for being in this place."

Intrigued, Eve followed him through the door. They negotiated a short airy passage and stepped out through a beautifully crafted arch onto a flat area roughly under the overhang where her room was. From here a staircase was cut into the sheer face of the cliff. The stairs were very narrow and precipitous but were perfectly flat and well maintained.

Freddy was showing signs of discomfort at Eve's nonchalance and had to exercise restraint, on several occasions during their decent, when she stepped to the edge to peer down at anything that caught her eye. This, of course, made her do it all the more. She was being given VIP treatment, so far with little explanation of why, and she wanted to test how important she was to whatever plans he had, and how free she was to do as she pleased. Would he try to restrain her? Best to find out whilst it was just him and her, and no cohort of warrior priests within hailing distance. When they reached the bottom, some of the colour had drained from his face but his relief was evident, if subdued.

Two horses waited saddled and ready to ride. Eve was impressed when he hitched up his robes and vaulted into the saddle of the larger. Turning his horse, he looked down at her, arms folded expectantly. She couldn't resist the bait and somersaulted onto her own horse. As her bum hit the saddle he gave a satisfied whoop and dug his heels into his horse's flanks, causing it to buck and lunge into a gallop.

"Race you to the other side. Last one there's a Greasy Kebab." Eve reacted in kind and was soon on his horse's heels. A couple of priests had to jump out of their way as the path narrowed ahead but Eve knew she could squeeze past and urged her horse on. As she drew level he leaned low. She saw the flash of a blade in his hand before he ripped up and through the saddle strap ejecting her from the horse. As she tumbled backwards he shouted at her. "Come on don't let that stop you. All's fair in war and religion!" The horses galloped on side by side. Eve had managed to kick herself into a backward role and landed on her feet. Frustration shot adrenalin through her system and she lunged forward with the speed of a Cheetah. Her horse had now lagged behind Freddy's but was still in the chase. Gritting teeth, she stomped on and before two hundred yards had passed, she was on its tail, then, with a determined burst, up by its head. Snatching out at its neck she bounced onto its bare back and was off in close pursuit. Freddy, was giving it lots of "yehaahs" and laughter, and shouting back insults.

"Get off and milk it. This is the sport of kings, not feeble women. Yeehaah!" He was almost at the wall but she reckoned she could catch him. He threw back a saddle bag that she had to dodge. The movement caused her mount to slow a fraction and Freddy was now within yards of the wall. Without thought, she was on her feet, on the horse's back. Leaping with fluid grace she landed behind Freddy, dislodging them both as he was drawing to a halt at the wall.

"Tie! You cheating bastard!"

They both landed hard on their backs and he burst out laughing. "I knew that would get you going. I heard about your leap at the crevice in the cliff and had to see for myself, and babe they played you down! You are the genuine article." His laugh was infectious and she couldn't help but join in.

"Sorted you out though, didn't I? Who's the daddy now?" She gave him a playful cuff around the head and he fell to the ground.

"Oh I'm sorry. Are you alright? I didn't mean to."

He jumped up like an acrobat. "Hah! Fooled you!" He rubbed his ear. "Did fucking hurt though."

Breathing heavily they tethered the horses in the shade of a rock fall. There was no vegetation on this side for them to eat but Freddy threw down a few handfuls of grain. He had sobered up from his excitement and was now more business like again. "Sorry about that, had to test you really. We have waited so long and ..." he hesitated, "you were not quite what we expected."

"So long? For what? And what were you expecting?"

"For you of course, but too many questions. You may begin to understand once we have been to the Temple. It's not far now." He guided her along a rock littered path that switched back and forth up a steep incline. Ushering her forward, rather than taking the lead, not wanting to offend, by insisting on following, she set a fast pace to create a reaction gap. She liked him but she was not about to trust him. Not yet.

Abruptly, they emerged onto a small ledge and a breathtaking vista of the opposite side of the canyon. A large out-thrust of rock blocked further progress. There was a low recess to the rear of this prominence through which a large person could not have passed. A cold draught issued from the black opening that carried on its vaporous breath the sick sweet smell of a funeral chapel. Eve did not wait for encouragement. Ignoring the precipitous drop, she swivelled her body to face the recess. Walking forward, she came square on to the opening. Her acute night vision revealed uneven steps plunging into a cavernous space that promised to be the equal of the drop to floor of the canyon that she had just turned from. Entering this space, it was as though the sun had been snuffed out. There was no transition, just bright sunlight then total darkness. Her other senses cut in immediately. She knew them to be sharp but had never realised just how so. It was almost like seeing with her feet, hands and ears. Every footfall conveyed texture and resistance; every sound bounced back an image of shape. Her feet chittered down the meandering steps as though she'd walked them every day of her life. Freddy cursed several twists behind her and produced an LED lamp from somewhere that threw confusing shadows into the gloom. He called a warning and asked her to slow the pace. Her nose was now registering a new smell. Somewhere below incense had been lit and there was rustling movement and a faint glow of light below.

As more candles were lit, the space began to take form. It was like an oval well shaft, about a hundred feet in depth. The walls were perfectly cut and as smooth as ice, inlaid with strange symbols and animal shapes overlaying an ancient sculpting of a giant tree that rose to, and covered, the entire ceiling of the cavern. It mesmerised her, seeming to writhe with sentient power. When she could draw her eyes from this wondrous art she looked directly down onto the dark grey slab of a granite altar in the centre of the cavern. Around which stood several cowled figures. Abruptly, a drape was snatched from an opening below and a shaft of sunlight struck the altar, throwing it into sharp relief, and causing something reflective in the wall above the head of the altar to shine like a star. A gust of air accompanied the sunlight that extinguished the candles with a hiss, and the creaking of shrinking wicks could be heard.

Sex Magic

She had paused. Freddy was now behind her, his lamp too, extinguished. She was unconcerned about him because she knew she could launch him to the bottom in a wink but this whole set up had her twitching. What the hell was going on here? Still, she was not going to lose the initiative now. Freddy placed a hand in the small of her back and gestured her forward. She took off at a bound, clearing the flights of narrow steps between each turn and was at the foot of the altar in seconds and eclipsing the man shaped opening that had admitted the sunlight from the foot end of the altar. Her senses gave her the advantage now. Before Freddy had a chance to switch on his lamp, she was across the altar launching blows at the four figures surrounding its sides and had manhandled the fifth, at its head, back over the altar to the opening that she had observed dropped a considerable distance to the rocks below, and over which she now held his struggling body with one outstretched hand. "Someone needs to start telling me what is going on here now! Before your head priest here takes a tumble and the rest of you follow suit pretty sharp!"

"Oh Shit!" this from Freddy as, with stumbled steps, he hurriedly descended, "this wasn't how it was supposed to go at all. Please bring Fadil back in from out there. It must be very uncomfortable for him."

"Fadil?" she screeched, and turned her head to glance back. Somehow Fadil managed a smile and a sort of a shrug. She brought him back in but kept hold of his throat, relaxing her grip just a little. She placed him in front of her, as a shield, hoping that none of them had any firearms with them. "I'll hear from you later Fadil. Start talking Freddy, but before you say anything else, tell me, what has happened to Ben? If you have harmed him, you will regret it."

"He is unharmed and is enjoying a well-earned rest and, almost as many comforts as bestowed on you. Although, he has been quite a handful and," he paused, looking for the right words, "somewhat threatening, about your whereabouts and safety. We have had to contain him."

She thought on this for a moment. It certainly sounded like Ben, so perhaps the rest was also true. "You're holding him prisoner?"

"House arrest, if you must. He has freedom to roam most areas but he is not a part of this."

She squeezed Fadil's throat a little. "Is this true Fadil?"

Fadil nodded, managing only half a smile this time, then to Fred "go on! Tell me everything." Fred sighed and shuffled his rump back onto the altar. At a gesture from him the other priests relaxed and began tending the wounds inflicted by Eve's attack.

"To tell you all we know would take decades and no man," he gestured at her, "or, I feel, any woman, however exceptional, can know everything. Yet I will attempt to give an overview and hope the tale will tug at the strands of that elusive knot of otherworldly knowledge hidden somewhere within your psyche, and so may fill in some of the gaps. Perhaps then you will find it fitting to assist us in our long-awaited transcendence from the state of imprisoned impoverishment in which humanity finds itself. Please release Fadil while we talk. I think he may be going into a state of shock."

This last comment caused her to look around and take in her surroundings. A sense of the ludicrous descended on her like a rumble of thunder. Squeezing her eyes tight shut she shook her head to shake loose this new layer of lunacy that was being dropped into the madness of her life, but when she opened them again, it, Freddy, and the rest of this insane tableau, were all still there. Mankind, it seemed, needed to tether itself to her, and to her uncertain hold on reality, in order to achieve the next step on its evolutionary journey. She needed to maintain a grip on something solid and real. Unfortunately for Fadil, this was currently his throat. Dropping swiftly to the ground, she used her weight and strength to force Fadil to do likewise. Freddy nodded in resigned acceptance and continued.

"Our story goes back farther than even your research has so far taken you." Answering her unspoken question, he explained. "Yes we have researched you thoroughly, since you first came to our notice Miss Fox, or Miss Gabriel if you prefer." She was unsettled by this but kept her expression neutral. She sensed he wasn't as sure of himself as he would have her believe, and was fishing.

"As I have looked at pre-Genesis that would be some feat."

"But the writings you have studied are from a time long after that event. What is more, they were looked at through an historical lens and so they are distorted. Our," he reached for a word to describe his thoughts and settled on, "images were created before Genesis, an indefinable time before. Time itself was still in a state of gestation, we could say, somewhere between zero and a trillion years. So, whilst they are a true and accurate account, they are also embryonic and cryptic and consequently beyond human comprehension. Yet, we have, in a very broad sense, had some success with comprehending them.

"There is a spark of divinity in us all that can shine light into the unfathomable. More than a glimpse, however, of that un-shadowed realm is, for us, death, or the slow and destructive poison of insanity and damnation. We have achieved many such glimpses and, equally, many such damning losses. What we have descried is that man was meant to be better than he is, but that faults were deliberately introduced into his making that would forever deny him his full potential, faults to enslave him to the higher being who created him. And that would have been our doom, eternal and unquestioning obedience to a cruel and self-absorbed master. Except that an intruder entity, the only such entity whom we, the black priests, accept as worthy of worship took pity on us and fought to redeem us from this fearful and unjust fate."

He gave a rueful smile, and added "he, or she, created a new father and mother of humanity more fitted to independent existence, and gave them vehicles to ease their access into this realm. He was defeated in this attempt, cast out, his work destroyed, but the divine remnants of his efforts were crafted well and were not wholly unmade. They continue, to this day, to exude empathic desire to their sundered parts, yearning to be made whole again to fulfil their allotted purpose and to deliver mankind from the malignant clutches of its creator. It has been our work to nudge events, to strengthen that empathy. It has been our hope that the time would come when such a creature and its unformed psyche would reform new and whole and fulfil its fate, to heal and to lead us to our completion."

This sounded familiar. Her mind took an inspirational leap. "You don't happen to know Isaac Abrahams by any chance?"

Freddy smiled. "We knew of his work, or thought we did, and some of our associates were in contact with him. What we did not know was how far his research had taken him. Perhaps you could enlighten us."

Eve felt deflated and finally released Fadil. He moved to the wall and sat rubbing his neck. She would get him to fill her in later on what he knew. "So what the hell is this altar all about? It looked as though you intended to sacrifice me."

"Hardly, you are, to us, the most precious thing in the universe. We did however intend a ritual that would have meant your voluntary presence on the altar."

Eve puffed out her exasperation. "As if ..."

"Please hear me out. I know how sinister it must have looked but it was to set the mood, and to create the tension that we have found greatly assists the mind to transcend its normal state. For you this may be unnecessary but, for us lesser mortals, we need every edge we can get."

There were a couple of drawn breaths of surprise at his comments from the ailing priests. He waived them to silence and continued. "We believe you to be in danger."

She puffed again. "Not the obvious physical dangers you seem to experience daily. I am talking about spiritual danger, demonic danger, if you like. You carry it with you like a cloud and anyone sharing your space, within the sphere of this malign force, for too long, is likely to suffer some mishap."

Eve was instantly alert. How could he have known? "You've spoken to Soames!"

"We know of your little ritual with Mrs Woolfe, if that's what you mean, but we did not need this knowledge to know that you carry around the substance of an evil spirit. It surrounds your aura like a cloying fog seeking weakness, feeding off fear and seeping into your dreams."

Not fishing then, she thought. Obviously he does know a lot, but probably not everything. Soames is a crafty bastard, he'd only release as much knowledge as he had to unless ... "Have you hurt Soames?"

"We are not your enemies, nor would we harm anyone who has aided you." You don't know about the ovaries then. She thought. Eve decided to cut to the crux. "Tell me about this ritual you intended."

"Something a little more sophisticated than that you performed with Mrs Wolfe, no blood-letting, or anything involving physical pain, but it was our hope that you might voluntarily agree to a sexual element. We thought you might find Fadil an agreeable participant. We understand that you and he are on quite good terms."

Eve glanced at Fadil. "So that was your game. You little shit! Try and touch me in that way just once and I'll rip off your balls and ram them down your lying throat." She had to admire his cocky shrug and broad grin. She turned her attention back to Freddy. "Well you can forget that part, but let's hear the rest."

"Unless your powers have grown considerably since you last tried it, it may not work without some stimulus. There is knowledge locked into your spiritual DNA. In times of danger, extremely heightened emotion, or sexual tension, a pathway, or a kind of feedback, can be forced into your spiritual mind. Above this alter, there is a shard, part of the original shattered pentagram, a representation of which you have around your neck. Doubtless, you saw its reflection when the sunlight entered this temple. It is not of this world alone. It also has a spiritual aspect. If you can perceive this aspect with your spirit senses, it can guide you to understanding of the knowledge contained in the images that are inlaid within the mural of this Temple."

Eve did not know why but she felt the truth in his words and also a sense of impending doom. She made what she hoped was not a rash decision. "Tell me what I have to do."

"Forgive me if I speak plain. You must prostrate yourself face up on the altar, in imitation of the man shaped opening at its foot. You should be naked." Observing her scathing look, he continued, "But, if this is likely to lead to bloodshed," he eyed her closing fists, "perhaps we should try it clothed first." He tried to ignore the killing stare she aimed at him as she crawled warily into place. "We must hurry before the sun is aligned with the navel and then the genital area of our man shape. Tilt your head back and stare up at the shard. Try to remember the ceremony at Soames' place and your earlier encounter in Texas. Place yourself and your thoughts, into the same zone you felt then. Try to remember the fear and the tension. If you can achieve this same state, encapsulate it in your thoughts into a bubble, make it solid, real, and move that bubble towards the shard."

Eve felt the warmth of the sun that had been on her breasts move down toward her navel gaining in intensity until it felt like a laser cutting into her. The shard above her began to glow bright with reflected light and to take on a three-dimensional quality. The sunlight lanced into her navel like a burning spear. She gasped out a scream as her abdomen erupted into a dark chasm. Convulsively, she gripped the gaping wound to try to close it but something was emerging. Two golden hands, dripping fire, suddenly snatched out from within, grabbing her own hands, and dragged her into the dark void. But it was not dark inside. It was star bright, and she looked down on her own perfect and unblemished body on the altar, and a piece of her mind was still in that body and still aware of her surroundings. She looked to the source of the light.

Above her, in the wall of the chamber, was the shard, but it projected inward rather than up and seemed to punch through the rock into a forest glade, from which there were a number of paths. She tried to step forward but was unable to move her legs. Freddy was speaking to her.

"Don't let the memory of the ritual fade. Hold onto the tension. Expand it. Take it with you." She concentrated and took a step forward. She could feel a breeze on her face and the glade drew focus from the movement of her foot but it was like walking through deep mud. She felt something detach itself from her. Something she had been unaware of, until she felt its absence. She knew what it was though. It was that same presence that had invaded her dreams and threatened and killed her friends. Afsoon! Afsoon had become aware of the shard's presence and was seeking the source. Eve knew she had to get there first. She spoke to Freddy. "Freddy I can't move. Something is here with me. It is evil and it wants to get there first, how do I move?"

"More tension Eve. Masturbate!" Her awareness was suddenly on Freddy.

"What! You sick bastard." She felt the other presence condense. "Shit!" She stuck her hand down her jeans and started to probe and rub. It was no good. The sun entered the head of the opening in the wall and struck her genitalia with a sexually charged jolt. She rubbed more vigorously and felt herself back where she had been, looking at the glade, but now it was obscured by a red mist that was gaining shape, the shape of a man of godlike dimensions. Afsoon was materialising. She had to get there first but her progress was so slow every step draining her reserves. She looked up from the slab. Fadil was pinning her shoulders down to prevent her thrashing. She knew it was impossible to beat Afsoon into the Glade. "Fuck it. I hate you all, you bastards." Punching her open hand straight up, she grabbed Fadil's robe at the neck and flung him onto the slab. Twisting on top of him in one move, she ripped her jeans off with her other hand. The sexual explosion building within her was unbearable. She didn't know whether he was willing or not but he responded physically, and that was all that mattered.

She lowered herself onto him with a hard thrust and felt a tidal wave of force surge through her groin, propelling her forward into the red mist at the entrance to the glade. The mist closed around her like a claw. She thrust again but no energy was coming through from Fadil. Insane with orgasmic panic, she threw him aside and reached for Freddy. He did not resist. As she lowered again, she felt raw power. Distracted for a moment, her lips twitched into a smile and she looked down on him. "A virgin Freddy?" A force uncoiled and catapulted her through the red cloud and into the centre of the glade.

She sensed, rather than saw, the cloud shredding and dissipating behind her, and contemplated the various paths before her. One seemed less forbidding than the others and she moved onto it. Immediately, it began to slither under her feet, then steadied and accelerated under the giant leaps she took over its surface. It became a living thing, writhing and undulating. Its serpentine scales contorting to bring around a massive head. Her momentum was irresistible. As the head turned she caught a glimpse of a red eye. From within the fanged opening of a gaping black throat, a forked tongue lashed out, coiling around her waist and ripping her into the pit of its slavering maw. Within the fetid stench of its contorting bowel, the world flipped over and she hung in utter darkness.

Time meant nothing in this place. Seconds or years might have passed. Her identity diffused into the nothingness but, eventually, something pierced the dark void. In the distance there was a speck of light. It moved fast towards the memory of what she was. With a crash of awareness she was engulfed by it, and found herself in a small compartment looking down on a floating corpse, held aloft in a web of glasslike micro-fibres. Baffled by the illusion, she reached out and touched the web. There was a gasp from the corpse and the fibres caressed her hand pulling gently at it, each strand feeling along the surface of her skin.

Then, all at once, and in unison, they penetrated her forearm, a thousand tingling needles jabbing into the nerve structure just beneath her skin, spreading like a net below its surface. To pull free would have been to pull out her internal organs through the pores of her skin and to turn her inside out. Her awareness shifted again and she tumbled, headlong, down through the fibres, and there he was, waiting.

"Afsoon." She breathed his name in a hissing sigh. They both hung in a grey sphere, her glowing silver aura merging with his flaming red one. He seemed confused for a moment then, in a blur of piston fast movement, his hands went to her throat curling into a grip she knew meant agony or death. Reflexively, she fended off with a chop to his forearm and saw him drop like a stone to the floor, retching and gasping. His aura shrivelled around his balled figure defensively. She pulled at the red flame experimentally, peeling it open into a flat sheet. His groaning body lay in embryonic spasm within. Reaching down she pulled him up by his windpipe. His eyes tilted up in pain, he gurgled, gasping for breath. "Got you! You bastard! You will never hurt me or mine again." Placing a hand on his forehead she wrenched back with all her might to rip the windpipe from his throat. For an instant she felt the sinews give and stretch and then, it was as though a grenade went off in her hand and she was blasted into a tumbling somersault to land exhausted across the comatose form of one of the priests.

After laying there for some confused moments she became more acutely aware of her surroundings. She was still on the slab of the altar. Freddy lay crumpled against a wall entangled with another unconscious priest. Fadil was propped up, seemingly lifeless against the opposite wall, being tended by a still conscious priest and another priest was praying with his hands splayed out on the altar above her head.

"Just nod my lady and I promise you there will be carnage in this chamber?" Glancing back she saw Ben standing in the man shaped opening wielding a machete. She rolled off the comatose and wasted priest quivering in ecstasy beneath her and turned to sit, facing Ben, having the uncomfortable and disgusting feeling of a flaccid phallus being pulled from her as she did so. She felt soiled and embarrassed but there were more pressing matters.

"You're always there for me you little shit. I'm beginning to think I can't get by without you. You haven't used that thing on anyone have you?"

"Only the handle, on Hakeem's head, he pointed at the foot of the altar. She eased herself wearily over the edge to look down on him. He looked a mess. There was a boot print on his face and blood seeped from his nose. His hand was outstretched with the forefinger and thumb looking as though they might be broken. "Took this off the creepy bastard," he fished a handgun from his belt and waived it for her perusal."

"Come on Ben we need to get these guys to some help. Oh, and by the way I want you near me from now on. There are times, it seems, when I need a bodyguard" He grinned and threw his head scarf at her.

"They should not look on your nakedness Lady Eve." Eve laughed at the absurdity of his comment and the fact that he still seemed to hold her in such esteem but she made a skirt of his scarf nonetheless. With the help of the two conscious priests they managed to get those lacking this commodity onto the horses and transport them back to the monastery. Eve was concerned about Fadil and carried him herself. Freddy regained consciousness but was unable to stand and kept slipping back into a troubled stupor. Armed priests met them halfway and escorted them back with deference, although, as before whether they were guarding them or taking them prisoner was unclear.

A revived, though weakened, Freddy sat on the veranda outside Eve's room. Ben stood in the shadows in watchful silence. The sun was dropping behind the red furnace of the horizon. The fizz of burning lamps merged with the distant clatter of Cicadas, releasing a jasmine scent that weaved through the wafting odour of exotic plants from the valley below. It was magical and Eve waited while the sunlight faded, to be replaced by a trillion shining stars winking into existence in the black moonless sky.

Freddy's low tones rumbled into the balmy night air, in perfect harmony with the meandering pace of Eve's thoughts. "Beautiful, isn't it?"

She answered, in slow low tones of her own. "Yes." But her mind drifted back to a similar magical night, in the broken wall of a volcano with the moon hanging before her, in the chalice of a different world, when she was not as she was now.

Any romance that might have settled on the moment was snatched away, however, by a coil of self-disgust as disturbing memories writhed out of the dark places of her mind. Resisting the onslaught was like pushing fingers into a crumbling dyke that was being loosened and turned to slush by an oily sea. A deep unsettling feeling infested her thoughts that very soon she was going to be engulfed by the deluge of all the ills contained within her recent past. There was a leviathan out there and it was getting hungry. Tightening her resolve, she pushed more mud into the spreading cracks of her psychosis and reminded herself of the purpose that was being remorselessly thrust upon her. She leaned across the table between them.

"What the hell is it with the sex, Freddy? Afsoon tried to rape me. Sadique and his men succeeded in doing so, and further attempts were made by others after that," there was a rustling of clothing as Ben shifted uncomfortably, "and now I, despite my loathing of contact with men, have done the same to you and your men, possibly killing Fadil in the process."

Freddy sighed wearily. "When you are manipulating the forces of creation, sexual magic is one of the most powerful channels through which to focus your efforts. Think about it. What is the most potent thing in creation if not the creation of life itself? Barring the first made, all life is produced through the act of sex. This is when creation itself is at work. If you would ply these forces and pit yourself against other adept users, then you must take control of the greatest power source available and direct it to your will. There are many places from which power can be drawn but few as strong as that taken during the act of sexual conjunction except ..." He paused and seemed reluctant to complete the sentence.

"Except?" He shifted uncomfortably.

"Except the opposing act, a blood sacrifice."

"And which is most powerful?"

He wriggled, in some distress, at being pressed. "That depends on the power of the individual performing the sacrifice and the power, or the quantity, of the life that is being offered."

She thought she could see where this was going. "If someone sought to amass or to manipulate power in this way, what, or who, would be the most effective sacrifice?"

Seeing his reluctance she pressed him. "Come on Freddy spit it out."

"Okay, okay. It would be you of course, or failing that, someone close to you, or, if possible, all of those close to you."

"And that's it! Those are my options? To kill my enemy, and to protect my friends and myself, I have to fuck or kill someone else?"

"Or your enemy."

"Sorry?"

"Anyone powerful enough to stand against you would also be a well of immense power as a lover or a sacrifice or ..." He looked at her directly, "or as an ally."

That explained an awful lot about Afsoon's motivations.

"That is not an option, what if I had no friends?"

"I think you already know the answer to that. You would be isolated and vulnerable and humanity would be at the mercy of the victor."

Eve's mind was doing back flips. She needed time to take it all in and so decided on a diversion. "Listen Freddy, I am deeply sorry for the way I have treated you and the danger I put you, and your followers, in. If there was anything I could do to make amends I would."

Freddy wobbled to his feet and moved around the table to kneel in front of her. "My dearest Eve, you fulfil a prophecy we have awaited for millennia and you apologise to us for allowing us to assist you. This is our purpose for being. We are yours to command or to use as you see fit." His abject need of her guidance, and his genuine concern for her predicament were discharged through his touch into the lightning rod of her pent-up emotions. She began to quake under the pressure, grappling with them to try and understand.

Struggling to maintain control, she snapped at Freddy. "Get off your knees! Do not grovel before me again! Ever!" Noting his pained expression, she gently assisted him back to his seat and continued in a softer vein. "Now tell me, what is the situation with Fadil? Can anything be done to restore him?" Freddy quickly recovered his composure and gratefully settled back into the chair responding in a seemingly unperturbed fashion. "His mind is gone I'm afraid. We have done all we can … but you may be able to help."

Eve sighed. "Please tell me this doesn't involve sex or killing, although, I can think of a candidate for the latter. You can tell me what you have found out about Hakeem later."

No sex or killing was involved, only a great deal of effort and, of course, ritual. She had done a similar process before, when interrogating the priest and also when protecting Helen, but this was different, harder. She had to delve into the darkest corners of the nightmare that now occupied Fadil's mind, seeking the refuge in which he had hidden. She found a frightened little toddler covering his eyes in foetal withdrawal and cowering under his cot. She learned a lot about the tenderness of maternal love in the process of persuading him to leave his refuge and come with her. Eve had to nurture his trust until he was willing to allow her to guide and accompany him through the valley of his fears, re-living the moments when his mind broke apart, and coaxing the pieces back together to reform a new whole. She had help, however. Freddy took control of the ritual and also gave her the shard from the temple in the cliff, that proved to be one point of what Freddy described as the original seal or gateway from a higher or heavenly dimension to this world, a complete if broken replica of which hung about her neck. She reluctantly parted from Fadil, leaving him with the mind of a child. Freddy believed this to be a temporary affliction and nurtured the belief that he would fully recover in time.

"I haven't asked you but I assume Fadil is one of yours?"

"Yes, a remarkable young man. When he first came here, he wandered the desert for longer than Jesus did, searching for this fabled place. We observed, as we always do, thinking he would surely die but, somehow he kept going, so we brought him in and healed and trained him in our ways. He was our first apprentice for over twenty years and by-passed all the usual initiation rites. During his near death he had some interesting visions. For a start, it was he who told us to expect a woman instead of a man. We thought he was crazy of course, but then you turned up, every bit as remarkable as he said you would be. He was waiting for you. If not for him, your reception here might have been rather more hostile. Indeed you may have found a cult of Afsoon worshippers, out for your bloody sacrifice, for that malignancy has come to the more adept of us in our dreams, offering power, rewards and immortality, but the dreams have an undercurrent of dark foreboding and grinding fear that stays with you like a dark cloak, although, strangely, it seems to dissipate when you, Eve, are near. Some have come under his influence, of course, but I am proud to say that most have sensed his evil intent and those few who were drawn into his sphere were …" he struggled for a word, finally finishing with, "removed."

"You killed them? Was that necessary? I tell you now, I don't approve. If you insist on raising me to the status of a deity, then I assume I can make certain dictates. And here is my first; you will only kill when there is no other option. Is that clear?"

He gave her a pained look.

"They were not killed Eve. They were …" he paused again, "neutralised. You might say their current mental state is similar to that of Fadil, except that they are in an adult faze. We will return them to life in the locality of their birthplace. We had," he fished again for a phrase, "what the ignorant might term, a sorcerer's battle. We won and we set the terms. They no longer have any knowledge of their time with us, or of you. Although, I can't promise that Afsoon will let go of his hold on them so easily."

"When did this take place?"

"Just before your arrival here yesterday."

"I want to see them now!"

A shadow crossed Freddy's face and he strode quickly to the door. "And, before you leave, where is Hakeem?" Her acute hearing suddenly picked up a sound and she angled her head toward the terrace. Catching the gesture, Ben was already moving into the shadow of the overhang, none too soon. A spidery figure dropped onto the stone surface wielding a device in a throwing gesture. Ben reacted, chopping the arm off at the elbow, with sufficient force to hurl it, and the object in its grasp, out into the abyss of the valley. A shower of rock shards accompanied the shattering explosion that followed. Three more figures dropped onto the terrace, appearing as shadows in the dust and smoke. Ben managed to gut one, thrusting up from his, now, prone position on the floor into the groin of his assailant. Eve was on the other two in quick, lethal succession, sending one spinning into the open drop beyond the terrace, and wrenching the arms behind the other in a bone crunching manoeuvre that pinned them at angles no human skeleton was ever meant to adopt, followed by a jab to the jaw that cut off his curdling screams. She could hear the staccato fire of automatic weapons receding down the stone corridor outside her room. Freddy stuck his head back through the door, taking in the scene in an instant and, having satisfied himself all was under control, was gone again, in the direction of fire. He re-appeared minutes later with several guards, struggling to contain two bound and flailing creatures, barely recognizable as anything, human. This was less due to their battered condition than to the demonic growls, spitting, foaming wheezes, contortions and vomiting, as they struggled against their restraint.

Eve wasted no time in contemplation but acted on instinct. Grabbing the first by the windpipe she snapped upper arms and femurs to prevent further struggle, although, the creature continued to flail its useless limbs in impotent rage. Fishing the shard from her pocket, she slid the point effortlessly up the back of its neck between the cervical vertebrae and the base of the skull, releasing a jet of cerebrospinal fluid, as it slipped deep into the brain. Her captive went rigid, his eyes dilating impossibly, with a liquid darkness that ran from the sockets like black acid. Eve drew her face close to the steaming gore.

"I see you Afsoon! You got away this time you bastard but I'm not running any more. I know exactly where you are now. Maybe it's a long way off but it is a very small space and you're stuck in it, whilst I have a whole planet to move around in and a lot of time to prepare for your coming. And, by the way, if I catch you inserting your ethereal beak into my, or my friends' and followers', proximity again, I will come along that same dream way I was so recently expelled from, and rip your living lungs from your body." So saying, she head butted her victim with such violence that his skull was shattered, her own embedded within it, at the same time extending her awareness with whiplash force into the neural pathways, along which Afsoon was now in rapid and, panic stricken retreat, following his sudden realisation of her intent. All three captives dropped into instant lifelessness. Eve screamed in pain and frustrated anger as his presence extinguished like a snuffed candle at the far end of a long black tunnel. The ensuing dark imploded into the singularity of her psyche with devastating force.

The Abyss

Slowly, she became aware of her foetal position, and of Ben and Freddy pulling gently at her arms to help her to her feet. She let them guide her to her bed and the void of dreamless sleep. But it was not a comfortable void. Something was in there with her, not attacking, but invading her, probing with sciatic intensity into her core, extending curious strands of awareness into, and through, her at a cellular level. A snake crawling through her that might at any moment strike or, with agonising patience, slowly flex crushing coils around her gasping id. She mustn't move, mustn't let it know anything sentient existed here. It had not sensed her mind yet. Days passed. She remained still. Eventually, very slowly, it slithered out.

Eve awoke, weak, several days later, gasping of thirst to find Ben cross-legged on the floor and fully armed, located so that he had a clear view of terrace, door, and bed. He smiled at her. He did not speak, and she could not. He rose fluidly from the floor and came to her bed side, concern darkening his face. He scanned the room but sensed that any danger was inside her.

Tentatively he leaned close. "Great one, what is wrong? How can I help?" She blinked slowly. He seemed to understand. Lifting a glass off her bedside table he dribbled water between her lips so carefully and patiently that she did not gag. He laid his ear next to her lips.

She managed to breathe words. "Stay very close. Be ready."

"Always, great one." He could not protect her from the danger within but he could watch her back in this world and it bolstered her strength to know he was near. Controlling her fear, she allowed herself to drift back into a more natural sleep, filled with forebodings, but also with a grain of hope. She had struck back at Afsoon for the first time since leaving the habitat. It was time to prepare herself for the confrontation to come, and to consider this new phenomenon. She hoped it was just a dream but knew in her heart it was not.

Her amazing body and mind did what it always did and recovered in record time. Her system flooded with endorphins, her body pumped with adrenalin. She bounced out of a bed, largely destroyed by her nightly, unconscious, physical stretching and exercise regime. Ben on the terrace, machete in hand, turned away from her nudity. She ran a freezing shower, shook her head and climbed wet, into jeans, shirt and shoes. Striding for the door she called Ben. "Come on, we have work to do."

Somehow he was there before her, holding it open. She could not help but smile. Shaking her head she walked through into the future.

She had Freddy bring all his loyal people to the great hall further down, inside the cliff face. Again, it had a large undercut terrace looking out into the valley that was still far below. There were more than she expected, close to two hundred thronged the hall and these, Freddy assured her, were the tip of a small empire spread around the globe, six thousand initiates in all but each controlling many hundreds of believers. How many remained true to the cause though, he could not be so definite about. She set the facts before them in broad but brutally honest terms and received information and speculation in return. Eve asked nothing from them but offered to them and to humanity her undying loyalty. It seemed Afsoon had been busy raising his own army, exuding his presence into the minds of the weak through dreams and visions, corrupting the thoughts of many. Almost overnight, religious cults had sprung up in many locations around the world, and were gaining rapidly in impetus and strength. Every drug and alcohol clinic, homeless hostel and shanty town was being besieged by followers of the sleeping messiah.

Freddy's people were purging their own ranks but, unfortunately, it seemed many holding high office in his organisation had given their allegiance to the new cult. Rebel militia influenced by these cult factions were growing in numbers and seeking to destabilise vulnerable governments, whilst new political parties were appearing in the more established countries. These had little influence at the moment but there was a ground swell of interest. Some had become openly active only recently, during the time of Eve's residency at the order. Freddy suspected Hakeem had been the eyes that alerted Afsoon to Eve's movements and actions here. Hakeem it seemed had also, somehow, escaped.

"Afsoon has totally subsumed Hakeem. I think we will hear more from him." Eve decided the low key approach was no longer an option and made a decision to call in her own assets, such as they were. She sent a message to Soames.

And here they all were. Freddy had arranged a meeting room in a high tower with a panoramic view of the city and four helicopter landing pads on cantilevered arms, all viewable from the two semi-circular windows. On Eve's insistence, Freddy chaired the group at the head of the table. Eve to his right and Ben, the only one armed, next to her. Eve took the time to look closely at him. He had become a formidable companion. Gone was the slightly stooped wiry frame. She hadn't realised how tall he was. He stood here now, a perfectly proportioned, well-muscled man of six feet three inches with an unflinching gaze and exuding a strength of presence that was hard to ignore. At a nod from her, he finally sat. Matt and Janie sat opposite Eve. Soames and his advisors were at the far end, as far from Ben as possible. Eve had to elbow Ben in the ribs to get him to stop staring malevolently at Soames. Several of Freddy's priests including Fadil, who was making a remarkable recovery, if still somewhat vague and distracted, made up the remainder of the group, plus one other. Matt had asked to bring a guest. She sat between him and Janie. Eve was startled when she saw who it was, but the one she had hoped to see was visibly absent. Eve hadn't really expected her to come, she had not replied to any of her attempts to make contact with her, and there had been many. A gaggle of Freddy's and Soames' security guards occupied places outside, on the pads and on the floors below. Freddy rose and all went quiet. Freddy's presence seemed to expand to fill the entire vastness of the oval room.

"Gentlemen and ladies, we are entering the end of days. Whether it is to be an apocalypse or the dawn of a new and great era depends on our ability to withstand the might of the 'Sleeping Messiah' and, to unite behind, and shore up, the strength of our own, living Goddess. We must nurture her abilities and give her time to develop, and to wear, her destiny as the mother of a new chapter in the existence of humanity." Eve cringed. This was not what she had expected. She almost leapt to her feet in enraged indignation but Ben placed his hand on her shoulder and gave a fractional shake of his head. For some reason, she couldn't understand right now, she acquiesced and remained seated. "You know of whom I speak. There are none here who are not aware of her unique abilities. You all know her to be far more than human." Soames wriggled in agitation at this. "You have seen her great physical prowess, but it is her ability to influence the spiritual currents that control the universe, and all of life, that will save us, and give true purpose to the continued existence of our species. Note my words. If the 'Sleeping Messiah' awakes and takes control, humanity will know the true meaning of eternal damnation. There is only one who can withstand him, and she cannot do it alone. Already he wields fearful and malign power, capable of terrible destruction, and this, while he yet sleeps." A stunned silence followed.

The quiet voice of Soames breathed into it. "Far more than human," he parodied Freddy's words. "Is that a euphemism? To put it kindly, she is beyond human, another species. The better of two evils I grant you, but, as far as humanity is concerned, evil nonetheless." He looked apologetically at Eve. She could feel the tension in Ben beside her. "I like you Eve. I really do. I know your current intentions are good, and I will do all I can to help you defeat this greater evil. We may not be able to do it without you, but once that task is complete, I am afraid it will be impossible for the likes of you to co-exist with humanity."

Eve used Ben's shoulder to raise herself, as a warning for him to hold himself in check. "And exactly what danger is it that I pose to humanity. As you are aware, there is little chance of my being able to breed a new species. You having had that capacity removed when you stole and destroyed my ovaries." There were a few intakes of breath around the table and Ben went ashen but he held his ground.

"For all I know Miss Fox, you may be immortal, you certainly have an incredible regenerative ability and that is the problem. Have your ovaries regenerated? I would like to have you examined again, to make sure, because a breeding pair, most definitely, cannot be allowed to exist for one moment longer than is absolutely necessary."

"Are you suggesting that I would ever let that creature Afsoon near me? The next time we meet, I can assure you, one of us will be dead very shortly afterwards."

"Yes, your history has shown how adept you are at preventing men from copulating with you. And Afsoon, as you have been at pains to tell us, is far more than just a man."

Eve sunk her fingers into Ben's shoulder holding him to the chair, and speared a shocked Freddy to his with a piercing stare. Despite herself, she saw his point. She also saw an opportunity.

"Very well, if I allow your people to examine me, will that satisfy you?"

She could feel the weight of disapproval of all those in her camp but stayed them with a gesture.

"And will you agree to further surgery if necessary?"

"One thing at a time Soames, we will re-establish terms if, my future fertility becomes a fact, and, before any agreement is made, I have a condition. I want Helen back."

"She may not want to come. She has refused all contact with you. Do you really want to destroy any chance of future reconciliation by forcing the issue?"

"So you say. I want to hear it from her."

"I can remedy that here and now. I have a letter in response to your request for her attendance here. It is quite emphatic. You know her hand."

"It could be a fake. You could have forced her."

"She is a wonderful woman Miss Fox and she is human. I would never hurt her, and you hurt me by inferring it."

Eve shook her head in exasperation. "Nevertheless, I do not want her in my enemy's camp. If she doesn't want to see me then

Freddy will relocate her and ensure she has all she needs." She looked at Freddy and he tilted his head in confirmation.

"I will allow your ..." he drew breath, looked around the table and finished with, "disciple, to meet with her. If she is agreeable, I will release her into his care, but I will not force her to do anything she does not want to. And, Miss Fox," he hesitated, "Eve ... for the time being at least, think of me as an ally not an enemy."

"Very well, agreed, but your examination will take place on neutral ground with my people in attendance. Freddy will arrange a venue."

"We can do it here and now Miss Fox. My helicopter carries sufficient equipment for this eventuality."

Eve silenced objections. "Okay, Soames. I want Ben, Freddy, Matt and Janie present at all times. You may have four of your people. Set up here in this boardroom, and get on with it. Oh, and give me that letter." She staggered when he handed it over and had to be supported by Matt and Ben. It was addressed to John. Suddenly, and overwhelmingly, she was, for a few moments, completely John again. Eve couldn't bring herself to open it in company. She had noted Janie's look of disappointment when she had not been near enough to support her. Handing her the letter, she asked her to look after it until this business was done. Janie took it and put it in her pocket enclosed in a fist that Eve felt, even with her superhuman strength, she would be unable to prize open. Her four chosen, unconsciously acting as one, adopted a protective escort. Eve felt reassured, confident they would each die to protect her.

The scans showed no appreciable regeneration. Soames wanted to laser the scar tissue, but decided it could wait until future scans revealed any defined regrowth after Ben and Janie made it plain what would happen if he attempted to inflict any further surgery on her. Soames, having been given all the satisfaction he was likely to get for now, and the various staffs retired to respective rooms on the three floors below agreeing to re-convene the meeting the following morning. Her four chosen, plus Fadil and young Jackie Barnes waited in the lounge of Eve's suite whilst Eve read her letter and took a shower.

She sat on the toilet seat for support and, heart pounding, read the words she had waited so long for, and now, almost wished had

not arrived at all, because she was sure it was going to be bad.
Hadn't Soames inferred as much?

John

*Are you okay? Soames tried to track you but, even with his vast resourc-
es, he lost you? He really likes you, you know. He has been at great pains
to convince me that you are what you say you are, and how heroic and
honest your intentions are. I think he would love you for a daughter, or a
wife.*

*He needn't have bothered. I know my husband. I hid it from myself but
I think I knew, in some remote part of my being, from the moment I met
you again. What else could have induced me into such an encounter? I am
as straight as they come, but it was incredible (for you too, I think). It had
everything. The man I love, fit, healthy, and back from the dead, and
wrapped in a form that would entice an angel. A boat on an iridescent sea,
the thrill of taboo sex, and wow! You were always good, but that was
something else wasn't it? I will never forget those few days, and, whilst I
was able to carry on kidding myself, it was idyllic. But the fact remains that
you lied to me and misled me and, well, truth is, I'm past my prime, damn
it! And, from what Soames tells, me you may look the same a thousand
years from now.*

*We have tasted each other, but you got the best of me. I will only
deteriorate now, and I'm okay with that, growing old with someone you
love is acceptable, but that bit is not possible now is it? You will only get
stronger and more vibrant with each passing day. We are entirely mis-
matched you and I so, unless you can find a way to dip me in the pool of
eternal youth, there is no way we can ever be together again. Not in that
way and I don't think that I could ever be in your company again without
suffering a yearning that would probably kill me off, but oh, what memories you leave me with. I have known heights that would sustain me
through a dozen life times.*

*I wish you the very best of everything this world and this universe (which
I am sure you will explore every part of) has to offer John, but no, I do not
want to leave the care and protection of Mr Soames. I trust him. Although
he may one day try to kill you, for your sake alone, he would never harm
me, and I believe he is also very fond of me for myself. I am as content as I
am ever likely to be. He provides everything I need. He has housed me in a
beautiful location and I have nearly finished my book, which he has
promised to help me publish. I will send you a copy, if you wish. I love you*

*with every ounce of my being John but I am afraid this is goodbye. Please
don't try to contact me again. We occupy different worlds now.*
    Your loving wife forever.
    Helen.

Eve washed away her tears in the shower, and it was a very
subdued and sober Eve, but definitely Eve, who returned to the
lounge area to catch up with her friends. John was now, once
again, a part of the whole that was Eve Fox aka Gabriel, a person
fashioned from human, superhuman, man and woman, and
unique experiences that forced the development of a new and
totally unique persona.

It hadn't worked out with Matt and Janie. As Janie explained, "I
am lesbian after all, or at least I thought I was. Matt has rather
clouded the issue. We had the greatest sex but something, some
other thing, got in the way. Matt felt the same. We were ecstatical-
ly happy for a while, and we are still the very best of friends and,"
she actually flushed a little, "are still occasional lovers. I would die
for him and, I hope you know this, for you too, as would Matt."

Eve hugged her with genuine affection, and assured her that she
would think nothing of entrusting her life to her, or to Matt. Janie
ran out of the room. Matt assured Eve that she was anything but
upset.

Little Jackie Barnes proved to be a revelation. Once you got over
her youth and femininity, it was like having Vincent back. Her
body may have been young but her mind was sharp, original and
mature and she really did not blame Eve in the slightest for her
father's death. Rather, she seemed to have inherited his faith and
affection for her. It was eerie how, sometimes, she could forget it
was Jackie speaking and actually respond with Vincent's name on
her lips. Fortunately, Jackie didn't seem to mind in the least. So,
with faithful and trusted friends at her back, she went to build an
alliance that she hoped would be able to take on, and defeat, the
malignant might of her nemesis and rival Afsoon. She was not sure
she could win but, at least she would not know the desperate
loneliness and fear that had been the hallmark of much of her
existence, until now. With friends, such as these, she could fight
on.

The meeting reconvened and, finally, late in the proceedings, Eve had taken the chair and was making her proposals and demands. As ever, it was really a question of convincing Soames. The rest, for the moment at least, were all fully on board. She had had a brief private meeting with him earlier in her suite. She agreed that Helen would stay under his protection, and this seemed to allay many of his fears, but he was still driving a hard bargain. He had been surprised Eve was sending no response to Helen's letter but seemed to understand when she said, "Just tell her that you, Soames, know how much I will always love her. I trust you to find the words to make her understand that, and to frame a goodbye that I am incapable of making myself." She had choked then, but was able to quickly regain her composure and move on. She noted a tear on Soames' rheumy eye and wondered, absently, if he might have an infection.

All parties had stated their case and various agreements and contractual clauses were suggested and insisted upon. There were some heated exchanges, aising from Ben and Janie, which Eve had had to keep a firm check on. Curiously, no one had questioned that Ben was the only one armed, and he made no secret that he was prepared to make use of that privilege if the situation demanded, but since Eve had taken the chair and spoken with such calm and measured control, everyone stopped to listen attentively. It was agreed that Soames would focus his resources on locating the life capsule containing Afsoon and of trying to find some means to destroy it before it ever got close to earth. In return, Freddy, who had the lead on all spiritual aspects, would share all that he could learn from archives and texts, or from, for want of a better word, "magical" means, that might assist in that endeavour. Janie was to take care of security and the raising of a well-equipped and highly trained army, Matt intelligence. Soames and Freddy would supply finance. Soames insisted that Eve agree to regular check-ups on her regeneration, and that she would undergo further surgery if necessary, or he would pull out and go his own way. He also insisted that she give him the benefit of her presence and assistance with various translations of texts, artefacts, and spiritual and occult experimentations of his own. Freddy and the others also wanted her time and aid in these areas, and Freddy demanded reciprocal arrangements from Soames regarding both scientific and religious research and discovery. In fact, Eve suspected that, if calculated, she had promised in excess of somewhere, in the region of, 200% of her time to the various factions. She had a special job for Ben, and he did not like it, nor did Freddy and Soames.

All parties were in agreement that Afsoon was, somehow, able to greatly influence people and events on earth, even from his remote position, somewhere on the far side of the sun. How he achieved this was beyond the understanding of any in the group assembled, spiritual or scientific. His intent, it was conjectured, was to raise a flood tide of worshippers in preparation for his return. The message of an absent Messiah who will announce his imminent coming with visions, prophecies and miracles, was an old, but also powerful, one and both Soames and Freddy had provided reports of just such a new religion spreading through, and from, the third world like an epidemic. There were already rumours of miraculous cures, walking on water, and even one case of apparent resurrection from death. Eve made the argument that fire should be fought with fire and that her own pseudo religion should be promoted. Soames almost got angry at this and Eve truly believed it would have been a first for him, but to Eve's dissatisfaction he managed to wrestle himself under control when Freddy stepped into the silence and took over once more.

"There is nothing pseudo about it. I know this distresses you Mr Soames, but, by your own admission, Eve is beyond human. She also fulfils a prophecy that pre-dates the Bible or any other religious writings you care to make reference to. I will be happy to show you scientific proof positive of this, if you will visit my laboratory some time. I think you will find that this is the very definition of a religious icon, the likes of which this world has never seen. Further, when divinity enters into the dealings of humanity, a sure sign of validation of that divinity is that great evil will rise to resist it, and I doubt if anyone here would not conclude that Afsoon is just such an evil. The body and DNA that is Eve was created at the same time as that of your biblical Eve, the Eve that so defied and angered your God. She was the perpetrator of original sin. And what was that sin? The sin of trying to know what he knew. My order would say that she had the spirit to be our saviour but God made her too weak to mother or sustain a race capable of facing the universe without God. We believe that the

Eve who stands here now is the intended Eve, that God balked at
creating lest, as the mother of humanity, she would birth a people
capable of taking ownership of this universe, without the help of,
or reliance on, Him. 'The Dawn Star' Lucifer, God's right hand
man, fortunately, was able to mitigate the damage of his friend and
master, when that master lost his way and became jealous of his
own creation and limited its ability for independence."

Eve sat down, drained and slack mouthed, but Soames had
gained a new, grudging respect from her when he held his tongue
and simply nodded with neutral disdain. She was not happy with
the turn of events. She was sure that to be worshipped would be to
lose the closeness of all her hard-won friends, and to be brutally
separated from the rest of humanity, but her prime objective for
now, was the defeat and destruction of Afsoon and everything he
represented. She knew that the Eve so eloquently created by Freddy was exactly the sort of fabled narrative who would win over
worshippers. She needed, not only to rival, but to dominate,
Afsoon's own efforts in this regard. She was, however, going to put
her own mark on it.

And so, to Ben's role in this, she insisted that he was to lead her
new church. He, like Peter, would be her rock and she hoped that
both Fadil and Jackie Barnes would be his bishops. Ben objected
vociferously but acquiesced when Eve just sat looking at him until
he ran out of steam. Jackie looked surprised but agreed that she
would be happy to help where she could, but it would have to fit
around her studies. As these were, in large part theological, she
thought her new role might offer unique insights. Fadil just smiled
acceptance.

Privately, Eve spoke pleadingly with all her friends, begging
them not to see her as anything but simply Eve. Matt and Jackie
were the only ones she felt were really listening, although Freddy
seemed to be able to view her both as friend and divinity, in equal
measure, whilst Ben, well Ben was never an open book. She would
just have to wait and see.

And so the stage was set. The next few months passed like a
whirlwind. Fadil with his newly acquired childlike simplicity,
surprised everyone by returning to the desert peoples, in a new
incarnation as healer, seer and prophet. Stranger yet, he seemed to
have a remarkable talent in these areas and Freddy had sent two

scribes to document his successes. Jackie seized on this and was working with Freddy's PR team to spread the word with great subtlety, working locally through word of mouth and rumour and random media filler stories. His reputation was catching fire in the tribal imagination and gaining some notoriety in wider society, and the name of Eve, "The Saviour Goddess" from the dawn of creation, likened by many to Gaia, was spreading like an underground stream, shrouded in mysticism, spoken of in fearful whispers, and celebrated in secret festivals and ancient rites by exultant and joyous converts, longing for the salvation that had been so very, very long in the coming. Jackie really had an exceptional gift for this sort of thing. Matt worked with both Freddy and Soames consolidating and improving spy networks and trying to infiltrate, observe and disrupt Afsoon's following around the globe. He also had to work closely with Janie. To create special ops forces that would tackle terrorist activities and head on attacks from rival forces.

Ben insisted on returning to Eve's side as often as possible and, to facilitate this, set about the completion of his allocated duties with great zeal. Under Jackie's guiding hand he set up churches in many deprived areas on the South American continent, where his streetwise nature was of great benefit. Eve would at unexpected times, however, often trip over him sleeping on the threshold of her room. She could not dissuade him from this activity and eventually had Freddy create an alcove to her room with a comfortable bed and facilities for his ad hoc use. Truth be told, she slept easier when she knew he was there. Eve herself was kept out of the limelight, except for the odd fuzzed photograph or video clip of her visiting one of her churches, or Fadil's hermitage, or addressing a street crowd (Jackie again). In truth, they were often not her at all. Eve had had an exhausting schedule, meeting her commitments to both Soames and Freddy, and just about everyone else. Soames now speculated that they had been looking in the wrong place for Afsoon. Neither, ground nor space telescopes or scanning devices had found anything. His belief was that they had made trajectory predictions based on known technologies. He now felt that the capsule's twenty-five year path could be travelling close to the speed of light, which would mean an orbit of vastly larger proportions. He was further concerned that it was stealthed, or cloaked, in some way unknown. He urged her to try to enter the spiritual, shard path, in the cave again, to try and find something that would locate Afsoon. Eve refused to rape more priests or to take part in any form of sacrifice and reckoned this barred any effort in that direction.

Freddy agreed. He was sure Afsoon would have taken protective measures and that Eve would be at extreme risk. "The fact is," he stated, "that, at the moment, Afsoon is by far the stronger of the two. Our only advantage is his current predicament, and our remoteness from it."

Soames countered. "But our best chance is to tackle him before he gets to earth. If what you say is true then his arrival will spell the end for us all." Eve resolved matters by agreeing to study the cave text with her unique vision and to probing the various paths revealed by the shard. She had been intent on this course anyway. Now she had good reason to take time out for the purpose.

Soames, struck to the heart of the matter, as usual. "We need a weapon to give us superiority. Have you been exploring the merits of the shard? I understand it is of unknown metal and has some unusual qualities in your hands. I would be more than happy to have it examined." Eve declined his offer. "Nevertheless, the pendant you wear shows five shards. At present you have only one and, I think it safe to assume that Afsoon has none at this stage. I would guess though that his followers are hard at work looking. It is likely that whoever gains the most shards will have the components of a weapon of unknown potential and, having more of them, it seems likely, would also give that party the advantage. I'm guessing though, that Afsoon might have a greater knowledge of how to use them. Also, the fractured nature of the depiction on your pendant suggests that, were all the shards brought together, and assembled whole, the wielder of that device might well have a great power indeed in her, or his, hands." Eve had been thinking along similar lines and so had Freddy. It was agreed that the search for the other shards should take priority over all else and the writings in the cave were the obvious place to start.

Eve visited the cave every day. She tried at different times of the day, starting at the altar at the time when the sun struck where the shard had been located, as it had been when she was last able to enter onto the spirit path. Shard in her hand, or shard relocated in its niche seemed to make no difference. She could not get back onto the path. She tried reading the golden thread in the story on the walls whilst holding the shard and then again after relocating it, or leaving it back on the other side of the valley in Freddy's care. Ben or Freddy sometimes accompanied her but she preferred to go alone and, oft times, insisted that she do so, entering and leaving at odd hours of the day and night. On more than one occasion she would find one or the other of them waiting patiently at the exit or at the base of the cliff. Janie was there more than once, and her guards were never far away. Eve had made various discoveries.

The altar was the least important part of the cave complex. It was kind of like the capsule at the tip of a rocket. A launch point, or opening, for the vastly complex mechanics and power of the entire cave system, above and below, and there was an awful lot of below. The system penetrated deep into the earth under the cliff base. Eve thought it would probably take years to search it all, and it would be easy to get hopelessly lost down there. Fortunately for Eve however, even in the pitch darkness she could always see the golden thread that ran though the pictorial, and written, events exhibited on, and in, the walls. This would always guide her back by the most direct route and it fed off of the whole system in a way that condensed miles of depictions into single words, that somehow, made sense of the whole to her. The shard, she grew to understand, was an enhancement and guidance tool. It seemed to expand her consciousness, allowing it to seep and flow into spiritual dimensions. She was becoming attuned to it. She had started to dream very vividly about it.

Tonight, having located it in its niche, she wandered the caves and came to a spot where she struggled to find meaning in the golden narrative. She would normally have fallen back on the shard to guide and sharpen her focus. There was something important here. Lacking its physical presence, she studied more intently the piece she was reading and drifted into daydream memories about the shard and her first sighting of it in the altar cavern. After a time she felt a pressure in her hand and found she was holding the shard, but it was not the shard. It was a kind of solid, three-dimensional image, and it sharpened her abilities just like the original. On an impulse she pushed it into the thread on the wall and that part of the narrative enfolded her.

She was floating just above a seabed. It was lightless yet she could see. She stretched long sinuous limbs, gave a powerful double kick and pulled webbed fingers through the shifting currents. She was mistress of this domain and the golden thread stretched before her. She followed and became aware she was accompanied. Small serpents were swimming along with her. They multiplied with every stroke she took, nuzzling and entwining around her body and limbs, until she must appear a moving nest of vipers, a Gorgon, a Medusa of the sea. And there below, a deep fissure in the seabed and somewhere, deep inside that fissure, a presence, agonised, malign, insane, and malevolent. The shard dropped from her hand and, with a slight rocking motion disappeared into the chasm and was lost. Suddenly she was back inside herself looking at the cave wall. Her jeans were wringing wet and she realised she had urinated. Touching the thread, she again summoned the image of the shard but, when it came, it was a ghostly insubstantial thing, not the solid object of before. Nevertheless, with great concentration she pushed it into the thread. Nothing happened. She left it there as a bookmark, knowing she could summon its whereabouts whenever she wished, and made her way back to the surface.

To her, she had been gone, perhaps, a night but three days had passed and, as she approached the surface, she could hear shouts and running feet and see torch beams. She walked into a melee of concerned people in near panic. Janie was almost hysterical. The only calm in the storm was Ben. He approached and patiently helped to disengage Janie from Eve's shoulders, which she had seized as if to reassure herself that Eve was real, and looked to hang on forever. Ben handed Eve a drink and a pack of sandwiches that she wolfed down with deep gratitude. Freddy helped to calm everyone down while Ben led Eve through a subdued crowd who parted before him like reeds before the prow of a boat. Such was his presence now. As soon as they were clear Eve left him, ran to the altar cavern, and was very relieved to see the shard still there. She took it and returned with Ben to her suite on the other side of the valley.

A meeting of the "disciples" (as they had now started referring to themselves, jokingly at first, following Soames' quip at Freddy in the conference suite) was called. Janie insisted that Eve was no

longer to go anywhere unaccompanied. Freddy said it was for Eve
to do as she pleased; her knowledge was divine and superior to any
of theirs. Matt, too, felt she should be given a free hand, but for
different reasons, basically it had worked so far and she should not
be hampered. In fact, Janie was outvoted by everyone present,
which left her in a terrible sulk. Matt moved things on to the more
important issue of what her experiences might reveal. Everyone
was baffled by her vision. Fortunately, Jackie was at the valley for
a few days. Her quiet voice dropped into the general hubbub of
debate and all stopped speaking. Everyone had come to understand that when Jackie spoke, it was always worth listening to.

"It seems obvious that the question is not, what this dream is
trying to say. I'm sure everyone knows it is suggesting the whereabouts of another shard." Most had realised this much but one or
two blank faces registered enlightenment. "The problem is the
spiritual realm often communicates in riddles and metaphors, so
we need to work out just how much of a metaphor this is. Is the
shard actually in a fissure on the sea floor and, if so, in what sea or
ocean, what latitude and longitude and how deep? And, if it is very
deep, I think you said it was lightless Eve, then, do we have the
technology to get down there? Last and this could be the most
worrying of all, what was the menacing presence you sensed there?
The appearance of serpents would seem to indicate Satan himself."

Fadil now interjected to raise a point. "Eve, I think you should
remove the ghost shard from the thread. It will be a beacon to the
'other' who would have knowledge of this. We know he has the
ability to walk the path, he followed you there before. Surely it
would be even easier for him to access this thread." As he spoke,
she reached for the shard on the table in front of her. It sang in her
hand. Reflexively, she projected into it to banish its ghostly counterpart in the caves under the valley by pulling it free. It was like
trying to contain an exploding bomb. Another hand was gripping
it too, but the ghost shard was her construct and she would have it.
With a superhuman effort of will, she disengaged the other, and
dissipated the object back to the ethereal realm from which she had
summoned it. The effort caused an implosive shock wave that left
her reeling. In a weakened state, she recounted to the others what
had just occurred.

Freddy asked. "Was he watching? Did he see?" Eve could not say. "Then we need to decipher this vision as quickly as possible. I will put all our resources, spiritual and scientific, onto this and Soames will need to know. Is there anything else you can tell us that might help with this, Eve?" She shook her head and everyone left to do their own research and make preparations. Jackie lingered behind. Ben sensed she wanted to talk with Eve privately and went outside. He had taken to meditating on a rock that overhung the valley floor at the edge of her terrace. His closeness to the edge made Eve fretful.

"What is it Jackie?"

Jackie looked uncomfortable. "I think I know where the second shard is. Not exactly, but I reckon I know which sea, and I would guess, from the reported instances of strange events happening in that area, that some power is at work influencing that whole section of the sea, so dead centre would be a good place to start."

"Well where is it, and how do you know this?"

"Describe the serpents to me." Eve did so. Jackie responded, "Eels."

"Eels?"

"Yes, eels, don't you see? It's the Sargasso Sea where eels go to spawn, that's what was crowding around you, hardly any metaphor at all really, and what sits right over and on the Sargasso Sea?"

"The Bermuda triangle." They said it together.

"Of course, that has to be it. Jackie you are a genius, but why didn't you say this at the meeting?"

"You like to work unhampered don't you. I wanted to give you the chance to slip away from all the back up and support required for that kind of operation. It is bound to attract the wrong sort of attention."

"You're right but on this occasion I think I am going to need a lot of technical support, if it really is deep down like you said, and maybe some fire power, to deal with whatever menace is down there."

"I don't think so. Speak to Fadil. He thinks you should keep this as small as possible. Since his experiences in the," she hesitated, "since you," she paused again, "you know, in the altar cavern." She wriggled in embarrassment, "he has become aware of certain things. He has insights regarding your vision. You need to talk with him. I told him to come here tomorrow. I need to make some arrangements but I will be here too."

Fadil was much changed from the flirtatious and energetic young man she'd met in the Bedouin encampment. He now had a serene air of inner calm and a subtle dynamism, quite different from the youthful energy of before. He was much more mysterious and contemplative and, although, sometimes vague and distracted in conversation, he would at times suddenly seem to contract from a great awareness inside himself and look directly out at you with a power that was like a cresting wave poised to crash in a cascade of wisdom. Not this time, however, and indeed, never, when speaking to Eve. With Eve he was always deferential, offering his insights and knowledge like a vendor displaying wears for a buyer's approval, ever eager for confirmation of his ability, and good intent.

"I have been having dreams and visions and I have been speaking with Jackie and Soames and, at Soames' suggestion, whilst I have taken great care to impart to him as little information as possible, I have also spoken with Helen." Eve's head snapped up at this, but she remained calm and contained, and allowed Fadil to continue. "Helen described an incident when you swam together and argued. She said you disappeared under the waves and communicated with a dolphin. She also said you were down for a very long time and quite deep."

"What are you getting at Fadil?"

He continued, "In your vision you were surrounded by serpents and you felt mistress of your domain, and ..." he took a deep breath for emphasis, "you communicate with dolphins." He waited for that to sink in. "As stated, I too have had dreams and visions. In them I have seen you in the unsettling guise of a Mer Queen, commanding the denizens of the sea and the very waves themselves." Eve could not help but turn her eyes upward but she resisted the temptation to tut. Visibly flustered he, nevertheless, carried on, but now in some haste, lest she stop him before he could finish. "I know my visions are more fanciful and vague than yours, I am only a man," he added defensively (it struck her that he was going to say human but she let it pass), "but I think the meaning is clear. I don't believe you will be able to command seas, it is just that I have been granted a vision, of many layers, from which I have divined truth. This is my skill, that I put at your service and I do think, I truly believe, that you will be able to call upon the creatures of the sea to elicit their aid. You must have faith in your own abilities, divine one." He started to stammer and could not get his words out. Eventually he just gave up and adopted a distracted and vacant stare.

Eve went to him and, taking his hands, brought him gently to his feet. She kissed him lightly on the forehead.

"Fadil, you are a true friend. I thank you for your wise words and skilful guidance. I know you will be discreet and tell no one of this. You must leave now and continue your valuable and important work. It is a great weight off my shoulders knowing you are there amongst the people promoting our cause. We will talk again soon but for now I must consider my next move and make plans. Good health and strength to all your endeavours." She ushered him gently out of the door. Jackie made to leave too.

Eve placed a hand on her chest. "Jackie, please stay. There is something I wanted to ask you." She waited in the passageway until Fadil turned out of sight then returned to the room, closing the door behind her.

Treachery

"What do you make of that?" Jackie sat down and thought for a few moments. Eve gave her time.

"Hmm, it was strange. In essence, it was no different to my own conversation with him, and he has convinced me of the likely truth of what he says. His visions and interpretations have been amazingly accurate until now, and it makes sense. If you are of a kind with the biblical Eve, then scripture would support that you have command over the creatures of earth, but when he spoke with me, it was with absolute authority and confidence, more important though, with loyalty and strength of purpose. The man here, just now, was completely different, unsure, defensive and, well, shifty! Perhaps he is just overawed by you."

"Overawed? Or emasculated and scared? It was not the Fadil I know. This was not just the usual diffidence and respect he affords. Who knows what horrors have come back to haunt him. I misused him in the most terrible way. Perhaps I put him back together again wrong. And isn't this all just nonsense. I am neither divine nor a goddess. I can't command creatures and tell the sea what to do. I have some enhanced abilities, that's all."

"Far more than that Eve, and didn't you also give some rather complex instructions to a pack of dogs, when you were trapped on that rock in the sea with Ben, and didn't they obey to the letter?"

"I can't explain what happened there but this is a lot more than communicating a few vague wishes to a group of dogs. If the depths are as great as we think, instructions would have to be relayed through a chain of very strange, even monstrous, creatures of the deep. Even a dolphin can't hold its breath forever and the pressures would crush it, wouldn't they? Impossible, it's ridiculous even to think about it."

"Not at all, you were surrounded by eels and felt yourself to be their mistress. Eels swim very deep. Listen Eve, you have to experiment and to realise all of your abilities. One day, not too far from now, Afsoon will arrive. In many ways he's here already, and you need to be in full possession and command of all of your abilities if you are going to stand a chance of defeating him. You are our best hope Eve. If you fail, we all do. But I agree something is not quite right with Fadil. We need to bring Freddy and Matt in on this.

Freddy sat quietly whilst Matt spoke. Eve looked at him searchingly. "Really Matt? You think it wise to bring Janie in on this?" She looked at Jackie and Freddy for support. "She can be a bit heavy handed. I don't want Fadil beaten to death, just to find out why he is acting a bit strange."

"You've got her wrong you know and she has changed too. She can be subtle when necessary."

Eve looked doubtful, "Anyway, she has already raised concerns about him with me and has been keeping an eye on him since your sojourn in the caves."

"Why?"

"Because he disappeared for a while when we were looking for you and Janie noticed a change in him afterwards."

Eve started thumbing her nose, as she usually did when she was in deep or agitated thought. "And what has she found out?"

"Well, for a start, he has made several further visits to the caves, and he always goes down."

"Do we know where exactly?"

"No. It would be impossible to follow him closely without him knowing of it and without him in sight, as a guide, the only person who could follow him, and be sure of getting out again, is you. Janie suspects he is trying to find where you inserted the ghost shard."

"Then I had better get about following him as soon as possible."

"No need. Fadil was entering the caves just before I came here. Janie is following him in."

"But I thought you said ..."

"I've fitted her with a very high powered tracking device and a relay of receivers to plant on route, with back up officers at intervals behind her. I reckon we should know something soon."

Everyone had run out of things to say and had all settled into their own private ruminations. Matt was quietly drumming his fingers on the arm of his chair when there was a raised voice and disturbance outside the door. Ben seemed to materialise from thin air, machete in hand into the space between the door and Eve. Matt slipped smoothly into a crouch behind the sofa with a pistol aimed steadily at the door and Jackie moved next to Eve, who stood poised and relaxed as a cat observing its next kill. The door burst open under the force of Janie's boot and a bound and spindly creature was thrown across the floor at Eve's feet. She was also gripping another entity's wrist in her left hand and dragged, what turned out to be, a disoriented and confused Fadil into the room.

"Sit down over there you bloody fool and don't talk until I say you can, understand?"

Fadil wobbled over to a chair and sat quietly, with a confused and guilty look on his face.

Janie addressed Eve, "May I sit please, Eve?"

"Of course, and never ask me that again. You are my friend and my equal and you may sit wherever you want without my permission. Can I get you something to drink?"

For a moment a wave of unreadable expressions fought for dominance over Janie's features before she managed to regain her usual dour look. She shook her head and sat, back straight, hands on open knees, and nodded to the petrified thing on the floor that was currently looking along the edge of a machete, pressed to its throat, and into the vengeful and penetrating gaze of Ben, who was flashing a shark like grin.

"He is probably unrecognisable now but that invertebrate at your feet is your old friend Hakeem, or so Fadil tells me. When you were missing in the caves, Fadil wandered off alone using intuition and his eerie visionary talent to search for you. He found instead this thing, or rather this thing found him. It seems in your last encounter with Afsoon you managed, largely, to nullify his observation of, and direct interference in, your activities. But Afsoon maintained a strong connection to Hakeem and set him to watch and wait, and to learn what he could in the caves. He seems to have been living on vermin, insects and cave moisture these last months but I'm guessing his eyes have transmitted much information back to Afsoon. For all I know, Afsoon may by now be aware of where all the remaining shards are hidden.

"When I caught up with Fadil this evening, he was wandering around in the cave system, muttering and seemingly arguing with himself. There was some sort of red mist surrounding him. When I listened closer he seemed to be trying to exorcise the mist, as though it were the breath of Satan himself. He was clutching a talisman and garbling something in Arabic, and making sweeping gestures with his arms. Frankly, he looked like he was losing. He seemed to be hunching over. After a while I'd had enough and challenged him. I caught hold of what I thought was his shoulder. It was not. It was this creature wrapped around him like a leech and feeding off the vein in his neck whilst whispering instructions into his ear. Those instructions had such force that I was almost overcome myself. I had to be quite violent to silence and subdue him, so I'm afraid you may find him very broken. As his struggles abated, so the red mist thinned, but it was poisonous and choking and I was exhausted and disorientated. The tracker supplied by Matt had somehow got lost. Thank God Fadil still maintained his ability to guide us out.

"I questioned Fadil on route. It seems he has suspected Afsoon had an agent in the caves and has been seeking him out. The fool didn't think that you or anyone else needed to be bothered with this. From what I have pieced together, he was totally unaware of this parasite feeding off him and thought that he was returning to the cave each night and fighting off the malevolent presence there that was hindering your own exploration and research. I suspect this thing has been feeding off, and weakening and distorting, his will on every visit and, from what I saw, he was about to be completely consumed. I think you need to speak to him ... May I have that drink now please? I think I might be about to faint."

Eve was at her side in an instant, turning her so her legs were on the arm of the sofa and her head was low, and was dripping water into her mouth. When she was comfortable Eve faced Fadil with a look heavy with expectancy.

Fadil looked to be on the edge of collapse and was dripping blood from a gash on his neck but he was recognisable once more as the person Eve had brought back from the dead. He smiled weakly. "I owe my continued existence to you my mistress of the desert but it seems I now owe my soul to this warrior woman. I have been a fool. I sought to take some of the stress from you all and fear I may have made matters worse. I have allowed a bad situation to continue and myself to be contaminated. If this brave woman had not rescued me, I would have become as this entity before you, a creature of the sleeping Satan, and I am afraid I may already have been his instrument. I was with you, that first time, on the spirit road. Afsoon knew me and was able to penetrate my id through my visions and through my blood. Hakeem not only took my blood but I fear he has shared his with me. I think his mind, and the mind that controls him, are working for dominance in me as we speak. Kill me now. I would not be compelled to betray you."

"Information first Fadil."

"Of course my lady Eve. The hand you felt on the ghost shard was not that of Afsoon. It was Hakeem, acting as a proxy channel for the power of Afsoon. Otherwise, it is unlikely you would have wrested it from his grasp. Had you not done so, Afsoon would have been able to absorb much power from the shard, weakening our advantage greatly. Through Hakeem's connection with me, he has used my visionary skill, and my spiritual communion with you, to observe you and to read through many of the cave inscriptions. He is knowledgeable Eve. He knew where to look. He has discovered the location of the second shard and has also divined the whereabouts of the third."

"But if he was working through you, you must have seen what he saw."

"No, it was mostly hidden from me. I have nothing else to tell you."

Eve had unconsciously picked up the shard and it was now pulsing in her hand like a beating heart, urging her to action. Having believed herself free, at least temporarily, from the crushing and all-pervading presence of Afsoon, she now felt all her plans were crumbling under the sheer weight of his malignant will. Eve felt she would suffocate if she didn't act now. She came to a decision. Whipping across a left hook to the back of Fadil's jaw, she threw his unconscious body over her shoulder, then, stuffing the shard in her waistband, she leant down, grabbed the loose flesh of Hakeem's waist in a crushing grip and rolled him up under her arm. She spoke to the unconscious Fadil as she strode from the room. "I saved you once, you incredible little man. I'm not going to lose you again to the likes of Afsoon and his warped creature Hakeem."

Rage and anger, and the need to act, were swamping all reason and judgement. Afsoon would threaten the lives of her friends and loved ones no more, not in this her haven, her house. She would rip this thorn from her side once and for all. "Freddy come with me and bring what priests you need for a ritual. You are going to help me get back on the spirit road. I have vermin to destroy."

At the alter cave, Freddy was fretting. "Eve you can't do this. Sex with Hakeem and Fadil, whilst Afsoon continues to possess and manipulate their wills, may get you on the spirit path but Afsoon will be waiting and it is quite possible he will overpower you and gain access to this place through you. You must build your strength. Do not dance to his tune."

"Where's your faith Freddy?" She did not pause. She laid Fadil on the foot of the alter and Hakeem, whose struggles had ceased, on the centre, where she straddled him, hooking her feet over the torso of Fadil. She was following some inner dialogue, revealed to her from the throbbing sensations of the shard that was now almost writhing in her hand. "You told me once Freddy that sexual magic was powerful because it was the act that created life but that the act of taking life away was perhaps stronger. We need a sacrifice Freddy." As she said this, her hand arced through the air, clutching the vibrating shard. Hakeem started to struggle when realisation of his fate dawned on him but then, as the point of the shard smashed through his forehead dragging splinters of bone in its wake, a sly smile died on his lips before agony subsumed him.

Eve exploded onto the spirit road accelerating at breath-taking speed towards the tiny star she knew to be the hurtling sarcophagus, transporting the body of Afsoon through the depths of limitless space. Landing like a hawk in full stoop, she wriggled through the skin of the hull and scuttled with the dexterity of a spider (although, on encountering the web of fibres supporting Afsoon, she felt more like a fly). Avoiding the seeking and sentient tips that waved like sea anemones, she squirmed through the forest of tangled roots, slithering closer to his inert form before they, or he, became aware of her presence. Summoning another ghost shard she slashed through the fibres and plunged it into Afsoon's head, exactly as she had Hakeem's. They were now one. She could not kill Afsoon, but she could make him experience death through Hakeem, and she could prolong that death and make it tortuous. Afsoon screamed and the wires writhed but whilst she maintained this connection they could not distinguish her from Afsoon. Instead they created a bubble of awareness in which Eve stood facing Afsoon with her fist, bearing the shard buried in his skull. They were floating in a silvery white sphere. He appeared relaxed and calm but her senses were acutely attuned to his pain and torment. His eyes were dilated, black as obsidian, and deep as the vastness of space.

He was first to speak. "You are full of surprises aren't you, Eve? I feel I can call you that now with confidence. There is little left of John in you. Your humanity is melting away. Soon you will despise them."

"I am still more human than you have ever been."

"Are you Eve? Are you really? You have spiked a living creature, a human being, to an altar table, like a butterfly to a collector's board, and now you are slowly and agonisingly killing him, for no other reason than to demonstrate your power, and to exact vengeance on me. And what good will it do? What purpose does it serve? I will recover and you will have the devil of a job escaping this vessel's protective security, and my own wrath of course. Once the power provided by Hakeem's dying leaves you helpless and alone here, you are lost. But I like this new Eve. She is far more fitted to rule than the old. I will make you a once only offer. Be my wife and concubine willingly and I will let bygones be forgotten. We shall rule together as equals."

"I'd rather eat shit for eternity than spend another moment with you."

"The first part can be arranged. You will never escape me Eve. Give up this pointless resistance. I am your destiny. You will be my wife. And that could be a truly pleasant experience, if you agree to my offer."

In her mind's eye Eve drew a fingernail across Hakeem's navel. On the altar, his intestines spilled out through the wound. Afsoon tried not to react but was brought to his knees with the pain. In spasm with the effort to articulate, he ground out his words, "I take it you refuse. That is a pity but it is good too, because it frees me from my offer. The pain I now suffer is terrible, but you have a very limited imagination. Not even very original are you? Drawing out entrails like that, seems to me you've seen that before, when I shared the mind of that very promising young man Sadique. I thought, his application of the medium rather more artistic than yours, but then I was prompting him so perhaps that is understand-able. You on the other hand are becoming a very substandard imitation of myself. Still, your ruthless streak is really starting to show and that is a good start. You might be interested to know that Hakeem, unlike Sadique, is a total innocent."

"I could not control Sadique, only prompt and coax his actions. His wickedness, although delicious, was his own. Hakeem though is a weak mind, quite a goodly person really, in a shallow sort of way. Everything he did was totally at my bidding, and against his own will, and look at how you have treated him. Not with the sympathy and kindness he deserves. That is certain. I'm not sure that even I could have been so cruel. You truly will be the perfect receptacle for my seed Eve. Our sons and daughters will be entirely unhampered by any form of weakness or useless pangs of con-science, and they will be born from your suffering which will make them vengeful and merciless. They will need those qualities if they are to rule effectively. We will have such times you and I. I will take great delight in teaching you what real pain is and I shall have forever to do it. The experience will be good for you. I will temper and mould you for all of eternity. The process is already begun."

Eve was starting to doubt the wisdom of her rashness in coming here but her course was set. There was no changing her mind now.

"Release Fadil from your influence! Sever the connection now, and permanently, or you will find my imagination for pain can reach further than you can ever conceive. Don't try any tricks. I am connected with you through the shard. I will know if you try to deceive. In fact, sever all your earthly connections." Afsoon shook his head mockingly, then, would have screamed out in pain, but could not, because he was gagging on the proxy entrails being stuffed into his mouth, and which he was being forced to swallow, as Eve pinched on Hakeem's nose and massaged his throat, knuckling down the organic mess with her fist. Afsoon, somehow, managed to get to his feet and square his shoulders. Despite Eve's efforts, Hakeem was fading, and Afsoon was gaining strength. Something had to be done, and done now! Her attention was being dragged towards the disc formed by the base of the shard, still held in her bunched fingers, when, a vision swamped her senses and a premonition drove her to action. She commanded and manipulated the disc, expanding its diameter until she was engulfed by it. She then swam into the diminishing cone with powerful strokes, against an equally powerful outwash.

She could hear Afsoon's panicked shout. "Eve don't!"

Then she was at the apex and drawing herself through. A black cloud of pain and hatred engulfed her. She fought for breath against the in-pouring entrails, and felt pincers of blackness pulling at her mind, drawing out her essence. With a supreme effort of will, lent strength by her own fear and panic, she dispersed it and crawled into the womb of a soft red tunnel, where lay Fadil sleeping. Other tunnels branched off in every direction and she could hear a thousand dialogues going on.

"Yes Mesiah, we will kill them all."

"Oh great Afsoon hear our prayers."

"The false Goddess will soon fall."

She listened intently trying to sift out the most relevant. "We will obtain the false one's stolen shard. She seeks the second but it is protected. We can bargain."

"When we have the third shard, the location of the fourth will be revealed."

"When we have all five, we can summon the sixth."

"Hush! Be quiet, we are observed."

The walls began to undulate and contract violently like a bowel squeezing faeces. Eve snatched up Fadil's body and pushed it through, ahead of herself, into the punctured end of the apex, of the, now giant, shard. As she crawled through, she was caught in a tornado of black treacle that flopped her down onto a hard surface, and into its own congealed gore. A blinding light drove a jagged edge of searing pain behind her eyes, as she struggled to raise herself from the ruined remains of Hakeem's desiccated body. "Get that bloody torch out of my face will you?"

Nobody said anything. They wiped off the gore as best they could and helped her back to her suite of rooms. She was puzzled by their quiescence but was content not to talk, apart from instructing that, "Fadil would now be alright and should be given rest."

Eve allowed them to help and support her back to the sanctuary of her bed and the sleep of the innocent, but, despite her exhaustion she did not sleep. She was no longer even remotely innocent. With her unthinking murder of a blameless and anguished man, she had forfeited all claims to that respite. Afsoon was right, God help her. She was different from him only in the limits of her imagination. What had she become? She had become the shit on the shoe of a tyrant, repugnant and worthless. During the twilight of her restless semi-slumberings, the world began to rumble and heave and, finally, crashed in on her in a riptide surge of dark murk and horror from which demons prodded and slashed at her dark thoughts and self-loathing emotions, and then were gone to make way for the next queue of tormentors.

On and on it went, each slash and prod, carving scars of despair deeper into her soul. Echoing whispers pervaded her mind. What had she done? She was a failure, had let everyone down, all those who loved her. They would all hate her now, those who were not yet dead, as surely they soon all would be. How they would regret their loyalty to her. Craven and weak, a traitor to humanity, killer of friends, deceiver of lovers and loved ones, a slut and a whore, worthless and unfit to exist. She could bear it no more. Loss, failure, bad decisions and unfulfilled responsibilities choked any residue of motivation. Her own stupidity turned her to black despair. Doubts and misgivings poured shame and self-hatred into her mind. Her will to resist her own condemnation shut down and scuttled away. She slithered into a nightmare dreamscape where she was John, drowning in a vat of black treacle, being topped up by herself opening the wheel of a giant faucet.

Afsoon above, on a Zeus-like throne, hurled thunderbolts, imbued with his words, that crashed about her ears in a shale of broken razor blades, each tearing a little bit more off her soul and slashing it into disintegrating shreds. "Full of surprises aren't you Eve? ... Losing your humanity ... are you Eve? Are you really? ... Spiked a living creature ... Killing him for no other reason ... A butterfly to a collector's board ..." This last became a sea of humanity, row after row, nailed to a vast undulating red board. She was just hammering in the last nail through John's chest at the end of a row that included all her friends, both dead, and alive. Next on the pile to be added was Helen. And all the while Eve was sobbing and muttering. "Vengeance is mine. An eye for an eye, and she gouged one out, a tooth for a tooth, she pulled one, a life for a life."

And Afsoon's mocking words continued to crash around her. "This new Eve ... more fitted to rule ... Receptacle for my seed." She looked down at her hand and saw she had crushed Helen so completely her entrails were squeezing out through her fingers. She started to scream hysterically and insanely, with Afsoon's laughter echoing in her ears. "There is little of John left in you now ... Poor, poor Hakeem, so innocent so abused so ... murdered! MURDERER! RAPIST! TORTURER! Hakeem held her firmly in his giant fist and was plunging her, head first, into his stomach, using her as a hook to pull out his intestines and, all the while, screaming in agony.

When she could draw breath, she begged and wept, each tear releasing a fetid stench that reminded her of the faeces that Afsoon was waiting to feed her with at every meal for all of eternity. "Please, please, forgive me, please, please, PLEASE!" Afsoon LOOMED LARGE wielding a serrated hunting knife, gouging the nose out of her face again and again with slow, bone crunching, sawing movements, inflicting unbearable pain, with each pull and slow, deep, grating push of the blade.

"Eve. You have to be punished for your vile and evil treatment of my people. I am your God now, and I am a vengeful God. The punishment must fit the crime." As he cut, she screamed, but she could not drown out his voice. It ate into her brain. "I think I will keep you in this disfigured state forever to remind all of the cost of defiance. I will let you regenerate occasionally so that you can demonstrate your desperate need to satisfy my lusts. If you are well behaved, I may let you keep your beauty until you displease me. Then it will all begin again. I am interested to see how many times you will recover, until your disfigurement becomes a permanent feature. Then, I can always cover your head and work with the rest of you. You will still be able to bear my children after all, and you will make a wonderful mother Eve, and an obedient and depraved wife." And all the while her own screaming deafened her as though she were a giant bell and her screams, and his words, were dual clappers clanging against the inside of her skull, and going on, and on, forever.

She saw a sanctuary, a dark velvet black space spilling into a hole in the ground. A frightened little boy again, scared to go forward but terrified to go back, he crawled on shaking hands and knees into the hole, and dug like a dog into the coal, until he found the darkest, deepest corner. Curling into a foetal ball he shivered and hid and prayed. A thunderous tread shook the world and a giant eye looked through the hole, searching, He made himself small. A lid clanged on the hole and the light went out forever.

A whisper in the dark disturbed the all-enveloping blackness. The nothing, the no one that he was, blocked it out, but it was persistent.

"John?" It was seeking him. It must not find him. Curling tighter, he sunk further into the corner covering his ears, squeezing his eyes tightly, shut in case the light came. "JOHN! COME OUT!" John scuttled away clawing at the cellar wall. Then, like a hand, groping beneath the shingle of insanity, Soames' voice reached down to him and found the hidden psyche below. "Come John. I've been searching for you. You don't have to be afraid. I will be with you ... Helen is here ..." A wavering little voice whispered into the gloom.

"She died ... All are dead ... I killed them ... He made me do it ... He wants to hurt me really, really bad."

"Helen is here. She is alive and safe. She has come to see you."

"No! I squeezed her, and he took my nose, and I'm ugly, and it hurts, and he's going to do things to me for ever and ever." He crawled deeper into the coals, then, another voice.

"John, I'm here. I love you John. Come out John. We're all here, all your friends, Matt, Jackie, Janie, Fadil and Ben."

"All?"

"Yes."

"And Ben?"

"Yes."

Soames spoke again. "Let's kick him out John. You're not a little boy anymore. You're a man … for Helen, John."

"Yes for me John. For us, do it for us." The whisper steadied and grew stronger.

"And Ben will be there too?"

"Yes."

"I hurt Ben."

"Ben loves you too John. We all do."

Soames spoke again. "Come John. It is time to get rid of this bad thing. This is your house, your body. He has no power here. Get up! Take my hand!"

"Will, will Eve come?"

"Oh yes, John. Eve will come and she will be a fury, and she will be you, and you will destroy this spiteful and twisted thing that has invaded your house. Come!"

John reached up and took his hand and rose from the coals, and thrust a hand through the ceiling, and clambered out, and became John the man, and Eve the avenging goddess. And her voice was a hurricane, and she called for Afsoon. And Afsoon was there, leaning nonchalantly on a post office letter box.

"I see you brought your friends Eve. Nearly had you there, didn't I? It will do you no good in the end though." He walked forward and looked at Soames. "I might have guessed you were involved Exorcist. How did you keep yourself hidden from me for so long? Cat got your tongue? No matter. I see you now."

"You do not frighten me Afsoon. You were always a spiteful, nasty and evil little child and that's all you ever will be at heart. It's time you left. Get out of here, now!"

"That's not for you to say though, is it Soames? You can only support and assist, so I think I'll stay a bit longer. Perhaps I'll cut your nose off again Eve, and rape you a few more times. What do you say, you up for another round? Soames and your other friends can watch if they like." So saying he gestured and the manhole to the coal cellar spun into existence over his left shoulder. "Or you can go hide again. Much quieter in there, safe, you can sleep, lose yourself. You don't want to listen to Soames. After all, he's in your mind as well, aren't you Soames? Taught me everything I know about how to get in, and now he wants me out. You might say I'm here because of him. Perhaps I should exorcise you Soames, tell you to GET OUT!"

Soames staggered and lost substance but kept his feet and solidified again. "Oh bravo Soames, you always were a strong one. You were a good teacher too." Sensing her surprise, he turned to Eve. "Oh! He didn't tell you did he? Tut, tut, Soames."

"Shut up and leave, Afsoon. It didn't take long to discover you for the viper you are. I am here to restore to this body its rightful owner, not to trick an innocent soul into vacating it for my possession. Don't listen to him, Eve. Throw him out. He has no power here that you do not give to him."

"Well, Eve, it seems we have a quandary. You are currently possessed by two spirits. He says you can throw me out. But this is not actually your body, is it John? If you try to throw me out and I win, well, then I would occupy two bodies. How delicious. Sex would be incredible don't you think? And where would you go John? You lost your humanity some time ago, so no biblical God would want you. I'm your God now and I think I can supply a suitable hell for your helpless soul, but I will have to deal with two of you. I can do that but it will drain my resources, so I am open to negotiation. Crawl back into your hole John. In return, I will leave all those dear to you alone and I will give you ... oblivion. Sounds good doesn't it. You're tired, John. You are long past dead now. Accept my offer. It's the best you're going to get. Fight me and ... well you know how vengeful I can be."

Eve snatched out with devastating speed and gripped Afsoon's face, squeezing until his eyes popped. "This is my body Afsoon and I don't need you to leave here. Why don't you stay? Be my guest you bastard, because I am going to make you pay for every hurt you ever did to me or mine." A golden cloud, laced with black, started to coalesce around Afsoon. He was instantly aware of it and was suddenly behind, and clear, of it.

"Clever girl, I can see I may have underestimated your instinctive and intuitive grasp of your hidden abilities, but you will never match me Eve. I was way ahead of you when we started and by the time I arrive in person you will know the futility of all your pitiful efforts. Oh, and Soames, you may not be frightened of me now but you will be. Stay alive Soames, I have a special fate reserved for you."

Soames' weary voice cut through the air again. "Just cast him out Eve. Do it with force and do it now. There is no gain in listening to his spite and deceits."

But Afsoon had one last thing to say. "And, by the way John, Annabel misses you."

Finally, at the exact same moment of Afsoons' last utterance, Eve roared, "GET OUT!" The dark cloud imploded, releasing a crackling white hot photon whip that slashed into the vacant spaces previously occupied by the groin and chest of Afsoon.

He was gone already. Eve felt his true absence for the first time since they had met. And it was like a mountain had been removed from her shoulders. Soames offered his hand again and solidity began to form in the white space that currently surrounded them. Objects began to take shape. She was in her room in the cliff face of the valley. It was evening, and the last rays of the setting sun lanced in, lining objects and the occupants in the room in a reddish glow.

A New Quest

Ben and Janie had been trying to restrain her and had failed badly. The room was wrecked. A crystallised wave of reason and clarity broke inside her, to wash and lap gently through her being but in the disturbed gravel of its passing the seed of Afsoon's last, lost comment took root and swayed unseen in the murky wash. She floundered out from the cloying residue of her madness, finally coming into full cognizance, amid a coughing fit to find herself sitting up on the splintered remains of her smashed and broken bed.

"Soames?" She looked at Soames, holding her hand. He was stooped over her, and looking for all the world as though he actually cared. Then, with more focused concentration, she looked around at the room. It was all but destroyed. Fadil sat on the wreckage of a chair in the corner, looking exhausted. Janie and Ben were sweating and dishevelled, with all the appearance of having been in the front line of a riot. Matt looked little better. Jackie stood, awkwardly, by the door, and there, behind Soames, stood Helen, the embodiment of all hope and reason.

"Jesus John, things you'll do to get a date." She looked around calmly and said, "leave us for a bit please?" There was reluctance and hesitation but nobody argued. Janie helped Fadil to his feet.

"How long have I been raving?"

"Five days."

"And you? How long have you been here?"

"Three hours."

"Shit! You heard what I did?"

"Yeah ... It was cruel John."

"John ...?" He looked down at his breasts then back at Helen.

"I know who I am speaking to. You are tough John, and you will never shirk to do what you have to, but you were never cruel before." In the heavy silence that followed, she gave him time to absorb her damming words ... "Come on, shove over. The night air is cold here and I need some body heat." Kicking off her shoes, she wriggled in beside him and laid her head on his chest. Old habit and reflex guided his arm in its encirclement of her shoulders.

"What made you come?"

She looked up at him. "Not fooled are you John? You know how much convincing it takes when my mind is made up. It was Soames. When I saw how worried he was, I knew it was bad. He begged me to come but he needn't have. Once I knew you were in danger, nothing could have stopped me."

"You never came when I was cut."

She huffed and sighed deeply, "Ah that. I never knew John, at least not at first. Soames kept it from me. I did enquire once but you had instructed that no one, least of all me, should see you like that. That hurt John. Then later they hid you and, after that, Soames persuaded me that this was something you had to live through on your own, that my interference would only weaken you and you needed to learn and to grow stronger."

Eve went silent for a while, whilst Helen watched.

Biting her lip and fearful of Helen's reaction, Eve spoke, "I don't know what happened, Helen. I made what I thought was a necessary choice, to save Fadil and others, and even, perhaps, to give release to Hakeem. It seemed like a clear choice, a decision that had to be made fast, or be lost but, somehow when I was confronted by Afsoon, I lost all perspective and reason. You know, I was never particularly religious, ironic given my current status, but that guy is Satan times a thousand. He really frightens me Helen. I think he may be unbeatable and, even if I could defeat him, I am just as frightened of what I am becoming, and worse. Helen, forgive me for this, the sexual attraction he exerts over me is almost impossible to withstand. Soames is right. I should be killed. It would put both me, and everyone I come into contact with, out of our misery."

"Don't wallow in self-pity John. It has never been a part of your make up. You are the only thing that stands between humanity and Armageddon. Whether you like it or not you are in this fight until the end, and you have never avoided a fight, but you are not alone. You have wonderful friends, and now you have me too, but you will only keep us, John, if you stay true to who you are."

"But who am I, Helen? I'm not John any more. I think I am slowly becoming a monster. And what are you? Wife? Lover? Absent friend?"

She held his eyes for several moments. "Just friends for now John, but extremely good friends, and absent no more and you are John, the man, and now woman. I have always known. You will not fail John. Soames tells it well." She drew breath and quoted from memory. "'You were transformed from an ageing, terminally ill fatalist, waiting for death, into a young sexually dynamic female athlete with expanded physical and paranormal abilities.' You are the same person inside but the pressures and influences on you are incomprehensible. There is no precedent. Flash flooded with a torrent of raging hormones, power to crush all those around you, and adrift in the maelstrom of an unstable universe. In this cauldron of chaos you have had, somehow, to adapt. Add to that the loss of everything dear to you and the threat of torture, humiliation, sexual domination and annihilation by demonic forces no one could begin to imagine and he, and I, and probably the rest of the world, find it astounding that you are able to function at all, let alone to have adopted the care of humanity as your prime concern."

"And Soames said all this, did he? And what does Soames say about my current bout of insanity?"

"He says it is not insanity, it is humanity. He says he was wrong. Whilst Afsoon is alive, he still fears any union between you, but he also feels that without you, there is little hope of defeating him. He thinks you made a terrible mistake in trying to confront Afsoon head on, but that your reaction to the callous enactment of your failure, which he has been anticipating for some time, was better than he could have dared to hope. Only someone completely in touch with their humanity could react with such self-loathing and punishing remorse."

"It was me who did this terrible thing Helen, me who has watched, with futile impotence, whilst my friends, and those I loved were, and are being, destroyed, no one else."

"He said you would say something like that, and that it was a crossroads you had to encounter sooner or later, and besides you were at the mercy of cataclysmic events, having to think and learn on your feet, whilst fighting against a formidable and deadly foe who held all the cards. Your mind, since your transference, has never been entirely your own. Afsoon took the place of your cancer and sat there gnawing away at you but you resisted and you have won. It is your mind again now, John. You may be called Eve and have the body of a goddess but it is still you inside. You know John, Soames dreaded the prospect that you might never recover. He loves you as much as the rest of us, but he fears the loss of humanity even more.

"His hope was that, if he could stimulate your return to something approaching normality, your incredible mind and body would redress any chemical and psychological imbalances and bring you back to sanity. To help, and to facilitate that, he needed a strong emotional and sexual stimulus, hence the need of my presence and ministrations." She slapped his shoulder when he squirmed at that. "Although, Freddy says that, if we were successful in bringing you back, there are certain rituals that should be performed, to make sure any lingering influence, from your mental union with Afsoon, is completely purged. He is making preparations now.

"What this all amounts to John, is that you are still you, and you still have friends who love and support and need you. It is just that, while you were dying, fate took a hand and traded in your clapped out banger of a body for a shiny new, atomic rocket variety. Snatched from the clutches of a premature death, you found yourself instead at the controls of a dangerous machine in a very vulnerable and unstable environment, and you were overwhelmed by the potency of its performance, and the responsibility of handling it. So stop hiding John and come out of there." She straddled him and leaned in close to his face, rapping on his forehead with her knuckles. Holding his gaze for several seconds, she folded back onto his chest and sighed. After a few moments she spoke again and sent her hand questing downwards. "So, tell me, what's this about an overwhelming sexual attraction? You withstood him. Can you withstand me?"

Eve stiffened then melted. "Just friends you said."

"No one said there couldn't be benefits."

Eve performed the rituals with Freddy. Although she was very reluctant to exploit the shard again, she could not argue against the necessity of it. Helen had returned to her sanctuary with Soames but promised to be a more frequent visitor when either had need for the other. They had re-defined their relationship. It was now a friendship but with recognition of each other's needs that may, or may not, adjust and develop as time passed. Soames did another scan of Eve's reproductive system and was satisfied there was nothing of immediate concern. After this, Soames felt it was time they talked and they spent some hours together sitting by the river in the valley or, at least, Eve sat. Soames fished. Soames re-affirmed that he thought her body an abomination but conceded that John was a good spirit and that it was he who occupied this deified form. He gave a little ground and said that, perhaps, there was another way, and that a good soul was a good soul, no matter what shell it inhabited. He said he would think hard on it, and left her to recover.

He had said little about his tutelage of Afsoon, only that she had approached the Vatican, when she was a student, to learn about Christian exorcism, and that he had been given the task of instructing her.

Jackie came to her one night, not long after, and urged action in her hunt for the second shard. She was concerned about Eve's overheard exchanges when she was in the mind chamber of Afsoon from where Fadil's captured psyche had been rescued. She now quoted one such: "She seeks the second but it is protected. We can bargain. This is worrying Eve. It sounds like you will encounter a foe in your search, a foe with whom Afsoon believes he can communicate and strike a bargain. You must maintain the initiative. Our advantage is your ability to be physically mobile on earth. We cannot afford to squander the time we have while Afsoon is trapped in his meteoric prison. And those other comments, what the hell was that about the 'sixth shard'? There are only five depicted on your pendant, but Matt, Soames and Freddy are all working on that. For now we need to get you moving. What's your plan?"

She waited. "You haven't got one have you? It's a good job I have then. Fadil has camels waiting just outside the valley. A night's ride into the desert will bring you to a rendezvous point. Soames has obligingly provided a helicopter and pilot for your use. No one knows the whereabouts of your boat except you and Ben and it is probably best kept that way, the less people who know the plan the better.

"The two of you will be dropped wherever you tell the pilot to drop you and you can make your way to whatever place you have hidden it. I'm sure your boat is well equipped but, just in case, you will be provided with an extremely powerful radio pack. Anything you need in the way of help and equipment, and a call to Soames will have it flown there post haste."

Before Eve could respond, Jackie raised her hand. "You are probably thinking you could get to where you want to go a lot quicker but Fadil tells me he has foreseen a need for you to do it this way. He said you need time to re-acquaint yourself with the sea and its creatures, and advises that you take time to do that on route. I trust his visions Eve. This is a time of prophecy. I think we need to realise, it is also a time to have faith."

Eve kicked Ben gently in the ribs. "Get up you lazy bastard. We're going on a quest." He was on his feet in an instant. Eve thought if his grin was any wider the top of his head would fall off.

End of Book 1